TRIAL BY FIRE

THE ARCHEMI ONLINE CHRONICLES

VOLUME 2

By James Osiris Baldwin

A GIFT HORSE PRODUCTIONS NOVEL

COPYRIGHT NOTICE

For permission requests, please contact James Osiris Baldwin:
author@jamesosiris.com

A huge thanks to Stacy Schonhardt and her excellent copyediting!

Layout and design by James Osiris Baldwin.

ISBN: 9781718105256

TABLE OF CONTENTS

This book would not have been possible without the support of the following people:

My editors – Canth, Stacy, and Bryan. You guys rock.

The ArchOn Crew on Royal Road, inclusive of Ekmo, Dave, Krushah, Ant01440 and many others. Their comments and contributions are a huge help!

My awesome Patreon patrons: Jed M, Moonspike, Charlotte Pease, Brenden, James, Lolz, and everyone else who has helped support me and my family during the creation of this work.

To the GameLit Society for support, information and companionship.

I am super grateful to all of you – and also to you, the Reader. We literally couldn't do it without you.

Enjoy the story!

James Osiris Baldwin.

CHAPTER 1

Riding an angry, hungry dinosaur is hard at the best of times. Riding an angry, hungry dinosaur through a crowded city port with a stuffy nose and a baby dragon kicking you in the kidney? Welcome to the glamorous life of a virtual reality video game adventurer.

"Karalti! Can you *not*!?" I hissed down toward the struggling bundle that wriggled inside my cloak, struggling to control my mount as she snapped and lunged at passersby.

"Karalti see!" The hatchling scrabbled with her feet again, thrusting her gleaming black opal nose out from underneath the cloak. *"Ahh! Smells good!"*

"Karalti!" Fighting not to sneeze, I reined in Cutthroat with one hand, and shoved Karalti's snout back under the cloth. She squawked with indignation.

"Nuuuu! Hector!" Her telepathic voice whined inside my head. *"Karalti see!"*

"Karalti keeps her snoot out of sight before the bad men come and take her away." I thought back, trying to sniff back the mucus that was threatening to run out my itching nose. It was the Common Cold debuff, which I'd picked up from sleeping out in the woods on a cold night. The debuff wasn't serious – a 5% reduction in my Perception skill – but it had me on edge. About a week ago, before I'd been uploaded to Archemi, I'd died from the flu in real life. I hated being sick.

"The bad men aren't here," Karalti grumped back.

"You don't know that, and neither do I. Please stay hidden."

"Bleeh. Oki."

She managed to contain herself for all of five seconds before her snout poked out again, nostrils working. *"Smells sooo good-!"*

"Stop it!" I immediately regretted growling aloud, because the itch in my nose built to a sudden sneeze – and Cutthroat lost her goddamned mind. The hookwing roared and spun her body to the right, and rammed us into a stand loaded with ice and teetering piles of freshwater fish.

"What the- ARRGH! MY FISH!" The vendor sprung up as the stand collapsed. "My godsforsaken FISH!"

My irritable Allosaurus-sized war machine bellowed down at him. Swearing as only an ex-soldier could, I hauled on her reins and got her back under control. Only for a moment. The fishmonger ran out in front of Cutthroat, screaming: "My family will starve! Starve! My fish are ruined!"

Cutthroat was a hookwing: a feathered raptorine dinosaur who was eight feet tall at the shoulder, about twenty feet long from nose to tail, with tattered plumage as black as pitch, blazing golden eyes, and a temperament that could only be described as 'nuclear'. Each one of the hooks her species was named for - the fused digits of her hands - were wickedly sharp scythe-like claws as long as a bastard's sword blade. I barely even had time to wince before she lowered her head like an angry bull and charged the man down.

The vendor screamed. I screamed. Karalti screamed because screaming was fun. Cutthroat roared as she knocked the man to the side and darted her head towards his gut, and the only thing that saved his life was the iron muzzle that encased her head like a cage.

Instead of eviscerating him, Cutthroat nipped his shirt through her face-cage, picked him up, and threw him. I didn't even see where he landed – Cutthroat was off down the road, boiling with saurian road rage, and I couldn't do a damn thing to stop her.

"Sorry! I'm really sorry!" I called back over my shoulder.

"Funny fish guy! Karalti see!" Karalti's entire head popped out through the gap in my cloak this time.

My HUD flashed an alert. *[[You have lost -250 Reputation in Bryos. Current Reputation -125: Troublemaker. Law enforcement has been alerted.]]*

It was enough to make a man weep.

Cutthroat charged all the way down the main boulevard beside the docks, scattering people out of the way. I hauled on her reins, but it wasn't until the rings were about to tear out of her nostrils that she finally stopped, sneezing with irritation. Karalti giggled the entire time, and she kept trying to stick her fucking head out.

I took several deep breaths, fighting down the twin urges to yell at her and plead with her, and marched Cutthroat down the dirty road. *"Karalti - I know it smells great here, but you need to stay under the cloak. We now have T-minus ten minutes before the Mata Argis arrive."*

"Oopsie." Karalti said soberly.

"Yeah. Big oopsie."

The city of Bryos was the largest in Ilia, bigger even than the capital, Liren. It was, however, by no means the prettiest. The Bryos Skyport was a filthy sprawl of markets, docks, taverns, inns, whorehouses and warehouses. Sailors, beggars, and merchants vied for space. The magitech engines of flying ships from all around the world hummed, roared, and surged at the ends of the wharfs. The air was full of the smells of fish, frying food, dung, magic, and machine grease. Behind the racket, the thunderous sound of Archemi's harsh oceans could be heard below us, the sound of waves the size of mountains washing up against even taller cliffs. If it weren't for the HUD - my Head's Up Display - the HP rings that flashed into view when I focused on people, and the way that certain objects were framed by rings of different colored light and labels, I'd have completely forgotten that Archemi was actually a videogame.

My hope was that Bryos had enough ships coming and going that we could vanish before the Mata Argis showed up. They were the reason that I had a cold, and why I was still only Level 8 – barely – and Karalti was only Level 1. We were currently marked with the Fugitive status. Every time I'd attempted a sidequest, visited a merchant, tried to stay at an inn or made any trouble after escaping the Eyrie of Saint Grigori, Ilia's finest appeared out of thin air and began to hunt us. Each time we'd fought them, they'd gotten harder. The last group, in some podunk Ilian village I couldn't even remember the name of, had been ten levels higher level than me. There had been no fight: we'd had to run.

"*Not even little peek?*" Karalti asked, as we cut down an alley toward the docks.

"*Not even little peek.*"

"*Ooookaaayyy.*" Karalti wheezed a long-suffering sigh, and withdrew back into the cloak, leaving only the tip of her nose and her nostrils outside. "*Karalti smell?*"

"*Karalti can smell. But keep your head covered.*"

"Eeep!" She made a happy chirp, nose working overtime. "*Smells good! Like fishies!*"

I rolled my eyes, but couldn't help but smile.

Since fleeing the Skyrdon of St. Grigori with Karalti four days ago, we been relentlessly hounded by the Mata Argis, the secret police who enforced the Warden's rule in Ilia. They wanted to kill me and drag Karalti back to the Skyrdon, the dragon knights who would force her to breed the next generation of enslaved dragons for their order. As a result, we had been making do by hunting and brewing potions, killing monsters, and dispatching mercenaries and bandits. The EXP had been pathetic, but the potions I'd been able to sell for a silver here, a silver there. Still, without the ability to do much in the way of quests, levelling had all but ground to a halt. Entering Bryos was a huge risk, and the only reason we were in the city at all was because it was the only way to escape the reach of Ilia for good. I intended to get on a skyship for my fictional homeland, Tuungant, and leave this stinking shitheap of a country behind.

Gold rolled and clinked inside my pack as we turned a corner and lit on the inn I was supposed to be looking for.

The Whistling Clam - yes, really - was a large ramshackle inn with three stories and two balconies, the kind that was sure to be smashed during dramatic player-vs-NPC bar fights. The entire building was painted sky blue, the color flaking off in patches from the damp filthy wood beneath. Anxiously, I walked Cutthroat over to a noticeboard highlighted by my HUD. A blinking blue arrow hung over the flight schedule for Tungaant.

Glancing back down the street, I reached out to it and ripped a copy into my Inventory, turned Cutthroat around, and nudged her to walk back down the alley beside the inn as I had my HUD read it to me telepathically.

"Let's see..." I muttered aloud, reining Cutthroat to a stop. "Oh man, we are so frickin' lucky."

"Huh?" Karalti's nose lifted up the edge of my cloak.

"There's a flight boarding in thirty minutes. Long trip with about ten port stops... but still." I said, folding the timetable back into my Quest Items. "And the fee listed on the Archemipedia checks out. All we have to do is stay down and stay cool, and we're out of this pigpen."

"I'm hungry," Karalti said, her tone dreamy with longing.

"You're always hungry, little Tidbit."

"*Can we find something to eat?*" Karalti pressed in against my back, shivering and hot.

Ever since hatching, Karalti had been ravenous. She hadn't grown much in size since she'd hatched, but I'd noticed that the closer she got to Level 2, the flakier and duller her scales had looked and the more she'd wanted to eat. And damn, the kid could eat.

"There should be a stable around here somewhere," I replied. "I can smell it. Come on, Cutthroat. Move your butt."

Cutthroat stopped trying to scratch her muzzle off and began to pad forward, tail lashing.

Most riding animals in Archemi were meat-eaters, so public stables provided them with offal, spoiled hides, rodents and probably the odd murdered pickpocket in 'hospitality troughs' outside inns and taverns. The troughs and stalls reeked terribly, but hookwings were scavengers capable of stomaching even the rottenest meat. I'd learned this when Cutthroat returned to camp one night chewing on a human body she'd dug out of a bog. She'd been fine. I, on the other hand, would never be okay ever again.

I basically let Cutthroat guide us to the nearest stable, which was on the other side of The Whistling Clam in a small courtyard facing Hell's Walk, the street dividing the buildings from the docks. She surged eagerly toward the stalls and the trough of sun-ripened, fly-blown pig guts inside. Surprisingly, there were no other hookwings in there already. No stable hand, either.

I kept an eye out behind us, and finally opened my cloak up. "Okay, Karalti. Go grab something to eat."

"*Yay! Food's the best! Yay!*" Karalti kicked off my leg, flapping like a bat. One wing hit me in the jaw, snapping my head back. Once the stars faded, I dropped down to the ground with a sigh, catching Cutthroat by the reins. While she foamed at the mouth, I unequipped her [[Iron Muzzle]] and folded it into my inventory. "Don't eat too much, Tidbit. You have to be ready to fly."

"*Oki!*" The little queen dragon landed gracefully on the edge of the trough and began to chow down like her life depended on it.

I was worried that I was doing something wrong with her. According to her character menu, dragons grew and matured by levelling. Karalti was still the size of a small dog, with feet and hands too big for her scrawny neck and wedge-shaped head. When she'd hatched, her gleaming black skin had rippled under light with colored fire, like opal. Flashes of blue, orange, green, gold and red glowed between every dark scale. Now, her skin was dull and flaky.

While my saurian buddies pigged out, I went to the outside of the stable and kept watch over the strangely empty yard. From here, I could see out the gate and onto the street with perfect clarity. I kept an ear out for strange noises or conversations, and restlessly brought up Karalti's Path information.

Dragon Character Information

Leveling Your Mount

Your NPC mount has her own EXP pool that is independent from your own. Like you, she levels by gaining experience from combat, training, and practicing her skills. Unlike you, your dragon only gains three kinds of EXP: Combat EXP, Skill EXP, and a special type of EXP called Lexica.

Combat EXP is gained by going on adventures, fighting enemies, and completing quests. When your dragon completes a quest with you, the two of you each receive 100% Combat EXP from the quest. Any EXP you gain from winning combat is split. If you fight and kill a monster but your dragon doesn't help, only you gain that EXP. If the two of you kill it together, you each earn 50% of the total EXP from that monster.

Lexica

Lexica is a form of EXP unique to dragons that allows them to comprehend the Words of Power written into their blood. As your dragon gains more Lexica, they can learn spells and unique abilities in addition to their Path and Advanced Path. All dragons are born with the ability Gift of the Blood, which allows them to begin interpreting and manifesting Words of Power without needing to use any special tools or extra mana. At Level 2, they have enough Lexica to manifest their most important Word: their breath weapon.

Lexica EXP is gained as your dragon matures. Between Level 2 and Level 31 (when she is fully mature), she will gain a total of 60 Lexica points that can be spent on spells or unique abilities. This is enough to select 10-20 possible spells/abilities. You cannot change these abilities, so choose wisely!

Most spells require 3 Lexica points to acquire, but some spells/abilities require as many as 6 points.

Dragons are immune to mana toxicity and do not need any tools to control or contain mana when performing magic. However, the tradeoff is that the dragon's abilities have a long cooldown period, and casting too many spells in a row while airborne may cause the dragon to faint while flying, as each spell depletes their blood. They are also restricted to the spells and abilities determined by their type. Your dragon's character menu lists their type and sub-type (if applicable).

Your dragon is a Queen dragon, which means that the Words of Power in her blood are unique to her, and the combination of abilities and spells available to her are not shared by any other dragon in Archemi. Her skill trees and the advanced paths available to her reflect this.

My dyslexic ass was still no good at reading, so I had the HUD telepathically narrate the page to me for the millionth time while the noise of the street filtered in. Even with the mental chatter, I could hear and distinguish every conversation going on outside and on the balconies of The Whistling Clam. That was because I was now literally a mutant. I had passed the Trial of Marantha, the test given to aspiring dragon knights so that they could withstand all of the challenges that riding and fighting on a dragon presented. G-forces, extreme temperatures, vertigo, and perhaps most importantly, mana poisoning.

"...What do you mean you saw him with Kella?!"

"...Clams and cockles! Fresh clams, six for six!"

"...I don't know. That hulk looks like it couldn't make it crosst me gods' damn bathtub, let alone the Sea of Blades..."

"... girls at THAT place got the pox. Last time I went there, woke up three days latah with blistahs down there...makin noise no blistahs ought to make."

And a different voice: more cultured, out of place. "...Yes, foreign. He's quite distinctive, with long hair like in the drawing... yes, he has it tied back, like a savage. You saw him? Where did he... is that so?"

My eyes snapped open.

"Karalti," I said aloud, turning to stalk back inside the stable. "Go hide in the rafters."

The little dragon chirped and cocked her crested head, a fillet of meat still dangling from her jaws. She regarded me with innocent violet-white eyes, radiating confusion.

I pulled the Spear of Nine Spheres off Cutthroat's saddle and spun it around until the long, glaive-like blade pointed down. "Go. The Mata Argis are here."

Karalti hissed, and then sprung into the air. At Level 1, her wings were still long enough and strong enough to carry her short distances, even when weighed down with food.

I went to the edge of the stable, the head of the Spear held low to the ground. The weapon wasn't much to look at: a seven-foot long, dark metal polearm with faint engravings softened and dulled by age. The head of the glaive was a full-tang, curved metal blade. I'd scrubbed the tarnish off, but even after close to a month of use the weapon – an ancient magical relic – still looked like a broken antique:

Ruined Spear (Spear of Nine Spheres)

Soulbound Weapon

Slot: Two-handed

Item Class: Relic

Item Quality: Ruined

Damage: 25-55 Slashing or Piercing

Durability: 27% (-6 damage)

Weight: 1 lb

Special: +2 Dexterity, Soulbound, +50 HP, +2 Defense

A weapon reputed to be the Spear of Nine Spheres. To repair it, you will need to find a Mastersmith capable of reforging Lazula (bluesteel) magical artifacts.

"Time for me and you to do what we do best, my girl." I adjusted my grip on the Spear. "Break shit and kill things."

CHAPTER 2

From the shadows, I watched the seven men move into position. One Mercenary stayed outside of the fence while the other six filed in and fanned out. They acted like professionals who knew how to work together, but the way they were moving told me that they weren't a hundred percent sure where I was. Either that, or they had someone approaching from behind the stable. They were probably DPS: a Thief, Rogue, Assassin, or similar Path.

I pulled Cutthroat around by her reins, pointed her in the direction of the approaching vanguard, and swatted her as I gave her the codeword command for 'attack'. "Icecream!"

The hookwing knew what that word meant. Murder.

She lowered her head and charged out of the stable, breaking out into the open with a roar while I bounded out back to face the unseen rearguard.

Two Level 10 Mercenary Rogues, one with a net, the other with a crossbow, had jumped the fence and were coming up from around the building. I nearly ran into the net-carrier - and reflexively brought the butt end of my Spear around to hit him on the side of his head. As he staggered, I triggered one of my skills, Shadow Dance. I shot to the side, a blur of darkness, as the other man aimed and fired his crossbow in the wrong direction. I emerged out of Shadow Dance almost right behind him, slashing at his neck.

[[You Backstabbed Mercenary Rogue!]]

⟦Critical Hit!⟧

The Mercenary's head went flying, hitting the other guy as he scrambled up. He was hardened enough to not juggle it and scream. Covered in blood, snarling obscenities, he hurled the net at me and drew a pair of daggers. I heard men screaming in front of the stable, then a saurian shriek of rage - and pain.

"Don't worry, sweetheart!" I called to Cutthroat, knocking the net away with the butt of the spear and whirling it to parry the first sword strike with the pointy end. "I'm coming!"

Mercenaries called to each other, and boots thundered around both sides of the stable as I dodged, blocked, then hit the soldier's blade with a powerful strike, sending it flying out of his lacerated hand. I triggered Lunge, and drove the foot-long spear blade and part of the haft through his chest. He was a high enough level that it didn't kill him outright, but the kick to the chest to get the spear out of his body and the ⟦Bleed⟧ debuff sure as hell did.

There was a cry from the yard. "He's out back!"

"Where's the dragon!?"

Hiding, assholes. I ground my teeth, and charged out to join Cutthroat.

The hookwing was surrounded, trying to fight in multiple directions at once. Men with pikes kept her from their throats, while crossbowmen plugged her full of bolts. Three ⟦Mercenaries⟧ were torn apart like wet rags on the ground.

I willed my body to become immaterial again. The tattoo on my right hand blazed with cold, sending shooting numbness through my body. My HP drained fractionally as I slithered into a haze of dark smoke. I dashed in past Cutthroat, supernaturally fast, and reappeared just behind one of the Mercenaries who was attacking her. He spun, panicked, and struck a glancing blow off my shoulder armor as the others rushed in. I danced back like a ghost, blowing around one of the pikemen and reappearing behind and to the side of him. The mobs converged on me, and as soon as they massed up, I deployed the nuke: my newest ability and first AOE attack, Umbra Burst.

"Hrragh!" I slammed the end of my spear into the ground, discharging the built-up dark energy in my body. Twisted thorny vines of shadow sprung from the ground, lashing out to capture - and puncture - legs and arms. The men screamed in confusion and fear as ice crawled up along their flesh. I capitalized on the short Frozen debuff with another ability: Blood Sprint, which powered a slashing strike that knocked three of the men off their feet and sent them to the ground, and its combo chain ability Blood Storm.

The dark mana swirling around my spear turned dark red as I whirled the polearm around and cut a swath through the Mercenaries. Each successful blow restored health, and my HP jumped well above what I'd lost using Shadow Dance. Three of them screamed and fell to the ground, their skin dry and stretched tight over the bones of their faces.

Two weeks ago, I'd have been disturbed by what I was doing. But now, I had Karalti – and I would have eaten a man alive if that's what it took to protect her.

"*Oriaysal!*" The Mata Argis Agent, who had stayed out of the battle until now, leveled his hands at me. Only then did I spot what he'd been hiding under his cloak. He was wearing gauntlets reinforced with black matte crystal capsules and flexible tubing, the leather glowing with runes.

A spellcaster. He'd been letting his men wear us down. And he was Level 25.

The spell went off like a flashbang, blinding Cutthroat and me. It was like being stabbed in the eyeballs with a needle. NPCs who had been drawn to us to watch the fight fled, while screams of terror echoed from the street.

I struggled to keep position, hold a fighting stance, but I took hits from all sides as the Blindness debuff ticked down. Worse, I heard the mage speak another Word of Power. "*Thoram!*"

Thunder cracked, and suddenly I was flying, and not in the fun way. The energy slammed into me and surged through my limbs. Like a bowl of wet noodles thrown at a wall, I hit the side of the stable, limbs turned to jelly, then bounced and clattered onto the ground.

Or at least, I thought it was the stable. My vision swam back into view, and I saw that I'd actually flown across the yard, through the open gate, tumbled across the road, and hit the side of a large shipping container at the water's edge. Barely ten feet away was a flimsy knee-high barrier and a sheer five-hundred-foot drop into the churning abyss that passed for Archemi's oceans. 300 HP had vanished like a bad dream.

Groaning, I picked myself up to see the spellcaster whirl around and cast on Cutthroat as she charged him down. This spell engulfed my hookwing in a cloud of ice. Cutthroat gave a croaky squawk as she toppled to the ground.

Fuck, this guy was fast. I gulped down a couple of healing potions as I dashed for the gate and slammed into the swordsman who barreled at me, clumsily swinging. I slashed him to the side, and he fell, clutching his spurting throat. I bounded forward, leaping like a cricket in a bid to land on the mage, but my spear and feet slammed into an invisible barrier. My eyes widened, just before he casually blasted me with the other hand.

This time, I hit the corner edge of the shipping crate and crunched instead of bounced.

⟦Warning! You are Stunned!⟧

⟦Current HP: 25/440⟧

⟦Warning! This enemy's challenge rating is dangerously high!⟧

"Urrgh..." The blood beat in my temples. I had to keep this fucker away from Karalti.

"You there! Search the stable!" The mage called back over his shoulder as he stalked through the gate and out to the street. The Stun counter was still ticking down, and I struggled to move as he closed in on me, hand raised. Lightning danced around his fingers. "And you, heretic! Where is she? Where is the queen?"

"Have you checked your ass? I heard it's pretty roomy in there." I spat blood, moving to hands and knees. I still had the Spear of Nine Spheres wrapped in one tight-knuckled fist, for all the good it was doing me.

"You are in no position to sling insults." The masked Mata Argis Agent had a cold voice, dark with anger. "Where is she!? What have you done to her?!"

"The same thing I do to your mom every night."

The mage wrenched me to my feet with a spell, his gauntlet burning with blue fire. "Have it your way! We will extract the information at base without any need for your input. By the power vested in me by the Warden of Ilia-"

His speech was cut off by a furious black blur of claws and teeth. Karalti dove at the back of his head and hit him at full speed, sending him staggering toward me. He flung his hand out just before his concentration broke, but the spell was successful. I was whiplashed around in mid-air before being slammed down onto the rough ground. I hit the knee-high cliffside barricade hard, and felt something crack in my chest on the rebound. My arm went numb, and my spear skittered off across the dirt.

"Karalti! No! Stay back!" I yelled, rolling over to scramble up.

The little dragon's neck swelled. She hissed and spat, kicking with her powerful hind feet. She caught her sickle claw on the edge of the mage's mask and kicked it free, baring a surprisingly young face. He looked like a Mormon: pale, pointed face, wavy nut-blond hair. Karalti got one good slash across his eyes before he caught her by the neck like a turkey.

Karalti squealed, and my guts froze cold.

"Let her go, you jackbooted piece of shit!" I roared, blood pouring from my nose, and charged at him, desperate to provide any distraction at all. If they took her...

"Hold fast!" The last swordsman was running towards the pair of them with a net outstretched.

"No!" I screamed now, real terror overwhelming common sense, self-preservation, even the need to breathe. Every day, I was haunted by what had happened to her mother, and what would happen to her if they took her. "Let her go!"

"*Hector!*" Karalti screeched, little limbs flailing as the pair of men closed in.

The soldier reached them before I did. He threw the net over Karalti's struggling body, snaring her wings, and grabbed her in a bear hug.

"Stand by! Hold her! Don't worry - she's too young for fire!" The mage was struggling to see and catch his breath. He went to go pick up his mask. I bellowed, charging him, but he wasn't distracted enough to ignore me - with a dismissive sweep of his hand, his magic sent me sprawling.

"HECTOR!" Karalti twisted in the soldier's arms like a fish, slashing and biting. he tried to pull away from her, but a lucky claw caught him in the neck and he went down, blood spraying from his carotid. He dropped and she fell with him, still struggling in the net.

[[Karalti lands a devastating blow! X5 damage!]]

[[Mercenary Soldier is hemorrhaging!]]

[[Congratulations! Karalti is Level 2!]]

"Time to end this," the mage panted, standing over me. He levelled his smoking hand at my chest. "The Knight-Commander sends his regards."

CHAPTER 3

Six feet behind him, Karalti's body was consumed by a kaleidoscopic haze. The opal seams in her scales spread over her entire body. The guard nearly dropped her as she seemed to liquify, then doubled in size. It distracted everyone, even the mage.

Before she'd even stopped glowing, the dragon reared her head back and opened her jaws wide. "CHAAAA!"

A thin plume of burning liquid, like ghostly white napalm, burst from her mouth. The net caught fire, and when it hit the Mata Argis Agent, he caught on fire, too. It spattered the ground, and wherever it landed, white flames erupted.

The Agent's cloak caught like he'd dipped it in gasoline. The heat was so intense I could feel it from the ground. I recoiled as he jumped back and to the side, shouting a new spell. "*Bla'pahaz!*"

Water condensed out of the air around him in a sphere and dumped over his head, like someone had poured a bucket over him. The water sloshed down, saturating his clothes... but the flames were not extinguished. Clouds of steam spewed into the air.

"AAAAIIIIIEEE!" Now he was boiling alive instead of frying. He spun away from me, clawing at his robes to get them off. I rolled to the side and clapped a hand down on the haft of the Spear of Nine Spheres. Maybe we could pick away at him like this? Maybe we could...?

The mage snarled another Word of Power, whipping the dust and dirt on the street around himself like a tornado. The earth covered him, and when it fell away, the flames were extinguished. His HP was still in the green - the fire had distracted him, but Karalti was still only Level 2. It hadn't injured him that much.

"Bad man!" Karalti's raspy, parrot-like speaking voice cut through the air as she charged the Agent at a run, leaping into the air with great beats of her wings. "CHAAAA!"

"Karalti! NO!" I shouted, but it was already too late.

The mage blocked the napalm stream with an energetic shield, and then swatted the little dragon from the air. She cried out as she tumbled away, rolling to stillness in the churned dust of the street.

We weren't strong enough. We just weren't strong enough, and I wasn't strong enough to protect her. Teeth gritted, I burned through my healing items and prepared to charge anyway... except that someone else got there first.

"FOR TALTOS! FOR HONOR!" The man who emerged out of the cloud of dirt was massive. Six and a half feet tall, shoulders wider than a door, a saber in his hands. The Mata Argis mage got a shield up between him and the newcomer just in time, but the blow of that sword against the magical barrier send him skidding across the ground.

The mage looked nearly as confused as I did. He was preparing his return attack when a bright bolt of energy slammed into him from my other side. I glimpsed a small, wiry man in bright blue robes, with a steel-gray ponytail and mage-gloves that crackled with energy. The Mata Argis Agent staggered, reeling close to the barrier overlooking the cliff, and I saw my chance.

Wheezing from broken ribs, my HP throbbing in the red, I charged the mage and tackled him off the edge.

Whatever magic school the Mata Argis mage had been to, they apparently hadn't taught him how to fly. He howled all the way down, plummeting like a comet into the crushing hundred-foot waves that thundered against the base of the cliffs. Archemi's physics was a bitch.

[[You have defeated Mata Argis Agent!]]

[[You gain 200 EXP!]]

[[Congratulations! You are Level 9!]]

[[You have unspent ability points!]]

[[You have unspent skill points!]]

"Karalti!" There was no time to gloat. Struggling for breath, I ran to my hatchling. She was up on her feet, but she was down below half HP. A man in bright blue robes moved away from her as she flapped toward me.

The dragon hit me in the chest and knocked me on my ass. She clung to me with four sets of pointy claws, wings beating wildly. "*Hector! Hector is hurt!*"

"Hector's gonna be fine." But Cutthroat wasn't. With Karalti pressed in close to my hip, I limped across the smoking ground and back into the stable yard, to the huge body sprawled on the ground. I dropped to my knees beside Cutthroat, a lump rising in my throat. The hookwing was, to all appearances, completely dead. Out of habit, I jammed my fingers under the edge of her jaw, feeling for a pulse, even as my HUD display showed me her level and remaining HP. It was at 5 out of 460, and dropping slowly.

[[Your Mount is in a critical condition! You must restore HP equal to one quarter of her total HP to stabilize her.]]

"Shitballs," I said to no one in particular. I raided my inventory - there were ten Bonebreak Poultices that each healed 50 HP, six

Moss Tinctures that healed 70 HP, and a bunch of mana-infused potions that *I* could use, but would be toxic to Cutthroat.

I slapped a poultice onto her wounds and pulled the dinosaur's head onto my lap. Her skull was as long as my torso, but I pried her jaws open and poured two Moss Tinctures down her throat and returned the empty bottles back into my inventory. Cutthroat twitched, then kicked spasmodically along the ground as she regained consciousness, tearing long furrows in the dirt. Then she whimpered.

⟦Cutthroat has been stabilized! HP: 145/460⟧

"The creature is badly wounded." The blue-robed man had joined us, brow wrinkled with concern. He looked to be in his early fifties, and he had a scholarly, handsome face, with wise dark eyes. The huge knight who had intervened in the fight hovered by his left shoulder. He was a tall, broad-shouldered man with an impressive moustache and strings of black runes tattooed over his cheeks and under his eyes. He was dressed in a fine chainmail tunic underneath black and red lamellar armor, which made him look like some kind of Slavic samurai.

"Yeah, she is. Stand back." I uncorked the second Moss Tincture and poured it in, shoving my arm into her mouth to make sure it went down.

Putting my hand in Cutthroat's mouth wasn't the stupidest thing I've ever done, but it was definitely in the Top Ten Dumb Ideas of Hector Park. When her eyes flickered open, dark and hazy, I had about a second to pull my arm out and scramble away. I barely managed to stay out of reach as Cutthroat snapped at me, jaws clapping together barely inches from my face.

Karalti hissed at her and drew a deep breath. Before I could stop her, she exhaled wheezily in the hookwing's direction, but only a few tiny drops of burning liquid and saliva sprayed from her mouth. None of them landed on the dinosaur, and Cutthroat almost looked offended.

"*Oh.*" Karalti hunched down, looking up at us from the ground.

I turned to regard the pair of men who were still shadowing us. "Thanks for the assist."

To my surprise, both men went to their knees. The big knight bowed to the hilt of his sword. Blue Robes flattened himself down on the ground.

"Please forgive our imposition, *rytier*," the smaller man – mage? priest? – said as he rose back up. "We saw you and your *draak* in distress-"

"-We could not let these rogues continue their assault on this holy creature, or you, her sacred guardian!" The knight finished. He had a deep, booming voice to go with the moustache, but gentle eyes. He gazed at Karalti as if she were an angel fallen from heaven.

Karalti leaned in to sniff them curiously, wings buzzing. I rolled my shoulders and grimaced. People were beginning to stare at us, which was literally the opposite of what I wanted right now. "Well, thanks. I really appreciate it, but we have to find a ship and leave. The next wave will be here any minute."

"Please lend us your ear for a minute more, *rytier*," the knight said. He had a strange, thick accent. Not Russian, but definitely somewhere east of Germany. "I am Ur Kirov, Knight of Taltos and a representative of His Majesty Andrik Corvinus the Wise, and this is Father Petko Matthias, priest and scholar. We come from Vlachia, where your *draak* is a most holy being. We were, in all honesty, on our way to a royal vessel when we spied your entanglement with this knave and his-"

I groaned. "Well, thanks again, but we don't have much time. Where are you going with this?"

"Ahh, well... we have been recalled to mighty Vlachia at the Volod's request following a great tragedy in the kingdom." Kirov sheathed his sword, nodding thoughtfully and with a disturbing lack of urgency. "I was sent here to protect Father Matthias, but by the power invested in my office as a Knight of the Red Star, I would offer you and your *draak* sanctuary aboard our vessel."

My eyes narrowed. I'd had enough of Archemi's knightly orders to last me a lifetime, but this guy was too ridiculous to not be sincere.

"The Volod ordered that we should bring any skilled adventurers with us to address the problems of the kingdom," Father Matthias added softly. "But to find a true draak in the company of a skillful warrior... it can only be a sign from the Nine."

The Nine? That caught my attention. I caught Cutthroat's reins in one hand as she tried to limp past me and pulled her to a stop. "Wait. You're a priest of the old gods? The *dragon* gods?"

Matthias glanced at the nearest bystanders. "Please be a little more discreet, *rytier*. Their worship is outlawed here."

Kirov clasped his hands together, beseeching me. "We cannot in good conscience abandon a *draak* and her guardian in these barbaric lands. I would beg you to consider our offer."

I frowned. The gamer in me said that these two were about to offer me a quest - a juicy one, given that they directly served their king. But I'd been avoiding people ever since leaving Fort Palewing, and the string of betrayals and the gross abuse of the dragons that the knights of the Order of Saint Grigori committed had left a bitter taste in my mouth. Still, the name 'Vlachia' rang a bell somewhere... and after a couple of moments thought, I remembered. Vlachia was the country where I was meant to meet up with Matir.

"Hold on a second." Keeping one eye on the two men and one on my hookwing and dragon, I opened up the description of the first major quest I'd ever received:

Ongoing Quest: The Temple of the Hidden Seed

When the Dark Star rises to the sky, journey to the Thunderstones at Myszno, a village in the east of Vlachia.

Reward: ???

Difficulty: Level 12-15

"Do you happen to know where the Village of Myszno is?" I asked Kirov.

"Myszno? Why, of course!" His moustache bristled, and his eyes turned distant and dark with emotion. "Myszno is both a village and a province, down near the southern border of Vlachia. It is a sight that would melt the heart of any painter. The endless forests, the rolling hills, the mountains soaring into the sky like..."

"Myszno village is a place of pilgrimage for the local natives," Matthias added, rapping Kirov's armored sleeve to shut him up. "There is a holy place up in the mountains near the town, but rumors of monsters and worse have grown in recent times. However, it is not anything I can speak of comfortably out of doors, especially on Ilian soil."

Interesting. I was betting that 'holy place' was the Thunderstones, whatever they were. I nodded sharply. "Alright. I'll talk with you. You said something about a ship?"

"Yes. Our mighty steed awaits." Kirov nodded. "Now, please, come with us so that we might see you aboard, and journey with you to safety."

CHAPTER 4

The Vlachian royal ship was called the *Hóleány* - pronounced 'Hoo-lan'. It was easily the nicest ship in the port: a sleek cruiser with four huge magictech engines and layers of waxed silk sails.

The pair of men led me and my saurian friends down the harborfront with some urgency, half-sheltering Karalti and me with their cloaks. Guards were pouring from the city now, stopping and frisking people, pulling back robes, harassing dark-colored hookwings and their owners. We reached the gangplank just ahead of the tide of angry soldiers.

"Shelter, at last," Kirov said hoarsely. He looked to Father Matthias. "Please, Father, you and our guests must go first, lest these rogues try to breach the deck. I will stand guard until you are hidden."

Kirov seemed to be a real, honest-to-gods chivalrous knight. I didn't argue with him. I just scooped Karalti in my arms and carried her up to the ship like a big puppy. Cutthroat limped up without complaint, too injured to be her normal rage-driven self, while Father Matthias followed up behind her. *Well* behind, so that she didn't knock him off into the sea with her lashing tail.

"We have facilities for your hookwing," he said, once we were on board. "We will stable her, and then retreat to the guest quarters to discuss our dilemma."

"Thanks." I looked back over the railing, watching as a unit of black-cloaked soldiers swept down the road. They were about five hundred feet from us, but I could see them clearly, zooming in my vision like a sniper scope. "We need to hurry. The Mata Argis are going to be on us any minute."

Matthias was looking at my eyes and face as if he were seeing it for the first time. "You have the dragonsight? That means you trained with the Skyrdon of Ilia. And she-?"

"Karalti escaped a fate worse than death, and so did I." I blinked, refocusing to close range. "Let's go to the below deck."

The priest escorted us there. Cutthroat was anxious on the ship, hissing at every shadow until we locked her into her stall. I unequipped her muzzle just as the ship's engines began to roar. Her feathers flattened against her skull, and she crouched down, eyes darting from side to side.

"That's a good girl. Sit down and don't murder anyone, okay?" I patted the door, and left with Matthias for the main deck. "Thanks, by the way. You didn't have to do this."

"It is our honor," he replied, leading the way back up the stairs. "Our vows include that of hospitality. Your Karalti is a rare and precious creature. How did you come to accompany her?"

I liked his choice of words: 'accompany', not 'own'. "The short version is that the Skyrdon of Saint Grigori enslave their dragons, including Karalti's mother. Her mother gave me Karalti to protect. She asked me to give her a good life."

"The gods judge us by the way we treat those in need," Matthias said, slowing to turn and duck his head. "Do your people worship the Nine, then? You're not Ilian."

I rubbed my arm. "I don't worship any gods, but I work for one. It's kind of like a side job."

"Meaning?"

I shrugged, and pulled my glove off to show him what lay beneath. "Meaning one of them put a stamp on me, and asks me to run errands for him."

The Mark of Matir was a nine-pointed star that was similar to a chaos star, with an extra arrow and a question-mark like symbol at the center. It was burned on like a primitive tattoo, but the black lines almost seemed to float underneath the skin.

"*Bogdi vris!*" His hand flew to his mouth. "The sigil of Chernobog!"

"You mean Matir, right?" I pulled the glove back on and tucked my sleeve in.

"He is The Keeper of Night, the Prince of a Thousand Names. The dragons called him Matir. In Vlachia and the Sathbar Plains, we call him Chernobog, the Black God. And you... you are more than an adventurer." Matthias spread his hands. "I cannot believe my eyes, but... here you stand. Is it true, then? Does Chernobog stir?"

"Seems like it." I nodded. "I don't really know much about him though, to be honest."

"It is something for discussion later. For now, we should get a drink. I will send someone to see to your hookwing and restore her health."

Karalti yawned, flashing rows of needle-sharp teeth. "*Soooo sleepy.*"

"*We'll get you to bed soon, Tidbit.*" I thought back. I spoke aloud to Matthias. "A drink sounds good. Is there any way we can arrange a bed for Karalti?"

"Of course! Come, we shall see to it at once. And perhaps I can tell you what I know of Chernobog... his mark on you surely explains why you desire a pilgrimage to Myszno."

So much had happened in the two weeks since my death that I'd barely had time to sit down and think, let alone grind out levels and skills. I'd arrived in the game in a slave ship, led a rebellion, and in short order found myself trying to join an order of dragon knights. They'd turned out to be assholes, and since escaping with Karalti, we had been running and hiding from them and their agents. For the second time this month, I was back on an airship. But this time, I wasn't a slave. And thanks to Karalti's mother, neither was she.

We were well out over the Bay of Knives, the channel separating the Ilian Peninsula from the rest of the continent of Artana by the time that the four of us – me, Kirov, Father Mathias and Karalti – gathered together in the Royal Suite on board the *Hóleány*. There were thankfully no royals aboard, so we spread out like fat men on a sofa. Karalti was a snoring ball of wings and scales on the grand bed, curled in the middle of the red silk sheets. Me, Kirov and Matthias sat around a small but well-stocked bar, drinking a little bit of everything and a lot of some things.

"Slivovitz!" Kirov boomed, setting a shotglass of clear liquor in front of me. "This will put hair on your stones, *rytier!* To the Volod!"

"To the Volod!" I picked it up and threw it back. It was fruity, but strong enough that my eyes watered. Still, before being uploaded to Archemi, I was a Korean-American dropout who'd hung around bikers and then soldiered for five years. All of those circumstances meant that I could definitely hold my own in the liquor department.

"*Rytier* Hector, we come to you with a grave matter indeed," Kirov said, shaking his head and setting his glass down. "It is no exaggeration to say that Taltos, and indeed all of Vlachia, owes the dragons its foundation. Our cities, our culture, even the land itself was shaped by the mighty *Solonkratsu*. We venerate their gods, but especially Khors, the God of the Forge. The Church of the Creator is the closest ally of the state, giving us inspiration and a moral framework by which to live."

"Okay." *Ugh, religion.* Not entirely sure where this was going, I helped myself to another shot of slivovitz.

"Something is preying on my brothers in the city of Taltos." Matthias gestured animatedly as he spoke. "Priests of Khors have been murdered by some manner of terrible spirit."

Kirov muttered. "Ghosts. Bah."

The priest shot him a sharp glance. "Do you really think a flesh-and-blood assassin could have convinced Franz Darko to commit suicide? Impossible. The ocean would rise to the skies before that happened."

"Wait a sec." I held up a hand. "You just said these guys were murdered."

"They were. Franz would not kill himself: suicide is anathema to Khors, a coward's death." Matthias' scholarly face hardened. "No... something killed Father Abel, and something killed Darko, and the same being has killed one of our great prodigies, Brother Orban."

"So two senior priests and one junior priest have been murdered so far?" I asked.

They nodded.

I studied Matthias. "Why do you think it's a ghost?"

"I am a scholar of the supernatural, among other things." Matthias shook his head, then reached for the bottle. "Kirov, tell him the details of what you told me. They nauseate me to repeat them."

"Very well." Kirov slouched back into his chair, his hands resting on his stomach. "The first to die was Father Lazlo Abel, a patriarch of the church and tutor to the royal throne. He was beaten to death in his own study with one of his own books, and a quill forced into his eye."

"Jeee-zus." I grimaced, and threw back my next shot.

"The second to die was Father Franz Darko," the knight continued. "As His Grace said, he appears to have committed suicide. He was found hanging from the rafters in his sacred forge. The room was locked from the inside. We did not assume it had any connection to Father Abel's demise-"

"But I do," Matthias interrupted. "I know Franz like my own brother. He was a ferocious man, full of fire and spirit. He was a man of honor, and even if he were to kill himself, he would do it in the manner of a warrior. He would not hang himself like a brigand, and especially not inside his place of worship."

"The third victim was found only days ago." Kirov's dark eyes glittered with worry as he spoke. "Brother Orban... he was a great

Mastersmith, a senior monk and a protégé of the High Forgemaster, Agoston Toth. Orban went missing in the catfolk ghetto, where he was serving the poor with his craft. Two days later, he was staked out in the public gardens for all to see. I received a letter detailing the scene. What I read was... grotesque."

I frowned. "Give me details. How did they find the body?"

The knight sighed. "His neck was wrapped with barbed wire, the kind found on the district wall separating the ghetto from the rest of the city. His body was drenched in sewerage, a chamber pot left on his head. We found a rat in his mouth, rammed down into his throat so only the head protruded. That was what killed him."

"Not the staking or the wire?"

"No. The staking was... surgical in its precision. It is possible to keep a man alive on such a device. The wire was not tight enough. And the rat was still alive, though barely. It had kicked his throat apart."

"That is some horror-movie-level shit right there," I said. "That kind of murder doesn't scream 'ghost' to me, though."

"No one saw or heard a thing," Matthias replied, lighting up a small pipe. His hands shook as he coordinated the match and sandpaper. "The city guard did not see anything. Not the staking, not the screams... nothing. He did not have time to fight back. It is as if he materialized in the gardens in the dead of night."

"Nothing human could do this," Kirov insisted. "But there are creatures with the kind of strength to commit such atrocities. This assassin – monster, ghost, whatever it is – has been named the Slayer of Taltos. It must be destroyed. That is why the Volod ordered that we search for suitable adventurers capable of dealing with such a creature."

"And you are a Starborn, are you not?" Matthias added.

Yep – this was leading to a quest. A big one. I folded my hands on the table. "Yeah. I'm Starborn. What is your Volod offering to the person who brings this creature in?"

"That, I cannot say. It will be exceedingly generous, but you will have to discuss the reward with him," Kirov said. "But to start with, you and your dragon will be given full hospitality and guaranteed sanctuary in Vlachia. Will you help us?"

New Quest: The Slayer of Taltos

Priests of Khors, the draconic god of Fire and Craftsmanship, are being murdered in the Vlachian capital of Taltos. Matthias, himself a priest of Khors, and his bodyguard Sir Kirov have been recalled from their mission in Ilia and tasked with finding a hero capable of bringing the Slayer to ground. They believe you can help them restore order in Taltos and bring the murderer to justice.

Difficulty: *Hard*

Recommended Level: *12-15*

Rewards: *EXP, Fame in Vlachia. Speak with the king, Volod Andrik Corvinus III, to negotiate your material rewards.*

Special: *This is an evolving quest. Updates will appear in your log.*

The offer of sanctuary by itself was tempting. Wherever we went, the Mata Argis was bound to follow – even if I took Karalti back to Tuungant, like I'd originally intended. But if I was directly under the protection of a foreign king... well, that offered a measure of safety. Not only that, but I had to get my ass to Vlachia soon anyway. I still didn't trust Matir, but I was willing to fulfil the terms of the quest and see where it led. I could do this quest and level up, then head to Myszno.

I looked over at Karalti. She had rolled partly onto her back, her foreclaws clasped over her eyes. She was sound asleep, snoring away despite the noise we were making. The fight with the Mata Argis had exhausted her.

I hit confirm with a small nod, then stood and offered a hand to Matthias to shake. "Fine. Count me in."

CHAPTER 5

Three days later.

We woke with the sun onboard the *Hóleány*. Or more accurately, *I* woke with the sun. I was curled around Karalti under a down comforter, her back and wings arched against the front of my body. The single level gain had made a huge difference to her. She had doubled in size, and her scrawny hatchling neck was filling out, becoming smooth and muscular. She was still smaller than me, but even though she was the little spoon, she still somehow managed to take up two thirds of the bed.

I didn't wake her straightaway. Instead, I slowly pulled back the covers and drank in the sight of her. The little dragon slept on her side, with all six limbs curled against her body, her head tucked down, the tip of her nose sticking out from under the blankets. The flaky dull scales had been replaced by new, bright blue-black ones that practically glowed under light. They were smooth and warm to the touch. By the dawn light, her dark scales rippled with deep veins of color. It was an eerie, beautiful effect, as if she was sculpted from perfect black opal.

Now and then, I reminded myself that she wasn't real, but inevitably concluded that it didn't matter. Archemi was my reality now, and not a day went by where I wasn't grateful to have Karalti in my life. She was curious, mischievous, adorable, and needy, but she was also deeply loving, with a powerful need to please and to learn. I stroked over her folded wings, her horns, her shoulder. She continued to snooze on while I bought up her character sheet for review.

Karalti - Queen Dragon

Level 2 Hatchling

Strength: 12

Dexterity: 17

Stamina: 13

Will: 15

Wisdom: 5

Intelligence: 12

HP: 250/250

MP: 50/50

Affinity: Darkness/Life

EXP: 374 (233 to next level)

Lexica: 2

Spells: 0

Skills:

Acrobatics 3

- Aerial Acrobatics 4

Dive

[[Karalti has two unspent skill points!]]

Abilities:

Gift of the Blood: See detailed description for more information.

Eviscerate: A power attack with the front claws.

(New!) Ghost Fire: 65-90 damage; sticky fire that burns underwater. 2 Charges, 30 min recharge time.

Bite: 25-30 damage.

Gore: A dragon's unarmed attacks do double damage and cause Bleeding.

Spells:

None.

Karalti had two unspent Skill Points from her last level and one new Lexica point. She was also halfway to Level 3 already – probably because she'd landed some fire damage on the Level 25 Mage. At Level 3, she'd be able to take her first spell, but I was going to hold off selecting one until Level 4 or 5. Each one of my dragon's levels came with a selection of two possible spells. Provided she had the required number of Lexica points, Karalti could learn either of the spells before or at her current level. This meant that if you hoarded points, you could get better spells later on – though when I brought up her Magic tree, I noticed that some powerful spells required 'lesser' versions of the same spell to be selectable. Greater Darkness needed Darkness as a prerequisite; Telekinesis needed Presdigitation.

Level 3 had a good pair of basic spells: Detect Magic and Shadow Double. Each one cost 3 Lexica points, so she would be able to take one. I was going to have to see what kind of combat role she played at larger sizes. Both spells were potentially very useful, especially as I was not capable of using any magic – just special abilities that chewed up Adrenaline Points and-or HP to execute powerful attacks and evasive maneuvers.

With a hand resting on her snoring flank, I brought up her Path menu:

KARALTI - QUEEN DRAGON (DARK/LIFE AFFINITY)

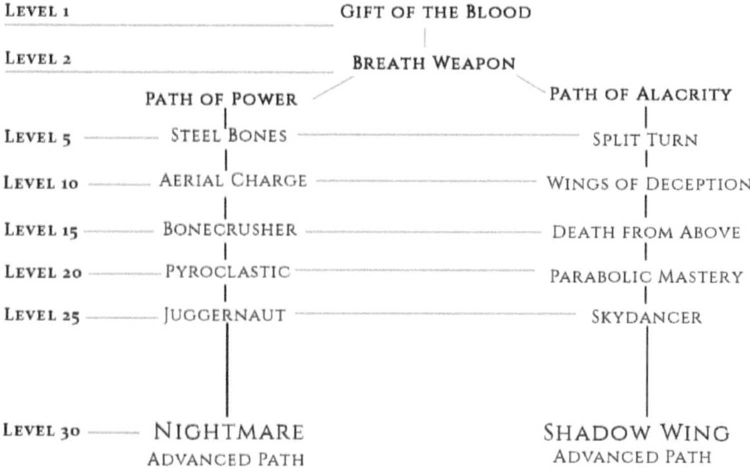

This was also something I already had to think about. Dragons levelled differently than players. Superficially, it was similar in that Karalti got to take a Path and then an Advanced Path, which in this game was equivalent to taking a Class. There were some differences. Players started out with a basic general Path – Warrior, Mage, Specialist, or Artificer. At Level 5, they had the option to take a specialized class, or Advanced Path.

Karalti had to grow to Level 5 just to take her basic Path, which was less like a character class and more like a developmental track for her that shaped her strengths and weaknesses. She wouldn't get to take an Advanced Path until her soft cap at Level 30. I assumed that was because of how powerful dragons were at levels 1-30 compared to the average player character or NPC. Advanced Paths were an endgame feature for dragons.

Draconic Paths: The Path of Power and the Path of Alacrity

Dragons mature slowly, and like humans, they can only take an Advanced Path when they are experienced adults. A dragon reaches adulthood at Level 30. From hatching to maturity, your Queen dragon can invest points into one of two basic Paths: The Path of Power and the Path of Alacrity.

Path of Power: *This Path focuses on your dragon's strength and offensive abilities, improving their ability to take and deal damage, and the strength of their breath weapon.*

Path of Alacrity: *This Path focuses on your dragon's mobility and defensive abilities, improving their speed, agility, and tactical movement at high altitude.*

At first, I'd been disappointed in the Path 'gap' between Level 2 and Level 5, but that gap had a purpose. It was there so you had time to think about what Path you were going to take your mount along. It was impossible to tell what kind of personality or native talent your dragon had at Level 1 or 2, but I knew I'd have a good idea by Level 5. Not only that, but at Level 5, I was pretty sure she'd be big enough to start flying – which meant we'd be able to experiment as a team before we committed to one of the two paths: Power or Alacrity.

My dragon had two unspent skill points. I decided to put another point into her existing Acrobatics skill, bringing it to Acrobatics 4, and one into a new skill, Stealth. Stealth covered both sneaking and hiding. At her size and level – and given that we were headed for an urban environment – it made sense to make sure she was able to fly nimbly and successfully hide if she had to.

"Morning, sleepyhead," I said, closing the HUD menu. "Time to get up. We've got training."

Karalti snored on.

"Come on, kiddo." I gave her a couple of shakes.

"Uugooo..." Karalti balled up like a cat, tucking her head under her wing.

"Yep. Training. You're gonna be the best flier in the world, remember?" I pushed off her and made my way around her tail to sit on the edge of the bed. "Come on, chop-chop."

"Nuu. Karalti sleep." Her telepathic voice was blurry.

"Nope. Karalti gets out of bed and embraces the suck." I was beginning to sound like my old NCO. "Up and at 'em, sunshine."

"Nuuuuuu. Sun can go die." But she untucked her head and peered at me blearily. Her eyes were even more stunning than her skin: a tight bicolor core of black and pure amethyst purple, shot through with silver. *"Karalti hate the sun."*

"Me too, but we need to get stronger. We're doing hoops and beams today."

While my dragon groaned and rustled around under the covers, I dropped and started doing push-ups. There were no Stat Points to assign in Archemi – you got what you trained for. If you wanted to raise Strength, you lifted weights, overloaded your pack and marched around, or worked a forge and hammer. If you wanted to improve your Dexterity, you ran laps, learned gymnastics, or practiced knife throwing, parkour, or similar activities. Same with all the others. You wanted more INT? You read books and learned stuff. Wisdom? I'd found that thinking about strategy and tactics, playing games, and getting to know NPCs reliably improved Wisdom. The difference between Archemi and IRL, the thing that made this process fun, was that you got immediate, tangible benefits for training. Your muscles pumped when you gained a point. Your mind got keener, your vision improved. You saw the improvements training made to your body, your mind, and your Attack, Defense, Evasion, and other abilities.

It reminded me a lot of the training program I'd used to get fit when I'd really started to get into motorcycle stunt work. Being an enormous dork, I used augmented reality apps that added an RPG element to my training, and had worked on becoming a 'Level 15 Barbarian' by checking off workouts over weeks and months. Karalti leveled her stats exactly the same way, and so did Cutthroat. Thus, training.

I'd finished two sets of 50 push-ups by the time Karalti slithered out of bed. She yawned, revealing twin rows of razor-sharp teeth, and smacked her jaws together couple of times. *"Karalti hates hoops."*

"It's time you started using first-person pronouns, Tidbit." I cracked my knuckles and then turned back to my exercises. Clap push-ups, then burpees. "You're a big fire-breathing girl now. No more baby talk."

Karalti regarded me pensively, her in eyelids half closed. *"So I can say stuff like... 'If you make me fly hoops, I'll set you on fire?'"*

"As long as you say it in first person."

"What about... I hate hoops, and I hate you for making me fly through them? And I want five chickens, aaand..."

"You're a Queen Dragon, not a dragon princess. You'll eat what you're given."

The little dragon finally hopped to the floor, stretching her wings and curling her back feet up against her ribs one at a time, like a bird. *"I'm so hungry though. Bleh. Well, I guess hoops are okay, but do I have to wear the...?"*

Her pupils contracted to points, and then she turned her head away from me, studying the ceiling intently.

I stood up, and arched an eyebrow. "The what?"

"*Nope! Nuthin!*" Karalti made a show of preening underneath her wing. "*Wow, I sure got really big after I levelled, huh?*"

I rolled my eyes, and went to get the source of her dread. My backpack.

Karalti whined aloud, flattening her wings against her body. *"Nuuuu! No backpack!"*

"Yes, backpack." Everything we owned was loaded in my pack, which weighed about sixty pounds. Karalti was still too little to carry all of it while flying, so I sorted about half of the weapons, junk, and tools onto the floor while she griped and stamped her feet.

"*Don't wanna!*"

"Of course you don't wanna. But you're already twice as big as you were at Level 1. Think how strong you'll be by your next level after some resistance training."

"*I don't care! It's heavy!*"

I sighed, standing up with it over one shoulder. "You want to carry *me* some day, don't you?"

Her wings drooped. "*Yeah.*"

"I weigh a hundred and eighty pounds. This weighs less than a quarter of Hector. Do you remember why we use the backpack for training?"

She looked sidelong. "*Because you're a fatass?*"

I mock-scowled, and reached back to grab my butt. "I'll have you know that my ass is a supple, perky marvel of nature, young lady."

Karalti play-bowed to me, tail lashing with mirth. "*Yeah! Because it's fat!*"

I narrowed my eyes. "If you want to make your stand on that hill, be prepared to die on it, because I *will* twerk on you."

Dragons were intensely visual creatures, and the rant made Karalti squeal with laughter and cover her eyes. How she knew what twerking was, I'll never know. "*Aaaaghhh, whyyy??!*"

"Me and my perfect ass have no shame whatsoever, and you *will* regret ever questioning the mass and might of my posterior. Now, unless you want to see Uncle Hector crack walnuts with his buttcheeks, try again," I said.

Karalti's eyes and nostrils scrunched up in a draconic pout. *"Because resistance training with balanced weight makes it easier to fly?"*

"That's right."

"*You better wear it too!"*

"I will. I'll even go first." I walked over and booped her on the snout with my finger. "I don't expect you to do anything I wouldn't do myself."

Once we actually got outside and got moving, Karalti's surliness was replaced by giggling enthusiasm. She bounded across the rolling deck and practically threw herself over the railing, chirping with delight as she swooped up into the cold, choppy wind. This time, her exuberant morning flight was accompanied by gouts of white fire.

I watched her for a few minutes, admiring the way she cut the air. That one skill point had made a noticeable difference in her agility. While she warmed up, I did two sets of ten while wearing the pack where she could see me. I hadn't told her it didn't actually weigh thirty pounds – it weighed forty. That was for my benefit, as well as hers. When I was done, I'd gained another point to Strength and Stamina. *"Okay, Tidbit. Time to work."*

"Oki!" Karalti swung around and backwinged to land on the banister of the ship, flapping to keep her balance, and turned to present her back to me.

"That's the spirit." I buckled the straps back around her wings and arms, then around her chest. "Soon we'll be able to do this together."

"*Yeah!*" She looked around inquisitively. "*Where should I train?*"

I pointed up at the ship's masts and overhead, horizontal sails. "I want you to cut figure eights through the rigging. That'll force you to keep with the ship, too."

"Oof. That's hard." She looked up at the rigging with trepidation. "How heavy is this pack?"

"Thirty pounds," I lied.

Karalti groaned under her breath. "*Thirty! I can't fly with thirty!*"

"Of course you can. You can do it, muscles." I clapped her on the shoulder. "Embrace the suck, enjoy the pain – it means you're growing."

She wibbled for a couple of seconds, but then looked back at me with determination in her eyes. "*Okay... I'm gonna do it! I'm gonna be the strongest! Watch me!*"

When I stepped back, my dragon stood on her back legs and stretched her wings out to their full ten-foot span. She had long, streamlined wings, like a sea bird. Karalti dove off the railing and dropped like a stone for a good twenty feet before she caught a thermal and rose, puffing with effort, and headed for the rigging. While she did that, I tied myself into an improvised rope harness, and knotted that to the railing before leaping up to balance on the edge. It was, in a word, terrifying. The ship was bucking up and down on the currents of air. To my left, there was nothing but sky and an eight thousand foot drop onto land. It was exactly what I needed.

My dragon had to build her strength to be able to carry me, and I had to build my mental strength to being able to fly on her – and fight on her back. Even though I was immune to vertigo and had no fear of heights, that didn't mean that I was immune to the very rational fear of falling off. I could look over the edge of a skyship like this and not feel sick or dizzy, but my inner monkey still screamed in horror whenever I wobbled on the railing. If I was going to be a good dragon rider, I had to be completely unafraid of falling. Even though Karalti was nowhere near being able to carry me yet, she wasn't going to be a gawky little hatchling for very long - and riding a dragon wasn't as simple as sitting on it while it flapped around. Archemi's physics were very real, and you didn't just magically stay on something diving at two hundred miles per hour without the proper skills and gear to hold on.

There was something else I had to master, too: using my HUD while suspended over extreme heights. I found stable footing on the railing and called it up, holding my spear out for balance while I glanced over my own character sheet:

Dragozin Hector - Dauntan (Tuun)

Level 9 Dark Lancer

==Stats==

Strength: 20

Dexterity: 24

Stamina: 22

Will: 21

Wisdom: 22

Intelligence: 19

HP: 482

XP: 2038 (576 to Next Level)

Adrenaline: 55

Renown: Notable adventurer (General); Wanted Outlaw (Ilia), Heretic (Hercynia)

==Abilities==

=Racial=

Blessing of Burna: +10% bonus to resist disease; +5% Stamina bonus to recover from illnesses. Immune to Pox and Lockjaw. +10% cold resistance. All physical needs accrue 2% slower.

Plateau Native: No Stamina penalties in thin air, -2 Stamina penalty at sea level.

Saddle Born: All Riding skills increase 5% faster.

Sun-sight: No vision penalties in bright or very bright light, -5% penalty in dark environments.

Blessing of Tarn: +15% movement speed.

Blessing of Hrrun: No airsickness, reduced inertia, no vertigo.

=Dragonforged Abilities=

Mana Tolerance: You have great resistance to Stranging and Mana Sickness, and may consume magical potions without permanent ill effects. Your toxicity threshold is now equal to your HP. See the Mana Tolerance ability entry for details and related skill and ability trees. Exceeding your Mana Threshold brings on symptoms of Mana Sickness and drains HP.

Eagle Eyes: 20/5 eyesight with enhanced spectrum, 340-degree visual field.

G-force resistance 1: You can remain conscious at up to 5 g of horizontal or vertical pressure.

Stone Bones 1: +10 resistance to crushing damage, 5 damage reduction.

Deep Breather: 1.5x lung capacity.

Iron Body 1: You are practically immune to extremes of heat and cold. You can safely weather extremes between -20 and 120 degrees Fahrenheit.

Gyroscopic orientation: You cannot be disabled by extremes of motion. You are immune to disorientation and vertigo, and suffer no penalty to vision or concentration while spinning, falling, or while upside down.

Blood Pact: By undergoing the Rite of Marantha, you have become dependent on dragon blood to sustain your metabolism. Every week, you must consume at least one Dragon Blood Elixir to maintain your abilities. Failure to consume the potion will trigger the Starvation and Withdrawal statuses. All abilities gained through the Rite will become unavailable, and AP will regenerate 50% slower.

Stranged: The Rite has resulted in permanent mutations to your body which are visible and identifiable by some creatures. In places (or with people) where Stranged or magical beings have pariah status, you suffer a Severe penalty to all social interactions.

=Traits=

Curiosity: You are an open-minded and engaged person, willing to question your modes of thinking and doing and readily accept new ideas. Combat, craft, and class skills gain 5% more quickly.

Introvert: With a preference for your own company or small groups of loyal friends, you gain a 5% bonus to accumulate skills in solitude, provided you are not disturbed. Fatigue accumulates 10% faster in large groups and crowds outside of combat situations.

Dyslexic: The written word is something of a mystery to you. Books take longer to read, and all language-related skills gain -5% slower.

Natural Leader: You have a natural inclination to take charge. Social skills increase 2% faster when engaged in leadership activities.

Endurance: You are becoming accustomed to pushing yourself, even when you are exhausted. You may spend adrenaline to offset starvation, fatigue, or bleeding for +1 minutes x your Stamina.

Mark of Matir: This may convey special abilities at higher levels. When the Mark is activated, it will drain health from enemies on a critical hit. HP regained is equal to remaining AP + Will bonus. 300 second cooldown. You are immune to undead fear effects. – 500 Infamy in places hostile to worship of Matir.

=Path Abilities=

Doubletap I

Jump II

Bluster II

Shadow Dance II

Whirlwind Butcher I

Blood Sprint II

Chain: Blood Storm I

(New!) Umbra Burst I

=Gifts of Matir=

Fury Drain: When your HP falls below 20%, you can drain 10 HP per good hit from a single enemy (Cost: 5 AP. Cooldown: 10 sec).

Blessing of the Raven: You call on your power and gain increased insight into knowledge and skills. +10% Skill EXP for 45 min.

Life for Life: Channel a blast of damaging dark energy into your enemy and drain their lifeforce to replenish your own. Inflicts Corruption debuff.

=General Skills=

Riding 15

Riding Specialization (Dragon) 1

Navigation 9

Stealth 9

Negotiation 6

Intimidate 10

Survival 16

Acrobatics 12

Acrobatics Specialization: Freerunning 8

=Crafting Skills (Common)=

Foraging 15

Improvise Shelter 13

Alchemy 7

Herbalism 10

=Crafting Skills (Advanced)=

Potion Creation 4

[[You have 3 unspent Ability Points!]]

[[You have 3 unspent Skill Points!]]

[[You can select 1 Gift of Matir!]]

[[New Knowledge!: Gifts of Matir B!]]

Since we were on the ship and not having encounters, I'd hung onto my Skill Points to think about how I wanted to invest them. I'd already maxed out Herbalism and Alchemy without an instructor, so I couldn't spend them on my favorite skills. I planned to hold onto my points until I reached Taltos and could find someone to teach me Intermediate Potion Creation. I'd actually forgotten about the Ability Points. I couldn't take any new combat abilities at Level 9 – probably why I'd forgotten – so I quickly assigned them to three of my combat abilities: Blood Storm, Whirlwind Butcher, and Shadow Dance.

Gifts of Matir were related to him having chosen me as his champion. Being Matir's champion was kind of annoying, because it meant that I got shoehorned into some quests - like the Myszno one - but it came with perks in the form of bonus powers. I got a small selection every four levels. *Fury Drain* was an ability I'd gotten when I first met Matir; at Level 5, I'd gotten to pick two powers. At Level 9, I was allowed to pick one.

Swallowing against the nauseating fear, I pushed the HUD to the side, then stepped forward and rolled into a beam handstand on the ship's railing. The ship bounced just as I got vertical, and for a crazy moment, I thought I was about to topple off the side... but I bent my arms, and held the position. Sweet, sweet adrenaline washed through my body, and I grinned madly as I swiped my HUD back in. Upside down.

I checked out my new knowledge first. It was a short update to my previous Gifts of Matir Archemipedia entry. It upgraded my knowledge from C-grade knowledge to B-grade:

Gifts of Matir (B-Grade Knowledge)

Gifts of Matir are powers bestowed upon you by the draconic god of Darkness, Matir. His dual nature gives you access to two branches of Gifts: The Gifts of Life and the Gifts of Entropy. Gifts of Life enhance your abilities, heal disease, and combat the undead. Gifts of Entropy ravage and destroy your enemies, but may physically corrupt you and those on whom you use the abilities. Choose carefully, and use your powers wisely! Gifts of Matir are permanent and cannot be changed.

"Hmm." Curious, I had a look at my current Gift abilities with this new information in mind. *Fury Drain* and *Life for Life*, which both sapped vitality from enemies, were Gifts of Entropy. *Raven's Blessing*, which gave me +10 Skill EXP for 45 minutes, was a Gift of Life.

"Probably best to keep this shit balanced." As the ship bucked, I folded down from the handstand and back to the deck, then had a look at what was offered for Level 9:

Close the Wound (Life)

You draw on your own raw lifeforce to heal another's injuries.

Heal other player/NPC 50 HP per sec while ability is active.

Cost: -30HP and -10AP per sec.

Suppurate (Entropy)

You channel dark power into a person's wounds, destroying the body's ability to heal and causing their injuries to fester.

Cost: 20 AP + 10 HP.

Damage: 120% + 5% max HP per hour until enemy receives treatment for infection.

+1% chance to cause Blood Poisoning per 5 Levels.

Inflicts Corruption debuff 15m (Target).

Bury the Dead (Entropy)

You can strike incorporeal targets with a normal, non-magical weapon.

Duration: 30 seconds.

Cost: 25 AP.

Spider Climb I (Life)

You gain the ability to climb and travel vertical surfaces, crawl across ceilings, and hang on walls. Level this ability to extend duration.

Duration: 20 seconds.

Cost: 30 AP.

"Spider Climb." I selected it without hesitation. Didn't even have to think about that one. It was a great ability for someone who was destined to fly – an ability that could one day mean the difference between life and death.

The Mark burned cold on my skin for a moment, sending shooting thrills of ice through my veins, and with it came the knowledge of how to do the Spider Climb maneuver. I reached out and grasped the ship's railing. I felt shards of dark energy gather on my palms and the pads of my fingers. They dug into the wood like a glove of tiny claws, and when I flexed my hands, the tendons in my arms, wrists, and shoulders contracted like steel cables. Awesome: I was a tarantula now. Or perhaps... a Hecturantula.

"*Hector! I did it! And I caught a seagull!*" Karalti's voice broke through my focus. I turned as she swooped down, panting around the twitching carcass of the unfortunate bird. "*And I saw land! Did you see me fly?*"

"Of course I did." I rubbed the top of her head, which now came up to my navel when she stood on her back legs. "How far away from land are we?"

"I 'unno. Maybe five miles? It's on the other side of the ship."

I checked my mini-map, and saw that she was correct: we were only ten minutes or so from making landfall. I nodded, then crouched down and smiled at her. "So... want to know a secret?"

Karalti cocked her head. "What?"

"I didn't tell you the truth about something," I said, pointing at the backpack. "That pack? It doesn't weigh thirty pounds. It weighs *forty* pounds... and look what you did. You did your exercise *and* caught a seagull. You did it with ten more pounds than you thought you could handle. How amazing is that?"

Karalti dropped the dead bird on the deck, and blinked several times. "*Why didn't you say so?*"

"You already thought you weren't going to be able to train with thirty. But that struggle? It's all up here." I tapped the side of her head. "Any time you think you've maxed yourself out, you've only really given fifty percent of what you're capable of. I hated the Army, but I learned that bit of wisdom there... and as much as I hate to say it, they were right."

"*Whoa.*" Karalti looked down. "*That's deep.*"

"Yep. Anyway, we better go pack up. Also, it's potion day today. Are you okay with me doing a blood draw?"

"*Sure!*" Karalti happily trotted ahead of me. We both knew that my health and our bond required me to drink a potion made from her blood, but I always asked her permission anyway. "*My strength went up! And so did my flying, and my stamina, and...*"

The recipe for the Dragon's Blood Elixir that my mutated body required to keep running had fortunately just appeared in my Recipes after I'd imprinted Karalti. The unfortunate part was that the ingredients were expensive to buy, and the potion itself was moderately complicated to make. I didn't mind that much - Alchemy was fun, and I'd been able to gather small amounts of the herbs I needed in Ilia. I could only hope the plants also grew in Vlachia.

FIrst up was the {[Saturated Aqua Regia]} I needed for the potion base. This was a mix of three parts hydrochloric acid to one part nitric acid, which made aqua regia, and then - wincing the entire time - I added a single gold coin to it. That turned the mixture bright orange, which meant I could add the other ingredients: {[Serpent Lily x 2]} and {[King's Grass x 1]}.

I assembled the acid and herbal ingredients into a flask, corked it, then took it over to Karalti while she preened and primped. Once I had the blood drawing tools ready, she paused, offering her wrist to give me access to the vein we used for this vampiric ritual.

"Little pinch." I warned her, just before I slid the curved needle in.

Karalti barely flinched as her highly pressurized, vivid blue blood sprayed into the collection bottle. She hummed under her breath, tail flicking. When I drew it out and put pressure on the small wound, she gazed stoically out the window. When her chest swelled with a gasp, I jumped. "What?"

"Outside! Look!" She lifted her head on her long neck and weaved her head, a motion she made when she was focusing her eyes on something in the distance.

I capped the bottle and made sure the bleeding had stopped before I stood up and followed her gaze. And then I smiled. A great city was on the horizon, its glittering gothic spires rising into the sky. Behind it the city loomed an enormous volcano: the cone was clearly visible, wreathed with clouds, and the slopes were heavily forested.

"Yep. That's a city. It's where we're headed." I sat back down, and swirled the potion base until the reagent had completely digested the rest of the ingredients, turning the liquid a rich golden yellow. I poured the blood into that mixture. The liquid frothed as it mingled, turning green, then brown, then colorless as the acid was neutralized and transmuted by the dragon's blood. The result was a clear, thick potion with an eerie blue glow.

Dragon's Blood Elixir

Magical Item

+5 Adrenaline Points for 1 week.

Sleep restores Fatigue at an accelerated rate for 1 week.

Relieves the Blood Pact debuff for 1 week.

Value: Cannot be sold in stores.

Special: Must be consumed immediately after brewing; no storage possible.

Karalti bustled over to the window. "*What's the city like? Is it like Bryos? Are there things to hunt?*"

I uncorked the potion and sniffed the contents. It smelled vaguely herbal and sharp, like bottled lightning. I was vaguely disturbed by just how much I wanted it, because my hands shook a bit as I put it to my lips and threw it back. It hit my stomach with a rush of heat and color and pure, unadulterated relief. The weekly timer reset, and the tension that had been building in my body suddenly released. I sat back on the bed with a sigh. "There's plenty to do there, Tidbit. We're going there to find a murderer."

"*Do you think I can get strong enough to eat him?*"

I snorted. "We'll see."

CHAPTER 6

The scene that greeted us at the Taltos skyport was that of armed chaos.

We arrived in the early evening, and the area around the docks teemed with travelers - a very large number of whom were non-humans. Elf-like Lysdian, the cat-like Meewfolk, and cliques of masked, hooded Mercurions milled around in crowds, marched up gangplanks onto creaking old airships, or got into shouting matches with soldiers from behind barricades. Some people were clearly departing. Others were stuck behind temporary fences that kept them from leaving the docks. Some were crying, others simply staring. Parents comforted wailing children.

"What the hell is going on down there?" I asked Kirov, leaning on our ship's railing.

The tattooed knight stroked the end of his moustache. "I am not certain, but... well. Brother Orban was found in the public gardens. The Volod... hmm." Kirov scowled thoughtfully as he trailed off.

"Hmm?" I lay a hand on Karalti's wedge-shaped head.

"My guess is that the Volod must have issued that decree he was 'discussing' with the Holy Forgemasters." Kirov scratched the thick stubble coming in on his cheeks. "Brother Orban was murdered while he was serving in the Meewfolk ghetto, as I believe we mentioned. When I left, His Highness was talking about a decree to ban all non-human travelers from entry to Taltos. Not a bad idea. Those females might have a litter of six kittens, and who's going to feed them? Clothe them? Their menfolk don't work."

"Stereotypes ahoy." I scowled, watching a lanky Meewfolk woman console a pair of young kittens while a guard shouted behind her from the other side of the fence. "Come on, man. I expected better of you."

Kirov's expression darkened for a moment, but then he shrugged. "Eh. You'll see how it is here. The Meewfolk bring nothing but filth and mummery wherever they go. At least the silverskins set up workshops and make watches and carriages."

"Can't say I like what you're saying," I replied. "People used to say that kind of shit about my family."

"Ah, but *you* were not born to a family of alley cats." Kirov ruimbled with a deep belly laugh, then slapped me on the back. "Come, don't trouble yourself. And - oh, look, speaking of carriages. Down there."

He was pointing at a fine, gold-decorated carriage waiting for us at the end of the wharf. Instead of horses, it had a spinning, glowing mana engine showcased in crystal, a smaller version of what was powering our airship. I grunted. "Fancy. Is that the King?"

"No. His Majesty must have sent his illustrious carriage to collect us." Kirov jerked his head toward the entry to the below-decks. "Go, get your beast. We'll need you to help clean a path through this mob, eh?"

From fantasy dictatorship to virtual racism: fantastic. Shaking my head, I went to collect Cutthroat.

My hookwing was drinking from her bucket, sucking her cheeks in to draw the water up along her tongue. As soon as she sensed me, her head reared up. She sighted down at me, golden eyes narrowing with menace. The intimidating effect was somewhat offset by the fact that the tip of her tongue was still sticking out the end of her muzzle. Blep.

"I know, I know. My fluffy little murderbutt's all pent up." Before I even opened the stable door, I got within range and re-equipped her [[Iron Muzzle]] from my Inventory.

"SCREEEEE!" When the muzzle materialized on her face, Cutthroat swung her head and bashed it against the side of the doorframe, splintering the wood. I winced, but I'd become something of a vicious dinosaur expert these last few weeks. Before I'd hit Ride 10, I'd only been able to directly equip her muzzle and reins. Now that I was an Apprentice rider, I could equip all of her tack without going through the physical motions of putting on the blanket, then the saddle, then the cinch and saddlebags. I equipped them all. When they appeared on her body, she hissed and lunged at the door, banging her muzzle into it and sending it flying out at me. I dodged like a flamenco dancer and caught her by the reins.

"That's right, girl. Time to go and oppress us some cat people." Dodging her strikes, I led her forward. Dark humor aside, the notion of oppressing the Meewfolk actually made me feel kind of sick. If the Volod was the kind of man to punish a whole species just because a guy was kidnapped from the place that species was supposed to live, I already didn't like him. "Why are humans such dicks to everyone, Cutthroat?"

Drooling through the bars of her muzzle, Cutthroat growled and tried to bite the back of my head.

"Because we're nihilistic voids of pointless rage, fear, and ignorance, huh? Sounds about right." I led her up to the deck, absently weaving from side to side to dodge her snout as it darted forward over my shoulders.

Karalti was still clinging to the ship's railing with her hind feet and wing claws, and cocked her head as I led Cutthroat toward the gangplank. There was no way I was getting onto my mount's back and riding her down to the wharf - she'd throw me off into the ocean and roar with triumph as I tumbled to my doom. "Okay, Tidbit. Time to play turret."

"*Oki!*" The little hatchling launched herself into the air and landed on Cutthroat's rump. The hookwing's growls turned into a high whistling screech, like a tea kettle. She swung her head around to hiss at Karalti as the dragon found her usual riding place just behind the saddle. Karalti flared her horn stubs and pulled her lips back over her fangs, leering back at her.

"Cut it out, ladies." Exasperated, I led Cutthroat across the gap between the ship and the dock. I mounted only once we were safely on land. Kirov and Matthias followed, along with a foppish man dressed in splendid black and red silks. He blanched when he saw us.

"Ready?" The knight's moustache bristled as he surveyed us. "This herald has informed us that we are to be taken to the morgue so that Matthias may view the remains of Brother Orban. Cremation is customary here, but the Volod's new investigator demanded that the body not be burned."

"Smart guy," I replied from my high perch. "Let's go."

"Are you... well... is *she* coming with us?" He gestured vaguely at Karalti, who chirped curiously and tilted her head to the side.

"What?" I chuckled. "Of *course* she's coming with us."

"Well, no offense intended, *rytier*, but the morgue is a grim place, and she is a child of her species, is she not?" Kirov cleared his throat awkwardly.

I blinked a couple of times. "She's a *dragon*."

"Yes, but, she is a sacred..."

"She rolls on and *in* dead things," I replied. "And poop. Dog poop, cat poop, she doesn't care. She rolls all over it."

Karalti harrumphed. "*I do, too! Cat poop is WAY better than dog poop.*"

"Ah. Of course. I guess even a child of the gods is still a beast." Looking a little green, Kirov joined Matthias in the carriage. "Well, Hector, please follow us through the city. We are going to the University District. The morgue is there."

I nodded, and Matthias gave an order to the driver. The driver lifted a crystal wand, and energy arced between his spell glove and the wand as the carriage lurched to life and rumbled off down the road, clearing people in a wave ahead of it. It moved about as fast as Cutthroat's canter, so I followed behind.

Taltos wasn't that far from Ilia, but it couldn't be more different. The earth and stone here were dark, and nearly all the Parisian-style buildings were built of the same gray-black limestone. The low, cloudy English skies had been replaced by clear and cloudless blue, like the kind in Arizona or Nevada, and the weather was warm and breezy. I'd been expecting the same cool-weather foliage here – oaks, pines, roses and grass – but the gardens here were dry and sandy, filled with desert flowers, succulents, jasmine, and agave.

The city was a maze of narrow cobblestone streets. It was dingy at first, but brightened up as we climbed the hill toward the city center. There, the cramped medieval streets opened up into bustling tree-lined boulevards with shops and cafes serving dinner, open-air bars and restaurants, flower carts and food stands. At the heart of the city was the Main "Square" - actually a round plaza with a grand statue-topped fountain and an enormous sun mosaic that started in the center and radiated out to touch the entryways of the main commercial buildings that surrounded the public space. A church with soaring amber steeples and no fewer than three working forges out front stood on one side. Across from it was a huge Art Nouveau-style market hall.

I'd always been a city boy, and found myself relaxing in the hustle and bustle of the people around us. Hookwings - lighter in coloring and smaller in build than their Ilian cousins - carried fashionable townsmen dressed in silk. Merchants wrangled the triceratopses that pulled their carts, while smaller, bird-like dinosaurs scurried around at knee-height. I spotted terrier-sized compsognathus with brightly colored feathers. The little dinos crooned in the laps of ladies playing cards at lattice metal tables, while less showy breeds of small insectivores ran alongside children playing soccer.

I listened to the Archemipedia entry on the city, which had unlocked now that we'd arrived:

Taltos

The capital city of Vlachia, the biggest country in Eastern Artana, Taltos was originally a dragon settlement built into the dormant caldera of Mount Racosul. It was settled by humans nearly a thousand years ago.

Taltos was formerly its own city-state in the midst of the Sathbari Empire. It was able to hold its own due to its intensely strategic position on the Racosul Plateau, its enduring construction, and the division of the city into eleven fortified Districts which restricted the movement of mounted Sathbari raiders. When the Sathbari Empire collapsed, Taltos remained, and it now serves as the political, economic, and spiritual heart of the East.

The ruling king of Vlachia is currently [[NUMBERFETCH 12-091g-2-TypeNPC-Vl-Nbl]]

The audio cut off at 'currently', and my heart thumped nervously on seeing the error code at the bottom of what looked to me like an unfinished entry. Archemi, despite its depth of world-building, had been a rush-job. Now and then, I was reminded of just how tenuous this new world of mine really was.

The districts the article mentioned were very clearly delineated by walls, checkpoints and portcullis gates that could come crashing down to seal occupants inside. Our destination, the University District, took up about ten blocks of hilly, narrow, paved streets near the center of the city, and it was crawling with security. It was easy to see why. A good number of clerics lived and worked here in the District's churches, classrooms, and the seminary. The students and clergy who dared to come outside watched us anxiously as we passed.

The morgue was attached to a small blocky building that looked newer than the rest of the stately, castlelike campus of Loroda University. Eight guards with torches stood around the entry. Six of them were normal city guards dressed in iron chainmail, like ancient Turkish warriors. The other two wore the same fancy black and red lamellar armor as Kirov. They also had lines of runic tattoos down their cheeks, distinguishing them as members of his chivalric order: The Knights of the Red Star.

"Ur Kirov!" The man who stepped forward might have been Kirov's brother. Same haircut, same mustache, but where Kirov was big and bull-like, this man was thin and gangly, the kind of man you expected to find in a Thieves' Guildhall. He had stringy hair, slightly bulging eyes, sharp cheekbones, and a long, thin-bridged nose. The pair of men clasped arms and then embraced like brothers. "Welcome home, brother. And you, honored sage."

"Thank you, Ur Pavel," Matthias replied heavily. "I wish it was for a better reason than this."

"If you're here, does that mean His Majesty is visiting this place of death?" Kirov asked, aghast.

"He is. And he's far too excited about it, in my opinion." Pavel made a sound of disgust at the back of his throat. "The Volod should not be mucking around in blood and guts, but he was determined to accompany that Dakhari he hired to help us. Pah. Who is your guest? And... by the gods, is that-?!"

"Yes, that's a dragon. Her name is Karalti, and she's not a goddess, no matter what she tries to tell you." I rested a hand on Karalti's head and smiled wryly. The dragon trilled, and Pavel's eyes bulged harder. "I'm Hector. Dragozin Hector."

"Khors heard our prayers, and has sent us a Starborn and a true dragon to help us," Matthias added piously.

The presence of a dragon seemed to lift five years of fatigue from Pavel's face. "Well, you can't do worse than the Dakhari. Three men murdered still there's no clue as to how or why."

"There is only so much one person can do." Kirov waved his concern away, then clapped his hands together. "Come, Hector. We shall get you masks with sweet herbs, and then we shall go and view this horror."

We all got cloth masks, except for Karalti, and trooped our way down into the bowels of the place, descending into a series of cold cellars. Talismans and prayers written on ribbons hung inside the doors to ward away the spirits of the dead, who lay out on slabs under sheets. The staff here wore long plague-doctor style masks and heavy leather robes with thick stitching.

"*Smells weird,*" Karalti remarked, pausing to sniff at some condensation on the floor. "*I wanna roll in it.*"

"*Come on. We're about to meet royalty,*" I chided. "*We can't have you smelling like roadkill.*"

The room where the Volod had taken up residence was fairly obvious: it was the one with the two huge knights guarding it. They were clad in forbidding black platemail and helmets decorated with backswept dragon wings. My HUD identified them as ⟦Royal Guards: Order of the Dragon⟧. They stood with their sword points resting on the ground, hands wrapped around the hilts, only moving as we approached. There was an argument going on beyond the doorway - a man's voice with a sharp, biting sarcastic note, and a woman's terse replies.

"Ur Kirov and His Grace, Father Petko Matthias have bought His Majesty a most esteemed pair of guests," Pavel flourished with his hands back toward us. "The Solonkratsu Queen, Karalti, and her protector, Dragozin Hector. I vouch for them."

"I vouch for them," Matthias echoed, stepping forward.

"As you say, Your Grace. Adventurer, you must leave your weapons with us." The Royal Guard held out his gauntleted hand in expectation.

I didn't argue – I just handed them over. My spear, dagger, a ratty crossbow, and a shortsword I'd picked up as an emergency weapon all vanished into the Royal Guard's Inventory. He seemed to sense when I had no more weapons, because he nodded and waved us through.

"Let me lead the way," Matthias said to us softly. "His Majesty has a cutting intellect, but he has reservations about strangers."

Resigned, I nodded, and let him take point.

We entered into the cold room beyond in a single file. It was brightly lit, with five or six lamps illuminating the mutilated body of a muscular, light-haired man on the slab. Another Royal Guard stood watch in the corner of the room, keeping an eye on the animated conversation between the man I assumed was His Majesty Andrik Corvinus the Third and 'the Dakhari'. Whatever I might have noticed about Andrik vanished into a film of white noise as my world focused on the woman.

She was tall and athletic, with dark, coppery skin that gleamed gold under the torchlight. She was stripped down to bloodied gloves, buckskin leggings that hugged every curve, and a faded rose halter top that was snug enough to be practical, but low-cut enough to be intensely distracting. Her short, flyaway hair burned with all the colors of fire. She knew I was looking at her, because she stared back at me with defiant golden eyes, as fierce and beautiful as an eagle's. She radiated confidence, competence, and power... power that made her seem more royal than the man who strode toward us from the other side of the slab. She was gorgeous. Not only that, she was Starborn. She had a blue player halo like mine.

"Aha! If it isn't the Devil of Yorca, and he has brought me Petko Matthias! And just in time, too!" The Volod's sharp voice cut through my trance. I swallowed and tore my gaze away, fixing a polite grimace to my face and turning to face him.

"Your Highness, we have brought you a most worthy candidate to assist in the hunt for the Slayer of Taltos," Kirov said, bowing and gesturing across to me. "May I introduce you to Dragozin Hector of Tungaant: Starborn warrior of the Nine, chosen emissary of Matir, and the holy guardian of the Queen Dragon Karalti, first of her clan."

Andrik Corvinus was younger than expected: a sharp, roguish, handsome man with eerie white-gray eyes and elegantly styled, short black hair that gleamed with health. The King was dressed entirely in black and red. He wore a black Byzantine tunic with crimson trim, a pectoral collar of glistening rubies, and rings that flashed with dark jewels. He pulled a scarf down from over his nose as Kirov talked, revealing a sly, thin-lipped mouth. When Kirov said the d-word, the King's eyes widened. Then he looked down and behind me, and his eyes widened more.

"Magnificent," he whispered, stepping away from the body. "How marvelous. A dragon, here, in my capital!"

Karalti, nearly invisible in the dark and half-hidden by my leg, bobbed her head and trilled a small, friendly chirp.

Andrik looked me up and down, hands on hips, then nodded. "Who would have thought that Khors would answer our prayers so directly. And where are you from? The Western Continent, if I'm not mistaken?"

"You're not, Your Majesty," I replied. "I'm from Tungaant."

Andrik smiled a wry, challenging little smile. "A Tuun? Well, honored guardian, I wish the circumstances of our introduction were better. Were it not for these infernal murders, the nation of Vlachia would be offering you and your dragon a far more gracious welcome."

"No worries, Your Majesty." I shifted from foot to foot. All the olde-world formality was getting uncomfortable.

"And you, Father. You're looking well," Andrik opened his hands to Father Matthias as the priest bowed. "I am heartbroken to be here, and to be witness to the loss of Brother Orban and all the others."

"As am I. It is good to see you again, Your Majesty," Matthias said carefully. He bent a knee and leaned in toward Andrik's hand, but the Volod pulled it away before he could get his face near it.

"Please, do not kiss my ring today. We've been poking around down here in this cadaver for half an hour already, and I have all manner of vileness under my nails," Andrik grinned, a little awkwardly.

Matthias bowed from the neck, getting back to his feet.

"We thought that Dragozin Hector would be of great benefit to the investigation, Your Majesty," Kirov said, laying a friendly hand on my shoulder. "I have offered him provisional sanctuary, dependent on your approval, of course..."

"Sanctuary?" The Volod regarded us curiously. "What for?"

I steeled myself, drawing in a deep breath, and held my hand out for Karalti to approach. I heard her claws clicking on the damp stone, and she brushed her head up from under my palm. "The dragons of Ilia are laboring under slavery. My dragon's mother entrusted me with her egg, and asked me to flee with her and see her somewhere where she could be free. The Mata Argis of Ilia have been pursuing us ever since, and thus, we share this moment."

"Unsurprising. Backwards country... it only recently went through a bloody revolution that replaced the king with some soldier rabble and their pet merchants." The Volod nodded sharply, then looked back down to the body. "Yes... I think a man of your ability would benefit this investigation. But I will make the same offer to you that I have to this lovely woman: I am offering a reward of ten thousand *olbia* and a royal favor to whomever brings me the Slayer's head. However, before I am willing to sign the bounty contract, I must have compelling evidence of the Slayer's purpose. In the interim, I will compensate by extending full hospitality to the hunters seeking to bring this madman to bay... and hospitality includes provisional sanctuary for you and your dragon."

The red-haired woman was looking less impressed by the minute.

I nodded at the Volod's words, and my HUD flashed a quest update alert:

Quest Update: The Slayer of Taltos

Priests of Khors, the draconic god of Fire and Craftsmanship, are being murdered in the Vlachian capital of Taltos. After accepting the invitation of Sir Kirov and Father Petko Matthias, you have met the Volod (King) of Vlachia, Andrik Corvinus, who has offered you provisional sanctuary on the understanding that you will investigate the Slayer and return to him with a report on the Slayer's motives.

Reward: *10,000 gold Olbia, Royal favor, EXP (Progressive), +500 Fame in Vlachia, Faction relations go from Neutral to Good.*

Special: *While you are undertaking this quest, you have Hospitality in the nation of Vlachia. The capacity of foreign actors* *to pursue and attack you is greatly reduced. You are able to undertake quests and side quests in Vlachia without attracting attention.*

Special: *Failure Conditions – Fail to bring evidence to Volod Andrik Corvinus at the Vulkan Keep within 3 days.*

There was an option to accept the conditions of the quest. I confirmed it with an affirmative thought, and the title blinked green before vanishing.

"Excellent. I shall give you my mark, so that the guards of the city know you are in my employ." The Volod stared at me for a moment, and then the mark added to my HUD as a new status – it looked like a stylized raven wearing a crown with five points. Karalti got the same mark.

Once that was done, Andrik inclined his head to us with a stiff little smile, then turned his piercing gaze to Father Matthias. "Now, Father, if you would come to examine the body-"

"There's no point in examining the body more than we already have," the woman interjected. Her voice was exactly what I'd imagined it: a smooth contralto, dark as burned honey. She had a thick accent that I couldn't immediately place. "Which is what I was getting to, when we were disturbed. Any evidence there might have been was obliterated when the city guard trampled all over the scene of the murder."

Her blunt words effectively shut down the niceties, to my relief. Andrik scowled, turning back to her. "What were we supposed to do then, Suri? Leave him there in the commons for all and sundry to gawk at?"

Suri. I repeated the name inside my head as her player name tag appeared. I had mixed feelings when I saw it. On the one hand, I'd been hungering for contact with people who could give me insight into what was happening in the outside world. On the other, the worst experiences I'd had in this game had been with other players.

"Have the Captain of the Guard put up curtains around the body and call your investigator." Scowling, Suri motioned to Orban's corpse. "When your guardsmen picked him up and carried him out, they destroyed all the forensic evidence that might have helped us nail the murderer. Fingerprints, bootprints, all of it. So with all due respect, Your Majesty, next time this happens, you need to order them to preserve the scene, then call me in before anyone touches it. You wanted to know why we weren't getting anywhere? *That's* why."

Forensics? I blinked. *Jeez. She sounds like a cop.*

The Volod scowled back at her. "How are fingerprints supposed to help with anything?"

"Every person's fingerprints are unique." I dared to step up beside her at the slab, Karalti trailing behind, and looked over the corpse. "And if the murderer forgot to wear gloves, you can find their prints and match them to suspects."

Suri's head snapped around as I approached, flashing me the kind of look I was used to getting from Cutthroat. "Exactly."

Faced by two Starborn saying the same thing, the Volod's hostility turned to visible curiosity. He rubbed his thumb across his jaw.

"It still can't hurt for me to examine him," Matthias said gently. "And in any case, I must give him his funeral rites before he is burned."

"Was he working alone, or with a group of priests?" I asked.

"Brother Orban was not a priest, *rytier*. He was a Forge Brother, serving as a craftsman for the poor and needy." Matthias gently corrected me.

"He was working as a smithy in the catfolk ghetto," Andrik replied. He was struggling not to stare at Karalti. "He may have had contact with any number of commoners there. I don't know if Meewfolk have fingerprints."

"They do. Not that it matters now." Suri gestured impatiently at the body. "Who was he with? You never answered me when I asked before."

Andrik's mouth sloped to one side. "Alone. As I understand it, this was some sort of test for him. You would have to speak with the High Forgemaster himself to get the details of the assignment..."

"Then that's where I'm going. Cheers." And with a curt nod, Suri turned and strode toward the door.

"Wait." The Volod and I both said at the same time.

The woman turned back around in the doorway.

"Why are you going to see His Grace? Why not go to the ghetto?" The Volod spoke before I did. "The Catfolk there surely did this."

"No. They didn't." Suri cocked her head to the side.

The Volod gave a testy little sigh. "And *how* do you know this?"

The woman grimaced. "You told me nothin' was stolen from his workshop, right?"

"Yes, but-"

"*And* you enacted the laws that prohibit Meewfolk from owning or carrying weapons, didn't you?"

"Yes-"

"Do you see any claw marks on him?"

"No, but-"

"Do you see any shiv marks? Bruises that look like they were left by hands with feline finger pads? And do you really think a Meewfolk mob would leave his gold earrings in?"

I glanced down at the body, struggling not to smile or laugh as the King of Vlachia wilted under the glare of Suri's reason.

"That's what I thought," Suri replied. "Now, by your leave, I'm gonna go to the Seminary and talk to his High Forgeness."

"Mind if we tag along?" I asked her, patting Karalti to indicate the other half of 'we'.

"Actually, yeah. I do." Suri flashed me a ferocious glare, and stalked off through the door like an atomic bomb on legs. She paused to collect her gear, then kept going.

Chasing Suri upstairs gave me a magnificent view of her ass, but it made communication difficult. I hissed to her as we clattered up the steps. She turned near the top, glaring down at us as we caught up.

"Lemme guess," she said, eyes narrowed. "You want to party up with me."

"I'm pretty sure the only kind of party you're into is the Donner party." I tucked my spear under my arm, and re-equipped my brainbucket ⟦Militia Helmet⟧. "I'll put a raincheck on that, thanks. My name's Hector."

"I heard, in case you forgot I was in the room ten seconds ago." Suri grinned mirthlessly, flashing a mouth full of sharp white teeth. She'd re-equipped her armor and weapons: a coat of mail with plate armor for her arms and legs, a pair of axes, and a huge scimitar-like sword nearly as long as she was tall. "Well, Hector, you're a good judge of character. This is my bounty, and no, I don't want to share it. This city has plenty of quests. Go find your own."

"Uh-oh, Karalti! Someone just told me to forfeit my story quest." I held up both hands and rolled my eyes. "I'll be right on that ma'am, just as soon as you go fuck yourself."

Karalti threw her head back and emitted a sound disturbingly close to a human laugh.

I'd pegged Suri as the sort of woman to respect people who were capable of giving and taking shit, and the gambit paid off. She smirked. "Well, that won't be happening any time soon. But seriously, bugger off, mate."

Mate. That was the word that finally tipped me off, and that made her accent – filtered through the fictional Afro-Arabic accent of a Dakhari woman – suddenly click with me. "Wait. You're Australian?"

Suri had been about to stalk off again, but she froze in the doorway, her back tense. Then she slowly turned back to face us.

Yeah, ouch. She was Australian. That was awkward.

America and Australia had been on opposite sides of the Total War.

CHAPTER 7

I'd never actually spoken to an Australian before, short of screaming 'DIE, YOU ROO-FUCKING SCUM!" while we rained machine gun fire down on each other in the jungles of the Crescent Front. I'd been born and conscripted in the UNAC. Australia had been part of the Pacific Alliance. We'd killed each other a lot.

"I'd like to establish something before we go any further, alright? I really don't care if you were Australian. I don't hate you, the Alliance, or *anyone* except the fuckwads that started the War." I held my hands up in mock-surrender. "Yes, I was an Imperial Stormtrooper. No, I didn't want to do it. I was a conscript. All I wanted to do was ride my motorcycle, play old video games, and eat a lot of pizza. If you like one or more of those three things, we'll probably get along just fine."

Suri's expression soured more with every word that tumbled out of my mouth. She folded her arms and thrust her chest and jaw forward. "What the fuck are you talking about?"

"Which one? The bikes, the games, or the pies?"

Her eyes narrowed. "The *war.*"

"You know... *the* War. Twenty years of global conflict, nuclear winter in the Middle East, billions dead from an apocalyptic plague?" I gestured up and 'out', as if toward the Real World.

"Out there in the sky?" Suri snorted. "Alright. So not only are you a pest, you're a nutcase, which makes you exactly the kind of person I do *not* want hanging around."

I peered at her owlishly. "Do you... not remember the war in which you probably died? The one where you learned concepts like 'forensics' and 'pizza'?"

She sighed. "In case the dark skin, red hair combo wasn't enough to clue you in, I'm *shallatu*. Fireblooded, from Dakhdir. Last twenty-year-long war we fought there was close to a thousand years ago. Now, sod off."

"All jokes aside, I really can't." I laughed. There didn't seem to be any point in forcing a reality check on her, so I gestured to Karalti. "This dragon doesn't pay for her own groceries, so to be frank with you, I don't give a shit where you're from or what you want. My little scaly princess needs food, shelter, and safety, and Andrik's going to give us that."

On cue, Karalti deployed her ultimate weapon: cuteness. She looked up at the woman with great big puppy eyes, her crests held flat to her skull. Not even Suri's resolve could withstand the pathos of a quivering baby dragon. She pressed her lips together, glowering back down at her, but I could almost hear her ovaries swell.

"Fine," she growled, turning on her heel. "Just try to stay out of my way."

We set off again. As soon as Suri wasn't looking, Karalti dropped the cute act and stalked after her, her tail lashing stiffly. *"She's mean. I want to burn her like how I did with the bad mask man."*

"No, Tidbit."

"But burning bad people is fun! And she called me a pet."

"No fire," I said. *"No setting anyone on fire. I want to get to know this lady better."*

The hatchling harrumphed. "*You're only saying that because her chest is bouncy.*"

Dammit. I'd forgotten Karalti could sense my... "interest." I blushed despite myself. "*Okay, yes, but it's not just that, okay?*"

"*What is it, then?*"

"*She's a Starborn, like me,*" I replied. "*But... I don't think she remembers who she is. Or maybe even what she is. She's clearly Australian, which in and of itself is really weird. They were our enemies... I don't know why there's a Pacific Alliance citizen in Archemi. Like, how the fuck did she upload in? This an American game.*"

"*Oh.*" The real world metagame stuff flew over Karalti's head, as it usually did. "*So is she good or bad?*"

"*I don't think she's bad... or at least, I hope she isn't. She's probably just grumpy.*"

"*So grumpy people can be good?*"

"*Sometimes. I have a feeling this lady's grumpy because she's seen some bad shit.*"

"*Oh.*" Karalti pensively dropped her head. "*You mean she's done a lot of bad things?*"

"*Maybe,*" I said. "*Or had bad things done to her.*"

We emerged into the fresh night air outside, and I gratefully drew a deep breath.

"The High Forgemaster lives in the monastery on the other side of this college," Suri remarked, stretching her arms back in a way that was both alarming and distracting. It wasn't just the boobs. Suri was built like an MMA fighter. Her biceps were bigger than mine.

"That's a long hike. Want a ride?" I asked.

She gave me the side-eye. "Cheers, mate, but I'll walk."

"Suit yourself." I shrugged, then summoned Cutthroat from the stable. The big, black dinosaur materialized in front of us, swinging her head from side to side to orient on her surroundings, and then on us. I froze. Someone had taken her damn muzzle off.

The sour expression left Suri's features, and she beamed like I'd just teleported in a box of kittens. She approached Cutthroat fearlessly. "A *black* destrier? I thought only royalty got to ride those. She's beautiful! Hi there, baby girl...!"

"Uh..." All the hair on my back and scalp lifted as Suri strode up to my vicious, unpredictable hookwing. Cutthroat took a step back from her, pawing the ground and rattling warningly in her throat. "I'm going to say right now that trying to pet the slavering hookbeast is a very bad idea."

Suri clicked her tongue and bobbed her head, circling around. To my surprise, Cutthroat didn't lunge forward and rip her head from her shoulders. Instead, she took a cautious curving step, then another, and then made a low crooning sound in her throat. Suri smiled and repeated the head bob gesture. Cutthroat's nostrils flared, snorting, but then she tentatively bobbed back.

I squinted at them. "Are you... are you some kind of wizard?"

"Hang on." Suri clicked her tongue, and went in closer. Cutthroat's feathers flinched as she lay a hand on her neck, but she didn't turn her head to bite. I watched in disbelief as Suri began to scratch, and Cutthroat not only let her, but turned her head to the side to guide her hand to the best scritchy-spot.

"She's a lesbian," I said. "That is literally the only way I can rationalize what I am seeing right now."

"Are you a little birdy dyke, Cutthroat?" Suri was clearly into it. Her whole face lit up, and she got that high-pitched voice women reserve for babies, puppies, and best friends they haven't seen for years. "Yeahhhh, *there* you go! Who's the baby bird? *You're* the baby bird!"

"I cannot fucking believe this." I crossed my arms. "That raging hairy anus of a dinosaur has been the biggest learning curve of my entire life, and you just waltz up and lesbian-seduce her."

"I always liked hookwings. All animals, really." Suri shrugged, and reached up with her other hand to give a double-barrel scratch. Cutthroat's eyes rolled back with pleasure. "Haven't you ever tried the pack greeting with her? Hide your hands, bob your head, move around in a circle?"

"Of course I have." Scowling, I watched my hussy of a hookwing preen under her arm, then shake her feathers out. She looked like a puffy black canary. "I've done that, and I've tried to scratch her like how you're doing... and she bit my head off. Literally. All I was trying to do was give her love. Because I *do* love her. I mean, it's terrifying, co-dependent, masochistic love..."

"*You can scratch* my *head,*" Karalti said, huddling against my leg. "*My head's better anyway. And it's REALLY itchy.*"

Suri laughed a warm, rolling laugh, and my skin prickled for a totally different reason. "Well, you know, birds of a feather and all that. Big, scarred-up old bitch like this knows another one when she sees her. What's her name?"

"Cutthroat." I slowly approached to try and join her in the scritchfest. I got within two feet before the hookwing's head whirled around, jaws gaping wide. Out of reflex, I Shadow Danced six feet to the side, evaporating as her teeth chomped together in the space where my shoulder would have been.

"Cutthroat? Good name. Rolls off the tongue better than Guillotine." She pronounced the word like 'Gilla'teen'. "Ooh, she's feisty, isn't she?"

"You have no idea," I replied. "Now, stand back. We have a launch procedure."

Suri chuckled as she moved away. Cutthroat moved to follow her, chirping like a hungry chick, but then I equipped her muzzle. It was like lighting a tank of kerosene. The hookwing shrilled with fury, spittle flying everywhere. I tucked my hands behind my back and bobbed my head at her, but there was no friendly return greeting. Sticky drool streamed from her jaws, and she lowered her head menacingly, moving it from side to side in time with her tail.

"See?" I sighed as I tried to grab the saddle, but she turned in a circle away from me, darting her head out and banging the muzzle cage off my boot. "Muzzle or no muzzle, she's hated my guts from the moment she saw me. The only time she's fine is when she's killing things. Most of the time, she's like the incarnation of PMS."

"I always seemed to be able to get along with 'em." Suri said from the sidelines. "They like the red hair."

"Really? That's it?" I dodged Cutthroat's hind sickle claw, and jumped up onto her back in the brief interval between her attempt to eviscerate me and the stumble to recover her balance.

"All of them like red stuff. You should try waving a pair of red flags when you walk toward her."

My eyes narrowed. "Fuck you. You're trolling me."

Suri only grinned.

"I like red!" Karalti chirped. As soon as I found my stirrups and gathered the reins, she flew up to perch on the hookwing's butt. *"So do you. You like Grumpy Lady's hair."*

"Hey, you know what my dragon calls you?" I called back to Suri, wrestling Cutthroat into walking the right direction. "You're 'Grumpy Lady'."

"You wanna know what I call your dragon?"

"Go ahead, but keep it PG-13. She's a baby. Kid-friendly insults only, thanks."

The woman scoffed, jogging ahead of Cutthroat. The effect was instantaneous. Cutthroat trilled happily, and pranced off after her at the same speed, completely ignoring the reins, me, or anything else other than the new love of her life: Suri, the angriest and most athletic Disney princess in the world.

"So," I began, once we were out on the street. "You're Australian, but you *think* you're from Dakhdir... and you don't remember the Total War? So either everyone in Dakhdir is Australian, or your upload must have screwed up even harder than mine."

Whatever goodwill I'd earned by introducing her to Cutthroat vaporized, and suddenly, Suri had her rage face firmly back on. "How many times do I have to tell you that it's none of your bloody business, mate?"

"Is calling someone 'mate' in that tone of voice more or less friendly than calling someone a cunt in Dakhdir?"

"Less. But you're a real annoying cunt, anyone ever tell you that?"

I beamed. "After my morning bacon and eggs, I sit on the toilet with my acoustic guitar and make up sad country songs about how annoying I am while I take a big ol' cry-shit."

"Jesus fucking Christ," Suri muttered.

That's right. Dragozin Hector, Ladies' Man.

The Temple District, which was adjacent to the University District and the Trades Quarter, looked more rundown than you'd expect of a holy area. The winding street that led to the Seminary was lined with stone apartments, guild halls, and open-air smithies. Bald monks in heavy leather aprons poured sweat as they hammered out farming tools, weapons, and machine parts in forges that looked like open dragon mouths. To my surprise, there was a players-only bar here, too. It was currently closed, something I noted with a twinge of regret. Archemi simply didn't have enough players to populate all the cities.

Yet, I thought to myself. A nuclear strike had probably taken out Aurora Shard, one of the huge sealed megastructures in the USA and the joint Japan-American development center for Archemi. It was currently running off the off-world orbital servers, but that didn't mean there weren't survivors. Any day, the Devs who'd survived could come back online.

We approached the massive seminary, a star-shaped building with interlocking archways and a huge onion dome made from translucent amber. The central hall was big enough to admit a full-sized dragon. A burly guard took Cutthroat, and they made us peace-bond our weapons with red silk rope before we were admitted. It was like walking into an aircraft hanger: a huge open space with airship hulks, giant sails, crates and pallets stacked high. Layfolk craftsmen mingled with more worker-monks, and priests in red or blue robes. The ones in blue poured over diagrams and books, led prayers around giant forges, cleaned and swept. The red-robed ones had their sleeves rolled up and were instructing people on all manner of repairs and craft skills.

"We could grind Crafting like crazy here," I whispered to Suri.

She grunted her agreement, and slowed warily as one, then a dozen heads turned toward us. And they were all staring at Karalti.

"By the gods!" A young man exclaimed.

"They come with a dragon!" A woman cried.

"A goddess!"

"It's a sign! They've come to stop the Slayer!"

"It's beautiful!"

I took a step back, shielding Karalti with an arm as a crowd formed and pressed in around us.

"*Yeah!*" Karalti puffed her throat out, flipping her wings as she strutted back and forth. "*I'm the best!*"

"So, how's it feel being popular?" Suri squinted, a hand resting on one of her peace-bonded axes.

"Kind of terrifying," I mumbled back.

"What's going on here?" A gravelly voice boomed over the chattering people gathering around.

The crowd parted as a thick-set man rumbled forward. He was dressed in red and gold, his sleeves tied back over muscular tanned arms, and a heavy, brown leather metalsmith's apron loaded with tools. Worshippers and craftsmen bowed as he passed. The newcomer's thick beard, square face, and graying blond hair gave the impression of an old lion. When his dark eyes lit on Karalti, he turned pale.

"*Yeah! Worship me!*" Karalti flared her crests up and came to stand beside me, and I jabbed her in the ribs with my elbow. "ACK!"

"High Forgemaster Agoston Toth?" Suri asked. She put down her weapon.

The big man looked between the three of us. "Why... yes?"

I nodded. "The Volod sent us. We hear you've been dealing with some murders."

CHAPTER 8

"Orban was still young. A true prodigy." High Priest Agoston Toth was just about the least priestly-looking man I'd ever seen. Tall, wide, with a broad heavy face, a neck like a bull, and hams for fists, he seemed to take up most of the room. The small parlor where he had received us was connected to the main cathedral. It had bookshelves and plants, a jug of wine, and murals of dragons, battles, and men working a forge. "I took him under my wing, knowing he would exceed my ability in the coming decades. I looked forward to it. For a man with no children, your students are the hope for the future. Not only was he talented, he always strove to embody the virtues expected of a servant of Khors. The only reason someone would kill him would be to strike a blow against the church, generally, and me in particular."

"Did he have any enemies?" Suri tapped her lips with a finger. She sat at the end of the table, one leg crossed over her other knee. I was still standing, mostly to watch Karalti while she happily gnawed on a huge marrowbone in front of the fireplace.

The big priest spread his hands. They were calloused, and he wore a lot of rings, each one forged of a different kind of metal. "Not to my knowledge. There are the usual arguments and conflicts among the men here, conflicts which are resolved through mediation by senior brothers. A functional brotherhood relies on good communication."

"What did you do for him?" I asked. "Andr... His Majesty said you sent him to the Meewfolk."

"I did." Toth bowed his head.

"Why?"

He looked down at Karalti, who was making short work of the bone. "The priests and monks come to me with their troubles, and I counsel them. This can be anything from simply listening to their woes through to issuing penance for lapses of duty. They come to me knowing that what I order will be fair and just, and the penance will be in line with the oaths they swore to maintain. Orban came to me not long ago with a confession."

Suri nodded. "Which was?"

The priest sighed. "He admitted to me that he held prejudice against the Meewfolk. He had grown up being told that they are plague-bearers and thieves, and he confessed that he looked down on the catfolk who visit the House of the Maker. Not for any particular reason... a matter of upbringing and simple bias. However, the faith of Khors does not discriminate. It was the dragons, actually, who taught us that all peoples are equal under the sky, and all may seek to uphold the values of Khors and light a fire against the Void. One of the values we uphold is courage. The courage to face fear, and admit when we are wrong."

"You sent him on a solo assignment to the ghetto to prove his fears weren't real?" I rubbed my face thoughtfully, thinking back to Kirov's description of how his body was found.

"Yes." The craggy lines of Toth's face deepened with sorrow. "I confess I feel some guilt now that this has happened. He was a good man, and so young. He sincerely wished to overcome his fear, and now... now this."

Suri spoke next. "What are these values? Are they a code, or less defined?"

"Khors is a god of principle and action, and he extols seven virtues," Toth replied. "Hospitality, honor, courage, self-reliance, wisdom, discipline, and honesty. His faithful, whether they be lay or brothers in the faith, always strive to embody these virtues."

I glanced aside at Suri, and found her momentarily looking up at me with understanding in her eyes. I nodded a little.

"Orban was found with stab wounds in his back," Suri said. "But those didn't kill him. Someone went to the effort of forcing a live rat down his throat. He choked on it."

"Symbol of cowardice," I said, with a short nod. As I talked, I scanned the room. "The others who were murdered..."

"One was a tutor to the royal family," Suri said. "He was beaten to death with a book and a quill."

"Yeah. Safe to say that could be wisdom."

Toth's brow furrowed as he listened to us.

"Father Darko doesn't fit that pattern." Suri scowled, massaging one of her hands as she thought. "He hung himself. Nothing fancy or symbolic. Unless he really wasn't murdered."

"No." Father Toth fiercely shook his head. "No no no... Franz Darko was a ferocious and honorable man. If he desired death, he'd have strapped on his armor and gone into the woods to battle monsters until he could no longer fight. Suicide is a great disgrace."

"The opposite of disgrace is honor. That's the virtue, then," I said. "Father Darko's death just wasn't as... I hate to use the word, but it wasn't as 'flashy' as the other murders."

"Yeah." Suri picked at her lip ring, brooding. "That's how assassins kill people. Make it look like they did it themselves."

"You truly believe this?" Father Toth looked between us. "We thought perhaps someone was targeting us because Khors has... well, because the church is such a strong supporter of His Majesty, I should say."

Suri nodded. "What makes you think that?"

"The Volod is concerned about national security, and after the events in the Southeast and unrest among the non-humans of Taltos, he has focused a great deal of time and money on fortifying our borders and modernizing the army," Toth replied. "Khors is the god of the fire that protects us against the night and the forge on which we create the tools that feed and defend us. He is also the patron god of House Corvinus, who is said to be descended from him via his human-born son. His Majesty has begun a great push to modernize Vlachia, and has leveraged taxes on the common folk to pay for the weapons, armor, infrastructural components, and siege engines we build. He is training smiths and soldiers under the banner of Khors."

"What about the other eight gods?" I asked. "I haven't seen any big churches like this one here."

"There used to be," the High Forgemaster replied. "But the Nine are the gods of the dragons, not humanity. Of them all, only Khors exalted humankind. It is said he fell in love with a human woman, an artist of great skill, and she bore Taltos - the first prophet and patriarch of our faith."

I grunted. "Then it could just be some religious nutcase, but we won't know until we have a suspect in hand. How does the murderer know who's breaking which virtue, or who best embodies a particular virtue so they can murder them to make a point?"

"*Duhhh,*" Karalti said, chewing on her bone. "*They listen. That's how you learn stuff.*"

"You're far more likely to be murdered by someone you know than someone you don't," Suri said grimly. "My thought is that it's someone either in the priesthood, or who has a lot of access to the Church."

Father Toth rubbed the bridge of his nose. "Fire and Sky preserve us... I can't even bear to think of such a thing. But your idea is compelling... though we could simply be applying our ideas to a tragedy which is far simpler."

"It's always a risk, but it gives us something to go on." I jerked my head toward the room. "Out of curiosity... did you talk to the other murdered men shortly before they died?"

Father Toth's eyes narrowed, and his chest swelled. "Are you implying that *I* might have done this?"

"No." I glanced at Karalti. "I'm wondering if anyone might have overheard you talking to them."

"Confession and counselling is done in my chambers," he said stiffly. "But now that you mention it, yes, I did talk with Father Darko and Father Abel not long before they were murdered."

"Do you remember what you talked about?"

"Father Abel came to drink, report on the state of the university treasury, and we played a game of chess. He was my good friend." Father Toth shook his head, looking down at his hands. "Franz... *he* came in to rant at me over some matter of protocol. I don't remember. Much as I valued him, he was hot-tempered and quick to see insult or transgression where there was none."

Karalti might not have been that far off the mark, then. My stomach thrilled nervously. "Anyone else in the office at the time?"

"No. I receive my subordinates privately."

Suri nodded, her mind made up, and stood. "Then we need to search your office."

The priest bristled again. "To what end?"

"There might be some way the killer is listening in to your conversations," I said. "A painting with the eyes cut out or something. And if they're using your office to spy on priests and monks here..."

"You could be in danger," Suri finished.

"This is... I..." Father Toth looked at us, briefly at a loss for words. "I... suppose that's possible, but the temple guards watch the doors night and day. The windows are barred."

"Well, Matthias said he thought your killer might be a ghost," I replied. "Let's go find out if he can walk through walls."

Toth waited anxiously by the door while we went in and searched. Karalti trotted after me with her bone clamped tightly between her jaws, sticking her head in around me as I peered behind tapestries and paintings. By the way that Suri searched, I felt more confident that she had been either a cop, a soldier, or both before her upload to Archemi. She was brutally thorough, looking in spots most people would miss. Under carpets, inside drawers, and to the High Priest's dismay, through his papers and then underneath the drawers, which she pulled out one at a time to check.

"I don't think there's really any reason to disarrange my entire study," the priest objected. He clutched the doorframe while he watched us work.

"You'd be amazed where people can hide themselves or listening devices." I swept the room, zooming in on objects of interest, bookshelves, vases. The high priest's study had a collection of beautiful weapons and forge tools displayed in glass-fronted cases. My HUD highlighted them with glowing blue rings.

"Best place for a listening device is on the inside or underside of things," Suri mentioned from across the room. "Drawers, inside electrical outlets, windowsills."

"A listening device?" Toth looked even more taken aback. "Is such a thing possible?"

That was something I wondered myself, but given that Archemi had airships, firearms, and steampunk cars, I was betting the combination of magic and technology meant it was feasible. "*Smell anything, Karalti?*"

The little dragon turned her wedge-shaped head from side to side, tail lashing with curiosity. "*Smell fire! Aaaannd...big man over there? Annnd... OOH!*"

Two things happened all at once. There was a glimmer of gold light and movement in the corner of my eye; Karalti dropped her bone and then dashed off in a flash of black scales, obscuring my view of the scuttling thing.

"*Ratty! Rattyratty-OWW!*" Her mental voice was shrill with delight as she gracelessly slid across the marble floor and crunched face-first into the base of one of the High Priest's ornate wooden bookshelves. As she scrambled to recover, chomping wildly into the crevice underneath the shelves, it began to tip forward.

I didn't even think. I sprinted to her and put myself between her and the bookshelves as they crashed down on top of us.

⟦You have taken 25 bludgeoning damage!⟧

⟦You have taken 12 damage!⟧

⟦You are Bleeding!⟧

⟦You have earned a new Feat: 'When furniture attacks!'⟧

Medieval books don't have soft paper covers: they're made of wood covered by leather. I took a couple of hits to my face as they tumbled out. Straining, blood running into my eyes, I pushed the shelves upright and put my back against them. Nearly 50 HP down the drain for that little stunt. It was easy to see how one of the priests had been beaten to death with a book.

"You alright over there?" Suri called.

"Karalti! What the hell?" I wiped my arm across my face so I could see. "What have I told you about chasing rats and not looking where you're going?"

"But I got it!" My dragon reared up with the 'ratty' in her mouth. *"Weird ratty though. Too stabby."*

"That's not a bloody rat," Suri said.

She was right. The thing struggling in Karalti's jaws wasn't an animal at all.

It was a machine.

CHAPTER 9

The clockwork bug Karalti held in her mouth looked something like a tarantula with a round speaker device embedded in its back. It was about the size of a large mouse, writhing and kicking with eight needle-sharp legs. Karalti pranced up with it, and was about to offer it to me when it managed to jam one of its feet into her tongue. She squealed and tossed it down onto the floor, where it clattered onto its back, kicking its little brass legs. My HUD flagged it as ⟦Masterwork Arachnoid Artifact⟧.

"What the hell...?" Suri said. She and Father Toth converged on us, arriving just as the robot flipped itself over and tried to make a run for it. I stomped down and trapped it against the floor with my boot. Despite its size, it was tough; I had to put a good part of my weight on it before the damn thing stopped struggling - and even then, it continued to paddle its feet in the air, whirring and clicking like an irritated insect.

"By Khors' breath," Father Toth said. "That's an artifact. Mercurion work. It must be."

"A Mercurion made this?" I moved my foot so that I was standing on the legs instead of the body. The machine immediately began to struggle, lashing its body from side to side. "Is there a way to turn it off?"

"You would have to know its command words." The priest squatted on his heels, absently taking out a pair of tongs from his smithy's apron. "Let me see if there's a maker's mark."

I waited until the priest seized the bug around the edge of its carapace before lifting my foot. He held it up as it flailed, squinting at it as he turned it around and around. "Hmm... fascinating. And marvelous. I've only seen work of this quality a few times. There is no maker's mark on it, which I suppose is to be expected for a spying device. But this craftsmanship... it's superb."

Suri grimaced. "You're right. This is a Mercurion automaton. It has to be. One of those little buggers costs at least a hundred gold on the black market, too."

"I've never met a Mercurion," I said. Now that I had a good look at it, I could see that not only was the brass and silver thing tough as hell, it was a work of art. Tiny gears and levers whirled inside its abdomen. The brass was etched with elegant arcane designs. "This would be controlled by an Artificer or a Mage, right? I know next to nothing about magic."

"Yeah, an Artificer," Suri replied. "But look at the materials. Brass, silver, diamonds, bluecrystal mana... that shit's expensive. Whoever commissioned this has to be rolling in gold. I take it this doesn't belong to the Church?"

"It most certainly does not," Toth replied. "The Temple serves the people by producing staples needed to live a good life. Ploughshares, carriage parts, rebar, construction parts. Swords and armor. We are not Artificers. If we need magic or magitech, we outsource to the Mercurions or a very few human craftsmen."

I tapped the round disk on the machine's back. It made a small, tinny, hollow sound. "That's a speaker. Someone's been listening to your conversations."

"Given that its got legs, it might not have just been listening in this room," Suri said. "This thing could move anywhere around in the building."

A nasty thought occurred to me then. I pointed at a big glass jar full of what looked like cut tobacco and mimed dropping the bug into it and screwing the lid closed.

"Of course, of course. Let me... Hmmm..." The priest bustled over to his desk and dumped the contents into an empty metal vase, then brought the jar back. Suri dropped the spider in, and it began to scuttle around inside. We got the lid on just as it jumped.It hit the lid and began to crawl around again.

"The other priests," I said urgently, once I knew it was no longer recording us. "Has anyone come to you since Orban died? To confess their sins, or whatever?"

He nodded, swallowing. "Yes, though they did not discuss any sins they may have committed. There have been two: Brother Moricz and Father Erik. They came with separate concerns. But they're under heavy guard-"

"What did they talk about?" Suri demanded.

Father Toth hesitated. "I am oath-bound to keep their confidence."

"Where are they? Where can we find them?" I asked.

"Brother Moricz lives in the seminary. He's an instructor there. Father Erik teaches young orphans how to craft, so that they might have skills after they leave the orphanage and not turn to thievery or suchlike."

Suri set her jaw and rolled her shoulders. "Those are in opposite directions. Let's split up."

"I can ride Cutthroat. I'll take Erik," I said. "We should party up so we can-"

"I don't 'party up' with anyone." Suri shook her head, her scarlet hair flying out from her face, and stalked out the door.

Quest Update: The Slayer of Taltos

There are two priests of Khors at risk of being struck down by the Slayer: a seminary tutor in the Temple District, and a crafts instructor who teaches at the orphanage near the Skyport. You must reach the orphanage, quickly!

⟦A new location has been marked on your map!⟧

Father Toth blinked in confusion. "I thought she was your fellow investigator?"

I sighed, dismissing the quest update. "Long story. Come on, Karalti."

We jogged out of the room, but when I rounded the edge of the door, I was confused to not see anyone outside other than guards, priests, and congregation. I grimaced. I swiped my HUD over and summoned the 'Known Players' list to message her. When I bought it up, there was no 'Suri' listed there. The only names were the players I'd met at the Eyrie of St. Grigori: Violetta, Baldr, and Lucien, who were grayed out because I'd blocked them as soon as I'd left Ilia. Two others I'd met before taking the Trial of Marantha, Nethres and Casper, were also listed and were online. But no Suri.

"*Suri?*" I queried her name in the database.

⟦No such player found.⟧

I felt a twinge in my gut: my intuition, warning me of something. I tried a different spelling, but got the same system message. Had she blocked me already? But no... that couldn't be it. I'd seen her player's corona in the High Priest's office just a second ago.

"Ugh." I scratched my head and sighed. "Why do I even care, Karalti?"

"You told me *you wanted her on our side, but that's gonna take longer than one day. Grumpy lady is smart and brave."* Karalti bobbed her head. *"And bouncy."*

That made me chuckle, but I was still annoyed. At Suri, at myself, at the murders. I picked up my pace and hustled for the outside courtyard, whistling for Cutthroat. The hookwing appeared, and before she could give me any shit, we climbed onto her back. I pulled her around, and kicked her into a run, following the glowing marker on my mini-map. Between the quest update and the fact that the listening device had been discovered, I had a feeling our murderer was going to strike soon, and strike hard.

The orphanage was down near the Skyport: a three-story wooden manor house with an attached warehouse I assumed was a workshop or school. Both the house and warehouse had definitely seen better days. We pulled up with a screech at the front doors, and I vaulted off Cutthroat's back to the wet cobblestones. The doors were guarded by two men in the chainmail-and-plate uniform of the city guard, and they pulled their swords, scowling with suspicion.

"Halt! Who-"

"High Forgemaster Toth sent me. Father Erik is in danger," I said, holding my hands up. "Has anyone else come in in the last thirty minutes or so?"

"What? No." The guard on the left, an exceptionally thin man, shook his head. "Father Erik has a guard posted in his quarters. I see you work for the Volod, but...

"We're not supposed to let in anyone with weapons due to there being children inside. Captain's orders," the other one said. "Hand over your steel, and you may enter."

"The Slayer is in there!" I snarled. "I work for the Volod, and we need to get inside! Let me pass!"

"We can't-"

Karalti marched forward past me. She threw her head back and emitted a shrill roar, splattering droplets of flaming spittle everywhere. *"Bad men! Out the way!"*

Both guards jumped out of the way with cries of terror, brushing frantically at the burning spots on their armor.

"That's my girl," I muttered, and barged in past them.

The inside of the building reminded me of a school. Kids' drawings covered sheets of curling, yellowed parchment on the walls and the side of the wooden staircase. I fought the urge to barrel to the top of the stairs at full speed. Instead I stealthed it, dropping to a crouch and using one hand to guide my way across the old wooden floor. Karalti dropped down as well, and we silently followed the quest icon to a room behind a pair of double doors. I listened at the keyhole. Instead of the normal sounds I'd expect of a teacher's bedroom at this time of night: throat–clearing, the rustle of papers, the scratch of a quill, chit-chat between Father Erik and his bodyguard–there was nothing except the swish of fabric, and a soft metallic clinking.

"Claws and teeth only. No fire," I thought to Karalti, tightening my grip on the Spear. *"The building's made of wood and there are children in the rooms below us. If you breathe fire here, you'll kill them all."*

"Oki." Her telepathic voice was a whisper. *"On count of three?"*

"Yeah. One, two...three." On three, I kicked the door and charged in.

And then nearly stopped cold, because holy shit.

Father Erik and the guard were both dead. The guard lay on his face, a crossbow bolt protruding from his eye. Father Erik was naked, kneeling on his bed, and kept upright by an intricate net of ropes with hooks that stretched his skin out from his body. Standing over him was a tall, lean figure in a hooded cloak. His face was covered with a flat steel mask that burned blue with magical sigils.

Before I could even open my mouth, the Slayer of Taltos dropped what he was doing, spun in a flurry of black cloak, and dashed for the window.

CHAPTER 10

"Hold it right there, asshole!" I barked, sprinting after him.

The Slayer didn't hold anything. He dove through the window with inhuman agility and confidence, leaped across the alley below and onto the next roof. Without slowing, he hit the tiles with a crunch. Broken ceramic skittered to the street three stories below, and he kept running.

Pulse thundering in my ears, I vaulted the windowsill and triggered my core Lancer ability, Jump. Dark power gathered in my legs and then snapped out. I bounded after him like a cricket. Karalti was right behind me, flinging herself into the sky with powerful beats of her wings.

"*Flank him!*" I sailed through the air and landed behind the fleeing murderer, scattering loose tiles beneath my boots. He jumped to the next roof, swung around a metal chimney, and fired something at me: a crossbow no bigger than a Beretta Model 12. I dodged reflexively, already partially off the ground. Just as well. The bolt slammed into the roof and blew a hole in it, sending shards of brick flying into the air.

Explosive rounds. Wonderful.

The awkward mid-air correction threw me off course, and instead of landing on the level part of the roof, I hit the slope of it and slid down in a wave of broken tiles. I sprung up desperately at the edge of the gutter, jumping again before I fell to the street below.

That last minute effort propelled me across the gap, and I triggered my new Spider Climb ability just before I hit the waist-high wall of the balcony on the opposite side. Power surged through my limbs, crystallizing as I slammed into the wall with a crunch.

"Ow, ow, *ow*!" Snarling, I scrambled up like a gecko, vaulted over, then ran along the balcony as the killer's cloak flickered in and out of view above. The obstacles of the city ahead of us seemed to present no challenge to this guy at all. Like some sort of parkour prodigy, he hurdled and pivoted, vaulted and slid through it with eerie precision. Meanwhile, I blundered like a drunk rhino through tables and potted plants, getting on top of one and jumping to the next, wash, rinse, and repeat, until we reached the main road. He turned left across the roofs along the strip. I had nowhere to go but up.

"*Follow him, girl! Be careful!*" I urged as I got onto a balustrade, bunched my legs, and Jumped.

"*Oki!*" I heard Karalti's *chaaaaaa* and saw a burst of white light above. "*I got him!*"

I sailed up through the air and managed to grab the edge of the gutter at the height of my flailing arc. I scrambled up in time to see the killer trying to shoot Karalti as she flew rings around him. Her napalm fire was bubbling and flaring on the rooftop. He fired at her, missed, and dodged the next stream of flame, even managing to twirl the edges of his cloak away from it as he fled. My world narrowed down to that retreating back.

He fled to an adjoining belltower with an open door at roof level: a tall, narrow building where Karalti and I would be less effective. I was gaining on him by the time he vanished through the doorway. For a moment as I followed him through, I really wished I had a gun. He was sprinting up the spiral staircase inside the tower, taking the stairs two or three at a time. I spotted the motion of his cloak in the darkness and ducked as another explosive crossbow bolt shot out with a bright flash,like a tracer round. It slammed into the wall and bounced. The explosion cracked up and down the hollow center of the tower.

"*Fly up from the outside! Cut him off at the top!*" I called to Karalti as she tried to follow behind me through the door.

She reversed course as I ran up behind the murderer, sweat pouring down my face. I burst up onto the deck of the bell tower. The wind whistled over the railing, the heavy bell still and silent. Karalti spiraled up, beating her wings to hover in mid-air to my left.

"*Can't smell him,*" she said. "*Bad man has no smell!*"

"No smell?" I leveled my spear and advanced cautiously, ears prickling as I turned each corner and tried to see down to the roof below.

Like a ghost, the man slid out of the shadows behind me in a wave of rippling black fabric. I saw him in my peripheral vision, and he froze momentarily in surprise as I met his backstabbing blade with the haft of the Spear of Nine Spheres. It hit him in the gut with a dull 'thud', as if I'd rammed it into the side of a log instead of human flesh. It apparently still hurt, because he doubled over, his glowing sword skidding off in a shower of blue-white sparks, and the ozone smell of mana seared my sinuses as I sent it skittering away with a foot and carried the kick around. He blocked the strike with one arm, almost absently. There was no crunch of breaking bone. It was like hitting a mannequin made of hard rubber.

I lunged for him with the spear blade, and he dodged once, twice, and then spun into my guard. I headbutted him. The mask fell off, but all I saw of his face was a silver flash as he grabbed me, spun around, and threw me over the railing like I weighed nothing.

I caught his clothing as I went over the edge, and pulled him down with me.

"*Hector!*" Karalti screeched and dove for us, catching my hair and belt and flapping to slow our descent, but the murderer must have been built out of lead bricks, because he weighed a ton. Karalti almost fell with us, but she helped me orient in the air - when we slammed into the enclosed courtyard beneath the tower, I was on top.

[[You have taken 84 points of impact damage!]]

I grunted with pain as the impact bounced me like a basketball, but managed to avoid sticking myself with my own weapon as I tumbled over the ground and flipped up to my feet to confront the Slayer as he climbed up from the broken paving stones. He staggered briefly, hunched and limping, but turned to stare me down.

The Mercurion's face was not that of a vicious psychopath. He was angelically handsome, his delicate countenance twisted up into a mask of fear and desperation. His eyes burned blue, mana spiraling in around white pupils. Silver hair clung to his face and stuck up strangely around the winglets that curved back from in front of his ears. The cuts and tears on his silvery skin were leaking glowing white mana, not blood. I had just enough time to notice that before he bared his glassy teeth and threw something at Karalti.

Karalti, while agile for a creature of her size, could not get out of the way in time. The gas-spewing device struck her, but she swatted it back toward us with a squawk of alarm. The smoke that billowed from it swept over me with the wind.

[[Warning! High concentrations of mana in the area may cause Stranging in nearby NPCs!]]

[[You resist the dispersed mana!]]

For a breathless moment, I waited. Nothing happened, and the Mercurion's eyes widened.

"*Tarn takhrar*, motherfucker!" I triggered Bluster, regaining a few Adrenaline Points and some HP, and spun at him through the smoke with Blood Sprint, dark energy crackling down the length of the spear and into his body. The strike smashed into him, and the Blood Storm combo chain blew him off his feet.

⟦You hit Mercurion Assassin for 228 Damage!⟧

⟦You inflict Bleeding!⟧

The man backflipped midair, righting himself, and managed to land in a crouch.

"KIAHH!" I slammed the spear down along the ground. The energy gathered from Blood Storm burst out through the Umbra Blast maneuver. It tore the cobblestones and knocked the Mercurion off his feet a second time. This time, he couldn't get up. He was visibly panicked now; his crossbow was out of bolts, and the mana flare he'd pitched at us was obviously some kind of last resort. I Jumped forward and pushed the end of the Spear up beneath his jaw, pinning his head to the ground.

"Mercy," he croaked. "You don't understand."

"I understand that you're a sick fuck who just tried to mutate us," I snapped.

Karalti was rolling on the flare like a cat with catnip. The white gas turned dark on contact with her scales, like thunderclouds charged with violet lightning, then was absorbed into her body. "*Funny gas!*"

The Mercurion reached up to push the Spear away, but I dug it in until his fingers slipped away and a thin trickle of mana ran along his jawline. I glared down at him. "You. You've got five seconds to tell me who hell you are before I cut your head off and take it to the Volod on a platter."

His eyes narrowed. The magic in them roiled like lava, folding into the white pupil and then blooming out again.

"Three seconds, psycho." I drew on the Mark of Matir and sent a flash of dark energy down the length of the weapon. The Mercurion cried out, writhing in pain.

"There are… things worth dying for…" he gasped. "What I am doing is… for one of them."

"Alright. Suit yourself." I put pressure down on the blade to cut his throat.

"HECTOR!" Karalti shrilled from behind me.

I sensed the disturbance before I saw it: a puff of air, a cold shadow swimming overhead. I spun away just as something crashed down where I had been standing only a second before. It was a brass-and-steel automaton: a crab-like turret the size of a pit bull. It had four spiked legs, and a body that was little more than a platform for a repeating crossbow.

It fired bolts in a strafing line, chasing me away from the prone assassin. I Shadow Danced away with a snarl of frustration, reappearing as the Slayer, wide-eyed with terror, scrambled to his feet. Karalti spat a gout of fire that incinerated a crossbow bolt, flapping back up into the air as a second dog-sized artifact bounded into view. This one shot wildly at the pair of us as it approached. I took two hits: one to the arm, one to the calf. Their metal bodies were almost entirely soundless, save for the sharp **tang** of their feet as they stamped the ground.

Karalti's fire splashed the newcomer and sent it tilting away with a crown of flames, while the other backed off. *The Mercurion!* I searched around wildly, and saw him jump from a pipe to a windowsill to a roof and then vanish behind a chimney. Furious, I chugged a Brightlace potion, recovering 75 HP, and started running.

Another shadow figure, the one I hadn't seen, peeled away from behind a pillar and tackled me to the ground. I hit hard, brought down by the desperate bear hug of what felt like a stack of bricks. I cursed as we wrestled there in the dark. My attacker crawled away, shielding their face with their hands, and rolled onto their back as I clambered to my feet and leveled the Spear at them.

It was a girl. Another Mercurion.

"Please," she said. Her voice was high and breathy, her eyes wide with terror. "W-wait, please. Don't kill me!"

Nostrils flaring, I took a step away from her. This Mercurion was, in a word, adorable. Big eyes, an open, expressive face, a bob of translucent glassy hair, an up-tilted nose and a slim, girlish body. Like all of her race, she was unearthly. She was also flagged as a player character, with a strange-looking HUD ring: her blue corona had a gold ring around the edge.

She put her shaking hands up in the universal gesture of surrender, and didn't try to rise off the ground.

"Get up." Breathing hard, I took another step back. The Mark of Matir sent spikes of ice through my blood, charged with power just waiting to be released. "And call those death machines off my dragon, or I'll kill you."

Slowly, the girl picked herself up. "T-Their names are L-Lovelace and Hopper. Not 'D-Death Machines'."

"You don't say." I reached up, twisted the bolt buried in my arm, and pulled it out. With the combat rush pounding through my body, it didn't hurt as much as it should have. Even so, the pain replenished some Adrenaline Points. I threw the bloody bolt at her feet, and she flinched back, covering her face.

When she cowered, I hesitated - but not for more than a second. This girl screamed 'honeypot', from her ankle-length scarf to her cute little short-shorts and her wide-topped boots. She had spell gloves on both hands, which meant she could do magic.

"That man you just let go? I caught him murdering an NPC." I whirled my spear around into a combat position and stomped a foot down to center myself. The maneuver recharged some more AP, and distracted her from my dragon. Karalti was slowly flanking the girl. She vanished into the shadows, while the pair of automatons skittered back and forth uneasily hanging back to either side of me. "And YOU just stopped me from bringing him to justice."

The Mercurion girl shook her hands, and when she spoke, her voice was shaky with fear. "Please... he's not like this. He's an artist, a Master A-A-Artificer. He-he-he wouldn't n-normally do this! I-I..."

"Call. Your. Fucking. Robots. Off." I wasn't buying the 'panicky little kid' act.

The girl's hands shook as she held them out, and gestured. The mana in her gloves flared, and the two artifacts obediently scuttled around to their mistress. They fell in to either side of her.

As I tracked their movements, I saw a small flash on the ground where I'd just about dropped the male Mercurion: a pendant with a broken chain.

"*Hold steady,*" I ordered Karalti. "*Stay hidden. And if she tries to cast anything, blast her.*"

"*Oki.*"

"He's going to murder other people now. You know that, right?" I said aloud, moving slowly toward the necklace. "He's already killed three others. Don't you care about those NPCs?"

"Of course I care!" The girl shook her head, her hair flying out. "I'm trying to say that Kanzo wouldn't normally do this. He w-wouldn't-"

"Except that he would. He did. I literally caught him skinning a man in his actual goddamned office." I gestured angrily in the direction of the hospital.

"I mean that someone's *making* him kill these people!" There was finally some heat in her voice, and she advanced half a step. "He's not doing this willingly, alright?!"

"And how do you know that?" I demanded. I covered the necklace with my boot.

"Because I'm his apprentice," the girl said, fingers quaking beside her cheeks. "My name's Rin. And I'm a Developer."

CHAPTER 11

"A Dev?" I didn't drop the Spear point. "Guess that explains the gold ring."

Rin pressed her lips together in a thin line and nodded, glancing nervously at the blood leaking down my arm. "This doesn't look very good, does it?"

"No, it really doesn't."

"I'm sorry... but I have a quest too." The girl looked away from me, clutching her arm with the other hand. "I have to find out what happened to make Kanzo do these awful things, and then try to stop it and save him."

"*Save* him? What are you, a Jehovah's Witness or something? The guy's a serial killer." I was increasingly unimpressed. "It doesn't matter how much you like him - he needs a dose of the King's justice. Besides, you're a Dev, an Architect. You're a god above gods in this game. Why the fuck are you intervening in player quests?"

"Because I *am* a player," she replied, exasperated. "I *worked* on the game, and I was supposed to become a Mod, but then Aurora Shard was blown up and the servers reset from the orbital backups... Now I'm just a player until someone from the outside reinstates functioning Mod and Admin tiers."

I blinked. "There are no Mods in Archemi right now?"

"No. And there won't be until we re-establish outside contact. OUROS can moderate the game using ASE," she replied.

"ASE being...?"

"Oh! It stands for Administration and Social Exchange. It's one of the OUROS slave AIs that regulates NPC and player interaction." The physical signs of fear began to fade as her speech sped up, flat and a little fussy. "When the game rebooted from SOPHIA-1 and 2, all of the human-controlled Mod accounts were disabled as a safety feature to protect the refugees, because the human element is statistically less predictable than the OURO's ADEE and the ACE Engines. The risk of cyber psychosis goes up exponentially with externally imposed stressors like, um, global nuclear apocalypse, and... well, any apocalypse, really..."

"Cyber psychosis?" I blinked again.

The Mercurion blushed a bright silvery blue. "... I was babbling again, wasn't I?"

"You seem to know your shit," I replied cautiously. Her robot buddies still hadn't moved. "Don't suppose you knew a guy named Steven Park?"

Rin brightened a little. "Of course I knew Steven. Why?"

"He was my brother."

She gasped. "Really!? Oh my gosh! I didn't work in his department, but I, umm, I was part of the Environmental Design Team before I got HEX. He was one of the Core Devs who worked on OUROS. I was just a psycho-social advisor and architectural modeler mostly, but he was one of my nerd heroes, umm..."

Rin trailed off shyly, not quite able to meet my eyes.

I sighed, and dropped the spear point at last. This was like trying to hold a puppy at knifepoint. Rin was clearly not a combatant, despite the crossbow-wielding deathbots.

"Keep talking." I crouched down, and mimed adjusting my boot while I palmed the broken necklace that I'd been trying not to grind against the pavement. "Why are you in Taltos? Place seems kind of racist against anything that isn't human."

"I was one of the artists who created Taltos. We based it on old Bohemia, and I worked on, umm, modelling the buildings and base materials and logistics for the region, so when I crossed over, I wanted to settle here and become a crafter. Kanzo is my bonded NPC."

I squinted in confusion. "Your what?"

"Oh. It's a crafter thing." Rin fidgeted in a way that was oddly familiar to me. Fingers pattering, unable to meet my eyes for long periods, social awkwardness... hmm.

"Meaning?"

Rin twisted the edge of her scarf in her fingers. "When you make a character, you choose between combat and non-combat roles. If you don't take a combat role, you don't get the same paths or the same kinds of adventures as combat characters... and you get a bonded NPC who starts you off in your chosen profession. If you're a farmer, they might be like, your adopted dad or sister or something. If you're in the sciences or crafting, they're usually your craftmaster. I'm an craft-specialized Artificer, so..."

"So you got Kanzo." I sighed, and relaxed my guard. "Come out, Karalti. Stay chill."

Karalti stalked out of the shadows. Rin nearly jumped out of her skin as the dragon padded over to my side, her head held erect and stiff, tail lashing. While Rin was distracted, I slipped the necklace into a pocket. As I eased down out of combat readiness, I got new updates:

Quest Update: The Slayer of Taltos

After catching the Slayer of Taltos in the act of murdering a priest of Khors, you have discovered his identity: a Mercurion by the name of Kanzo who is a renowned Artificer – and a pacifist exile from Zaunt, the war-torn Mercurion homeland. You would have gotten him, too, if not for those meddling kids.

You have also collected your first piece of evidence for the Volod.

Reward: *502 EXP, Mysterious Necklace ⟦Quest Item⟧, 20 gold Olbia.*

As the EXP added, Karalti got an odd expression on her face. The seams of color between her scales glowed brightly. They licked out across her skin, obscuring her in a glowing swirl. She underwent metamorphosis rapidly, and when the colors retreated, she had nearly doubled in size once again.

"*Oopsie.*" Karalti still had a skinny hatchling look about her, but when she reared her head back, it easily came up to my collarbones. Her round horn stubs now had tiny, sharp, polished tips.

"Oh my goodness!" Rin exclaimed, her fingers fluttering up to her mouth. "She's beautiful. I... umm... didn't even see her before..."

Karalti narrowed her eyes, and huffed a spurt of white fire from her nostrils onto the ground. Rin jumped back about four feet. "*Weird rubber lady hurt you?*"

"*Not badly,*" I thought back to her.

The dragon flicked her wings along her ribs, pawing at the ground and weaving her head like a snake. "*I don't trust her.*"

"I've never seen a dragon in the game before!" Rin squeaked. "Did she just level?"

"Yeah, she did. And she's not too sure about you, which means that neither am I." Frustrated, I checked Karalti for damage. She was missing about fifteen HP, so I took a Bonebreak Poultice from my Inventory and applied it to her wound. "Look, I have to go report to the Volod about what I saw. You need to come too."

Rin shook her head vigorously, stepping back. "I can't."

"Why?" My tone sharpened again. "Your master's going to kill again. The King has a right to know."

"Because this isn't just about one or two people anymore," Rin replied. "You said it yourself... Volod Andrik doesn't like non-humans very much. The Mercurions already live in the Tanner's District ghetto and can't even own property. The Meewfolk have it even worse in the International District. If the Volod finds out the Slayer of Taltos is a Mercurion, he'll punish *all* the non-humans in the city more than he already does. He might even order a massacre."

I groaned and rubbed the bridge of my nose. Just what I wanted in a role-playing game: genocide. "Great."

"It didn't used to be that way... something changed between the end of the history acceleration process and the time I was loaded in," she added quickly. "This city is very centrally located in Artana, so it was expected that a lot of crafters would set up here and it would become a big market hub. Andrik isn't even supposed to *be* the King. The Volod should have been his brother, Ignas, but Ignas committed suicide. I guess OUROS didn't think we had enough conflict here."

I thought back to what the High Forgemaster had said about suicide being a disgrace, and the Taltos Archemipedia entry with its bugged out character code. The optimist in me hoped it was a coincidence... a small oversight in the game that hadn't been corrected once the story had changed. But I was holding the Spear of Nine Spheres. That was a bug, too – and that bug had nearly been the death of me.

"Apparently, the Architects forgot to account for human nature." I patted Karalti on the head, rubbing her horn stubs until she began to relax. The predatory focus in her eyes softened, and she crooned and butted against my hand. "Look, we can't just stand around. I need to investigate the scene of the crime, and at least alert the city guard to what happened at the hospital. And I'm going to find Kanzo and finish this quest. How did you know where he was, anyway?"

"In the last murder, the one in the park... he-he left me a message," she said, rubbing the knuckles of one hand with the fingers of the other. "A kind of code that we use together in the workshop. My quest updated and told me to meet him here. That's... that's how I know he's not doing this of his own free will."

"*That don't make no sense,*" my dragon grumped.

I was with Karalti on that one. If what Rin was saying was true, then Kanzo had led us straight to his precious apprentice. Rin didn't seem like a much better liar than she was a combatant, but she was the best lead we had. I was going to push her excuses to their limit. "What could cause him to do something like this?"

"I don't know." She shook her head miserably, looking down at the ground. "I'm trying to find out. The message he left for me... it was a plea for help. You have to understand - Kanzo is a good man, a good teacher! That's why he's in Taltos, and not the head of a House in Zaunt. I-I care about him a lot, and I want to know why he's doing these terrible things, but I can't let you hurt him."

The work I saw going on in the hospital was just about the opposite of anything a 'pacifist' was likely to do. I planted the end of my spear on the ground. "Look, the sob story is great and everything, but I can't just drop this. I'm on a time limit."

Rin blinked. "I... uh..."

"The fact remains that a bunch of priests are dead." I jabbed a finger in the direction Kanzo-the-Pacifist had fled. "That guy hasn't just been killing people. He's a butcher, and none of those men deserved what they got. I'm not letting you out of my sight."

"You don't know if they deserved it or not. But... I guess." Rin's small shoulders slumped.

I nearly resumed chewing her out, but then paused for a second. Yes, my first instinct was to argue. My second was to think back to the Order of St Grigori: to Knight-Commander Arnaud, who was so polished and righteous on the outside, and so rotten at the core. The whole Order had been that way, Charismatic to the point of seduction, but built on a lie. What did I know about the Volod, the priesthood of Khors, or the men who'd been killed? Fuck all, really.

I cracked my neck. "How about we set up a time and place to talk more about this? We can't just stand out here."

"Oh. Okay." Rin bit her lip. "How about I give you the coordinates of my workshop? I have to repair Lovelace and Hopper after your dragon... umm... cooked them. Maybe that would help you trust me?"

"Maybe." *But don't count on it.* I eyed the turret twins. "Lovelace as in Ada Lovelace?"

Rin smiled shyly. "Yes. And Hopper as in Grace Hopper. They're both nerd heroes, too. Hopper was a Rear Admiral and one of the first programmers of the Harvard Mark I in the 1940s, and she popularized the idea of machine-independent programming languages, which led to the development of COBOL, which is... ummm... oh, I'm doing it again, aren't I?"

She blushed, turning her cheeks a bright turquoise blue. Goddammit. I was starting to think this Kanzo asshole had led me here because he knew there was no earthly way anyone could fight Rin. She was a Scottish Fold kitten in humanoid form. I sighed in defeat. "Which one's which?"

"That's Hopper." Smiling, she pointed at the one Karalti had managed to roast a little more thoroughly. Parts of its armor had melted, and it was walking with a limp. "They're encoded with different Words of Power. Do you, umm, want to come back with me to the shop? I can send you a Friend Request..."

I hesitated. I was banged up and exhausted. It was close to three a.m. Karalti was already only 14 EXP from reaching Level 3, and I was only about a hundred from Level 10, which was going to be a gamechanger for me. It was the level where I could either take a new Advanced Path, or reuse all of my skill points and redistribute them back into Dark Lancer abilities. I planned to do the latter, because I understood this class a lot better than I had when I first took it. Not to mention, I needed to find Suri and at least do her the courtesy of telling her what I'd discovered.

"I really have to get some crafting supplies, re-gear, and everything." I held up my spear. "And get this fixed, if I can. It's down to nineteen percent durability now."

"Oh my gosh! Is that *lazula!?*" Rin rushed me, nearly crashing into me as she clasped the Spear. Her eyes were huge and glittering, as if really seeing my weapon for the first time. It put her uncomfortably close to me, so close that I could smell the strange, clean chemical scent of her breath. "Wow, this is an amazing artifact, where did you...?"

Karalti lifted her wings and rushed at her, snapping her jaws. Rin squealed and threw her hands up. She tripped over herself and fell on her ass. "Eeek!"

"Leave it, Tidbit." I reached out to catch Karalti by the edge of her wing.

"Bad lady!" Her head snaked, and she hissed, drooling white fire from between her teeth. *"No touchy!"*

"I'm sorry! I'm sorry!" Rin wailed.

"Hey, cool it. It's okay." I patted my dragon on the neck. She eased down slowly, but her stare bored into my back as I offered Rin a hand up. The Mercurion accepted shakily. "I-I-I'm really sorry, I didn't mean to frighten her."

"Don't worry. She's protective of me." I swallowed down the laughter pushing at the back of my throat and pulled her to her feet. Like Kanzo, she was heavy – really heavy. Rin was only five foot two and petite, but she weighed at least two hundred pounds. "Yeah, this spear is made of bluesteel. Lazula, whatever it is. I don't suppose you know how to fix it?"

"No. You need a Level 20-plus Master Artificer with Grade-A Aesari technology knowledge to repair lazula artifacts like this one." She shook her head. "There's only one Level 20 Master in Artana that I know of, and he's... well..."

I facepalmed. "It's Kanzo, isn't it?"

Rin nodded, keeping her hands up close to her face. "Yes. But I have B-Grade knowledge of Aesari Artifacts. And this is... this looks like the Spear of Nine Spheres?"

"Yeah, but it's probably a good fake," I replied. "The Spear of Nine Spheres is supposed to be soul-bound, and this one *says* it is, but it's really not."

Rin's brows creased. Now that she was closer to me, I could see that her eyebrows weren't made out of hair. They were filigree lace metal. "That's strange. Where did you get it?"

"Ilia," My throat tightened a little. "As part of a World quest from the Court Sorceress, Rutha."

A strange expression passed over Rin's face. She glanced at Karalti, who was looking at her the way she'd usually look at a plump mouse. "Rutha of Vasteau? If you don't mind me asking, is that where you got your dragon? There's only two places you can take the Dragon Knight class in Archemi: The Order of Saint Grigori in Ilia, or the Lysidian school in Lustria."

"Door number one. Though I'm not a Dragon Knight." I edged back cautiously, keeping an eye on Lovelace and Hopper. "And I don't want to become one. The Skyrdon are fucked up, slaving assholes-"

Rin blinked rapidly. "What?"

"Yeah, I know," I said. Once the story started, I couldn't stop myself from blurting it out. "The Skyrdon had the Matriarch – Karalti's mother – chained up in this pit in the middle of the Eyrie. All the dragons and the knights are bound under this magic spell that basically makes them slaves to the Knight-Commander..."

Rin gasped, pressing her hands to her mouth. "Oh, no."

"Yeah, 'oh no' is about right." I gestured angrily at the sky. "I don't know what sick fuck decided this would make for a fun game, but they need to get their head checked."

"No... no, that's not how it was supposed to be at all." Rin caught me urgently by the hand. "We need to go and talk. Now. Follow me."

The Mercurion's palm was hot and dry. I paused in confusion. "I thought we were going to put a raincheck on-"

"This is bigger than our quests here," she said urgently. "Before we do anything else, I need to tell you about a Dev who called himself Ororgael."

CHAPTER 12

"His name was Michael Pratt." Rin was sitting beside a work table, her head resting in one of her slim silver hands. Under light, she wasn't just adorable – she was gorgeous, a living sculpture with opalescent color dancing through her Valkyrie-like ear wings, her translucent hair, and over her lips and nails. "Ororgael was his gamer handle. Your brother would have known him... They were on the same team, OUROS Neuromorphic R&D."

We were sitting inside of Rin and Kanzo's workshop. It took up the entirety of a small warehouse crammed in among the countless shops, machine shops, smelteries and tanneries of the Tanner's District on the outskirts of town. This was the Mercurion ghetto, and the site of nearly all the city's factories, mage shops, and artificing workshops. The place was cozy. Half-finished projects littered tables, counters, and rolling tool cabinets. Nearly everything Rin and Kanzo worked on was clockwork, magical, or both. They made watches, carriage parts, and animal-shaped artifacts as masterful as the magitech spider we'd found in the High Priest's chambers. It was half-garage, half-wizard's laboratory. The room was dominated by a pair of forges and a small smeltery.

Karalti snored away on a nest of blankets in front of the hot forge. She was now around seven feet from nose to tail-tip, almost big enough to ride. I watched her thoughtfully, cradling a steaming cup of real, honest-to-god coffee between my hands like a precious treasure. It wasn't necessarily that coffee was rare in Archemi – the eastern and southern parts, at least – but thanks to the Army, I hadn't had real coffee for years. Conscripts weren't given coffee in their rations, and it wasn't served at mess. Not only was it delicious, it gave me a buff to learning Craft skills.

"I don't even know what 'Neuromorphic R&D' is," I admitted. "I have no idea what Steve was doing all these years. All I know is that he was on a first-name basis with Ryuko's CEO."

"Yeah. That was because of his breakthroughs on the radiant AI framework that generates our NPCs, ATHENA. Michael was close to Ms. Hashimoto as well."

I shook my head. "Shame they both died of HEX. I knew Steve was smart, but I didn't know he was like... *brilliant.*"

"Michael didn't have HEX. He got cancer. Prostate cancer, I think," Rin continued. "He was amazing at his job, but he was a really intense person. You know that Ryuko has... had a military contract division, right?"

"Yeah."

"Michael was one of the military guys who came over to our campus as part of the OUROS handover team," Rin said. "He was reporting back to the government on us. Like, he never said it, but we all knew. I'm surprised Steve didn't tell you about him. Michael was, well, he was kind of a prima donna, to be honest. Everyone had an opinion about him. You never met him through your brother? They worked together."

If I remembered correctly, GNOSIS was the system that copied human minds and consciousness over to OUROS, which was the AI that ran Archemi. I sort of nod-shrugged uncomfortably. "Me and Steve weren't on speaking terms for a really long time. We only made up because we both got HEX and realized we were going to die hating each other. He grandfathered me into the refugee program, but... he didn't make the transfer."

"Oh." Rin looked down at her hands in her lap. "I'm sorry."

I had a sip of coffee in the awkward pause that followed, savoring the earthy, sweet flavor. "Anyway, what happened to Michael?"

"Umm, yes... Well, his treatment for the cancer didn't work, because it had spread into his bones and even the nanite treatment couldn't stop it. This was around the time the HEX refugee program was being worked out. He volunteered to go in as a 'vanguard', and was the first person permanently sent to Archemi." Rin still didn't look up at me, picking a bit of lint off her glove. "We had this joke about him being the 'Archinaut'."

"Did something happen to him?"

"Yeah." Rin winced as she pulled a trolley over to her broken Artifact. She took up a small crowbar, and began to lever off the slagged armor plating. "Michael was how we learned about cyber psychosis in perma-uploaded players. OUROS and GNOSIS were considered safe by the time we beamed him in, but it was confirmed only for immersion sessions, not for upload. Our version of OUROS was still being rated for permanent transfers. Michael's upload was successful, but..."

"But what?"

"Something went wrong," Rin admitted. Now that she was concentrating on fixing Hopper, her voice was more confident, less hesitant and girlish. "He got stuck in some glitch and the system didn't recognize him as a character. It self-corrected, but he kept spawning in the wrong place. He incarnated in the sky somewhere over the Northern Continent and fell through the map into this void, then died. Every time he died, he'd respawn in the same place, and... well... *smoosh*."

It was my turn to wince. I hadn't repeatedly fallen to my doom, but I'd definitely had some variant of the same problem. "Jesus."

"The game corrected itself after about a dozen iterations, but it was too late. It turns out dying a lot is like... really bad for you, psychologically."

"Gee. Who'd have thought?"

"I know, right? Well, there's a temporary amnesia thing in place now to stop what we called the 'Michael Effect'. We didn't know dying would be so much of a problem, because the testers who hadn't perma-jumped had no problem with dying in game. They were nervous the first time, but after that they'd just laugh it off like a normal game experience."

"Seems like something that should have been picked up."

"Sure, but they didn't." She shrugged. "The Transference Team predicted it would be a bigger deal for permas, but they didn't know how much of a bigger deal. Mind you, Michael hid his psychosis for a good long while."

I shook my head. "So what happened?"

"Michael seemed okay to me," Rin said slowly. "We were all following his progress on our screens, you know... it was kind of a company-wide miracle. He was obviously still *him*, even though his body was now in cryo and everything. He performed for us, showed us all around Ilia... but that whole time, he was modifying the game from the inside. Little bit by little bit. That corruption you're describing in the Knights of St. Grigori? That's not part of the game canon. That was all stuff *he* did. He started this secret personality cult, the 'Cult of the Architect', elevated himself to demi-god status, and rewrote bits of Ilia's history. Then, one day he just... upped and killed King Rosvin and took over the country."

"How?"

Rin shrugged. "He had access to the developer panel and he knew how to program ATHENA to make it look like the NPCs around him were acting of their own free will. Of course, as soon as the company realized he was treating Archemi like his own personal sandbox, they removed his Developer access. And then he just... got it back, and kept screwing with the game. He told them this is why he thought the HEX refugee program was a bunch of baloney. 'Imagine if someone who wasn't responsible did this.' He used to say that all the time."

I blinked. "What do you mean he kept 'screwing with the game'?"

"They kept taking his Dev access away. And he kept getting it back somehow." Rin replied, tooling around on Hopper's frame. "They changed his character type to NPC and rolled back the changes he'd made, but then the AI organically carried out Michael's version of events and gave him back his special character status and access to the Dev Panel. He blocked out other players from uploading and continued to just... taking over the world."

"He turned himself into a virus?" I looked down at the Spear of Nine Spheres resting in my lap, and swallowed.

"Basically. The CEO had to make the decision to... well... delete him. It was horrible, but they had to. They deleted him and rolled back his changes to the game, because otherwise the refugees would be compromised. I know that the AI kept executing his version of the Ilian civil war, but I didn't know it had kept going with all the other horrible stuff he decided was fun. The incident with Michael destabilized OUROS and ATHENA and made perma-uploads for new players more dangerous. It nearly derailed the entire refugee program."

I grimaced, rubbing the back of my right hand. "Did anyone ever say whether or not his glitchy upload was a factor in his turning into some evil overlord of suck?"

"Almost certainly." Rin replied fussily. "I mean, if the data is corrupt to start with, it's just going to corrupt further over time. Entropy is the natural trajectory of things. Even if a human profile preserves consciousness, the perception of the conscious individual is warped by their corrupted data. Especially if they die over and over. No one ever said porting our minds to a game was an ideal solution, you know?"

I felt my heart sink with every word. Swallowing, I glanced over at Karalti. She was sleeping peacefully, her tail wrapped around her body, her foreclaws clasped over her eyes. Her chest rose and fell, and now and then, her tail twitched in time with her dreams. Had my brother known about the Michael incident? He had to have known. Why hadn't he said anything to me, or even told me about the risks?

"Listen, there were some really dodgy quests in Ilia," I said quietly. "Michael – Ororgael – was Rutha's teacher, and *she* gave me the Spear. Like I said, it's a soul-bonded weapon that doesn't really seem to be soul-bonded. As far as I can tell, it's only purpose was to trick a player into opening this Pandora's Box thing down in the ruins of Cham Garai. Do you know anything about that?"

"Well, I have a read-only mod overlay, so I can tell you the Spear is definitely real." Rin looked back uncomfortably. "What you're describing sounds like something Ororgael would have done. He set up trojans for the other Devs when they were trying to clean him out. Did you complete the quest line?"

"No." I got up restlessly. "Someone else took the Spear from me and did it. He's a dragon knight now... or I assume he is. His name's Baldr Hyland. Last I saw, he had the Pearl of Glorious Dawn embedded in his face."

"Oh." Rin looked down. "That's not good. I think the Pearl is the key to... goodness, who's Dragon Gate was it...?"

"Solnetsi," I replied, pacing in front of the forge.

"I don't know anything about her lore. I think she's a goddess of war or something." Rin shook her head, and as she did, I saw a glint of metal at her throat. A thin chain, just like the one on the necklace I'd picked up on the ground. I still hadn't had a chance to look at mine.

"Well, nothing I can do about it in Taltos," I said with a sigh, and jammed my hands in my pockets. "Hey, I'm feeling pretty strung out after that chat: do you mind if I try my hand at some Crafting? This is the first place I've seen with player-ready crafting stations."

"Sure!" Rin nodded, leaning over to look at something underneath her artifact. "What are you going to make?"

"I REALLY need new armor. Not that I'm probably going to be able to craft any."

"What's your Armorsmithing skill level?"

I checked. "Uhh... Zero."

"If you're just starting out, refine some materials and practice making leather bracers." Rin pointed at a bin full of what appeared to be raw animal pelts. "It'd actually be a huge help if you can refine all those pelts into Leather and turn some of that scrap metal into Iron and Copper ingots and fittings. I don't get any EXP from that kind of work anymore, but you'll level up five or six times if you do it. You can use any of the ingots you make."

"Aren't those expensive?"

"Not really. Kanzo and I craft clocks and crucibii for the House of Corvinus and the Forgers. We're not short on supplies or money."

I stared at her. "You craft for the Church?"

"Of course. The Volod is - well, *was* - our patron. Humans farm out their magical crafting to us whenever they can."

Listening to a former Dev refer to 'humans' as if they were a different species was surreal, but I shrugged it off. I was glad to be thinking about something other than Ororgael and Baldr for a while. I got heartburn every time I thought about that backstabbing albino asshole. "Okay – anything in the shop I can't use?"

"Not that I can think of." She shook her head, picking up what looked like a small welding torch. She twisted around to get a small glowing capsule that she slotted into it. As she twisted, I saw a glimmer at her throat – the necklace.

I jerked my nose toward her. "Hey, one last thing before I start: did you make that necklace you're wearing? It's pretty."

"What? This?" Rin looked up, and then reached up to pull the delicate chain out from under her shirt. "No, Kanzo made this. He gives one to all of his apprentices. I'm not the first. He mentored several other NPCs who are Journeymen... we all get one of these."

At the end of the chain was an unusual pendant: a stylized bee, about an inch long, with a spiral seal embossed on the back and magical runes on each delicately-worked section of its abdomen. The body of the bee was partially hollow, and a straight metal axle ran down the center of its body on the inside of the pendant, visible through the gaps in the design. I carefully felt my captured necklace with my fingertips. It was a replica of the same pendant.

"Bee bling. Nice." I chuckled, and pulled my hand out of my pocket as I headed over to the Forge. "What's it mean?"

"It's Kanzo's personal House Mark," Rin replied. "And the Maker's Mark of this workshop. He was exiled from his House in Zaunt – our homeland – because he refused to make war machines for his *Tlaxican*. He was disinherited, which is an awful thing to happen to a Mercurion. But he made the best of it: he was from the House of the Hornet, a very wealthy House in North Zaunt, so he took the honey bee as his own House symbol. He told me that he'd rather be like a bee than a hornet, living a humble life and making things that are beautiful and useful for people. He told me that the only use for weapons was to defend yourself."

Or to do kinky murder-bondage with helpless priests. I nodded and smiled anyway as I approached the forge. When I was close to it, a prompt jumped up in my HUD. *⟦This is your first time using a Crafting Forge. Do you want a tutorial?⟧*

"Sure," I thought back.

Using a Forge

Realistic as Archemi can be, Crafting is supposed to be fun! You will be using a simple system that can be roleplayed in a realistic fashion, if desired.

To use a Forge, you need Forge Tools. Smelting metal ore into ingots requires a lit Furnace, Tongs, and an Ingot Mold. When you pour molten metal into Ingot Molds, they will cool and be added to your Inventory.

You can smelt certain types of ingots together to create alloys, which are required for many types of items. Try smelting ⟦1 x Pure Charcoal⟧ with ⟦2 x Iron ingot⟧ and see what you get!

To make tools, you need Tool Molds. Mold blueprints can be found in Smithing craft books. Once you learn a blueprint, forge it the mold, then pour melted ingots and any other required ingredients into the mold to create the tool.

To turn ingots into armor, weapons, and tools, you will need a Hammer and Anvil. Anvils can nearly always be found beside Forges.

To make weapons, you will also need a Plunge – a bucket of water (or other liquid) which you will use to quench your crafted weapons.

To make Heavy Armor, you will need a Dishing Form.

To make Medium and Light Armor, you will need a Riveter.

Once you have the correct tools and ingredients, you will be walked through a crafting minigame that will determine the success of your crafting attempt. The more you practice, the easier the game gets and the more items you can craft, so don't give up!

You can only craft the items available to you at your current level. As your skill level increases, so does your understanding. Unless you have the Prodigy trait, you can train yourself to Beginner 5 in any craft. You will then need an instructor to unlock the next set of levels, which will take you to Apprentice 1. NPC Instructors can be found in most towns and all large cities, and other players might be able to help you as well."

I heard banging from across the room, and glanced over to see Rin's eyes flicking from place to place as she hammered out a brass plate with what looked like lightning speed.

Based on that tutorial, I could guess that refining pelts into leather required a knife, so I drew mine as I went to the bin of unrefined skins. It contained Tanned Deer Hide x 200, so it was going to keep me busy for a while. The first thing I did was check my own inventory to see what I already had:

[[Iron Ore x 49]]

[[Copper Ore x 32]]

[[Charcoal x 225]]

[[Fox Pelt x 19]]

[[Wolf Pelt x 5]]

[[Monster Skin]]

Yeah, I had a lot of charcoal. It weighed nearly nothing and it made starting fires easy, so there was no reason for me not to have a ton of it.

I set up my tools. The leather was first. I got a very brief tutorial on how to deal with hides:

Leather Goods

Creating [[Leather]] is a four-step process.

First, you must collect a hide by skinning an animal, then you must cure it. To cure the hide, apply salt to it and use a knife, dagger or scraper to scrape the fur away.

The next stage is tanning. Tan hides by applying [[Tanning Solution]] to the cleaned hide. It will turn into leather.

Cut leather by equipping any appropriately sharp tool - a Leather Trimmer works best.

You can further refine leather by boiling it to make [[Hard Leather]] or cutting it into [[Leather Strips]].

By riveting together two sheets of [[Hard Leather]], you can make [[Leather Plate]].

I nodded after the narrator finished speaking, and got to work. My pelts were uncured - fortunately, they weren't the sort of items that turned gross with time, because I'd had them for a while. I rubbed salt on the wet side of the hide, drying it, then used my dagger to scrape them down. That was my first introduction to the rhythm-based minigame. A blue line would light up on the hide, and when I touched the pelt with the blade, it would travel down in a straight line at a certain speed. The edge of the knife had to remain inside the borders of the line. The bigger the hide, the more swipes you had to do. The [[Fox Hide]] took 5; the [[Wolf Hide]] took 10. I discovered that I was also able to salt and scrape the Monster Skin, turning it into a Monster Hide. That was worth 20 silver Rubles - not a bad price for a single component.

The workshop had a big barrel of foul-smelling tanning solution, so I took all of the hides over there and began working. It was fucking nasty. I called out to Rin. "What is this stuff made out of?"

"Do you really want to know?" She called back.

"Yeah. If nothing else so that I can brag about sticking my hands in it."

She laughed, a high, musical sound. "Mostly pulverized oak bark. Oh... and urine."

I made a face. "I said it before, and I'll say it again. Whoever thought up this game is a complete fucking sadist."

Hides turned to leather at a 1:1 ratio, and [[Leather x 1]] could be sliced into [[Leather Straps x 10]], but hardening leather required [[Leather x 2]] to produce one piece. I tried them all, and even got a Riveter and made some [[Leather Plates]], which were used for most kinds of Medium Armor.

[[You have reached Leatherworking 2!]]

[[You have reached Leatherworking 3!]]

"When you reach Leatherworking 5, we have some Skill Tomes to allow you to keep going until you hit Apprentice 1," Rin said, pointing a small bookshelf close to where Karalti was sleeping. "It's the one with the red cover."

"Aren't those one-time use only?" I asked.

"Sort of. Kanzo is a Master Artificer, so he can inscribe and recharge each of the Tomes. He only keeps the ones here that he can easily replace."

Puzzled, I went to collect the one I needed. "Why are you giving me this stuff? I mean, I appreciate it, but..."

Rin shrugged. Her back was to me as she worked on Hopper. The automata was now moving, waving its legs. "Nearly all the

NPCs of Taltos think we Mercurions keep to ourselves so that we can hoard our jewels and gold and look down on everyone else. The reality is, if we're on the mainland, then we're all refugees running from a terrible war, and we work jobs that most other races can't, so of course we stick together. Some Mercurions can be cold to strangers, and I guess I just want to show you that we're not like that. You know, before you go back to the Volod."

I walked back to the smelter. At no point had I generalized anything about the Mercurions, but I knew that if I was a serial killer and I needed cover, becoming a kindly, respected craftsman in a law-abiding community was a pretty good disguise.

The first fruit of my labor was a leather sock. I had intended to Craft an Archer's Bracer, but it didn't end up that way. I got a sock. A leather one. About the only thing it was going to be good for was jerking off into. Needless to say, it was a [[Junk]] category item.

Things got better on from there as I got the hang of the crafting minigame. Similar to what happened when I was scraping hides, I got lines and circles highlighted on the materials I was working with, showing me where to cut, trim, fold, and stitch. The ghostly instructions would appear in a sequence, showing you what to do, then fade. If you matched the sequence, you got the item you wanted. If you screwed up, you either got a lesser item – like my sock – or a lower-quality item of the same type you were trying to craft. The minigame pattern-sequence thing was the same each time you attempted the item, so there were no surprises if you failed once and tried again.

I stopped at Leatherworking 5, then switched to melting down scrap and pouring ingots to build my Blacksmithing skill. Soon I had plenty of iron, steel, and bronze ingots. I checked my crafting recipes to see what I could make, bursting with creative anticipation:

Chest Armor

<None>

Trousers

<None>

Boots

<None>

Gloves

Archer's Brace

Weapons

Steel Militia Spear

Other

Leather sock (Junk)

I reached up and tugged at my braids, staring at the nearly-blank menu. "Rin? Do you happen to have any beginner crafting recipes?"

CHAPTER 13

I hit the wall at about three in the morning. Fortunately, Rin had been able to furnish me with some recipes: Raider's Breeches, Heavy Boots, Lancer's Gauntlets, and Steel Vambrace. I made the leather items first, and then tackled the metal one.

Working with metal was far more complicated than leather. Sweating, I carefully banged the curve in the vambrace in time with the colored minigame prompts – red, blue and yellow – that told me how hard to hit, where, and with what tool. When it was done, the vambrace flashed, a three second timer counted down. I quickly lifted the hot steel and plunged it into the bucket of hot water at the end of the anvil.

⟦Crafting Success! You made Steel Vambrace (Regular Quality)!⟧

"Hell yeah!" Grinning, I pulled the wet vambrace down and patted it with a towel. Despite the prompt, it wasn't quite finished. I riveted some leather straps on it, and eagerly tried it on. The vambrace protected my entire forearm and tapered out above the elbow. Perfect fit. "Look, girl! I did it!"

"*Hector needs to sleep,*" Karalti grumbled, burying her snout under her wing. She had moved as close to the furnace as she was able to. Rin had gone to bed hours ago.

"Party pooper." I flexed my fingers, turning my arm to look at it from all angles. My old Light Vambrace gave me 15 Armor; this piece gave 30, plus +7% resistance to slashing, bludgeoning and piercing damage.

All of the new pieces together increased my total Armor from 95 to 140. My main chest piece was still the old Jack of Plates I'd worn since my visit to Dinant Palace in Ilia, but I'd been able to repair and improve it. I'd also made myself a Militia Spear for the hell of it. It had stats that were nearly identical to the broken Spear of Nine Spheres, but none of the special perks: no Dex bonus or anything like that.

A bittersweet smile played over my lips as I equipped it all and swung my arms to test the weight and quality of the new gear. "You know... I think this is the first time I've ever made anything useful."

Karalti shifted her wing so that she could peer at me with a brilliant violet eye.

"I just never had the chance to make anything before," I said. "The Army taught me how to shoot shit and dig foxholes. I improvised some stuff... but I never *created* it like this. I'm too dumb."

"Hector's dumb sometimes because he thinks he's dumb," Karalti replied, yawning. *"And because he's awake late banging metal things together."*

I yawned too. "You say that now. Wait until I have to make you a saddle. You'll be grateful I spent all this time on Crafting."

"Saddle is for later. Sleep is for now." Karalti rolled onto her side and partly unfurled her wing, revealing up a length of cloak for me to lie on. *"We have to find bad man in the morning."*

She had a point there. The little 'Zzz' icon in my HUD was warning me that I had the Exhaustion debuff: penalties to carry weight, movement speed, and reflexes. I needed to sleep.

Archemi required that you take care of your basic needs, but fortunately, it didn't grind your face in it too hard. With the

Dragon's Blood Potion buff at work, four hours of sleep was enough. We woke with the sun, moderately refreshed and ready to start the day.

We left Rin's shop at about 8 a.m. She saw us off at the door with a wave, and I rode out with some nice new gear, her master's pendant in my pocket, and a deep sense of satisfaction mixed with odd longing. The talk with Rin about Ororgael and Rutha played back like a recording.

"*You thinking about white elf lady?*" Karalti asked me. She was perched behind me, holding onto one shoulder with a foreclaw, her head beside mine. "*I never met her. What was she like?*"

"She was pretty great." I urged Cutthroat to a high-stepping trot, keeping her on a short rein. The hookwing was irritable, as always, but she'd had a meal at a nearby public stall and was about as mellow as she could ever be. "Smart as a whip, really kind. She was fierce when she wanted to be, gentle when she needed to be. And she was gorgeous. Big eyes, long ears, beautiful long white hair..."

"*You think she's as nice as grumpy lady?*"

"They're not really comparable. Rutha was nicer, for sure. But 'nice' isn't always what you want in a friend. I'll take hostile honesty over nicey-nice liars any day."

"*Did Rutha lie to you?*"

"Yeah." I felt a pang in my chest. "I don't know if she meant to lie to me or not, but she did."

Karalti 'hmm'd' aloud, nibbling the stubble on the side of my head. "*I don't lie to you ever. You think Suri is honest like me?*"

"You know, weirdly enough, I do think she's honest." We pulled up at an intersection to let traffic pass. I swept our surroundings, taking in cover, potential threats, passersby, and ambush points in a single glance, then moved on. "Suri could be a

Pacific Alliance Party fanatic who'll hate my guts forever on principle, but at least she's the kind of person who'd tell me to my face. I knew a lot of bikers and soldiers like her. Tough, hard, but real. If we earn her respect, we'll never have a better friend."

"*You don't NEED another better friend, 'cause she'll never be a better friend than ME,*" Karalti said grumpily. "*And if she does, then I'll fight her. See how tough she is then.*" And then, as if to soothe herself, she began to mimic the sounds of the streets around her under her breath.

We soon broke out onto the main market street, which went through the center of the Market District and up towards the University District. The food stands were setting up for breakfast: vendors were basting kebabs, uncovering trays of bread and pastries full of fruit, cheese, or ground meat, and brewing coffee. My stomach rumbled.

"*Hey, Hector?*" My dragon plopped her head on my shoulder. I reached up to scratch around her horns. "*You gonna make a saddle for me?*"

"*Yeah, I guess I'm going to have to try that out, soon. But we probably need to find a blueprint for a dragon saddle before I can make it.*"

"*Maybe rubber lady can help?*"

That was a possibility. Rin had spent the early morning cooing over Karalti, petting her and feeding her pieces of beef jerky and small cakes they kept for human guests. This had vastly improved Karalti's opinion of her, and smoothed over the fact that she'd ambushed us and plugged me full of crossbow bolts. Still - Rin was probably the one to go to with design ideas.

I found a place to hitch Cutthroat, and left her to find something to eat. I got a frothy cup of coffee whisked with butter, cream and a lot of sugar, and a spiral wheel of fried bread stuffed with beef and garlic. This divine foodstuff was called *burek*. It was hot, flaky, and soft on the outside and savory in the middle, and it was enough to convince me that yes, heaven did exist, but instead of choirs of angels, there was nothing but fields of cheerful street food vendors selling burek and coffee for five copper coins a piece. Forever.

We had to run through a gauntlet of food stands, and Karalti watched with increasing trepidation as I succumbed to basically all of them. I had chicken *burek*, beef *burek*, some kind of sour cherry danish, and then another kind of delicious stuffed-bread thing called *katchapuri*, which had a well of melted cheese and an egg in the middle. I put away every last crumb.

"*Are you about to level up?*" My dragon squeaked. *Dragons eat a lot when they're about to level up.*"

"*Nope. No leveling. Just obesity.*" I replied, as I waddled toward the Armorsmith's shop.

A bell tinkled overhead when we opened the door and entered, barely audible through the *bang bang bang* of a hammer striking steel. Beautiful suits of armor were on display: hanging on stands, mounted on the walls. Most were full plate, fluted and embossed with delicate designs. Most of it was too heavy for me, but one suit of leather and chainmail armor caught my eye straight away.

The armor looked like it was intended for rogue-type classes. The main piece of the set was a bodysuit not unlike a motorcycle racing suit. Over that was a plate-reinforced leather vest. The dark steel segments tapered in such a way that you could bend at the waist, from side to side, and backwards. Soft, thick leather flaps formed a V-shaped kirtle over hip armor, also flexible.

Small metal plates were sewn into the leather bodysuit on strategic points: knees, shoulders. The hard leather pieces were carved with intricate Middle Eastern designs. I had a look at the Body piece stats:

Nizari Leather Armor Cuirass

105 armor

+30% resistance to slashing damage

+15% resistance to bludgeoning damage

+5 Attack power

+20% Elemental resistance

Light armor

Body Slot

100% durability

Required Level: 10

Price: 1200 silver Rubles

Light, tough, maneuverable armor worn by the assassins of the Cult of Malek in Dakhdir.

"That Nizari set comes with a helm that's not on the stand. The whole set gives two-hundred and fifty armor, and it don't weigh more than thirty pounds." The gravelly voice of the smith - my HUD highlighted his name as Fyodor - rang out from behind me as the rhythm of hammer blows paused. "The helm has a hood that ties on. We make the whole set dyed any color you want."

Two-fifty Armor was way better than my current total of 180, and this gear weighed about half of my Jack of Plates set. It also had twice as much resistance to slashing damage, and perhaps most importantly, +20% elemental resistance. Against magic, that was a huge advantage. My inner twelve-year-old wanted black with red trim. Or even better: purple trim. Purple trim with tribal dragon tattoos. Then I could get at least one pair of mirror shades, an e-cig and a katana, and lurk in tavern corners. Edgelord Hector Bloodzin: Dragon Assassin.

"Do I save any money if I get a less-fancy version?" I asked him, turning to face the counter. "Because I get hit a lot. I mean, like, a LOT. I need the armor equivalent of dad jeans. I want the bonuses, but don't need any embossing or tooling or anything."

The smith was an older man with stringy hair and a twisted mouth. He scowled, and was about to say something rude about barbarians when he saw Karalti. She gaped her jaws at him, imitating a smile.

"That's... that's..." He sputtered.

I sighed. "Yes. A dragon. We're holy representatives of the church here to... bless your forge, good smith. You know, Khors being the god of the forge and everything."

⟦You have learned a new Skill: Bluff. Sometimes, the only way forward is to lie your ass off.⟧

Fyodor the Smith swallowed. "I see. Well.... Please, allow me to discount this armor set for you. And what about for her? Does she require armor? I will give you an excellent price."

'Discount' was one of my favorite words in the English language. I regarded Karalti for several moments. Armor for Karalti? I hadn't thought of that. She responded by posing prettily.

"Karalti doesn't really need armor yet, but I'm looking for saddle blueprints. If you have one, or think you could work with me to design one, the, uhh, Brotherhood of Awesome Dragon Guys would be eternally in your debt."

"A saddle? You... you would ride this sacred creature?" The smith looked affronted.

"It's my sacred duty as one of said Awesome Dragon Guys," I replied. "Plus, she actually *wants* me to ride her. Or else I wouldn't do it."

"Yeah!" Karalti squeaked.

The smith jumped, visibly shaken by what he was seeing. "I only do barding, not saddles. But I can recommend a good craftsman for them. He's a silverskin, but he makes saddles for quazi."

"Kazi?" I asked.

"Quazi," he replied, blinking at me in confusion.

"Give me a sec." I surreptitiously swiped in my HUD, and telepathically queried it. "*What the fuck is 'quazi'?*"

Quazi

A flying saurian creature related to hookwings, these griffon-like creatures are the preferred aerial mount of Vlachian light cavalry. They are used as war mounts, beasts of burden and in sports, but are expensive to keep and difficult to train. Unlike hookwings, they are not pack animals and must be specially socialized by experienced handlers. Quazi are rarely found in the West of Artana (Ilia, Gilheim, or any other realm in Hercynia) but are common in the South-East of Artana (Vlachia, Dakhdir and The Shalid).

The picture that accompanied the short generic knowledge was of a splendid, proud creature that looked like a cross between a wyvern and a gryphon. It was fully feathered, but had a toothy muzzle, a wedge-shaped tail with a long central plume, and walked on its wing hands and hind feet.

"Right. That guy probably knows what he's talking about," I replied, pushing the HUD aside. "What's his name and location?"

"His name is Mik... Mixa... Ugh. We call him Mikhael. I can't speak their damn click-clack language." Fyodor made a sound of disgust. "You'll find him in the Tanner's District. Here, I'll mark it on your map."

A marker appeared on my mini-map: a location not too far from Rin's shop.

"In exchange for your blessing, I will give you this Nizari set for seven hundred rubles," he said, once the map was put away.

Ouch. Seven hundred rubles still translated to about a thousand Ilian Florins, which was basically all the money we had. But I could trade in my newly improved Jack of Plates and the gear I'd forged, and this armor would last me until early mid-game, especially if I could enhance it. If I kept training my Leatherworking skills, I'd be able to bump its stats up. It was worth the price. "Done."

He opened the Shop Inventory, and we got to trading. I offloaded my old gear on him, and spent the majority of my money on the new armor. Armor in Archemi was 'one-size-fits-all', so when I equipped it, it was a perfect fit. I immediately felt better. Faster. Stronger. Hotter, too, in a 'LARPing a Drow Rogue in the park' kind of way.

"Now, about that forge blessing?" Holding his hammer in both hands, Fyodor glanced hopefully at Karalti. "Business has been slow of late, what with the Volod cracking down on demi-humans and travelers."

"Sure thing. Go, Karalti! Bless this man's forge with fortune and fire!" I made some half-assed pope gesture as Karalti toddled off toward him. Fortunately, Fyodor was so taken by presence of a Real Live Dragon that he didn't even notice how lame I sounded.

We left Fyodor worshipping at the white fire now burning a hole in his forge, collected Cutthroat, and started the long journey toward Vulkan Keep: the Volod's castle, which loomed gracefully over the city from the top of the old volcano at the center. Karalti and I had just settled into the saddle when my HUD chirped, alerting me to a message. Curious, I pulled it over and blinked when I saw the name. It was Suri.

"Hector. I already heard about what happened at the hospital." Suri's voice poured through the comm link like warm toffee. "Body's been recovered, and we found evidence of a fight. SITREP?"

Of course she had amazing radio discipline. As if she couldn't get any hotter. "Slayer is a Mercurion Artificer, name of Kanzo. I caught him with the victim in his third-floor office. We pursued him over the rooftops, heading toward the clocktower, and forced a confrontation. Nearly killed him, but his apprentice interfered and he escaped."

"What are your coordinates? I'll RV there with some knights, and we can make an arrest."

"We can't arrest her. She claims her craftmaster is being forced to assassinate the priests and has been leaving her secret messages begging for help. She's a civilian, Suri."

"No, she's an accomplice."

"I'm not saying she isn't. I'm saying don't bring a SWAT team in through her door, because she'll be too terrified to talk. Station them around, if you want the backup, but meet me discreetly and we can interview her together. I bet you'd be better at this than I am."

"She needs to be arrested." The stubborn note was back in Suri's voice.

"If we drag her in front of the Volod, there's a good chance he'll order a pogrom and kill her and every other Mercurion in this city," I replied, angling Cutthroat toward the University District gate. We were moving steadily uphill, heading for the castle that loomed above Taltos like a dark crown. "They can shut down the Tanner's District and massacre everyone trapped inside, so unless you want that on your conscience, can we drop the Robocop act and gather some more data first?"

There was a pause. "Fine, where are you?"

"Heading into the University District through the South Gate. Do you want to join my-?"

"No." Suri hung up.

"*Wow. Grumpy lady really hates parties,*" Karalti remarked.

I sighed. "She sure does."

"It's okay. You got me."

At least now I could see Suri's name in my address book. It was possible that players could disable the search function for their names if they wanted privacy. Something to look into later.

We headed up a steep, narrow winding street flanked by three-story European style apartments when I suddenly noticed just how empty the road actually was. I scanned the rooftops, alley mouths and darkened doorways, eyes narrowing. We were alone. No one was out, in contrast to the busy morning chatter of the Market District. And that had me on edge.

We rounded the corner, and I reined Cutthroat in to a halt as the back of my neck prickled. We were just about to pass under an archway. Further along the road was a wagon without a dinosaur to pull it. It was plain wood, and the back of the wagon had a heavy door with small bars on the windows. Not exactly a luxury sedan.

"Something's off, girl." I brought my spear around and down, and unequipped Cutthroat's muzzle. "Fly up and scout the rooftops. And be careful.

"Oki!" Karalti bunched, then launched herself into the air, straight into a fan of arrows that flew out at us from three directions.

CHAPTER 14

Karalti blasted the arrows with fire, twisting desperately in mid-air. She avoided some, incinerated some, but took three or four missiles made it through and struck her in the wings and legs. The dragon floundered and then crashed to the ground.

[[Karalti takes 70 damage!]]

[[Karalti's has sustained Wing Damage: -15 to all Flight abilities]]

"Karalti!" I dug my heel into Cuthroat's side and pulled her reins across her neck, getting her to turn sideways to provide cover for my dragon as she got to her feet. As the hookwing spun, I loosened my feet from the stirrups. When she came to a stop, I vaulted up to my feet on her back.

"Charge! Get that hatchling!" A man bellowed from overhead.

Thugs began pouring from the alleys, from behind the wagon, and from behind me, converging on the three of us. Twenty, at least, including the archers I could see. They were mercenaries, and I was pretty sure the fucking Mata Argis sent them.

It was one thing for them to attack me. It was quite another to attack *her*. Something savage pushed up from deep inside me. A mad, dark, hungry power bubbled up like magma. I felt its lust in my teeth and jaws, behind my eyes, and through my hands on the spear.

Whoever these goatfuckers were, they'd hurt my Tidbit. And I was going to tear. Them. Up.

"Hrrragh!" I snarled and sprung off Cutthroat's back like a bullet. "Ice cream!"

Cutthroat didn't need to be told twice. I heard shouts and screams and the wet tear of flesh below as I soared up, straight into the face of one of the archers crouched on top of the arch, and met his shocked eyes just before the tip of my spear blew through his face and out the back of his head. I swung him around and kicked him off the arch. Bows creaked from three directions as they were drawn. I took one arrow from behind even as I knocked three from the air, blurring into shadow and reappearing on top of the pack of lightly-armored archers in front.

I lashed out with a foot, knocking a bow out of a man's hands, following up with a blast of dark power and then a sprint forward. One man fell screaming to the ground; one took the Umbra Blast to the face and reeled away, clawing at his eyes. The last had drawn a sword. He swiped; I dodged, dancing around him and slashing out at the pale length of his exposed throat. Blood fanned in an arc. I spun behind the gurgling archer, grabbed him by the collar and belt, and pushed him ahead of me like a tower shield as I ran at the others on the arch.

Bows twanged, and the body danced in my hands as the rain of arrows struck it. I bellowed, just before I burned a Power Attack and flung the arrow-studded corpse at the remaining archers, scattering their rank.

Down below on the street, I heard Karalti blast someone, and as the EXP added up, I got a notification: *⟦Congratulations! Karalti has reached Level 4!⟧*

I hit Blood Storm and bull rushed them, gaining back the AP and HP I'd just spent. My body blurred into nothingness, only to reappear around behind one of the archers. I ended up only landing a glancing blow, because something hit me upside the back of the head: a bow.

The world spun. With the sound of wingbeats in my ears, I stumbled down to one knee. It pitched me under the second strike.

Arrows zinged past overhead, and then a huge shadow fell over us all.

I threw my head up, disoriented, and my eyes widened. It was Karalti.

Karalti was now the size of a large horse, with a wingspan to match. Her horns and wedge-shaped head had lengthened. Her body was more muscled, her scales thicker and more gemlike. And she had gained some HP with the level-up.

Her jaws gaped. "CHAAAARRR!"

White, ghostly fire spewed in a slick wave across the archway, boiling across the stone. The remaining three archers screamed in terror, scattering. One ran toward me. I tripped him with the Spear, and he slipped and fell, wailing, like a flaming meteor to the ground below.

"*Hector! The guards are here! And my blood turned some of the men into monsters!*" Karalti still sounded young, but her voice was deeper, more mature. She landed on the edge of the arch and turned her back to me. "*They're killing the other men! Get on!*"

"You can't fly with me yet, can you?" Panting, I reached up and pulled an arrow out of my shoulder. Ooh yeah, that hurt. My vision blurred for a moment.

"*I can glide. Come on!*"

Puffing to focus myself, I ran at her and jumped, landing on her back. My pain seemed to fade into the background as I got into position, hanging onto my dragon's back with my knees the way I would a motorcycle, and wrapped my arm around her neck.

"*Hang on!*" She launched herself from the arch.

My stomach lurched with the moment of reverse gravity, and all the hair on my body stood on end as Karalti's wings snapped out to each side. I weighed a hundred and eighty pounds and was carrying over a hundred pounds of armor and gear. It was all my dragon could do to steady her flight path as we swooped down, teetered from side to side, then crashed into a brawling line of ⟦Foreign Mercenaries⟧, ⟦Taltos Guards⟧, and ⟦Stranged Ghouls⟧.

The impact threw me off Karalti's back, and I was sent careening through the air. I flew over Cutthroat, who was fending off two swordsmen with teeth and claws and brute strength, and crashed into one of them. He got his shield up just in time for me to bash it back into his face, and we both sprawled to the ground. Unfortunately, I also crashed into his sword. The blade slid into a gap in my shiny new armor, through my gut, and out my back.

⟦You have taken a Devastating blow! X4 damage!⟧
⟦You are Hemorrhaging! You must heal to stop the bleeding!⟧
⟦You have Internal Bleeding: -25% to all attack and defense⟧
⟦Warning! You are at 95/482 HP!⟧

Getting stabbed like that was like being punched really hard by something very cold, all the way through. When you're in the middle of a fight, things happen too fast for it to even really hurt. The pain comes after.

"Sorry." I croaked, leaking blood from between my lips. I slapped my hand over his face. "Life for Life."

The warrior emitted a garbled cry as I ripped his lifeforce out through the Mark of Matir. His skin aged ten years in five seconds, and the fluttering, uneasy sensation of the ⟦Corruption⟧ debuff seemed to curl around the frigid length of the sword that skewered me through the waist. I wasn't actually sure what Corruption did, because I lost no health, stats or AP, but I knew one thing - it made my injuries *hurt*.

With my pulse roaring in my ears, I reached down, and pulled the sword free with a snarl. The sound of battle around me had dulled to a droning roar. The Hemorrhaging debuff reappeared. I used my last Moss Tincture to stop the bleeding. The tincture brought my HP up out of the gray, but my vision throbbed red as I rolled to the side and picked myself up. The thrill of flight had fled with my health. Now there was only grim determination as I clutched my wounded side with one hand and bashed aside twisted, zombie-like talons with the Spear in the other.

The ghouls were recognizably human, but their flesh had melted on their bones. Some of them were Taltos Guardsmen, some were Mercenary Thugs. They roared and gibbered as they chased their comrades, tearing at them with their fingernails and teeth. One was shambling toward me, hands outstretched.

I braced my spear for impact, but then then an odd, confused expression passed over the ghoul's face, and its head split in a wet explosion of mana-warped brain matter. It collapsed, an ax buried in what remained of its skull, and I looked past it to see a vision of Valhalla.

Suri flung her second ax at a retreating soldier, hitting him in the shoulder and dropping him to his knees. As he went down, she pulled her huge curved sword from her back and carried it forward in a decapitating blow. The body was still clawing at the stump as she waded in, hacking monsters down with every other step.

She was barely wearing any armor, and I shouted out as a ghoul lunged at her, claws tearing at her midriff. "Suri! Right!"

The monster ripped a long cut in her bare flesh, but Suri didn't even slow. If anything, she seemed to get faster, stronger, more excited. She slammed the ghoul in the face with the hilt of her sword, grasped the man by the hair and neck, and tore his head from its shoulders.

Holy *fuck*. Suri was a beast.

"Run! The battle is lost!" The Mercenary Leader yelled.

Suri yelled something in Dakhari, throwing the bloody head at their retreating backs as she ran after them with Karalti and Cutthroat. Cutthroat caught up to the straggler first, and got him by the back of the shirt. It was enough for Suri to catch up. She cut him from shoulder to groin, then whipped around to face the remaining ghouls, who had turned their attention to me. There were four left.

"Karalti! Capture the leader if you can! Don't kill him!" I spat some red goo, grasped my spear in bloody hands, and charged.

"Okay!"

"Come on!" I drove my weapon through the first ghoul, twisted it, and followed up with a kick to push it back. They attacked in a swarm, like movie zombies. I felt a hand grasp my shoulder, and knocked it away with the butt of my weapon. I didn't have enough HP to risk Shadow Dance - but the massive damage I'd taken had restored my AP to maximum. I triggered Umbra Blast. Dark power surged through my body, numbing the throbbing pain in my abdomen as it blew out from my skin in a blue-black wave of shattering energy.

The ghouls stumbled away, injured, just as Suri gained on us. She dashed forward in a whirling cloud of red energy, lightning-quick, and swung her sword through the second ghoul's waist, cutting it in half. The other two ganked her as she drew aggro. I settled for good old-fashioned stabbing, and as soon as I gained enough adrenaline back for Whirlwind Butcher, I used it. The Stranged man fell, bleeding from the back of his skull. The other had gotten through Suri's guard and was savaging her chest and neck.

"Count to three and push away!" I ran toward them, spear leveled at the ghoul's back.

The Backstab connected with the man's spine for a critical hit. Suri cursed as she shoved him off, and before I'd even had a chance to finish him, she flipped one of her axes up with her foot, dropped the sword, and slammed the broad, heavy blade into the back of his neck. The ghoul collapsed like a puppet, twitching through its death throes. I immediately got a waterfall of notifications:

[[You earned 410 EXP!]]

[[Congratulations! You are Level 10! You may now redistribute your Ability Points and take a second Advanced Path. Visit your Paths menu for details.]]

[[Warning! Your primary weapon is badly damaged! Durability 17/100]]

[[You have two unspent ability points!]]

[[You have three unspent skill points!]]

[[Congratulations! Cutthroat is Level 8!]]

[[Cutthroat has learned Pack Tactics!]]

I gaped at Suri in amazement. "Wow."

"Wow yourself." Suri was covered in blood and looked like she'd just had the best sex of her life. Her lips were full and flushed, her short hair tousled, and her skin glowed like deep burnished copper. She had bite marks on her neck and deep claw wounds on her face, but she showed no sign of pain. "Nice armor."

"Why thank you." I smiled back at her.

"What's your score?"

I checked my HUD. "Eight."

She licked the corner of her mouth, her eyes hooding. "I got six. Aren't you just a little one-man army?"

"*Hector! We got him!*" Karalti's voice rang through my mind before I could shoot back something in response to the 'little' remark. "*You better come before Cutthroat eats him!*"

"Karalti's got the leader," I rasped. My voice was husky from shouting I didn't remember doing. "You as good at interrogation as you are at ripping guys' heads off?"

"I'm good at a lot of things." Suri pursed her lips and bent down to pull her ax from the ghoul's skull. She hung it on her belt before picking up her sword and swinging it over to rest on her shoulder. I noticed belatedly that she was left-handed.

"Here." I took my last remaining Bonebreak Poultice from my Inventory and offered it to her.

"Thanks, but you need it more." Her gaze dropped to the huge soggy red patch on my armor. "They fucked you up. Good fight, though."

"What's your Advanced Path?" I asked. "I've never seen anyone fight like that without powered armor."

Suri actually grinned. Like Cutthroat, killing things seemed to put her in a better mood than usual. "Wanna guess?"

"Are you a deadly Kangaroo-Taipan Sausage Dervish?" I replied, lifting my armor up enough that I could apply the poultice. In battle, health items were consumed instantly. Outside of combat, you had to stick them on or drink them like how you would in real life.

"I'm a Berserker, you dimwit." She rolled her eyes.

"It was either that or Vegemite Assassin."

Suri got an odd look on her face. Confusion? "Vegemite. I feel like I should know what that is."

"You should. But don't worry about it." The poultice healed me for 50, but that only brought me up to 215 HP, still less than half of my total Hit Points. Even so, the throbbing gut pain and nausea receded. I no longer felt like the contents of my stomach were mingling with my bloodstream.

"Hector! Come on!" Karalti scolded me from down the road. I could hear angry voices – human voices – from that direction now. *"The guards are here!"*

"We'd better go." I pressed my hand in against my gut, and started off at a limping run toward the dinosaur and dragon.

We jogged up to find bodies scattered on the road and guards standing back as Karalti and Cutthroat faced off. Some were bleeding, some were deep-fried. Only one man remained, and he was trying to crawl out from under Karalti's feet as Cutthroat circled her, lunging and nipping to try to savage the mercenary leader. Well, savage him more. He was already in pretty bad shape.

"Okay, ladies! Break it up!" I clapped my hands loudly, striding quickly toward them.

Cutthroat turned to face us with a snarl. Her feathered crests flared as she stood up tall, puffed her chest and throat, and brandished both of her scythe-claws at us.

"Rah!" Suri came up from beside me, and threw her arms in the air as well. "Move it, bird brain!"

Cutthroat reared her head back, crests deflating, and clopped her jaws together in frustration. Suri lunged at her, and the hookwing shrunk back, her feathers folding close to her body.

"Grrrgh..." The man on the ground made a wet rasping sound. "Help... me..."

As Cutthroat slunk off, the guards closed in. The man leading them eyed Karalti warily, but respectfully. "What in the gods' names happened here? Your group bears the Mark of the King... Were you attacked?"

"This was a foreign invasion." I was more shaken than I was willing to reveal to anyone here, least of all Karalti. This wasn't just a small snatch-and-grab operation. The number of attackers, their gear and the brazen shutdown of the street was an assault force. "These men were here to capture this dragon. Karalti, hold him down by the neck. If he moves, kill him."

Karalti put her foot down on the Mercenary Leader's neck, and flexed her killing toe until the huge claw pressed in against his carotid. *"Like this?"*

"Perfect." I bent down and began to rifle through the man's pockets.

"I... won't tell you... anything!" He tried to spit on me as I worked, but only succeeded in spraying a little more blood on my already-sticky armor.

"It's the Vulkan Keep dungeons for you, foreigner. We'll find a way to get you squawking," the guard closest to me said.

I found something small and metal in one of his pockets, and took it out. Then frowned. It was a brooch, some kind of token made of gold... but it was in the shape of the Ryuko corporate logo, sans text. I tried bringing up an item description, but all I got was a blank screen.

"What the hell is this?" I demanded.

The man spat at me again.

When you work in security, there's one thing you never learn to tolerate: spitting. Brawling? Whatever. Cursing? I'd heard it all. Spitting was my hard limit, so when this guy hawked a third time, I stabbed him in the leg with the pin of the brooch. His eyes flew open, and he spat all over himself instead of me.

"My dragon's claw only needs to stick in about a quarter of an inch to kill you," I said, grabbing him by the hair. "Start talking. Who hired you? And what is this?"

"Kill me," he said hoarsely. "I'll die before I talk. Whatever you people do to me, my soul will be safe from the Caul. I'll be reborn by the will of the Architect, and will live forever!"

"What the fuck are you babbling on about?" Suri looked down. "C'mon, Hector. Let's just have the guards take this joker."

"By your leave, Kingswoman." The guardsman close to us saluted and took a pair of manacles off his belt.

I nodded, and let go of the man's head to stand up. But as I was backing off, he gave me a piercing, defiant look, lunged up against Karalti's claw, and slashed his artery wide open on the razor-sharp edge.

CHAPTER 15

Karalti yelped out in surprise, moving her foot away, but it was too late. The pressurized spray of blood burst from his slit carotid and painted her entire belly scarlet. A guard pushed me aside, applying a healing item to his neck, but not in time. The Mercenary Leader burbled and frothed as his eyes rolled back. There was no healing that wound.

Suri grimaced. "Guess he wasn't so mercenary after all."

"Fuck!" Cursing, I bent down and retrieved the brooch. "Motherfucker!"

"Is this connected to the Slayer?" The guard looked back up at us, shaken. He was still trying to stop the bleeding by leaning on the saturated bandage he'd pressed down.

I glanced aside at Suri. "Not to my knowledge. These men were Ilian."

"We'll search the bodies and report to the Volod's Castellan." Another burly guard wandered up. His voice was deep and gravelly, with a thick Eastern European accent. "You are exempted from questioning, because you carry the King's Mark... but try not to cause more trouble. There was magic used here. We must close the street."

I swallowed and nodded, looking back at the scattered carnage down along the hill. The bodies were still there. Normally, bodies quickly dissolved and turned into loot sacks that could be gathered, but these bodies had not. I suspected that was because we were in a city.

"C'mon," Suri said to me. "Let's go meet with Andrik. You can give him that report on what you found out about the Slayer. It might buy us an extension on the investigation. We need more than two days."

"Yeah. Sure." I pocketed the Ryuko logo brooch, and as I did, I brushed against the honeybee pendant on its chain.

There was a chirp from behind us, and I turned to see Cutthroat standing there like a giant black canary. The hookwing had a man's severed arm hanging from her jaws. When Suri stared at her, Cutthroat trotted up to us and began to plunge and rear her head, her bladed winglets fluttering against her ribs.

"Is she...?" I watched in mild disbelief, reaching out to Karalti as she came up alongside me. "Is she flirting with you?"

Suri eyed her. "Is that what you're doing? Gonna sexy dance at me?"

"Purrr! Purrr!" Cutthroat wagged her head up and down. The hand at the end of the arm flapped in time with her dance.

"There is no way this is gonna work. We have incompatible genitals, Cutthroat." Suri chuckled as the hookwing deposited the arm at her feet, and motioned back with her head and hands before stepping in to scratch the hookwing around the edge of her jaw and ear. Cutthroat's feathers lifted, turning her into a giant black puffball.

"Well, there's my quote of the day," I remarked.

Karalti hopped from foot to foot with excitement. "*I should do that for you with a burek!*"

"*No. No mating dance. For one thing, you are* way *underage. For another, I refuse to be known across the realm as Hector Dragonfucker.*" I groaned, and then something occurred to me. "*But that reminds me. You're big enough to carry me at a walk now. We can't fly, but... what do you say to letting me ride you? Platonically.*"

"*Yeah!*" Karalti bobbed her head eagerly. "*No more stinky hookwing! What's 'platonic'?*"

"You know..." I said, watching as Suri caught Cutthroat's reins with the other hand. "She's yours, if you want her."

"What?" Suri turned to look back at me.

I grinned, and gestured at the dinosaur as she began to pant. "That big old bitch has hated me and everyone else who's ever gone near her, but she's decided that you're The One. You're her waifu. Regardless of the reality, she now fully believes your genitals are compatible. You might as well make your twu love official."

For a moment, I could tell that Suri was trying to figure out if this was some kind of trap. But then she reached out and absently scritched Cutthroat on the neck.

"What d'ya want for her?" Suri asked.

"Party up with me and work together like an adult doing adulty things," I replied. "And if it doesn't suit you, leave."

Suri gave a testy little sigh. She looked me up and down, and shrugged a shoulder.

"Two rules," she replied. "You keep your hands to yourself. And I can leave the party when I want, wherever I want, no questions asked. No nagging, no bullshit. Alright?"

"Fine with me."

She nodded, and pulled herself into the saddle. I took that as a yes.

My Ride skill was high enough that I didn't need a saddle to stay on Karalti while she was on the ground, but I couldn't sit astride her like a horse. Her back was a completely different shape than Cutthroat's: narrower, straighter and harder, with a pronounced spinal ridge that ran from the base of her neck and then grew up into hard, bony plates on her rump. At her current size, neither feature was particularly friendly to male anatomy. I had to ride side-saddle.

"I feel so strong now!" Karalti enthused, jostling me from side to side as she trotted up through the University District. *"But you need to eat less bread. You're fat."*

I nearly retorted with the incredibly mature 'your mom is fat', but in light of recent historical events, it was in pretty poor taste. *"I'll eat all the burek I like, Tidbit. Now hang on, I have to distribute some points."*

I'd been waiting to hit Level 10 for a while now. Several new combat abilities opened up, plus you had the option to take a second Advanced Path – if you wanted to. More importantly, you got a once-off opportunity to redistribute your Ability Points. This was great, because I'd learned a lot about my Dark Lancer class in the last five levels and gotten a sense of what skills and stats I wanted to focus on. I didn't have enough time or concentration to sit and redistribute everything properly right now, so I spent my Ability Points on upgrading Umbra Blast and Blood Sprint, my strongest offensive abilities. I would redistribute them later; I had a strategy for my 'final build', but would lock it in when I had more time.

"Hey, Hector?" Karalti's voice intruded into my thoughts. *"Aren't I too big to be a Tidbit now?"*

"I don't care how big you get. When you're some big shot queen matriarch with a half-dozen boy dragons doing your manicures and feeding you grapes off a plate-"

"Eww!" Karalti broke out in helpless laughter.

"- Old Man Hector is going to tell your boyfriends how he was there wiping half-digested cat poop off your little chin." I drew out the amulet Kanzo had dropped the night before, getting a good look at it. It was just like Rin's, which struck me as odd. Maybe I was just a filthy capitalist accustomed to the excess of corporate CEOs, but I didn't understand why a craftmaster would wear the exact same iron pendant as his students. For a crafting system that had defined ranks, it seemed odd that the ranks weren't indicated by different pendants, or at least different crafting materials for the same design.

"That poop thing only happened once!"

"Believe me, Karalti. Once was enough for me to remember that smell forever."

"Hate to tell you, but your dragon's giggling." Suri had gotten Cutthroat's saddle and tack with the animal herself. The Berserker wasn't a particularly good rider, but she was able to hold her seat, and Cutthroat - while still sullen to have anyone on her back - was far better behaved with Suri than she ever was with me, but she still had to wear her muzzle.

"Yeah, she's overcome by my razor wit," I replied. "What do you make of this?"

"What is it?" Suri took the pendant as I reached out and handed it over.

"This fell off the guy I was beating on last night. His apprentice claims it's his maker's mark."

"I recognize it," Suri said, looking over it. "The Volod has some carriages with this symbol on it. Belongs to one of the Royal Craftsmen. Nice bit of work."

That lined up with what Rin had told me, at least. "Yeah. He and all his apprentices wear the same necklace. My menu has logged it as a piece of evidence we need to complete the Slayer of Taltos questline. Maybe we could find a mage who could track Kanzo with it?"

"Maybe." With the reins resting in one hand, Suri began to manipulate the strange little pendant with the fingers of the other. "Huh."

"What?" I glanced over, just as the pendant bent forward, and the 'stinger' of the bee popped out from the end of its abdomen.

"Oh, yeah. That's tricky." She hooked her fingernail into the gap in the bee's back, pulling a tiny switch forward so that the pendant straightened and the illusion of an insect braced around a solid iron rod was back in place.

"You *are* some kind of wizard, aren't you? First you seduce my hookwing, and now you're giving my bee an erection."

Suri chuckled, flicking the pendant in half again. "Make that fuckin' party request already, won't you?"

Oh, yeah. I'd forgotten about that. I brought up my HUD and queried 'Form Party' while Suri held the pendant up and squinted to examine it. I sent the request, and a few seconds later, she joined. My eyes bugged a bit when I saw her level, class, and abilities.

"Holy fucking shit." I gaped, bringing up her sheet. "You have *forty* strength? At Level 17?"

"Yup."

"Forty. Four zero."

"Yup."

I shook my head in disbelief. "*Karalti* doesn't have fifty strength points, and she's a fucking dragon. How long have you been playing in Archemi?"

"About as long as you've been off your meds, if you think I'm 'playing' at anything." she replied laconically. "But you know what? I think this necklace you found is a key. Have a close look at the stinger."

She held the pendant back to me. I leaned over and snatched it by the chain, frowning. The stinger of the bee wasn't actually sharpened: it was a thin triangular strut that fit into the iron rod that formed the pendant's spine, just long enough that it nested inside the bottom part of it. The little thing was polished smooth, and etched with hair-thin designs around an oddly symmetrical pattern of tiny holes.

"See those little dots on it?" Suri asked, keeping an eye on the road. "Reminds me of a hexagonal laser-patterned matrix. My bet is that our master craftsman has some kind of mage lock rigged up that can read the Words of Power that are transcoded into those dots."

I stared at her in blank disbelief for a couple of seconds.

"What?" She glared back.

"Okay, let me get this straight," I said. "You're some kind of min-maxed barbarian chick born in medieval Dakhdir. But know what a hexagonal laser-pattern matrix is?" I asked.

"Sure I do," she replied. "Why wouldn't I?"

"Okay. Can you actually describe a laser?"

"It's... It's..." The woman's eyes glazed over briefly. "Some magitech artificer thing, I don't bloody know. I'm not a wizard."

I puzzled over that in the awkward pause that followed, and then it occurred to me. Whatever was up with Suri, I could probably talk to her using the language of Archemi's mythos. "You know, I think I know what's going on here. You're Starborn, right?"

"That's what people keep saying." She looked away uncomfortably.

"You probably know because of one of your, uhh, 'past lives'. You know how we Starborn types remember bits and pieces of those?"

"Probably. Which is why I don't give a shit. This life's been more than enough to keep me busy."

"Right. Okay then." I sighed. "So, what do you want to do? Go to the palace, or go back to Rin's shop and see if there's something this key fits? The more evidence we can take back to the Volod, the better."

"I reckon we could go check out Rin's place. We're not in any rush. There's forty-six hours left on the clock." Suri ran her tongue over her teeth, and reined Cutthroat to a slow walk. We were at the top of the hill, about to cross the grand bridge that led to the gatehouse in front of Vulkan Keep. "You have a point about the pogrom thing. Andrik's alright, but he's a racist cunt. Took a while to even come around to me, which is odd because of how keen he's been."

"Keen?"

"Keen, as in he's got the hots for me."

I shook my head and blinked a couple of times. "What?"

Suri gave a testy little sigh. "He wants to fuck me, idiot."

I framed my lips around a silent 'Oh' and nodded.

"Anyway. Even if we bring him the Slayer's head in a bag, he's gonna want to take it out on all non-humans... but if we bring him evidence that this guy is acting alone, it makes it easier to argue that it's only one or two Mercurions involved."

"That was what I was thinking." I nodded, and tapped Karalti on the neck. "Time to turn around and head back to Rin's."

Karalti made a noise of disgust. *"I'm hungry. I wish we could just fly there."*

"Me too," I said. *"Won't be long now. But you know what this means, right?"*

"Wat?"

"We have to start flight training. And you'll be carrying a hell of a lot more than forty pounds in the backpack."

"UGH."

It was mid-afternoon by the time we reached Rin's workshop. It was shuttered, and the door was locked. The lock didn't look anything like the little pendant key.

"Bugger." Suri examined it for a minute or so, twitched her lips, and then took a small rolled-up pouch from thin air. "Spot for me. I think I can open this."

"What? You think we should just like... break in?" I raised my eyebrows. "I'm not okay with that. Rin's not a bad person."

"You said she interfered in an arrest," Suri replied. "I'm not okay with *that.* Until proven otherwise, she's an accomplice to a serial killer. Accomplices have every reason to seem like good people. I'd rather search the house without her hovering around."

She had a point there. Resigned, I took up position to watch the alley. "How does a Berserker learn how to pick locks?"

"Sometimes you have to 'zerk with finesse," she replied primly.

"Finzerking?" I wrinkled my nose.

There was clicking and scraping from behind me, then a muffled 'click'. I turned in anticipation, only to see Suri get to her feet, fists balled.

"ARRRRGH!" She smashed the door in with one booted foot, nearly taking it off its hinges. I jumped about a foot in the air. Cutthroat hissed. Even Karalti flinched.

"What was that about finesse?" I asked, following Suri inside as she stalked ahead.

"Damn thing's Master quality. Broke my last lockpick," she muttered.

"Well, I guess 40 Strength makes anything finessable," I said, strolling in after her.

"*Wait! Hector!*" Karalti made a honking sound of confusion and distress behind us. "*I can't- I'm stuck!*"

I turned to see my dragon's head and shoulders wedged into the doorjamb to either side. She was looking at me with pitiful desperation, her horns flat against her head.

"Aww shit. Hang on." I went back to her as she shoved against the confines of the door. It was solid stone, and it wasn't budging. Her wings were too wide for her to fit. "Whoa there, girl..."

My little Tidbit, who had only been a bit larger than a cat last week, was now the same size as my war-bred hookwing. There was no way she was getting in here. As I walked over to her, she strained her head toward me, huffing blisteringly hot air across my face and neck.

"Wait, wait, wait," I said, trying to soothe her. "It's okay, girl. But you're going to have to stay outside."

"Stay outside!? What if something happens to you inside!?" She butted in against the stone, then swiveled her head around on her long neck. *"I can't -Hey! There's another way in over there!"*

I followed her line of sight. It was true: there was a pair of carriage doors at the other end of the workshop. But that still didn't mean she was going to be able to follow me around the way that she had three levels ago.

I reached up, and cupped her jaws to either side. "It's too small in here for you, Karalti," I said firmly. "You're growing, and getting stronger means getting bigger. We knew this was going to happen someday, and that day is now here. Go wait outside."

To my surprise, she hissed at me, jaws open wide, and tried to push through – but it was no use. She couldn't even get proper leverage in the narrow alleyway. Karalti sat down on her haunches right inside the doorway, throwing her head from side to side like a toddler having a tantrum. *"I don't want to be left out!"*

"I know, girl. I know... but..." I gestured to the doorway. "Don't worry, alright? You can watch from there and keep an eye out for Rin. I'll make sure that when we bed down, we get a space we can share. Okay?"

"No! I don't want to be out here while she's *in there! It's not fair! It's not!"* Karalti bellowed this time, napalm dribbling from her jaws. She got to her feet and turned, clumsily smacking the doorframe with her wing edge as she ran back down the alley. *"It's not FAIR!"*"

"Karalti!" I jogged to the door in time to see her shove past Cutthroat, who halfheartedly snapped at her on the way past. When she reached the street, she launched into the air at a sprint and a wave of boiling heat, sending pedestrians scattering with angry, frightened, and then wonderous cries.

"Let her work it off," Suri said from behind me. "She's... what? What level now?"

"Four," I said. "I think that's about twelve in dragon years."

"Girls are all like that at her age." Suri smiled ruefully. "Don't worry, mate. She'll come back."

I watched as Karalti spiraled up into the sky, roaring and flaming. When I reached out along our telepathic link, I heard only angry white noise. "It's not that easy. What if someone tries to capture her? What if-?"

"No one's gonna capture her. There's not a quazi in Archemi that can fly like that. Just let her work off some steam. She's been up your ass and in your business since she hatched, and now she's suddenly being left out. Even if it wasn't anyone's fault, I'd be pissed off. Wouldn't you?"

"Yeah." I dug my fingers into the edge of the door. "Guess we better find whatever this key opens. Rin's already going to be furious when she gets back... I don't want her to think we're stealing."

The forge and furnace were down to a simmer, and Rin was nowhere to be seen. Neither were her automatons. I found myself feeling oddly guilty as we began to search around, looking for chests or doors that would fit a key as tiny as the one hidden in the bee pendant.

"You have any idea what a mage lock looks like?" I lifted a small lockbox and tried to match the key to it, but no luck.

"Usually like a round... Christ, what did they call them IRL?" Suri frowned. She was walking along the walls, knocking every few inches to check for false panels. "Dead... bolts? Deadbolts? But with a crystal face and conduits for mana. You insert the key and the mana flows into the dots and along those designs."

"Really? Those designs are tiny. He must have sat there with a magnifying glass to do that etching."

"Probably did. That's what separates Mastercrafting from amateur though, right? The better you are at crafting, the less mana you need." Suri stood back and sighed when she reached the end of the wall.

I wandered to the back of the shop, scanning the walls, ceiling, and floor until supernaturally sharpened vision snagged on something in the far corner of the workshop: a break in the pattern of an old rug on the floor. I strolled over, crouched down, and lifted the rug up. Yup.

"Here," I called back. "Found a trap door."

Suri joined me, and looked down, hands on hips. The door I'd spotted was closely fit into the floor, with a thin wire handle to lift it. I pulled it up and to the side, revealing a ladder going down into a musty basement corridor.

"Can you see in the dark?" I asked.

"Nope," she replied. "Can you?"

"Sure can." I hung my legs into the hole and caught the ladder.

"Gentlemen first, I guess."

Then a high girlish voice pierced the air. "Hector?! What are you doing here!?"

There was the sound of items crashing to the floor, and Suri and I both looked over to see Rin standing inside her doorway. She was wearing the smooth metal mask I associated with Mercurions over her face, but there was no masking her sense of shock - or betrayal.

CHAPTER 16

"Why did you break in here?" Rin stood among her dropped packages, fists balled. Her automata crowded in behind and around her, crossbows swiveling to point at us. "This... this...this!"

Suri stepped forward, drawing her axes and flipping them over in her hands.

"Wait! Both of you, wait!" I scrambled back out of the trapdoor. "No murdering!"

"I welcomed you into my home! I t-trusted you!" Rin shouted. "Why did you break in like this!?"

"Because your master's killed four men in cold blood," Suri replied. She watched Rin cautiously. "And we're the investigators hired by the Volod to find out why."

"We haven't spoken to Andrik about Kanzo yet," I added quickly, "But we HAVE to investigate. You weren't home... and..."

"So you destroyed my door?! I should... I should... UUUGH!" Rin shook her head, waving her fists close to her face. Then she sunk down into a crouch and began to sob.

"Jeez," Suri muttered. Her aggressive stance faltered.

"You didn't have to b-b-break in!" Rin stuttered, burying her head against her knees. "I would have... I'd have..."

'Jeez' was about right. Deflated, I went over to Rin, doing my best to ignore the way Lovelace and Hopper turned to track my movements, and knelt beside Rin to awkwardly pat her on the back. "Hey, kid. I'm sorry, alright?"

"Its... its... its..." She couldn't seem to say anything other than the one word as she began to rock back and forward.

At a loss, I took Kanzo's honeybee necklace from my pocket. "Hey, look. Kanzo dropped this the other night. Did you know this necklace was a key?"

"K-k-key?" She looked up. The smooth bowl-like surface of her mask seethed with hairline runes, the mana flowing under a layer of fine glass.

"Yeah, look." I fiddled with the bee until the stinger popped out. "Bee boner."

"T-That's... what? M-m-my necklace can't d-d-do that." Rin didn't sniffle as she sobbed – Mercurions didn't exactly make mucus or saliva or anything – but her voice was tight and thin. "Kanzo d-d-dropped that?"

"Yeah. And I figured that might be the case. That's why we came here, alright?" I rubbed her back soothingly. "I get that this is your house, but we don't have much time. I'm really sorry we broke in instead of waiting for you."

Across the room, Suri sighed and hung her axes back on her belt.

Rin reached up with a slim hand, and took her mask off, revealing her face. She looked between us. "I-I want to know why Kanzo hurt those men too. But I-I don't think you're going to find anything here."

"That trapdoor over there. Do you know what's downstairs? There might be something this key opens."

She shook her head. "J-Just the boiler room, and cleaning stuff."

"We're still going down there." Suri joined us, keeping a wary eye on Hopper and Lovelace. "You want to know why we broke in?

Because either we can search this place top to bottom, or the Volod's soldiers will. Hector figured you'd prefer it was us."

"I get it, okay?" Rin looked up fiercely. "Who are you, anyway?"

"This is Suri. She was looking into the murders before I joined in," I replied.

"Yep," Suri crossed her arms. "And all roads lead here, kiddo."

"I'm not a kid!" Rin climbed to her feet, an impressive five-foot nothing, and scowled up at her.

"You come up to my sternum," Suri drawled back. "Anything below tit-height is either a kid or a dwarf."

Rin got to her feet. "Well... from here you... you look like a... like a pair of angry walking boobs!"

Suri and I busted up laughing at the same time.

"It's not funny!" Rin shrilled.

"Glad you noticed," Suri said.

Rin's cheeks flushed blue. "That's not what I meant!"

"Then what *did* you mean?" Suri leered down at her.

"That's not... I wasn't-!" the Mercurion spluttered.

"You want a better look, little girl?" Suri arched both eyebrows, bent forward at the waist, and pulled her collar down to flash her half-mile of clevage. Rin squealed and covered her eyes.

"Okay, okay... that's enough mirth for today." I waved them on. "Let's go and get this over with."

I went down into the basement first again, dropping from the ladder into a dim hallway. Rin followed behind, muttering to herself. Something about boobs and forced entry.

"Are there any lights down here?" I called back.

Rin stopped grumbling, and paused for a moment. "Oh, yeah. *Orisel.*"

When she spoke the word, torches came to life on the walls: glass spheres sparkling with mana. Suri whistled appreciatively.

"Your boss must be rich as hell if he can afford bluecrystal lighting," she remarked.

Rin nodded apprehensively. "He never really talked to me about money, but, yeah, I guess he is."

"You're his Number One Apprentice, and he never told you how much he earns?" I let Rin take the lead.

"I... uh... kind of panic if I have to deal with money."

"Meaning that Kanzo is your mana-crystal daddy?" Suri called from the back.

"No! It's not like that at all!" Rin threw open another door into a warm room at the end of the hall. It wasn't an especially large basement. Pipes fed down from the ceiling into a boiler, and the rest was cleaning and storage, as she'd told us.

"Here," she said sullenly. "Like I said. It's just the boiler and some storage."

"Did this guy Kanzo spend a lot of time down here?" Suri asked. "Or like... out of the house?"

"Of course he spent a lot of time out of the shop. He traveled to all these different estates and factories and things. I never saw him down here, though."

"But he *was* absent for long periods?" Suri looked up and over the walls.

"Yeah... but..."

"What about strange noises? Rumblings, things like that?"

"The boiler makes a sound when it's heating up. That's all."

"Any rituals he held to real strongly?"

"Uhh... well, he's an Artificer and very disciplined, so he had all kinds of rituals. None of them involved this room."

I scanned the room, wishing more than ever that Karalti were here. Her senses were even keener than mine. Frowning, I looked over the visible walls, but couldn't see anything interesting until I wandered over to the boiler and looked behind it. There was a span of stone wall that was whiter than the rest, but when I knocked on it, it sounded just like the wall to either side. But as I was moving back, my eyes caught on something out of place. The machine had multiple pipes coming off it. Most of them went up through the floors to power the furnace bellows. Others were connected to the water pipes that fed the boiler. But, one set of pipes went down into the floor, and beside them was a small spigot set with five tiny green stones that only someone with inhumanly sharp vision could have spotted. It was hidden by another mechanism.

While Suri grilled Rin, I crouched down to get a better look at it. Sure enough, there was a small hole in the center of the spigot that was the size and shape of the bee's stinger. I tried turning the spigot, but it didn't budge.

"Hey," I called back. "I found something. Maybe move back into the hallway, in case it's a trap or something."

After hearing them move away from the center of the room, I inserted the key into the lock. But it still didn't turn. Instead, a thin trail of light shot out and connected the stones in a pentagram. I turned the spigot slowly, pausing as the boiler groaned and then creaked. Water gurgled in the intake pipes, and the machine came to life as I stepped back and looked around, just in time to see a section of floor depress, then slide back with hardly any sound at all, just the wet rasp of smooth oiled stone. A damp, moldy smell rolled up from the dark narrow staircase that led down.

Rin's eyes widened. "I... uh..."

"You know about this?" I jerked my head towards the entrance.

She shook her head hard. "No! I-I've never seen this before, I swear!"

"Time to go see what old Kanzo was up to, then," I replied, pulling the Spear of Nine Spheres off my back.

[[Warning! Your primary weapon is badly damaged! Durability 17/100]]

[[Using badly damaged weapons in combat may destroy them!]]

"Aww, shit." I dismissed the notification, and after a moment of consideration, equipped the Steel Militia Spear I'd made the other night. It did about the same damage as the artifact, but didn't have any bonus effects or stat increases. At least it wouldn't break in the middle of combat.

"What?" Suri drew up. "Jeez. You've been fighting with *that* cruddy old piece of shit all this time?"

"That 'cruddy old piece of shit' is an orange-tier lazula artifact," Rin retorted.

"Doesn't change the fact that it's about to turn into matchsticks," Suri replied.

I folded the Spear of Nine Spheres into my Inventory, and it vanished from my hand. "Nothing I can do about it. The only person able to repair it is Kanzo, apparently."

"That'd be right." Suri jerked her head toward the hole. "Let's get moving. We need to dig up something more substantial than a necklace."

I went first. There were no lights down here, only the stench of mold and the relentless dripping of water. The stairs led down into a narrow limestone corridor, where a channel carried away the condensation that trickled from the ceiling.

"This is so weird," Rin whispered. She was following up the rear with Lovelace. Hopper had joined me at the front of the line. "I don't know why Kanzo would have a key for down here. This is part of the Lethos Cellars."

"The who in the what now?" Suri asked.

"Taltos is built on the ruins of an old dragon city, Kalla Kulesi. That city was flattened during the Drachan Wars, and when humans moved in, they started tunnelling," Rin said. "The limestone that was mined from down here is what most of the city is built from. There are all these old mine tunnels under the city. Around the tenth century, the mines were closed. Some of the network was sealed off. Most of those old mine tunnels were repurposed as catacombs where a lot of bones and dead bodies are stored. Some parts of the mine were turned into a network of cellars underneath buildings. The Lethos Cellar complex is mostly a grinding area for low-level players who don't want to leave the city. Maybe... maybe Kanzo had this key in case the Tanner's District was ever locked down, and we needed to escape?"

"Mines underneath a city? That doesn't sound very stable." I eyed the ceiling nervously.

"It's not exactly comforting, is it? We modeled Vlachia off Bohemia in the 1700s - Budapest and Prague, mostly. Rome, Paris, London, and most other old European cities actually all had tunnels like this," Rin chirped back. "Mining was done locally because there was no easy way to transport stone from distant quarries. It's sort of convenient from a Dev standpoint. Cities with catacombs are prone to sinkholes and stuff so... literal plot holes."

"*Bad-dum tsch.* Rimshot." From ahead, I heard an odd sound - a kind of squelching, gooey noise. "Shh... hang on. There's something ahead."

"I can't hear anything," Suri hissed back.

"I can. Trust me. Hang back and let me stealth down there."

The wet sucking grew louder the further we went into the musty cellar system, a rhythmic, lewd sound that honestly made me wonder if we were about to catch a guy getting a blowjob from some toothless under-city hooker.

I dropped into a low cross-step and slunk to the end of the hall, blinking to clear my eyes as I left the circle of torchlight. When I turned the corner and saw what was making the sound, my stomach climbed up into my throat.

It was a slime. And not a cute jello-drop slime, either. No, this was a {[Sulphuric Acid Slime]}, a misshapen yellow blob about ten feet around. It had engulfed the corpse of a man, oozing acid that bubbled on the wet stone. The slurping sound was the monster sucking at the corpse's torso, defleshing it and absorbing the blood and entrails into its mass. The man's legs hung out from the side of the monster, twitching and jerking. His sword had fallen from nerveless hands, along with a roll-up bag of tools. His torch lay on the ground, still burning. *Eww. What a way to go.*

Because we hadn't actually engaged with the slime, I didn't know what level it was – but I knew the little red skull symbol that hung beside it's grayed-out HP bar. It was a monster that was several levels higher than me. My guess was around Level 15.

"*Karalti,*" I thought out as I stealthed back to where Suri and Rin waited. "*Where are you, Tidbit?*"

There was no answer from Karalti, but I knew she was flying and hunting. I had a flash of her twin hearts pumping as she dived down from the sky.

"What've we got slurping down there?" Suri asked softly once I had rejoined them. "I can hear *something* now."

"Some kind of man-eating slime. It just caught a guy, so its busy right now," I said. "We're not equipped for this. Between us all, we only have piercing and slashing weapons. We need fire."

"Oh!" Rin said brightly. "I can go get the flamethrower!"

We both looked at her in disbelief.

"Why didn't you bring that down with you?" Suri asked flatly. "Or like... any weapon other than Tweedledee and Tweedledum?"

"Their names are Lovelace and Hopper," Rin replied testily. "And I thought we were just going to stick our heads in. I didn't know there'd be slimes!"

"Wait." I held a hand up. "You know, I have a better idea than a flamethrower. Rin, in the boiler room, you said you store cleaning products. Do you have any lye?"

"Sure we do," she replied. "We use it for all sorts of things."

I rubbed my hands together. "Time to murder this thing... with *science*."

CHAPTER 17

"There's no way this is going to work," Suri said, looking down from over my shoulder.

"That's the attitude of a loser," I replied, as I slopped water from a bucket into a pair of large, thin-walled jars that had recently held flour. "We manifest what we believe in, Suri. Give me winning thoughts. These negative vibes are killing me."

She rolled her eyes. "At this point, 'winning' would me be chucking your arse into the slime."

"Do you dare mock my cunning plan?" I replied, pouring a box of nails into the jars. I split it roughly fifty-fifty.

"I think your 'cunning plan's gonna get us killed."

"'Killed' is a state of mind," I said sagely, as I poured a large quantity of lye into each one of the jars. "Don't worry: we respawn."

"That's all you have to say? 'We respawn?" Her voice heated.

"What? Afraid of a little dying?"

"I don't want to die again. Ever."

I paused to look at her. "But you're a berserker."

"So?"

"So berserking is literally the opposite of being concerned about whether you live or die, isn't it?"

"It's a skill-set, not a fuckin' religion. Now shut up and build your bloody bomb."

Ahh... another layer of mystery added to the furious enigma that was Suri Ba'hadir. If I didn't know any better, I'd have said that she was afraid to die. I didn't exactly look forward to death, but I'd done it twice already – once IRL and once in Archemi – and it didn't really scare me anymore. Unlike some games I'd played, this one didn't penalize death in any substantial way. The worst thing that happened was that you either failed a quest or had to restart it, and you risked losing your non-soulbound items if you couldn't make a corpse run.

"Be one with the IED, Suri," I said. "And be careful, because this shit is about to get really hot, really fast."

"I know what lye does when it hits water, genius," she snapped back.

"Ah yes. But do you know what aluminum foil does to lye?"

"It's alu-mini-yum," she said sourly. "Not 'aloo-mi-num'. And I assume it makes this mixture explode."

I held up a couple of handfuls of crumpled aluminum leaf: the detonator to the bomb I was about to shove into the slime. The predatory goop was still sucking on the sagging meat popsicle it had made of the unfortunate explorer. "Aluminum goes in and reacts with the lye, producing a lot of hydrogen gas in about ten seconds. Jar expands and explodes. Lye also explodes on contact with sulfuric acid. It goes boom, and we exit one Sulfuric Acid Slime, stage left."

Rin balled her hands against her face. "How do you even know this!?"

"I used to bounce at a biker bar where all these scarred up, paranoid old Millennials and Gen Z Vets of the Second Civil War hung out." I shrugged. "They taught me this stuff in case I needed to blow up the government."

"Great," Suri replied.

"Here. You know what you're doing, somehow." I handed Suri some of the aluminum leaf.

She sighed, and accepted the foil.

The plan was simple: I would sneak up on the slime and get as close as I could without being suction-cupped by a pseudopod, shove the foil in the jar, screw the lid on, and either bodily push it into the slime or put it on the ground so that it would mindlessly engulf it.

From my extensive experience of being a stupid teenager who liked to blow things up, there was a short delay between adding al-foil to the lye and the jar exploding. That depended, however, on exactly how realistic Archemi's physics was. Thus far, it had been difficult to distinguish Archemi's physics from Earth's most of the time, with a few notable exceptions. I was hoping that realism extended into improvised explosives.

The first challenge was picking up the jar. The nails wouldn't melt in the caustic solution – bases didn't dissolve iron – but the jar was approximately the same temperature as the water now boiling inside of it.

"Okay. Let's do this." I held the hot jar away from me, with the foil held between my lips and the lid in the other hand. This made speech difficult, so I communicated via PM. *"Get ready to cover me if shit gets hairy."*

"Please don't blow yourself up." Rin had a crossbow and her Mercurion mask back on. The mask let her see in pitch darkness, which was just as well, because we really didn't want any open flames down here.

"I'll do my best." I waggled the tin foil at her, and then padded down the corridor with Lacy and Hopper trundling after me. As the sucking sounds of the jelly consuming its meal became more audible, I dropped into a careful, slow crouch, and came up on the corner to peer around and see where it was.

The man's torso was basically gone: his bones, daggers, coins, and other metal pieces were suspended in the jelly's mass, dissolving much more slowly than the flesh had. The monster was now half black, half yellow, and was chowing down on his lower half. The only body parts sticking out now were the man's feet. Mercifully, they were no longer moving.

"Okay," I P.M'd to Rin. *"On the count of three, have them step out and fire. One... two... three."*

On three, Hopper and Lovelace both jumped out into the corridor and let loose on the jelly. The crossbow bolts punctured its quivering mass without resistance. The thing reared up, gyrating violently.

[[Sulfuric Acid Slime takes 12 reduced piercing damage!]]

[[Sulfuric Acid Slime takes 8 reduced piercing damage!]]

The slime didn't turn: the closest side of it just surged right at us, a wave of snot-colored ooze traveling much faster than I'd expected. As the slime rushed forward, I jammed the thin-beaten aluminum into the glass jar, screwed the lid on, and ran out into the open with it.

"Get some!" I shook the jar a couple of times, and lobbed it.

The jar hit the slime and stuck to it, and for a breathless moment, I thought the monster was going to spit it back at me. But the moment passed and its mass enfolded around the payload as it kept shambling towards us, except *now* it was a [[Sulfuric Acid Slime]] with a nailbomb stuck in it.

"It worked!" I cried, pumping my fist in the air. Then I noticed how close it was, and began backpedaling away. "Oh fuck, it worked! Run, RUN, RUN!"

I heard Rin squeal, and rounded the corner to see her running, but Suri standing firm with the second jar ready to go. The jelly undulated after me around the corner and down the corridor.

"Watch out!" Suri yelled. "It's about to throw-!"

I turned just in time to see the slime spit out one of the daggers it had absorbed. It flew at me, end over end, and hit me square in the neck.

[[Sulfuric Acid Slime uses Mindless Luck!]]

[[Sulfuric Acid Slime lands a Devastating blow! X5 Damage]]

[[You take 220 damage!]]

[[You are Hemorrhaging! Stop the bleeding before you run out!]]

[[Congratulations! Karalti has reached Level 5!]]

The notifications were a meaningless blur. I croaked something unintelligible and reached up to clasp the knife in my neck to pull it out. It came free with a pumping wash of blood. The damage wasn't too bad yet, but I was losing about five HP a second. I tried to pull up a potion from my Inventory, only to remember something important. I was out of healing items.

Suri ran forward and grabbed me by the front of my armor. She spun me around and threw me back so hard that I tripped. From the ground, I watched as she poured the steaming lye mixture onto the ground.

"You bloody idiot!" Suri ran back, away from where the jelly was shying back from the spill. She grabbed me under the arm and hauled me to my feet, one-handed, half-dragging me back into the corridor. When we were a safe distance away, she poured a light green potion over my neck. The Bleed debuff stopped.

[[Warning! You are Hemorrhaging! 250/482 HP remaining!]]

"Fucking hell," she grumbled. "The bomb didn't even go off."

"It's... uhh..." I trailed off, watching as the slime froze in place. The monster got an odd, confused look about it.

"Duck!" I grabbed Suri by the arm and pulled her down.

The jar inside the slime went off like a stack of C-4. Nails and broken glass tore from its body, spraying the walls and us. Suri yelped as something hit her; I took a couple of nails to my arms as I shielded my face.

[[You take 20 piercing damage!]]

[[You destroyed Sulfuric Acid Slime!]]

[[You get 88 EXP!]]

[[Rin reaches Level 10!]]

[[You earned a new Feat: Combat Alchemist]]

"Yeah, bitch!" I wheezed down the goo-spattered hallway. "Science!"

"Ow, ow, ow, ow." Suri reached back, and pulled a shard of glass out of her butt. Then she threw it at me.

"Hey, what?! Wait! We killed the slime!" I shielded myself as she removed and flung more shrapnel at me.

"You numbnuts!" She pitched another bloody bit of glass at me, and then reached over and yanked one of the nails from my arm. I let out a piercing girly squeal.

"Stahhp it, momma! I'll be a good boy!" I hollered down the corridor. "Rin! She's beating me up!"

That was apparently what did it for her, because Suri's scowl cracked. For only the second time since I'd met her, she busted up laughing. So did I, until she friendly-punched me in the arm and drove one of the nails in deeper. I yowled again.

"Hector, are you...? Oh." Rin drew close enough to us to see what was going on. "Umm. Did you guys know you're bleeding?"

For some reason, that only made Suri laugh harder.

"Okay, seriously now," I said, once I'd recovered my normal speaking voice. "There was a door down where the slime axed that guy. We should go check that out."

"I wonder what he was doing down here?" Rin joined us, and offered us herbal potions. "Here: I can't use these. Mercurions have to use Silicone Gel and mana for healing and stuff..."

They were only Mint Potions, the weakest kind of healing tincture, but 10 HP a pop was better than nothing.

Five minutes later, we limped down the corridor and surveyed what remained. We were able to pick up the dead man's loot - Iron Scraps, 2x Moss Potions, 1x Iron Dagger blade, Lockpicks, Locksmith's Tools (Shoddy), 35 silver Rubles and a gold ring with the face of a cat - which Suri took from my hand without asking. She held it up to look at it more closely by torchlight, and grunted.

"Syndicate member," she said, handing it back. "That's a membership band. Interesting."

"How do you know?" I asked, searching around for anything we might have missed.

"Long story," she replied. "But this man was a member of the Nightstalkers. Their boss calls himself the King of Cats, so he's probably Meewfolk. They run most of the low-end organized crime in this city."

Rin hung back, chewing nervously on one of her bangs.

"There's two locks on this door," Suri said. "One mechanical, one magical."

"You any good with locks, Rin?" I turned to her.

She nodded, and silently came up to take the lockpicks from me. She got to work, and after barely ten seconds, the mechanism in the door clunked.

"This is definitely one of Kanzo's locks," she said grimly. "Give me the necklace with the key."

She held a hand back. I passed it over, and she inserted it into the mage-lock. There was a second clunk, and the door swung open. An odd smell filtered out: clean, earthy, and electric. The smell of mana.

"Don't think this leads outside," Suri said. "You first, Rin."

"You're resistant to Stranging, aren't you?" I asked Suri aside.

She nodded. "Yeah. I'm Fireblooded. Are you?"

"Dragon Knight, sort of. I've got some heavy-duty mutations. You could dip me in mana and I'd live."

"See, you say that now, but one day some... I dunno, a fuckin' mountain lion or something's gonna body-slam you into a river of mana and you'll..." Suri trailed off as Rin opened the door. "Wow. What the fuck?"

CHAPTER 18

I felt like we'd entered some android's nightmare. Or wet dream – I actually wasn't sure.

The nude husks of six unanimated Mercurions hung from the ceiling suspended on body hooks. A couple of them were covered in sheets, like spoopy ghosts. The others were just buck-ass naked, and very not-alive. Their eyes were nothing but empty sockets. Their mouths were slack, hanging open to show toothless gums. None of them had hair, or any kind of detailing beyond their basic features. They were sexless and indeterminate, but finely sculpted.

Further in the laboratory were big hourglass-shaped distillers, and tanks of liquid mana that glowed with pulsating light. They were empty. There was a workbench with a partially finished, mounted skull made of metal, and a surgery table, currently empty. Mercurion body parts were everywhere. Some of them were obviously being worked on. Some of them had obviously been cut off the bodies of other Mercurions and were being used as models.

"No... No!" Rin ran to the desk, frantically searching through the scattered papers on top of it. "No, Kanzo! No!"

"Eww. I feel like we just walked in on someone's porn collection." I took a step forward. "What the hell is this?"

Suri found a switch on the wall. Magelights came to life when she toggled it, illuminating the suite of rooms. The light should have made it better, but only served to make the scene more macabre. There were an awful lot of smaller body parts pinned to felt boards that we hadn't been able to see in the dark.

"This is..." Suri dropped her voice to barely a whisper. "This explains a lot."

Rin was shaking. She shuddered her way to the desk and dropped onto the stool, put her face on her arms, and wept.

"I get that this is creepy, but I don't think I get the implications." I looked around, not entirely comprehending the gravity of what I was seeing. "What was he doing? Experimenting on his own kind?"

"How much do you know about Mercurions?"

"Nada."

Suri rolled her shoulders, grimacing. "Mercurions have some real strict social rules. Firstly, marriage. Marriage is real important. They usually marry in threes, and the trio gets hitched in this big ceremony. Two partners from one clan, one partner from another. Part of the ceremony is that the dominant clan gives the three newlyweds the instructions on how to craft the next generation of Mercurions. They get special blueprints for their honeymoon, basically, so that they can have kids."

"Right." I wandered over to look at one of the hanging bodies, alert to the fact that this *was* an RPG, and thus a good chance they were Zombie Sexbots who'd come to life and attack us.

"Animating someone and giving them life is... hard." Suri kept her voice low, glancing at Rin as she cried herself out. "Real hard. And dangerous. Doing it alone, without some tried-and-tested blueprints, is usually a recipe for disaster. Mercurions shun anyone who tries to create a child without guidelines, *especially* if that person is doing it by themselves out of wedlock. Double the outrage if that person is desecrating the dead to learn how to create a child. What we're seeing here is..."

"*Juch'ik'haxi!*" Rin slammed her fist down onto the desk and pushed up to her feet. "This is... I can't believe you, Kanzo!"

Rin kicked the stool over, and I ran to her before she flipped the desk. "Wait! Don't destroy the evidence!"

The junior Artificer turned on me, eyes wide and furious and distraught. I had a brief impulse to hug her, which I brushed aside. She wasn't a kid, though I had to remind myself sometimes.

After several seconds, Rin backed up, swallowed, and picked up the stool.

"I'll start over there," Suri said, pointing to the tanks. "Try not to wreck anything. Look for stuff we can take to the Volod. No offense, kid, but the more evidence we find to paint this guy as a psycho and an aberration, the less likely Andrik is to shut down the Tanners' District."

"This isn't how it's supposed to be!" Rin began to sort through the papers on the desk with trembling hands. Her jaw was clenched so tight I could hear her teeth creaking, and she was fumbling with small, spasmodic ticcing motions. "He was supposed to follow the rules!"

I ducked my head to catch her eye and get her to look at me. "What rules? The Mercurion laws?"

Rin rubbed her hands, shaking her head. "No. I mean... yes, those too. When I-I came here, I'd just lost my dad to HEX. I was scared to be alone, so th-they gave me a craftmaster who could... who I would feel safe with. I didn't have anyone else but Dad. I still lived at home with him and went to work every day at Ryuko..."

At mention of Ryuko, Suri looked up from across the room and frowned.

"Hey." I dared to catch Rin by the wrist, and she looked up at me sharply. "It's gonna be alright."

"I'm sorry. I sound like a child." Rin shook her head, but didn't pull away from me. "I wasn't... I just..."

"You'll be okay." I dropped my voice, gently releasing her wrist. "You're on the spectrum, right?"

For a moment, I saw something in her face that I hadn't expected to see: shame. She nodded, cheeks burning blue.

"It's okay." I nodded back. "I had a friend offline who was Aspie as hell. That man was more my brother than my brother was. I'll watch out for you."

Mercurions didn't cry tears or get red-rimmed eyes, but Rin's expression said it all. Before I could stop her, she grabbed around my waist and pulled me into a hug. She buried her face against my chest and shook.

"*She alright?*" Suri asked over P.M. "*Looks like she's short-circuiting.*"

"*Sort of. She's autistic, I think, and kind of fragile,*" I replied. "*Don't worry, the reactors will be back online shortly.*"

Suri raised an eyebrow, then shrugged and continued pillaging her side of the lab.

"Hey, I have to go look for evidence, okay?" I patted Rin on the shoulder in what I hoped was a brotherly fashion. "You just take a seat and work it off."

"I'm okay. I'm okay. I just... too fast." She shook her head. "This is all happening too fast. I don't want to think about HEX or Dad or fight or see... I don't do blood and guts. I never wanted this kind of quest. I just wanted to make stuff with my friend."

"Yeah, I bet." I gently prised her off me, and helped her to the stool. Rin took a seat, rocking back and forth as she began stimming by drumming her fingers, becoming quickly absorbed by the pattering of her hands in her lap.

Once she was situated, I I turned my eagle eyes to the desk and shelves that stood near it, and picked out any odd-looking feature I could spot. My gaze snagged on a shiny copper container that looked kind of like a vacuum-sealed bread box with a hatch on it, complete with a small, spoked wheel to unlock and reseal it.

Curious, I drifted over and twisted it open, then flinched back as warm red light spilled out through the crack. It beat against the skin of my fingertips like sunlight, but the feeling didn't intensify or get uncomfortably hot. There was no alert from my HUD, either. I opened the hatch again, wider, and hmm'd when I saw what lay inside.

It was a collection of rubies. Some of them were as big as a golf ball, but most of them were smaller than a dime. They were all rough-cut and unpolished. Each stone had a glowing heart the color of blood: a deep crimson light that pulsed when I pinched a stone between thumb and forefinger and lifted it up.

Quest Updated: The Slayer of Taltos

After breaking into the secret laboratory of Kanzo, the Slayer of Taltos, you have discovered a mysterious, magically active crystal. Volod Andrik needs to see this.

Reward: *50 EXP, Mysterious Crystal* ⟦*Quest Item*⟧.

"Hey Hector, what did you just find?" Suri looked over sharply. "I got a quest update."

I held the crystal up for her to see. "This thing. Hey, Rin: do you know what kind of crystal this is?"

Rin looked up, still mute and obviously distressed, but when she saw what I was holding, her eyes widened. She held out her hands, and when I gave her the stone, she held it up to the light.

"I can't identify it," she whispered. "My Analyze ability doesn't work on it."

"Some kind of mana crystal?" I was thinking back on what very little knowledge I had of magic. "There's bluecrystal and greencrystal... could there be redcrystal?"

Suri shook her head as she joined us. "Never heard of redcrystal mana."

"This doesn't look like normal mana crystal. Too heavy." Rin passed it from hand to hand. "I don't know what it is. No wiki entry. It's definitely magical."

"Our quest says we should bag it, tag it, and take it to the Volod." Suri motioned to the notes on the desk. "Read anything interesting?"

I looked down. "If you need someone to read anything, I'm not your guy."

"You can't read?" Rin asked.

"Technically, yes." I held up a finger. "Functionally... we'd be down here for hours. I'm pretty dumb."

"Apparently, or you'd know that can fold the notes into your Inventory and get the menu to read them to you," Suri replied. "Just hand them back to us so we can each rip a copy."

"Right. I keep forgetting that we're virtual reality plague ghosts." I gathered up the notes, and didn't even have to stuff them in a pocket: my HUD flashed an alert as soon as I'd collected all the papers into a pile. Another 50 EXP, and a New Quest Item: ⟦Kanzo's Notes⟧. There was also another Quest Update, which told me that we'd now collected enough evidence to present it to the Volod.

Suri's nose wrinkled. "Plague ghosts?"

"Well, yeah. Me and Rin both died of the HEX virus in our, uh, 'previous lives'." I motioned to her with my head. "Hence, plague ghosts."

Rin nodded.

Suri tilted her head. "What's HEX?"

"How can you not know what HEX is?" Rin blurted.

I discreetly elbowed her in the shoulder.

Suri shrugged. "Whatever. Anyway, I want to get back to Andrik with these documents – they're all the evidence we need. Hurry up and read."

Rin nodded. After a second or two, her eyes began to rapidly scan back and forth, reading text on a display I couldn't see. Same with Suri. I stood there and let my HUD spoon-feed the information straight into my brain. Then I had it read me the entries. Most of them were developmental notes, written in a mixture of Common and Mercurion scripts. I couldn't decipher the Mercurion scripts, but the HUD narrator read me the others inside the privacy of my head. It even did it in Kanzo's voice.

"Mart 2, 1655: Failure, again."
"Temmuz 7, 1655: Failure. Body perfect, but did not wake. I'm going to have to scrap her and start over."
"Junia 8, 1656: This body is not at all like the last one. Wise humans say that the definition of insanity is doing something wrong over and over again... well, this time, I'm sure she will be right, even if her form is unorthodox. I will take her to the Seid fount in Mount Racosul and raise her on my Wakening Day. I hope she wakes... I PRAY she wakes."
"Junia 8, 1656: I did it! Sweet merciful ancestors, you have given me a child! All these years of scraping together and spending everything I could on mana. I bathed her in the vault at the heart of the volcano and she woke! She cannot breathe well yet but that does not matter. She lives! The cognition system with the linked crystals in suspension is so much more efficient than the orthodox pressurized seid methods. Already, she is unusually intelligent and quick-witted. Even better, she treats the memories in the Ruby Mana like her own memories! This old artist will finally have the proper vessel... someone who can pass along my work in its proper form and continue to instruct Rin. I can hardly believed my child is alive. I already have a name for her, but I dare not write it down."

"Well, shit." After a minute or so, Suri clicked her tongue and crossed her arms, leaning against the edge of the desk with a faraway expression on her face. "He did it."

Rin's expression crumpled as she read the same notes.

"Wait: there's more." I skipped ahead, to where the writing became more erratic, and got the HUD to start narrating where I saw a lot of exclamation marks and caps. The entry read: *"Julius 23, 1657: THEY TOOK HER! THOSE BASTARDS TOOK HER FROM ME! Phaedra, ancestors, what do I do now!?? I have to find her. At least she didn't have the memory stone in place already - my worst nightmare."*

"Wow," I said. "Check out Julius 23rd. It's 1657, isn't it?"

Rin ground the heels of her palms against her eyes. "Yes."

I clicked my tongue. "Looks like you were dead on the money. Someone *is* blackmailing him. They kidnapped his daughter."

"Did you know he had a juchi down here?" Suri asked.

Still covering her eyes, Rin shook her head.

"Not for an entire year?"

The Mercurion girl looked up sharply. "No! I didn't know, okay? I didn't know he owned this lab. I wasn't even *here* in 1655."

"Hey, guys - cool it down a bit. We've got our evidence now. Let's take these and the gem to the Volod," I said. "Rin, do you want to come with?"

"I-I can't." The girl hung her head. "If Andrik meets me, do you really think he'll let me go?"

I winced. "Prooobably not."

She looked up at me pleadingly. "Please, just let me stay. I want to do my quest, and it wants me to investigate this place more deeply. Why don't you come back to the shop tomorrow? I know you broke in here with good intentions, but... I just... I need some time alone. Here – let me send you a Friend Request. You can find me or message me whenever you need to. I'm a Mod – I mean, I *should* be a Mod – so I can't block anyone."

A second later, my HUD chirped. I swiped the interface in.

[[Player Rin Lu has send you a Friend Request. Do you accept?]]

I accepted the request. Suri shot me a dark look, and I didn't need to be a genius to know why. In pretty much every murder-mystery I'd ever played in a game, the murderer was the least-likely person in the room. In nearly all circumstances, that person would be Rin: adorable, vulnerable, smart but loyal to her surrogate dad despite him being some kind of freaky mad scientist. I glanced around the room. We knew it was actually Kanzo who was murdering people, but we didn't know if he had help or not. And if he did...

Suri seemed to be reading my mind. She crossed her arms. "Rin, you should be advised that I've taken snapshots of everything in here. This lab is a key crime scene, and if you disturb it any further, you *will* incriminate yourself."

Rin cringed away from her. "I won't do anything, I swear. I don't even want them to know that I know it's here. They'll arrest me."

I nodded. "Be careful."

Suri and I left her in there, carefully shuffling through other papers on Kanzo's desk. We headed back through the cellars to the workshop in companionable silence.

"Weird question," I said. "Do you have any past-life memories of being a cop?"

"You've got a real hard-on for this past life stuff, don't you?"

"Yeah, but seriously. I'm just saying you have a real police-y vibe about you."

She shrugged. "Why does it matter?"

"Maybe I have a problem with overbearing authority figures," I replied.

"Hah." Suri snorted. "Then you're just gonna love the Volod. He can be a bit of a knob."

Night had fallen by the time we left the workshop and walked to the roadside stable. Suri unhitched Cutthroat and saddled up, while I searched anxiously for Karalti. I could sense her nearby, but... *"Hey, girl, where are you? Are you alright?"*

"I'm right behind you," Karalti replied.

I swept my gaze over the darkened street, over the roofs, and then the stable. "Uhh... where?"

There was a shuffle from the alley beside the stable building. My head turned at the sound, and even though I knew she was there, I couldn't see anything - until suddenly, I could. Karalti had assumed dragonloaf form on the ground: legs bunched up underneath her, foreclaws tucked under her chest, her wings held close to her body. But it was like staring at an optical illusion. She seemed to phase in and out of the darkness. The parts of her obscured by shadow disappeared entirely.

"Whoa." I stumbled away from the stable as Karalti stood up tall, shaking out her leathery wings.

"What's that?" Suri called as she rode Cutthroat out into the street. "Oh. Wow."

CHAPTER 19

Karalti had grown again. As she paced out soundlessly into the open, my eyes widened.

The dragons of the Skyrdon had holographic hides that flexed under light – some kind of aerial camouflage that made them harder to spot while flying. Karalti's scales were on a completely different level. The parts of her immersed in shadow simply vanished, as if they had turned invisible.

From what I could see of her, I was guessing that she was now about thirty feet long, including her tail. Her head was now held up on a long, elegant neck. Her horns were longer and thinner, and crested around the back of her her skull like a fan - or a crown. Thick seams of opal glinted and shimmered between her scales. She was slimmer and smaller than the fully grown adult dragons I'd seen at the Eyrie, but Karalti now had the same regal bearing, the same graceful raptorine build as her elders. But even more so. Young as she was, there was an arresting presence to her that the other dragons hadn't had. It was the charisma that her mother would have been able to manifest, had she been free.

My heart rose into my throat, part pride, part confusion. I scrolled back through my notifications, and sure enough, there it was. She'd hit Level 5 somehow. My Princess Tidbit was already becoming a Queen.

"Karalti..." I approached her, hands held up. She crooned as I came closer, bent her muzzle down, and touched the end of her snout to my palm.

"I'm sorry I got mad," she said. Her voice was still youthful, but no longer childish. It was deepening, having moved from adorable-but-sometimes-irritating shrillness to a silken soprano. She sounded like a thirteen-year old girl... fourteen at the most.

"It's okay, Tidbit," I replied. I wasn't actually sure if it was or not, but I'd vowed to myself to let Karalti grow into her own person... dragon. Dragon-person. She had to have some independence if she was to be free.

"It's not. I ran because I was embarrassed and scared." She hung her head. *"But after I took wing, I remembered your encouragement... and I remembered the promise I made to you."*

"Promise?" I lay a hand on the side of her throat. The intense heat of her body radiated through my glove. Twin heartbeats thundered under my fingertips: one fast, the other slow.

"I told you I'd become the strongest. And when I felt more grown up, I remembered, and I listened to what you said. I embraced the suck."

I grinned, and then the grin turned into a chuckle.

The dragon crooned in her throat. *"I went and hunted the monsters outside the city wall. I accepted that I'm not a baby any more. I have to grow."*

I rubbed my hand down the length of her jaw, massaging the powerful, tense muscles that connected her head and neck. I couldn't stop marveling at the difference a single level had made to her. "You're... you're beautiful."

Karalti arched her head and shoulders against me, like a marking cat. The old mischief was back in her eyes. *"When I levelled, several of my Words spoke up in me. My Blood tells me that I'm ready to take my first Path. Can you help me?"*

"Of course." My chest swelled with an odd feeling. Pride? Sorrow? I wasn't sure. Barely a week ago, Karalti had been my little Tidbit. And now? It was weird to be sentimental over a virtual pet

evolving like this – I knew this is what she was supposed to do – but I couldn't help it. I had the feels. "*Karalti... I'm so proud of-*"

"Hey, Hector. I don't want to bust your bubble or anything, but Cutthroat's getting a bit narky over here," Suri called from across the street.

I wasn't sure what 'narky' meant, but given what I knew of Cutthroat, I could guess. I looked back to see Suri holding the hookwing's head back as she pranced and snapped in frustration, dancing from one foot to the other. She tried to turn her head and bite Suri on the leg. The Berserker whapped her, and Cutthroat squawked in irritation. Her affection for Suri apparently only went so far.

"Jeez. Guess the honeymoon's over." I rested a hand against the base of Karalti's neck. "Are you still okay with me riding on your back?"

"*Yeah!*" The dragon watched the hookwing's antics with quiet, predatory amusement, the tip of her tail lashing in and out of visibility.

"Then you.. uhh... you're going to have to crouch down a little," I said. "You got taller, remember?

Karalti yarped a saurian laugh, then bent down and put her foreclaws on the ground. I tried to remember how Knight-Commander Arnaud and the others had mounted their dragons. They climbed up their wings, but Karalti's wings still looked a bit delicate for me to do that.

"*You could use your Jump ability?*" she suggested.

"Oh. Right." I tensed, and triggered Jump. I leaped up lightly onto her back, dropping into a crouch as I landed. "So, we're going to see the Volod. You should be able to come into the palace with us. After that, it's training time."

"*As you wish. I've already eaten, but not enough to be earthbound,*" she replied, starting off.

"Do I want to know what you had for dinner?"

"Nope. Probably not."

Vulkan Keep was a cave castle hewn from the tough, brittle, water-rich rock of Mount Racosul, the dead volcano that rose over Taltos. To get there, you had to leave Taltos from the Temple District and travel up Mount Racosul along a heavily guarded switchback road. The entry to the Keep's gatehouse was across an arched bridge over a small chasm of dark, swift water. I didn't know a huge amount about castles – pretty much everything I'd learned was from playing tabletop RPGs – but I could tell that no one was breaking into Vulkan Keep without some serious firepower. The outermost barrier - the curtain wall - had small windows and plenty of murder holes and other defensive features. The battlements bristled with ballistae, slings, and spikes - a monolithic 'fuck you' to any would-be invaders. I wasn't sure that even dragons would be of much use here, because the majority of the Keep was inside the mountain. It was no wonder Taltos had been able to hold its own against an entire empire without falling.

We rode through the towering iron gates of the Keep with an escort, who left us once we reached the entry to the inner castle. Black and white marble floors swept us into the Great Hall, which was entrenched in the cave system interwoven with the palace. The Great Hall reminded me of a cathedral vault: Black and red Corvinus family banners hung from the walls and ceiling, which receded up into inky darkness far above. Sweeping red-carpeted stairs led up to a tall throne, currently unoccupied. All of the doors in here were big enough that Karalti could join us.

She padded behind Suri and I as a servant led us through several hallways, rang a little bell, and then opened the hidden door. Andrik was sitting in an overstuffed scarlet armchair in front of a roaring fireplace, his boots propped in front of the fire. He was wearing his crown, a dark steel and ruby circlet. An eagle in a hood slept on a perch beside his left hand, its head tucked back against the top of its wing. Across the room were two other men. The High Forgemaster sprawled on a gilt golden chair that barely contained his bulk. Father Petko Matthias sat on a smaller wooden chair, smoking his pipe. He smiled when he saw Karalti.

"Good grief." Andrik unfolded his hands from his belly, sitting up straight in his chair. "For a moment, I thought you'd brought your hookwing into the Keep, but then I saw her wings. Suri, and... Hector, was it?"

"Yeah. I mean... yes, Your Majesty." I cleared my throat a little awkwardly. The firelight dancing off the gems in his circlet caught my eye, and I noticed that they glowed in a way that reminded me strongly of the gem burning a hole in my Inventory.

Suri bowed from the neck. "Your Majesty. We have learned the identity of the killer and obtained evidence of his identity."

"Really?" Toth shifted up and leaned forward.

"Who is it?" Andrik sat up straighter. "I heard there was a battle at the orphanage... and that you did not arrive in time to stop him. You have not bought me a head, so I assume he lives."

Suri and I looked at each other. She began to step forward, but I blurted it out first. "His name is Kanzo. He is a Master Artificer and-"

"Mercurion." Andrik's dark eyes narrowed to dangerous slits. "Kanzo is the artisan we commission our mana-powered carriages from. And you're certain that *he* is the murderer?"

"Yes, Your Majesty. And I would like to emphasize that he is acting alone. But the situation isn't as simple as a single depraved killer running wild." I watched the Volod uncertainly. As his ringed hands clenched the arms of the throne, I remembered that this man had ultimate power over what happened to us in Vlachia. It felt like staring down a lion. "He is being blackmailed into committing the murders."

"An assassin is an assassin," Father Matthias said heavily.

"I would hear the circumstances anyway." Andrik waved him down. "But first, the evidence. How can you prove what you have discovered?"

I took the honeybee necklace and gem from my Inventory. Suri procured the papers. She handed them to me, and I passed them to the Volod, who barely even looked at the necklace or papers - just the gem.

"Where did you find this?" His voice was suddenly very tight and very formal.

I glanced at Suri again. I had no idea how to handle pissed off kings, and clearly, neither did she. By the way he was swelling up, I really didn't want to tell him about Rin. She'd be stretched over a rack before the night was through.

"He dropped them all when he escaped the orphanage," I lied. "I got a few blows in before he escaped out the window, and cut the bag he was wearing."

[[Bluff failed!]]

"Do not lie to me, Tuun. I am not a stupid man." Andrik looked up at me piercingly. "Speak the truth. This is your last chance."

"He was keeping a secret laboratory that he hid from everyone he knew," Suri said, butting in. "He was trying to create a new Mercurion child by himself."

"That is an extreme perversion by the rules of their society." Father Matthias spoke up again. "And that is what I assume is being used to blackmail him?"

"Yes," I replied.

"There is no way he could have gotten this gem." Andrik stood, a slim silhouette in front of the fire, and held the stone up to the light. "And yet... somehow he has."

I crossed my arms. "What is it, Your Majesty?"

"This is a Corvinus Ruby," Andrik said. "A gem exclusively collected by my House. It is an extraordinarily rare form of mana crystal. There is only one known cache of it in the world."

"In Vlachia?"

"No. In Dakhdir." Andrik gave Suri a little nod. "A mine with a secret location that only those of the House Blood know. The House of Corvinus learned this secret when my ancestor Izemir the Splendid went on crusade to Dakhdir. These gems helped him become the first of our House to rule Vlachia."

"Other than being rare, does it have any magical purpose?" Suri asked.

"Yes. Corvinus Rubies have a single, unique property that is unheard of in other forms of crystal mana." Andrik touched the gems in his crown. "They can store memories and knowledge. If you know how to access those memories, they can be replayed forever. It is how we earned our House motto: 'What the Raven learns, he shall never forget'."

"That explains why Kanzo would want them," I said, looking over at Karalti. She had been utterly silent since arriving in the room, resting back on the base of her tail. "To give his creation the capacity for memory and recollection."

Suri nodded. "Or to store his own memories. He's a Master Craftsman. He'd want to transmit everything he knows to his successor."

"It is absolutely forbidden for commoners to possess one of these stones." Andrik paced, smoldering with rage. "This disrespect to the Crown... only a non-human is capable of such insolence. I should burn the Silverskins' hive to the ground."

"This man was acting in secret, Your Majesty," I said quickly. "His own people would have killed him if they'd known what he was doing. This was his crime alone."

"Khors' breath... I know my own people better than you do, Tuun, and I've punished *my* subjects for less than what you just said." The Volod snapped back.

Karalti's eyes narrowed, and her head came forward, neck rippling like a snake's. I lay a reassuring hand on her shoulder.

Toth cleared his throat, glancing at the dragon. "Your Majesty..."

"Your Serene Highness, the Herald of Matir means no offense," Matthias said smoothly. He was refilling his pipe, and did not look up at either of us as he spoke. "It is the nature of the Black God to contest and challenge, in order to provoke us to our height of intelligence and reason."

Andrik grunted, but the words seemed to calm him down. His pacing slowed.

Distraction was probably the best tactic right now, so I nodded and moved on. "Where could Kanzo have gotten a collection of these rubies, your Majesty?"

"Were this stone cut and polished, I'd have said that this Keep is the only possible location it could have come from," Andrik replied testily. "But it is uncut. Therefore, the only place it could come from is the workshop where these gems are processed. The Royal Jeweler is a human Artificer by name of Stefin Milosevic. These stones must be carefully worked by a specialist because of their mana content."

"Then we know who we need to see." Suri nodded curtly. "We'll speak to him straight away."

Andrik shook his head. "Not alone, you won't."

Some system messages and two quest notifications popped up - one that I was expecting, and one I was not.

[[You have earned 100 EXP!]]

[[You have gained 200 silver Rubles!]]

[[Congratulations! You are Level 11! You have 2 unassigned ability points and 6 unassigned skill points!]]

Quest Update: The Slayer of Taltos

After returning with your evidence to the Volod, he has identified the gemstone you found as a Corvinus Ruby: a rare, magically-charged gemstone hoarded by the ruling dynasty of Vlachia. Your next stop - Stefin Milosevic, the Royal Jeweler, whose workshop is in the Market District. You must question him.

Reward: 75 EXP, 50 gold Olbia.

Special: You must remain within range of Volod Andrik Corvinus III.

Quest Updated: Restore the Spear of Nine Spheres

Learn about the Ravensblood Ruby, Herald. Discover its location and properties.

The second one made me swallow nervously. There was no reward, no conditions, no details... nothing. Just those two lines. It wasn't part of the viral questline seeded by Ororgael. There was only one being in Archemi who could assign a quest and usually referred to me as 'Herald'. Ye Olde God of Darkness himself, Matir.

"I will summon my escort and ready my mounts," the King said stiffly. "We will ride to Stefin's. I will have words with him."

"Your Majesty? Is that wise?" Matthias stood. So did Toth.

"I have decreed it. Our meeting is at an end." Andrik slashed a hand. He stared at Suri, then at me. "You will be accompanying me, adventurers. And the dragon. My jeweler will not dare tell a lie in her presence, even if he dared to tell one in mine."

CHAPTER 20

It was nearing ten P.M when we left Vulkan Keep. Suri and I rode with the Volod and his Kingsguard on destrier hookwings, war mounts with the same large, solid builds as Cutthroat. Andrik had shed his finery for a flame-scorched suit of armor and a fine, heavy cloak with a deep hood, which he kept pulled up as we traveled. Suri and I rode at the back of the procession, partially so that they could lead us to the right place, partially so that Cutthroat didn't maul anyone, and partially so that we could speak privately.

"This stinks," Suri muttered. "The whole damn thing stinks. There is no way we're coming out ahead on this quest."

"What makes you think that?" I said.

She pressed her lips together, and instead of speaking, she P.M'd me. "*Andrik. Who else?*"

"*Yeah. He's awful twitchy.*" I also grimaced. "*Thinking about backing out?*"

"*Not a chance.*"

I snorted. "*How'd you get involved in this mess, anyway?*"

Suri looked down at the back of Cutthroat's head, scowling.

"*Listen,*" she said. "*I'm not going to talk about my past. Not to you, not to anybody. If you're not happy about it, too bad. I don't owe you shit.*"

I thought about that for a couple of minutes, gazing out over the sea of lights shining up from the city below.

Before HEX, while I was out on tour on the Crescent Front, I'd fought beside, rode beside, and cared for men and women who've been through Hell. Their trauma had eaten through them like toxic waste, and I counted myself beyond lucky to have come away from the Total War without crippling injuries or bad PTSD. Something about my psychological makeup and the experiences I went through had spared me. Suri may not have been so fortunate, so it was time to man up and eat some crow.

"*You're right,*" I replied. "*And I'm sorry. I'm not going to lie, though. You're frustrating the hell out of me, because I want to get to know you well enough that we can work together moving forward. That's all I want, okay?*"

Suri didn't reply. In profile, her long neck was proud, her face painfully beautiful, but her gaze had a far-off, bleak quality I was all too familiar with. It was the thousand-yard stare of someone who'd seen too much, done too much, but survived.

"*I'll tell you one thing.*" Suri next spoke as we were passing through the North Gate and back into Taltos proper. "*I'm here for protection, too.*"

"*Roger that.*" I closed the P.M. and said nothing else. We'd built some kind of fragile trust, and I wasn't keen on breaking it just because I was curious.

"*Whoa.*" Karalti's thoughts intruded into my own. "*Bouncy Lady is intense, huh?*"

I snorted softly. "*I didn't know you were listening.*"

"*Of course I'm listening. I can't help it. Your Words wiggle around when you're think-talking to your friends. I hear them in your body all the time.*"

Friends, huh? I could see Suri clearly in my peripheral vision. She didn't know I could watch her so clearly from the corner of my eye, and so I watched as she sighed and slumped in the saddle. She looked tired. Determined, focused, but tired. And troubled. Very troubled.

"*Now that you're big enough to give me a proper answer, I want to ask you something,*" I said to Karalti. "*What do you get out of this? Out of being with me?*"

The dragon cocked her head from side to side while she wrestled with the question, just as she'd done as a hatchling.

"*Lots of things,*" she replied after a short time. "*You've always been there, encouraging me and caring for me. You were the first thing I saw, so your Words were written in with my own... and now we will grow together.*"

"*Doesn't it bug you to carry this hairless monkey around on your back all the time?*"

"*No.*" Karalti reared her head back and snapped her teeth – the draconic equivalent of a 'no' headshake. "*Neither dragons or humans are meant to be alone. That is why we form bonds of mind and blood together. As long as I'm with you, neither of us will* ever *be lonely... and that's how it should be.*"

I was taken aback – and no lie, her words made me blush. A small nagging voice in the back of my mind told me that Karalti was an NPC, an algorithm and a personality made up from a base set of two thousand different people. That same voice told me that she couldn't really love me, and she was telling me what I wanted to hear. I told that voice to shut the fuck up.

"*That's about the best answer I could have asked for,*" I said, patting my dragon on the shoulder. No way was I going to get misty-eyed while we were in the company of the Volod – or Suri, for that matter. "*Speaking of growing, I guess we need to assign your points... and maybe start thinking about your Path. We've got fifteen minutes or so before we reach our target. You willing to tell me what you know about Words?*"

We were walking through the city proper. Karalti reached up with a clawed finger to scratch her chin. "*Words make up everything in the world. There's many kinds... They all wiggle inside of everything. They come together to make new Words all the time. When you get lots of them Wording together, they might make a Human, or a Solonkratsu, or the city or the sky.*"

I chuckled, and Suri turned to look over at us before she resumed brooding. "*You're describing code, Tidbit. Or DNA. Names for the proteins that build life.*"

"*Yeah! The way Words work is like language... but even language is made up of Words,*" she said. "*Capital W-words, not just little w-words.*"

"*Right. And there's... 758 different Words?*"

"*Nope. There's lots more than that. But some of them are brighter and wiggle harder than others.*" She swept her muzzle around in a half-circle, eyes gleaming brightly in the darkness. "*And I think maybe some can be seen by humans, some by Meewfolk, some by Mercurions, and some by dragons.*"

In all honestly, I'd figured that Archemi's magic system probably sucked – mostly because of the resource limitations imposed on the core magic classes, Mage and Artificer. But even if a Mage had limited mana and their mana could possibly kill them, they had some pretty epic flexibility when it came to designing and implementing spells. I'd already picked up one Word myself - 'Ori'. Any time I'd heard someone use a variation of a Light-based spell, they always used 'Ori' in the incantation. The system probably meant that Mages and Artificers could become intense magic specialists of any kind, and there were probably Advanced Paths that facilitated them. "*That's actually pretty nifty. So... next question.*"

"*Yeah?*"

"*What spells do YOU want to learn?*" I asked. "*And of the two Paths... which one do you like the most?*"

"*I can't decide,*" Karalti replied. "*I want them all. You looked at my sheet yet?*"

I interpreted that as the game telling me that I - the Starborn P.C. - was meant to make that decision about my mount. "*Not yet. I'll check.*"

Karalti had 10 Lexica points now, more than enough to assign her a good range of spells. We now also had quite a list to choose from. Her spells were drawn from the Darkness element and the Life sub-element. I queried those first to learn more about what they meant, in terms of magic:

Elements

There are nine elements in Archemi: Earth, Air, Fire, Water, Gravity, Time, Darkness, Aether, and Light. They are divided into three groups: The Physical Elements (Earth, Air, Fire, Water), the Abstract Elements (Gravity, Time, Darkness, Light) and Aether, which is the Primordial Element.

Aether is the foundation of all the other elements, the Prime Word which permeates existence and coagulates into Mana. It is unable to be worked by humans in its pure form, as most Aetheric Words of Power can only be inferred, not observed. The exception to this are the Ten Universal Words derived from Aether. These ten Words are the keys to all magic.

Words of Power are used to manipulate and combine the other eight Physical and Abstract elements to magical effects. For example, if you speak the Words for 'Strong Wind' (Air), 'Control' (Universal) and 'Levitation' (Gravity) and channel those words into mana, the mana will react to your Will, transmute, and you cast the Fly spell.

The Physical Elements deal with material phenomena, and knowledge of the Physical Elements is very important for Artificers and Alchemists, as well as those who hope to become Conjurers or Elemental Specialists (Aquamancers, Pyromancers, etc). The Physical Elements are 'paired' in **opposition** *to each other: Earth and Air are a pair; Fire and Water are a pair.*

The Abstract Elements are subtler, dealing with unseen or immaterial forces that nevertheless exert a powerful influence on the world. They are important for all practitioners of magic, but especially for Thaumaturges, Spirit Knights, Paladins, Baru, and other similar classes. The Abstract elements function in **complementary** *pairs: Darkness and Light; Time and Gravity. Unlike Physical Elemental pairs, which clash, Abstract Elemental pairings support and energize each other to the point where they are functionally inseparable.*

Every element has sub-elements within its auspice. You must research more to understand the potential of each element.

I rubbed the bridge of my nose as I slogged my way through the info dump. I was sure there was another reason the Devs decided on this particular system - to weed out stupid people who wanted to become mages. Sadly, I understood why. There really was nothing worse than an idiot who thought he was the smartest kid in the sandbox min-maxing himself into infinity and then doing dumbshit things with spells he had no idea how to handle.

I decided to check out Life first, because Karalti had that elemental subtype, but Life wasn't listed on the Elements Archemipedia page. To my surprise, querying 'Life' redirected me to the Darkness wiki entry:

Darkness (Element)

Darkness is the element of potential in the absence of light: potential for harm, potential for life, potential for danger, power, growth, and decay. Along with its complementary pairing, the Light element, it is the element most strongly associated with living creatures.

Darkness can be functionally divided into four sub-elements: Death, Life, Knowledge, and Shadow.

Death magic relates to all matters related to death and dying: kill effects, life drains, spells that inflict potentially fatal damage to living things, and the control of spirits.

Life magic relates to all matters related to the generation, manipulation, sabotage, and restoration of living things. It is exceedingly rare. True Life magic has not been seen on Archemi since the Invasion of the Drachan during the Reign of Dragons. There are no Life-based Words of Power currently known to humans – however, it is known that there must be Life Words, as alchemical and herbal potions can restore HP, cure disease, and even regrow limbs.

Knowledge relates to learning, but also to all magic that affects the mind, senses, and perception.

Shadow is the 'pure' darkness element: Darkened Aether which manifests as the freezing energy of the Void. It is both generative and destructive. All Darkness spells have a Shadow element, but pure Shadow energy can be used to form damaging attacks, create curses that inflict debuffs, animate or destroy the undead, manipulate shadows, etc.

Darkness-aligned creatures take extra damage from Time and Gravity effects. They take reduced damage from Light and Aether effects. They gain +5 to most attributes during the night, and -5 to most attributes during the day.

"*Well, aren't we just a couple of special snowflakes?*" I chuckled. "*Here's me, chosen by some old god and saddled with the Mana Spear, and you're apparently the first dragon since the Drachan showed up to be able to do any kind of Life magic. If we get any more special, I might as well change my name to Gary Stuzin.*"

"*Wat?*"

"*Don't worry,*" I replied. "*Let's have a look at these spells of yours. I want to have them by the time we accompany King Tightass to see his jeweler.*"

Karalti only had access to Level 1 spells. She would gain access to higher spells every five levels from here on out: Level 2 spells at Level 10, Level 3 at Level 15, and so on, all the way up to Level 10 spells at Level 50. Well, spell. There was only one Level 10 spell slot on Karalti's character sheet. I was guessing it was going to be something like 'Nuclear Darkness Obliteration Five-Ways Kaboom'. Archemi seemed like that kind of game.

Whatever that spell was, it was a long way off. We currently had a list of eight to choose from:

Dirge (Death)

A curse that slowly damages enemies every turn and has a chance to cause the Deaf and Mute debuffs. (3 Lexica required to learn)

Bioscope (Life)

Analyze an enemy and learn their strengths and weaknesses. (3 Lexica required to learn)

Sense Aether (Life)

Detect and assess magical effects, artifacts, and locations. (1 Lexica required to learn)

Cursebreaker (Knowledge)

Cure one ally of status effects and debuffs. (3 Lexica required to learn)

Haste I (Shadow)

Increase speed on the ground or in the air. (3 Lexica required to learn)

Dark Power I (Death)

Double your Attack Power in the next physical attack. (3 Lexica required to learn)

Dark Focus I (Knowledge)

Double power of next magical attack. (3 Lexica required to learn)

Shadow Veil I (Shadow)

Cause an obscuring Area of Effect Darkness effect. (3 Lexica required to learn)

Sense Aether was a given. So was *Bioscope.* I knew from playing my fair share of JRPGs that these two abilities were indispensable for strategizing battles and for planning farming expeditions. *Dark Power* and *Dark Focus* were both good, because leveling the spell led to triple, quadruple, and eventually quintuple damage - not bad when a strike had the power of a dragon behind it already. *Cursebreaker* was useful, because if I were disabled - or if Karalti were disabled while we were flying with something like Blind or Concussion - then removing the Debuff quickly could make a huge difference in battle. It was also a prerequisite spell to others down the line that would be even better.

The others were all pretty solid choices. *Dirge* screwed with Mages and ranged attackers, and a quick check on Curse damage confirmed that it was similar to the Poison debuff, except that it couldn't be removed with antidote potions – it had to be cured with Light magic. That was handy. *Haste* and *Shadow Veil* would both be good for evasion, but of the two, I preferred *Haste.* Karalti could already vanish in dark environments, a natural ability I suspected would only become more prominent the more she leveled. A bubble of darkness flying around was far more conspicuous than her natural camouflage.

Despite being tempted by *Cursebreaker*, I decided on *Bioscope, Sense Aether*, *Dark Focus I*, and *Dirge.* If Karalti cast Dark Focus, and *then* cast Dirge in the next action, then the affliction rate of the curse spell would become doubly effective. She could potentially blind and mute an attacker while their health dribbled away, which was always good if you were a DPS character like me.

Dark Focus had another perk: it could be used with Karalti's breath weapon, which counted as a magical attack. That was indispensable. Her *Ghost Fire* currently did 199-205 damage, and she was now up to five blasts before she had to take half an hour to recharge. Doubling her firepower per round could only be a good thing.

When I confirmed the selections, I felt my dragon's body heat against my legs, a flare of energy that prickled the hair on the back of my neck.

"*Oooh...*" She shivered, rustling her wings. "*Yeah... Those are good Words. I gotta eat and sleep before I can use them, though.*"

We were coming up on the Market District now. The smell of food made my stomach growl, but we weren't here to eat. I took a piece of Venison Jerky from my bag, and chewed on it as the procession cleared a path through the winding streets toward our destination: Stefin Milosovic's jewelry workshop.

CHAPTER 21

The Captain of the Kingsguard swept up the short flight of stone stairs to Stefin's apartment, and banged a mailed fist on the wooden door, rattling it in the frame. "Open up!"

Something metal and heavy smashed on the floor inside, followed by cursing that grew louder as someone stormed for the door. My hearing was sharp enough that I could hear him muttering. "Cursed son of a fish-bit whore..."

A balding, beetle-eyed man with a beer gut pushing against the front of his fancy silk tunic opened the door. The color drained from his face when he saw who it was. He paled even further when he saw Karalti.

"Hello, Stefin." Andrik lifted his hood so that the man could see him better.

"Your Majesty!" The jeweler bowed deeply. "What are you... Why do you grace my business with your presence?"

"A private matter. We must discuss it indoors."

"By all means, Your Majesty, though my wife and child are upstairs." He eyed the Royal Guard Captain nervously.

"Thank you, Stefin." Andrik swept inside, followed by the thunder of hard-soled boots across the floor.

"Stay chill, girl. Keep an ear out." I dropped down off Karalti's back, and clapped her shoulder.

"Okay." The dragon withdrew under a nearby awning and lay down like a cat, unselfconsciously bringing traffic to a screeching halt - but also keeping gawking onlookers away from Stefin's store.

The door opened into the jeweler's storefront. A shirtless, tattooed man with a cudgel who had been idling near the glass display cabinets stood up straight when all of us poured in. Behind the displays was the workshop, where Stefin had clearly just been working. A teenage apprentice, a thin, sallow boy with short dark hair, stopped grinding a stone against a lathe and stared at us as the jeweler led us upstairs to a sitting room.

Stefin fidgeted as Andrik swept his hood back. "Your Majesty, I was not expecting a royal visit. I have not prepared any sort of reception. May I offer hospitality? Wine? We still have a bottle of that-"

"It does not matter. We will not be here for long," the Volod replied curtly.

The craftsman led us to a parlor crammed with rich furnishings and landscape paintings. It was set up for noble guests, with gold and red velvet chairs, oil lamps, a bookcase, and a bowl of mixed grapes and apples. We filtered in, and Andrik casually plopped down onto one the chairs. Stefin stood by, wringing his hands. He struggling not to stare at Suri, and the looks he were giving her were not friendly.

"We need to ask you some questions, and we expect you to answer truthfully," Suri said to him, as the Kingsguard stomped in and took their posts.

Stefin swelled up another couple of inches. "And who are you to be speaking to me in such a fashion?"

"This is the pair investigating the slaughter of our clergy by the Slayer of Taltos," Andrik replied before we could, crossing one ankle over his other knee as he leaned back. "And you will abide by their demands, Stefin, or you risk my ire."

Stefin swallowed nervously. "Yes, Your Majesty."

I stepped forward. "Some Corvinus Rubies turned up where they shouldn't. We're trying to find out how the Slayer got his hands on them."

The jeweler began to twist the edge of his leather apron. "So, you've flushed out the killer, then? Khors be praised."

"Don't deflect, Stefin," the Volod drawled.

"Y-Yes, Your Majesty." He looked between us fearfully.

"Let me handle this," Suri said to me by P.M.

"N.P." I hung back, curious to see how she worked.

Suri regarded the jeweler with cool curiosity, hands folded behind her back. "How long have you worked for House Corvinus?"

Stefin blinked. "We have been the Royal Gemcutters for three generations, my... lady."

Suri nodded as she strolled forward. "Then I imagine you have a *very* secure system for the jewels. You don't store them here, do you?"

"Of course not. We keep the rubies in a special vault, as we have for generations. They are, uh, magically active, as I'm sure you know, so we must carefully bleed off some of the mana from the raw stone before they are safe to polish..."

"Who brings the rubies to Taltos?"

Stefin blinked a couple of times. "The Volod's own men mine the jewels in Dakhdir, and once a year, an armored caravan brings them to the shop."

"Did they make a recent delivery?"

"Y-Yes. Three weeks ago. It is always in the summer."

"Was the delivery or the store compromised in any way? No robberies, no trouble on the road?"

"No, there was no trouble."

"And the Volod is the only one who buys these rubies?"

Stefin nodded. "Yes, of course. It is expressly forbidden to sell them to anyone else. Your Majesty, you would not believe that I sold some of your rubies to another buyer? Even if I had the stones, I would not betray my father and grandfather's heritage."

Andrik flinched, startling up straight in his chair. "What do you mean 'even if I had the stones'?"

"I mean... that the vault is empty, Your Majesty? You ordered them cut and polished and bought up all of the last delivery yourself. Your emissary collected the last batch."

"Excuse me?" The Volod leaned forward, staring at Stefin.

Stefin shrunk back under the scrutiny. He looked uncertainly at Suri and me. "Yes, Your Majesty. It was only the other week. You do not recall?"

The young king's face drew into hard lines. "I am not in the mood to be toyed with, Stefin. My city is in chaos, some undead monstrosity is preying on one of my provinces, my clergy are being murdered, and *now* my jeweler is lying to me."

"I am not lying to you, Sire!" Stevin held up his hands, backing away a step. "Please, not under any circumstances would I dare. I-I have the letter, I have the receipt stamped with the royal seal!"

"Keep going." Suri nodded to him.

"A-A Royal letter came with an emissary dressed in the colors of your House requesting that we cut all of the rubies and send them to the Keep," the man stammered. "The letter was of the usual sort, so-"

"Was this emissary a Mercurion?" I asked.

The jeweler nodded his head, swallowing hard. "Yes. She was fully clothed from head to toe in red, but I knew what she was by way she spoke."

"How?" Suri asked.

"Mercurions are simulacra. To someone who works with machines all day, the sounds they make while speaking do not sound human," he replied. "This one had an unusually rough voice. She did not give a name... but she claimed to be the senior apprentice of a Mastercraftsman who works for your court."

Rin? A nasty sensation curled in my gut, twisting like a knife. Suri lifted her chin, eyes narrowing, and then flashed me an I-told-you-so look.

The Volod sighed. "Bring me this letter and the receipt."

Stevin scuttled off. While we were waiting, the Volod helped himself to one of the apples in the bowl, but before he could bring it to his lips, one of his bodyguards shook his head. Grimacing, Andrik put it back.

"Such are the times," he said, heavily. "Ahh, Suri, Hector... I apologize for my foul temper. It is unbecoming of a Volod to be so curt with his subjects and guests. I only wish that you could have visited during saner times, instead of during this madness. Did you find anything else we didn't discuss at the Keep?"

"No. What we do know is that any of the priests who confessed their sins to Father Toth and who are not living inside of Vulkan Keep are in danger," Suri said. "We need a list of men who've spoken to him since the murders began."

"I shall have it ordered tonight," Andrik replied.

Stefin came back a minute later, bearing a parchment scroll. He unfurled it with shaking hands, and passed it to the guard captain, who stepped forward in front of the Volod. The knight pushed his visor up, revealing a ruggedly handsome face with intense blue eyes. He was older than I'd expected. His mustache was long and white, face deeply lined. There were several minutes of silence as he read the document.

"Let me see... yes, yes... and this is certainly your signature and your seal, Your Majesty." The knight handed it down to him.

"Nonsense, Garen. I signed no such order." Andrik accepted the scroll, scowling as he read over it. But as he read, his expression shifted to something new: fear and uncertainty. "And yet... you are correct."

"Forgery?" I asked.

"It must be." Andrik held the paper up to the firelight, clearly perplexed. "Either that, or I was signing off on priceless jewels in my sleep. But I will admit this is exceptional work."

Stefin's lip shook. "Please, Sire, I would never willfully betray-"

"Silence." Andrik squinted at the document. "Suri, you told me you can work some magic with a man's fingerprints? Do you think there is a way to use the fingerprints of whoever signed this?"

"Maybe. It depends how much the letter has been handled. Let me see." She held a hand out. The Volod passed it to her, and I craned my head to see around her arm. There was a wax seal with a double-headed raven, the House of Corvinus crest, and a looping signature in dark reddish-brown ink that looked similar to blood. Beside it was a clear thumbprint.

"You normally sign your letters with your print?" Suri asked him.

"Of course," the Volod replied. "I am a pious man. The hand is the tool of Khors the Maker, so I always sign my letters with a print."

Suri nodded thoughtfully. "I need finely ground charcoal and a soft brush."

"I have them downstairs," Stefin replied, bobbing his head as he looked between us. "I'll get them immediately."

While he was gone, the Volod turned his attention back to us.

"Did you know of this apprentice?" he asked.

"She wasn't a suspect until now," Suri said, before I could say anything. She was kinda-sorta lying, but Andrik didn't call her on it. "Her name is Rin. She's Kanzo's senior apprentice."

"And why, exactly, was she not a suspect? Given that she is closely associated with the murderer?"

"She's a fragile non-combatant who believes her master is being blackmailed," I replied. "The evidence seems to point to that. She didn't know what the stones were, or anything about what her master was up to."

The Volod was expressionless. "I see. So this harebrained notion that Kanzo is being blackmailed by someone came from her? How novel. I suppose she's very pretty and delicate, isn't she? Most 'female' Mercurions are. They are also consummate manipulators."

I opened my mouth, trying to think of a rational retort that was better than 'my instincts say she's innocent.' But I couldn't think of anything.

"She needs to be taken in as soon as possible," Suri said heavily. "I'd even advise you to do it now, before she has a chance to flee. She convinced us she had no part in this. We found the laboratory underneath their workshop. The address is 34 Solyom Koz, in the Tanner's District."

My gut tightened like a voice with every word. This wasn't right. This couldn't be right.

"Garen, go rally the city guard. You and Leo can see to this," Andrik spoke to the older mustachioed man and one of the other guards. "These six will see me safe to the Keep."

"As you command, Sire." Garen put his fist to his forehead and bowed from the neck. Before I could voice my growing unease, the pair of knights departed without any argument, clanking their way down the stairs. Stefin squeezed past them and offered Suri the bowl of powdered carbon and a brush.

And then it hit me: the rubies that Stefin had given to the messenger had been processed. The ones we'd found in Kanzo's stash had been raw rubies, not cut ones. Any that Kanzo had polished and ground, he'd done himself. The thief had taken them when they were cut... They couldn't have been the same batch.

While Suri applied ground charcoal to the Volod's thumb, I made my decision. I opened my Player Messaging menu, and discreetly rattled off a quick message to Rin.

"Don't reply to this. You need to get the hell out of the Tanner's District and hide, now. Run." I stared at the fire so that they didn't see my eyes or lips accidentally move, watching them from the corner of my eye.

Suri took the Volod's hand in hers, and for a moment, their eyes met and he smiled at her. She didn't smile back, but instead pressed his finger against the vellum, rolled it, then lifted it to reveal a perfect print beside the red ink one. It was actually clearer than the one the forger had left.

"Well, that's..." she trailed off, pursing her lips.

"What?" I wandered up, looking down.

"They look the same," Suri said. She sounded almost impressed.

"Not so unique after all, then?" The Volod frowned. "I did *not* sign this letter."

I turned back, and held out a hand. "Here. Give it to me. I've got a dragonrider's eyesight."

Suri passed it over. "I hope you see something I don't, because to be honest with you, I'm kind of stumped."

I held the letter up to the lamplight, positioned it until I felt my eyes focus, and then consciously tightened them in. I could see the pores in the calfskin the letter was written on, and after a few seconds, the subtle differences in the fingerprints. They WERE different. The Volod's was narrower, the spiral at the center tighter, and the forger had a loop at the center that Andrik didn't. But they were similar fingers. More telling were the little scar-like lines that split off the bigger loops and whorls. They were different.

"I'm about ninety percent sure these are different prints," I said, handing it back and closing my eyes before they unfocused too hard, too fast. "They look really different up close. The forger's thumb is wider, and he has more wear on his hands."

"You really expect me to believe that?" The Volod sounded incredulous.

I opened my eyes and looked right at him, and he must have noticed how inhuman I really looked for the first time, because he flinched back. I focused my pupils past his cheek. "Sire, there's a nick made by a fingernail on the very edge of that window over there. A depression about an eighth of an inch long. I can see it in about five thousand more colors than you can right now."

"This shit must look like an acid trip," Sui muttered.

"More like really good mushrooms," I said. "You get used to it."

A small smile lit Andrik's mouth. He stood and went to examine where I was pointing. And when he found the tiny groove, his smile broadened with approval and curiosity.

"Impressive," he murmured. "Well, we have our answer, then. I was not drugged and made to send for a shipment of rubies in my sleep."

"Please, Your Majesty. I beg your mercy." Stefin, who had done his best to fade into the wall while all this was going on, clasped his hands and shook them. "I swear on Khors' hammer that I thought her to be your genuine emissary, or-"

"Quiet. I do not wish to hear your begging or your excuses," Andrik said curtly. "Did you not think it strange that a lone courier would come asking for my rubies?"

Stefin looked utterly dejected now. "But... She paid with Sathbari gold! N-No one other than you can afford such coin!"

"We pay with Treasury Promissory notes, and have since my grandfather's day, you imbecile." Andrik pinched the fine bridge of his nose, and made a sound of disgust. "It is the middle of the night, and I can no longer think straight. Lazarin, Pan, you will remain here with this man and his family. Stefin, you and your family are under house arrest until I decide what to do with you."

Stefin hung his head. "Yes... yes, Your Majesty."

"I am disappointed. Get out of my sight." The Volod flicked a dismissive hand as he got up from the chair, knees cracking. "Hopefully, we will take in Kanzo's apprentice tonight. This blackmailing nonsense is just that, and I refuse to believe any Mercurion would only work alone or in pairs. They are a clannish species. There will be more of them involved in this conspiracy, I guarantee it. They are all atheists, worshipping only their machines, and they resent the Crown. Not only that, they school like army ants. When one grape goes bad, the whole bunch withers."

"Uhh, that..." I replied. Suri shot me a warning look, and I shut my trap.

"To that end, we will take action to flush out any more co-conspirators," the Volod sighed. "But I will tell you my plans in private. Come, let us retire. We can only hope we do not rise to find another good man slaughtered in the dead of night."

CHAPTER 22

I'd hoped to get some time with Karalti and our character sheets when we got back to Vulkan Keep, but no such luck. Andrik ordered his Chamberlain to prepare a late supper for us in his war room. He insisted that all of us, including Karalti, had something to eat, even though we weren't hungry.

This led to the awkward situation of having a young adolescent dragon at a table of food she wasn't interested in. This was a problem. Dragons are intelligent, sentient, carnivorous apex predators. Like all apex predators, they're assholes to the genetic level - especially when bored.

"Peanut butter!" Karalti croaked in a raspy, reptilian voice. She sat beside me at the table, wagging her head from side to side as if listening to a song only she could hear. "Peanut butter sausages! Tidbit! Fresh fish, ooohhhaaah! Best fish in Bryos!"

"Is this... ahh... avian behaviour a common practice of dragonkind?" Andrik was using a gold knife and fork to delicately saw a sandwich into small pieces.

"She mimics stuff when there's nothing else to do." I hunched into my seat as she began to burble like a crowded street. Karalti's mimicry was like listening to a recording. She could 'sing' the multi-layered sounds of a village street with perfect accuracy – cart wheels rumbling, people murmuring, hookwings screeching and yarping.

"What His Majesty means to say, Karalti, is that you sound like an overgrown parrot." Suri grinned from across the table. She wasn't using a knife and fork for her bagel, and neither was I.

"Look, Tidbit! A whore!" Karalti chirped the words in a disturbingly accurate imitation of my own voice.

For a moment, Suri looked confused, maybe even offended. But then she seemed to realize it was a joke, and flashed me a small, odd little smile. I elbowed Karalti in the ribs as the dragon narrowed her eyes.

Andrik pretended not to notice any of it. He gestured at the dragon with his fork. "She can understand us, then? And communicates fluently with you?"

"Yep."

"What does she say?"

"Tell him I say that he's a boring meat person and I want to set him on fire." Karalti hunched, shook her wings out, and then heaved a long-suffering sigh that blew a small vase of flowers over on the table.

I reached out and put it back. "All sorts of things. She's very philosophical."

"Then why does she not converse?" Andrik gestured to her with one hand. "I can only imagine the contained wisdom in such a creature."

Karalti leaned in to carefully sniff at my glass of wine. *"Why does this smell like pee?"*

I coughed a little. "Most dragons only speak to their riders, Your Majesty, but they will reach out to others if they need to. They think deeply and say very little."

"Oh, I understand that attitude very well myself," Andrik said, after a bite of food. "I am also inclined to deep thought, especially while immersed in my studies. "I admit I'm curious to talk to her, but it is the privilege of the sacred *draak* to hold her silence."

I fought the urge to roll my eyes.

"Why isn't it the privilege of the sacred draak to get proper tasty fish?" Karalti sniffed my barely-touched bagel for the fifteenth time. *"This stuff is weird. Why does it smell burned?"*

"It's smoked salmon." I wasn't a big fan of it myself – I liked my seafood killed at the table and grilled while it was still twitching. *"Just calm the fuck down until this meal is over and done with. You can hunt later."*

"Can you ask the serving man to bring me some proper fish?" Karalti reached up with an idle claw, and began to slowly bat an expensive-looking porcelain dish toward the edge of the table. I elbowed her again.

"Ask him yourself. I'm not your fish-bitch."

There was a knock on the door at the other end of the richly appointed war room, and all heads turned as Garen the Kingsguard pushed it open and clanked his way across to us. He marched up close and bent down to whisper in Andrik's ear. The Volod nodded.

"Thank you. Please watch the door," Andrik said.

Ur Garen saluted and stalked off, his black cloak snapping out behind him.

The Volod's handsome face twisted into a scowl. "That was an update on the Slayer's accomplice, that apprentice you told us about. Unfortunately, she seems to have escaped. But it is no matter. The Tanner's District is to be closed. My soldiers will ensure she does not escape the ghetto, and I have no doubt the fugitive shall be apprehended once her fellow Mercurions start feeling the pinch in their purses."

The wry humor in Suri's eyes faded. I clamped my own poker face on good and tight.

"I confess that, on the ride back, I was considering what to do about this mess." The Volod waved a hand toward the huge map of Taltos on the wall facing me. "These murders are gathering into a dark picture. A Mercurion assassin linked to the court, the intensely personal nature of the theft of my Corvinus Rubies, the mass attack on you, the dragon, and Suri in the middle of the street... I am beginning to suspect that we are not dealing with a single assassin. I believe we are being targeted by a terrorist cell. A Mercurion terrorist cell."

"The attack on us by Ilia doesn't have anything to do with the murders," I said. "The Knights of Saint Grigori have been trying to get their hands on Karalti ever since we left the Eyrie."

"We don't know that." Suri crossed her arms, and shot me a thoughtful look.

"I beg to differ," Andrik said. He gestured to Karalti. "Your dragon's blood is almost pure mana. If there is one resource the silverskins covet, it is that. *Seid*, they call it. Mana is what they use to breed as well as create their artifacts. It represents wealth in a way that gold never can. A Mercurion terrorist cell would have everything to gain from capturing Karalti. They'd lock her in a cage and farm her for her blood."

Just the suggestion made me sick. "I guess? But the guys that attacked us were Ilian."

"They could be hirelings from Ilia who do not care whether the hands giving them money are human or not. In any case, we shall find out tomorrow." Andrik pushed his plate aside and leaned back, drumming his fingers on his knee. "There is a fundraiser tomorrow night at the Kobayaz Auction House. We'd planned it to raise money and supplies for our troops, but we are now using the event to raise money for the widows and children who have been orphaned by the Slayer. I was scheduled to attend, but my attendance was cancelled after the murder of Brother Orban. However, I am going to reinstate my presence and deploy criers to inform the citizens that I will, in fact, be at Kobayaz tomorrow night. This means that High Forgemaster Agoston Toth, the Voivode Janos Lanz of Czongrad and I shall all be in attendance. The three of us are the most likely targets for the Slayer."

"What makes you say that?" I frowned. So did Suri.

"One moment." Andrik leaned forward, and picked up a wine jug. He filled Suri's empty glass, picked it up, and held it out to her. "You are looking dry, my lady."

"Uhh... cheers." Suri accepted the glass awkwardly. She clearly didn't want it. I felt my hackles lift a bit, and Karalti shifted restlessly as Suri had a small sip.

"As for what makes me say that we are the most likely targets... well, Toth and I are obvious enough." Andrik's gaze lingered on Suri for a moment, before turning to me and Karalti. "As for the duke, Janos Lanz is perhaps the greatest financier of church projects in Vlachia. He has a missionary fire in his belly, a powerful desire to help our people by promoting the Forge Father's gifts and principles. All three of us in a single location will be a tempting proposition for our terrorists."

My P.M. notification icon beeped. It was from Suri. *"This is the dumbest shit I ever heard."*

Yes. Yes, it was. I cleared my throat politely. "Your Majesty, the uh, security logistics are going to be a nightmare. We're going to be scrambling like-"

"Like weasels chasing after a rabbit. Yes, but so will our enemies," the Volod said, smiling from ear to ear. "We are laying out irresistible bait."

Suri sighed through her nose. "Yeah, no. Not only is this a huge risk, but more likely than not, the Slayer'll use the event for cover while he murders someone on the other side of town."

"Add me to that chorus of 'no way', Your Majesty," I said.

Andrik lifted his chin, and his pale eyes turned hard and arrogant. It was an expression I was all too familiar with from my days in the Army. I called it 'Resting Colonel Face'. "Do either of you have a better idea?"

"Use a body double," Suri replied. "Or make an announcement that you want to parlay with the Slayer and will grant him mercy, so that you can lure him out. If he's being blackmailed-"

"Even if he were being blackmailed, it is of no consequence to me." Andrik gripped the arms of his chair. "And I will *not* show mercy to this silverskin bastard who is slaughtering our sages, philanthropists, and sacred smiths. As for body-doubles, it is unbecoming for a monarch to hide quivering in his palace while his people are being killed. I lead by example. You two shall attend and prowl the crowd, aiding my security and searching for suspicious activity. I will arrange for some suitable disguises."

I got a notification, and winced to myself as I pulled it across and confirmed that, yes, really, this was something the game was inflicting on us.

Quest Update: The Slayer of Taltos

Volod Andrik Corvinus has concocted what could politely be referred to as a 'harebrained scheme' to lure out the Slayer and any of his remaining accomplices with a juicy target: a church fundraiser attended by the people most likely to be the Slayer's next victims. He insists that you attend the fundraiser and protect him, Voivoide Janos Lanz, and High Forgemaster Agoston Toth.

Difficulty: *Very Hard*

Reward: *50 gold Olbia, 100 EXP, renown, ???.*

Special: *You will fail the Slayer of Taltos questline if Andrik is killed. If one or both of the other targets are lost, you will lose all rewards and lose -50 Renown in Vlachia (max -100).*

"Christ on a crutch," Suri muttered. "Look, no. I'm not wearing a stupid disguise for this stupid fucking quest."

Andrik blinked several times. "Such foul language from such a lovely mouth is somewhat unbecoming of a lady of your beauty, Suri. I believe I just told you how the plan will go ahead."

Suri got the same look I often saw on Cutthroat's face just before she got ready to jump someone. She put her hands against the table, leaning forward as she stood up. "With all due respect, Your

Majesty, you can take your lady-this and lovely-that and go bugger yourself with it."

The Volod turned white, then red as he glanced down at Suri's cleavage. I had to choke myself on my own tongue to stop from laughing.

"Why do human men get so funny over those bouncy things?" Karalti asked me.

I patted her on the leg. *"I'll tell you when you're older."*

Suri straightened up, hands on hips. "No. If I have to do this, I'm not dressing up like some fucking castle stormtrooper, okay? We want these guys to think we're letting our guards down, right? Fuck incognito. Let those town criers know that the Starborn who are going to stop the Slayer are in attendance. Make us part of the show. Hector's holy fuckin' dragon will be there. I'll be there in a dress. He'll be there in a doublet and hose, or whatever the fuck he wants to wear."

"In your dreams," I said, grinning at her across the table.

She wrinkled her nose at me. "Nightmares, more like it. Point being, that if we look like we're there to party, then Kanzo's gonna be more likely to act. If we're not there because we're disguised or whatever, that raises a big red flag over the whole thing. Now, speaking of dresses, Your Majesty needs to pay up for tonight. We went with you to Stefin's."

"Fair enough. The lady speaks true." The Volod held up a hand and concentrated.

[[You and Karalti have each received 75 EXP!]]

[[You have received 50 gold Olbia!]]

"That amount ought to provide for you," he said. "You have tomorrow morning and afternoon to ready yourselves. Be at Kobayaz by six p.m., and make sure that you are prepared. I don't think our terrorists will pass up the opportunity to cause mayhem."

Resigned to my fate, I swiped the quest update back into the minimized HUD. Given this was a videogame and Andrik was our key NPC, he was probably right.

CHAPTER 23

A servant led Karalti and I to our rooms in the Keep after dinner, navigating us through spacious marble hallways to a pair of wooden double doors. He opened them ahead of us. "Your rooms, honored guests. The staff took the liberty of arranging food for Her Holiness."

"Thanks." I was getting ready to tip him, but he glided away in a swish of silk and leather.

"Guess they pay well here." I let out a tense breath. "Come on, Tidbit. Let's go-"

"I smell meat!" My dragon rammed me into the doorjamb, crushing the air out of my lungs as she squeezed in past me. *"Meat meat meat!"*

The room was panelled in dark wood, lit by tassel-edged gas lamps that wouldn't have been out of place in Victorian Britain. The suite had a regal air, with a smoky, old-books-and-tobacco smell currently overridden by the stench of blood. The servants who'd prepared the room left us a huge silver platter on a round wooden table. A freshly-killed doe lay there, her tongue hanging loose.

"Yeah! Real food!" Karalti bounded across, snatched the doe by the neck, and dragged the corpse to the ground. The silver plate slid off and clanged to the floor with an ear-splitting clatter.

"Just keep it off the carpets, you little psycho." Wincing, I shucked my pack off and went to check the rest of the place out.

The bedroom had a huge round bed covered in furs, like a four-poster nest. A smaller table in the room was laid out with drinks and a plate of small fancy sandwiches for me. God, what was it with this place and late-night sandwiches? Eating was about the last thing on my mind, now that my dragon was disemboweling a deer on the living room flagstones.

I was tired and dirty, restless after the events of the night, and in desperate need for some 'me time'. Fortunately, this place had an awesome bathroom. I stuck my head in and saw a big stone hot tub sunken into the floor. A pipe in the wall trickled a fresh supply of water in, and another pipe in the tub carried it away.

Satisfied, I went back out and called to Karalti from the bedroom door. "Okay, Tidbit. I'm going to take a bath, and I don't want to be disturbed. Literally the only reason you need to call me for the next hour is if a ninja assassin appears in the living room. And even then, if you can take care of it, please do."

"*Okay!*" She clamped her jaws down on the deer's skull, pulling it up and out of the carcass with the vertebrae still attached. Her eyes closed with pleasure as she used her tongue to pick through the gooey mess. "*This is great!*"

Gross as it was, I couldn't help but feel a touch of pride in how strong she'd become.

A little voice in my head sobbed with relief as I retreated, closed the door to the bathroom, stripped, and then slid into the hot water. It was bubbly, like mineral water, and my lingering HP deficit began to rapidly recover.

Once I was settled down, I pulled up my sheets and alerts and began sorting through the backlog of notifications, hoping I'd missed a reply from Rin. Nope. Chewing my lip, I crammed my worries back into their box, then brought up my sheet and did a double take. My Advanced Path was no longer 'Dark Lancer'. It was now 'Dark Dragoon'.

I checked the relevant alert, curious to see what had caused my Advanced Path to change names:

[[Congratulations! Now that your bonded dragon has reached Level 5, she is eligible to take her first Path. To reflect her new abilities, your Advanced Path has been changed from Dark Lancer to Dark Dragoon!]]

[[You have one new Ability Tree: Dark Dragoon]]

[[You can learn new skills and abilities!]]

Awesome. This had to mean that Karalti was big enough to carry me in the air. Just.

When I'd first started playing Archemi, my upload had been so weird, so chaotic, and so frenetic that I'd barely had time to get the hang of things. I'd only really looked at what abilities were available to me and picked the ones that had seemed the best at the time. Now that I wasn't rushing around, I could get a better look at my Advanced Path menus and submenus and theory crafting beyond the 'Hector Survives Dragon School and Doesn't Get Raped to Death by a Giant Tentacled Frog' build.

My character menu had an Active Abilities Tree that allowed me to have up to ten abilities in play. There were grayed out circles on the tree that indicated I'd eventually be able to have fifteen once I hit Level 30. Each 'sphere' contained one of the abilities I'd selected to use as I'd leveled up: Blood Sprint, Shadow Dance, etc. The one at the bottom contained the one Ability I *had* to have: Jump, which was the core ability of the 'Dark Dragoon' and other Lancer classes.

The Abilities were selected and managed in the Ability Submenus: *Attack, Defense, Special,* and now *Dark Dragoon.* They were fairly self-explanatory. *Special* contained status-effect and Area of Effect maneuvers, almost like magical abilities, which fit in generally with the Dark element part of the Dark Lancer class. I browsed over to the Dragoon submenu and groaned. Dammit. None of this had been there when I'd planned my build, and there were now ten more abilities to sponge up my precious ability points. And some of them were *awesome.*

At Level 11, I had 25 ability points to spread out. I queried 'Clear Character Abilities' and got a prompt in reply:

[[Do you wish to cancel all your current abilities and return your ability points to your pool?]]

"Sure do," I replied aloud.

[[Are you sure? This cannot be undone.]]

"Yep."

The Active Ability Tree glowed softly, and the glowing orbs that signified my abilities drained away. As they did, my vision blurred. I groaned as my head throbbed, and a nasty, creeping emptiness pushed in. Suddenly, the only thing I could remember how to do, both theoretically and in my body, was Jump.

I drew a couple of deep breaths to recenter myself, and then dunked my head under the water. When I rose, I felt better.

Okay. Time to get cracking.

Each Ability Submenu had ten skills, for a total of forty available combat abilities. Each one could be leveled up to Level 10. Level 10 abilities were pretty insane: *Jump X* basically let me leap 50ft into the air and deal x10 damage to a single target. It also chained with several other *Jump*-related combo moves that made this ability ideal for mass combat and David-and-Goliath boss situations. I was going be to flying around like some wacked-out Chinese martial arts movie hero by endgame, which was 200% okay with me.

Not all of the abilities were able to be accessed at my current level. At every level, I unlocked one or two new abilities. There was a cap to how much I could raise the abilities I'd selected that depended on my Path level. At Level 11, I could learn Jump III, but not Jump IV. That would have to wait until Level 15. The cap increased by one for every five levels I gained.

That meant that at key levels - 5, 10, 15, and so on - I faced the choice between leveling an old ability or selecting a new one – to a maximum of ten, because I only had ten active ability slots. No matter what I did, each one cost a single Combat Ability Point. I got a fixed two points to spend per level, plus the three I'd gotten at Level 1. That meant that my endgame build – Level 100 – would ideally comprise fifteen maxed-out abilities, with the spare points allocated to abilities that supported and enhanced my core set.

I didn't have to spend any points to acquire *Jump I* - that ability had been a freebie, thanks to the fetch quest I'd done for the librarian of the Eyrie back in Ilia. Surely I'd be able to gain other abilities the same way as my journey went on.

I used three points to bring Jump I back up to Jump III. It was my core skill for a reason, allowing me to avoid attacks vertically and chain strikes in all directions.

I had a look over the summary grid for my available combat abilities:

Offense

Dictum: *Strike up to six targets and recover 2% of HP and AP.*

Blood Sprint: *Strike up to 3 targets, deal +150 Bleeding damage over 10 seconds, boost attack speed for 5 seconds. Chains with Blood Storm.*

Blood Storm: *Can only be used after Blood Sprint. Strike up to 5 targets, +10 HP recovered on good hits.*

Whirlwind Butcher: *Hit up to 6 targets and recover 10 AP on every good hit.*

(New) Shattering Darkness: *An attack that freezes and cracks an enemy's (natural or man-made) armor. Reduces enemy DR by 5% every ability level.*

Defense

Shadow Dance: *Basic evasive dash reduces damage by 70% at the cost of HP (25 HP per dash). HP cost goes down with each ability level.*

(New) Lightning Reflexes: *Damage received while evading is reduced by 5% per skill level.*

(New) Death by a Thousand Cuts: *Chained with Blood Storm. Mark targets with a curse that lowers their attack power by 2% per skill level, and increases your attack by 2% and Damage Reduction by 5%. Percentages rise as you level the skill. Max 1 enemy per skill level (Max 10).*

Special

Mantle of Night: *Boost movement speed and special attack power 20% for 10 seconds.*
Bluster: *Taunt your enemies and regen 5AP + 10HP per skill level.*
Umbra Burst: *Draw Dark mana from the air and emit a chilling burst of enervation that deals Dark damage and has a chance to inflict the Frozen debuff.*
(New) Obscuring Veil: *Chain combo from Jump. Deal x2 damage with a very high chance of inflicting the Blindness debuff.*

Dark Dragoon

(New) Plunge: *Your acquired resistance to g-forces has increased, even if your head is above your feet. You are able to withstand an additional 5 negative G's per skill level.*
(New) Adrenaline Junkie: *You and your dragon regain +10% AP during flight. Scales with skill level.*
(New) Leap of Faith: *You gain the ability to better control your direction in the air if you fall off your mount, even while moving at high speeds. You experience time dilation of 1 sec per skill level while falling.*

I actually gasped out loud as I read over the last ability. Oh, the possibilities. One of the issues I'd had with the Dark Lancer/Dark Dragoon class so far was the question of how to integrate the flashy jumping and lunging lance attacks with aerial combat in any meaningful fashion. Jump, plus Plunge and Leap of Faith were the solution. The combat style I'd need to train for this was insane -

literally insane. Death's Head Mode level of difficulty, 'jumping-off-dragons-flying-at-high-speed insane'.

But it *was* possible, and I got a bit high just thinking about it.

I forced myself to lay back in the bath and calm the fuck down before I went too crazy, then made some quick adjustments to my character plan and went back into the Path menu to assign my points.

I dropped *Doubletap*, *Power Attack*, *Bluster* and *Umbra Burst* entirely. The first three were holdovers from my starting Warrior Path tree, and were now too weak to be of much use. I'd originally planned to keep Umbra Burst, but it was a basic damage attack and fairly Adrenaline Point-hungry, and I was better off spending the points on something else.

I went for the *Blood Sprint > Blood Storm > Death by a Thousand Cuts* combo chain first, and leveled both Blood Sprint and Blood Storm to III and Thousand Cuts to II. That was my main damage combo, crippling enemies with the Bleeding status, recovering HP, and cursing them with weakness I could then exploit with the *Jump > Obscuring Veil* combo. I leveled Obscuring Veil to III as well. Now I had one effective forward push combo, and one vertical jumping combo.

Next on the menu was *Shattering Darkness*. I leveled it to three. Dealing 15% DR reduction to an enemy was awesome, allowing me to make every strike count more. I also reselected *Whirlwind Butcher*, and leveled it to II. It was a solid crowd-control attack, and more importantly, it regenerated Adrenaline Points, which allowed me to use more special abilities.

Shadow Dance was a given: that move had saved my life more than any other skill I had. Shadow Dance II had a negligible 10 HP cost per dash, which was easily regained by landing some hits. However, there were better evasion-dash moves further along, so I didn't power-level this ability.

My last six points went to *Plunge* and *Leap of Faith*. Plunge III meant that I could do all kinds of wacky shit while I was flying on Karalti's back and not worry as much about passing out because she dived while my head was above my knees. Leap of Faith III improved my gyroscopic orientation and would dilate my sense of time by three seconds. Non-stunt people would probably be underwhelmed, but I'd been stunting bikes since I was too young to legally own a license. Three seconds to plan your next move was an awfully long time to make a decision while falling. On the front lines, three seconds of movement was the difference between getting shot in the head and a bullet whiffing past your shoulder. I trusted my reflexes, but this would make them even better. I had a feeling it would also help during Jump maneuvers – especially once I began leaping to truly supernatural heights.

I confirmed all of my selections, and a warm pressure blossomed inside my skull. My vision blurred, and my heart began to pound as knowledge - too much knowledge - flooded into my mind and body. I twitched and thrashed, splashing water over the sides of the tub. My muscles tightened, my jaws snapped together. When it was over, I was left panting for breath... but I could feel the swirl of new power and focus.

Grinning like a madman, I pulled myself up out of the bath and sat down on the edge to do my weird Tibetan-Viking hairdo. I shaved my face and my head on both sides, then braided the long, mohawk-like strip of hair tightly along my skull and down the back of my neck. It was split off into two thinner plaits from my nape. Each plait was woven with strips of faded red silk and tied off at the ends with a chipped bronze ring. I stood after that, and had a look at myself in the mirror. The training I'd been doing showed in the way that my body had hardened and leaned out. I looked like I'd been working with a Hollywood personal coach for six months. Not bad for just under a month of hard living.

There was only one thing that marred my studly appearance. On my left shoulder was a weird black void, a triangular patch of missing pixels about three and a half inches long. It was an artifact of the one and only time I'd died since my upload. It hadn't caused me any problems, but as I poked and pried at the numb, featureless scar, I couldn't help but think back to Rin's warning about 'corrupted data'. Meh.

After all that was done, I wrapped a towel around my hips and threw open the door. Karalti was already waiting for me on the bed. She took up about two-thirds of it, a gleaming black crescent of scales and tail, but she'd arranged the furs so that I could lie back against her chest and belly.

"In Soviet Vlachia, dragon spoons you," I said. "Let me put on some pants first. You're still too young to see me stark naked."

"Doesn't bother me," she replied. Her eyes half-closed as I moved to my pack and equipped my clothing. *"I'm naked all the time."*

"Seriously, don't make this weird!" Laughing, I crawled up onto the bed.

Karalti unfurled one leathery wing, arching it over me like a dark tent. As she did, her scent washed over me. It was becoming more adult, somehow: a rich, intoxicating floral scent, like something you'd smell in a rainforest. The name of the right flower was on the tip of my tongue. It wasn't jasmine... It wasn't honeysuckle or rose... What was it?

I was still trying to remember what Karalti smelled like when I fell asleep, and didn't even realize I'd passed out until the deep velvet darkness resolved into erratic, disturbing dreams. Dreams of war, both modern and fantastic, all of it warped and buzzing like a faulty VR headset. My brother without a face, reaching for me. At the end, as I was starting to rise out of sleep, I found myself floating over a raging battle between the players who'd betrayed me and a monster I'd never seen.

Baldr, Violetta, and Lucien fought alongside three young dragons in a crumbling temple, dodging falling rocks as their opponent - a massive golden ogre with pits of light for eyes - swung a tree-sized club at them. Dead soldiers and knights lay scattered on the ground like broken dolls, but several were still standing at the perimeter of the battle. Among them was Skyr Arnaud, the Knight Commander of the Skyrdon of St. Grigori, and the Novice Master, Skyr Tymos. Their fully-grown dragons were nowhere to be seen. They were holding off waves of glowing skeletons with hammers and shields and magic. The skeletons were not human... They looked like the skeletons of humanoid birds.

As I watched the trio of players rain down blow after blow on their opponent, I glimpsed what lay behind the ogre's bulk – a huge door. It looked like a cherry blossom, with five petal-like segments surrounding a small pentagram core. Staring at it, I felt an odd sense of recognition... a feeling that intensified as a man came up beside my disembodied self and turned his head toward me.

"*My Herald,*" Matir's voice was like a thousand dry leaves slithering over concrete. The god was tall and slender, dressed like a rogue in close-fitting leathers and a long cloak made of swirling shadows. Instead of a face, he had nothing but a spiraling void of sucking darkness with an ember of light burning at the very center. "*They have found the Gate. We do not have much time left. Heed the message and act.*"

...brrr-brrr-brrr- brrr...

The sound – faint at first – grew louder as Baldr teleported from the ground to the ogre's back in a swirl of white vapor. He rammed his sword in next to the monster's spine, hanging on with gritted teeth as the beast writhed around in agony. A bolt of frost leaped from Violetta's hand and took the ogre in the chest, slowing it enough that Baldr could climb up on his sword blade, using it like a step to reach the base of the ogre's neck. He drew a second, shorter sword from his belt, and plunged it into the base of the creature's skull.

...BRRR-BRRR-BRRR-BRRR...

I flailed awake and sat bolt upright, clutching soft fur under my hands. Sweat poured off my skin. Gasping, I searched around for the source of the sound. It wasn't Karalti. She was still curled around me on the huge bed, her nose resting on the tip of her tail, her wings drawn in against her body. Her breathing was clear and quiet and slow. The fireplace crackled softly with embers. Rain slapped against the thick glass window.

My HUD was flashing a yellow exclamation mark alert. I'd never seen an alert like this one before. With anxiety gnawing at my belly, I called up the menu, and the vibrating alarm stopped buzzing. The alert was in my Message Center. When I had my HUD read it out to me, my jaw dropped. So I read it again. And again. It got worse and more surreal every time I heard it.

World Alert: Ilia

The ruler of Ilia, Warden Scandiva, has fallen! This is a Server Alert to announce the new Warden Protector of Ilia and Knight-Commander of the Eyrie of St. Grigori, Lord Baldr Hyland.

CHAPTER 24

Holy shitdicks.

This was not good. Like, on a scale of one to bad - and in light of what Rin had told me about Ororgael - we had firmly entered FUBAR territory. "HOW? How the fuck did Baldr become the Warden of Ilia AND the Knight-Commander of the Skyrdon in two freaking weeks? He was like... Level Ten when we left?"

I sank back down, stunned. I'd been worried enough about fucking Arnaud. The Knight Commander had been the Prince Charming of dragon knights: blond, blue-eyed, lantern jawed, completely punchable. He was the kind of dangerous son-of-a-bitch who'd do anything to preserve the status quo, but at least he'd been largely honorable. Baldr Hyland was not, and I had an awful feeling that Arnaud – and probably his dragon, Talenth – were now rotting in shallow graves behind the Eyrie.

"There is nothing okay about this." I reopened my Message Center and brought up a new P.M. window with Rin. "Hey Rin – hopefully you're doing alright. I don't know if you got the World Alert about Ilia, but this is really really bad. Baldr is the guy I told you about in regards to Ororgael and the buggy quest. Get in touch when you can. Shit's going down."

I sent it off, and peeled myself out of the pile of furs. Karalti heaved a little sigh, tucking her snout under her foreclaw, and I reached back to lay a hand on her thigh, willing myself to breathe. She was here, unmolested, and far beyond Baldr's reach. The knots in my shoulders had just started to loosen when someone banged their fist on the door and I just about shat myself.

"Fuck!" I jumped about a foot in the air, fumbling for a weapon. Karalti reared her head up out of a dead sleep and swiveled it to point her nose at the entry to our quarters, hissing.

"Who is it!?" I called, once I'd clapped my hand down on my spear.

"It is Petko. Father Matthias." The voice was muffled, but recognizable.

Oh. Good. It wasn't Baldr, come to steal my dragon while I was in my pajama pants. I climbed over Karalti's tail and slid to the floor, stumbling over to where I'd left my shirt, and began to dress manually before remembering that I could just equip shit. I did so - my Nazari armor and the Steel Militia Spear, both of which now felt completely inadequate.

I opened the door to find Father Matthias standing there, fresh and tidy, but with the kind of strained pleasant expression I read as 'outwardly calm, but internally screaming'. He was smoking, as usual, and smiled around the stem of his pipe. "Good morning, Rytier. Is something the matter? You look like you've seen a ghost."

"Well, my mortal nemesis just became the Warden of Ilia and the Commander of the Skyrdon of Saint Grigori." I adjusted my belt. "That was a thing that happened."

The priest's lips twitched in a small wry smile. "Believe me, your concern is shared by many. Andrik just called an emergency meeting in the great hall and is holding audience with a number of very tired ministers, diplomats, and Suri."

"Guess I'm not in 'adviser' territory yet," I replied.

"His Majesty may wish to discuss the Ilian problem with you in private later on," Mattias replied tactfully. "I don't suppose you would be up for an early morning walk?"

I looked back at Karalti. She had flopped her head down onto the pillow I'd vacated and was snoozing away. "Sure. Why not?"

Ten minutes of walking later, Matthias led me along a marble path that went down into the natural cavern spring behind Vulkan Keep.

"Karalti is growing incredibly fast," he remarked, "I had no idea the Solonkratsu matured so rapidly, given that they are said to live so long. This is an incredible observation opportunity for someone like me. We have not hosted a true dragon in Vlachia for a century or more, and never one as young as Karalti."

"She just about doubles in size with every level. I think she'll slow down from this point on, though." I had my spear resting over one shoulder, swinging it from side to side as we walked. "And I guess it makes sense. Most baby animals don't stay babies for very long. Humans are kind of an exception to the rest of the animal kingdom."

"True enough." Matthias drew on his pipe. He had been hitting it continuously since we left my quarters, burning through the entire bowl of tobacco. Worry lines were etched around his eyes. "Speaking of the dragons – we never did have our talk about Matir."

"Nope."

"What do you already know of him?"

I thought for a couple of minutes. "I know he's one of The Nine. God of Darkness, old as dirt... and that's about it. I know his basic portfolio, but he didn't really enlighten me very much. I can only guess why he wants me to go to Myszno. Do you know anything about a Draconic prophecy regarding the 'Herald of the Hidden Seed'? He keeps calling me that."

"Unfortunately not." Matthias shook his head. "The dragons did not record their stories and prophecies in written form. They transmit their knowledge through oral traditions and the sharing of their blood. As with the Mercurions, blood has great power and meaning for them, being the stuff of magic."

I frowned. The dragons of the Eyrie had known of the prophecy, but they hadn't been able to talk about it because of the geas that kept them enslaved. "I'm pretty sure it relates to the Dragon Gates. I have two ongoing quests that touch on it."

Matthias nodded thoughtfully. "Well, I can't help you with those, but perhaps the history and mythos of the Black God will be of use to you."

"Hit me."

"Matir is the second eldest of The Nine. The eldest is Veles, the Lord of Time and Magic. Matir is the God of Darkness, and his twin sister, Rusolka, is the Goddess of the Ocean and the ruler of the Deep Hells. Matir and Rusolka were born without a mother, brought into being when Veles first manifested the 87 Names of Darkness by mixing his blood with the shadows cast by the moonlight spilling onto the earth, which bore Matir, and the sea water, which bore Rusolka."

"Huh. Neat." I nodded.

"Matir and his sister represent the two sides of the Darkness element. One is creative; the other, destructive. In all the myths and stories I've heard, Matir is demanding, mischievous, quixotic, and paradoxical. He was easily the most commonly revered god among dragons, though his worship was rarely conducted in the open. There are mystery cults dedicated to him here as well. We do not only worship Khors in this land. The preeminence of the Forge Father is a relatively recent occurrence in Vlachia."

I pondered that as we veered down another path and left the Keep's sculpted gardens behind us, passing into the humid grotto. Water trickled in thin streams down the walls, flowing into gutters that kept the path clear. It was as warm as a steam bath. "Are you hinting that you're part of one of these cults?"

"If I were, would I ever admit it? Matir is the god of secrets, after all." Matthias replied.

I was briefly taken aback by the sudden note of bitterness in his voice. "Something is stressing you out. What is it?"

"Nothing." He jerked his head toward the corridor, arched his thin brows, and kept walking.

As we pushed on into the caves, the sound of water got louder – loud enough that anyone would have trouble hearing a quiet conversation between two men. Matthias held up a hand when we reached a particular spot, and I slowed my pace.

"Here," he said. "One of Vulkan Keep's many small secrets. The steam and noise here makes eavesdropping difficult."

"I figured this wasn't just a social call," I said. "What do you need to tell me?"

Matthias sighed. "Where to begin with this rosszarcú...? Ugh. The short of it is that while you have been hunting the Slayer, I have been observing at court and counselling the Volod. The Slayer's motive is now utterly obvious to me."

"Go on...?"

"You should know, Rytier Hector, that I am a pious man." Matthias regarded me with wise, piercing eyes. "I began studying at the seminary in my teens, and dedicated myself to the path of the sage, studying medicine and crafting, the ways in which magic and machines interact with the body. In doing so, I traveled the country, and came to believe that the best expression of faith is when we act in a spirit of acceptance and kindness. All of the Nine are popular in the country... Khors is the god of the city, because the city is where most industry takes place."

"Okay."

"I have learned that His Majesty has been taking steps to use the Church of Khors – and only Khors – to cement his rule of Vlachia." The priest looked down. "Each of those murdered men was part of a secret ecclesiastical council the Volod established to plan for a takeover. He wishes for us to be monotheistic, and intends to enforce this on his nation."

Nothing like a good political conspiracy to start the morning. "But why? He's a Corvinus. He already has the throne. It's not like he's illegitimate."

"Yes and no. Andrik is not the Corvinus who was intended to rule," Father Matthias said. "Andrik is young, and his coronation was beset with controversy. He is city-bound, and he has still not wed or even produced an illegitimate heir - and not for lack of trying."

"I'd have thought that would be a mark against him, if he had fathered a kid outside of wedlock."

Matthias shook his head. "Bastards are entitled to inheritance in Vlachia. Historically, our kings rarely married. They had a harem of courtesans who competed for his favor. The first one to bear a son became Queen. We have adopted more continental habits of marriage and succession during these last few centuries, but the laws of inheritance have not changed. Even an illegitimate child is better than none, and given the number of affairs Andrik has had, the lack of an heir is disturbing."

I rubbed my jaw. "Hmm."

"Besides, that, a number of the Voivoidar are not happy with his decadence, or how he pushes the Church above all other estates."

"So this council is the target. We know that Kanzo is killing priests in line with the virtues of the Church," I replied. "I guess that symbolism could fit in with a political motive. What do we know about each one of the members?"

Matthias looked distinctly troubled now. "Yes. Father Abel was the court tutor and one of the greatest sages of the Church, though he was an extremely conservative man. Father Darko was a firebrand and would surely have supported a monotheistic takeover by Khorsian faith. Orban represented the Forge Brothers and was the Forgemaster's protégé - and Forgemaster Toth is very much an idealist, the kind of man who believes heart and soul in the benevolence of the church-as-ruler. Father Erik was a young and passionate priest known for his ability to fundraise and motivate crowds, and he was involved in the shaping of young minds. A lot of our junior clerics are recruited from orphanages. There are only three other members of that council who yet live: High Forgemaster Agoston Toth, whom I just described; Voivode Janos Lanz of Czongrad, and the king himself."

"The same people he named to me and Suri last night," I said. "Why don't you think he told us about this council of his?"

Matthias pursed his lips. "He has been clandestine, because it is not the sort of policy that will be readily approved by the lords of the land. You must remember that a king's rule is not absolute - it depends on the loyalty and consensus of his vassals, and they are nearly all older than he is. Besides that, you and Suri are foreigners, and I doubt he sees any reason you should know."

"Huh." I took a moment to digest it all. "If we're right, and they're being murdered according to the virtues, the first three men were killed in defiance of the virtues of wisdom, honor, and courage. My bet is that Father Erik's murder was a rebuke of hospitality."

"Yes. Leaving discipline, self-reliance, and honesty," Matthias finished.

"Yup." I grimaced. "What is Andrik trying to do?"

He turned his extinguished pipe in his hand. "The gist of Andrik's plan is this: he wants all the smiths in the country to be press-ganged into the clergy. That way, they would be oath-bound to be his eyes and ears in the provinces. He wishes for the Church to become the sole trader of metals and other products in the land, so that he can indirectly control the production of farming equipment and weapons. He also wants to deport every Meewfolk and force Mercurions into indentured labor. Given that he has been building our army and increasing the numbers of Khorsian faith-militant around the country, one can only imagine how he plans to execute this."

"That's, uhh, awfully totalitarian of him," I replied. "Why does he have such a hate-boner for non-humans, anyway?"

"His Majesty claims it is because it is because of the scandal that caused his brother to commit suicide," the priest replied. "Andrik did not originally wish to become king. His elder brother, Ignas, had been groomed from birth to take over from their father. He was well-suited to the role. Ignas was a tall, sober, serious man, not prone to excess or frivolity. Despite this, he was a great patron of the arts and sciences, open-minded and wise, and supportive of our diverse polytheistic traditions. It was known that he would be an excellent king."

I raised an eyebrow. "And you're sure this guy killed himself?"

"They recovered his body and held a state funeral for him. I wasn't there to see it, but I have no reason to suspect foul play, given the nature of the scandal that triggered it." Matthias shrugged.

Why? What did he do?"

"It is a stakeable offense to discuss the details of Ignas' fall," Matthias replied primly. He glanced at the walls. "Quite a bit more serious than my speculative gossip."

"Oh. Well... So, how about Matir, then? Because getting staked is definitely on the 'Top Ten Ways I Don't Want to Die' list."

Matthias laughed. "And fair enough, too. Anyway... you mentioned that the Black God has summoned you to Myszno. It is the Eastern-most province of Vlachia, nestled at the base of the Falker Mountain Range. The Range separates our southern border from the desert nations of The Shalid. What I have heard at court is alarming. The province is effectively under the control of some undead robber baron."

"Fantastic," I said flatly.

"It is a great embarrassment for Andrik. Our army has been sieging the borders of the ruined land, but to no avail. Surely another reason he is trying to consolidate his power through religion," Matthias continued, gesturing expressively as we approached the end of the cave and broke out onto a bridge across a small, steaming chasm. Glowing mushrooms lit the walls with soft blue light. "Still, when you told me that was where you were headed, I immediately knew why."

"Why?"

"Matir loathes the undead," Matthias replied. "They are an affront to everything he stands for. Myszno was also the site of one of the few immigrant worker towns in Vlachia. It was a Tuun settlement, actually, and the Tuun who survived have been passionate opponents of the monsters who have blighted the land. They have also been effective opponents, mostly because they host several of the Kara Ay Tuugandar."

It still felt weird that I understood that. The Kara Ay Tuugandar were the Brothers of the Dark Moon. Warrior-monks... worshippers of Burna, the fly-headed god, who was an aspect of Matir. "They're the order that produces Baru, aren't they? Those doctor-assassin-midwife monks?"

"Indeed. There are about twenty of them holding the line against this vampire that has taken over the place. They say one Baru is worth fifty normal soldiers."

I reached up to rub my jaw. "That has to chafe the Volod's panties a bit... knowing that foreigners are holding off an undead invasion."

"Yes. Though they are human, so..." Matthias rubbed his forehead nervously. "It is the Meewfolk and Mercurions he despises. Anyway, I'd advise you to keep this information to yourself until the Volod willingly divulges it. I have good reason to suspect that the female Mercurion you spoke of, the apprentice, is correct – that her master is being blackmailed by someone who is opposed to a theocracy under a barren king and an iron-fisted Church of the Forge Father."

"Well, my lips are sealed," I said. "Anyway – heard about the plan for tonight?"

"Do zla boda," Matthias muttered. "Yes... I am going with you, as is Ur Kirov."

I mimed a little jig. "You sound about as excited as I am."

The priest's mouth flickered with a sneer, but then he sighed. "When I left my country to travel and teach, Andrik had only been Volod for half a year. Now... I believe that he does not possess his brother's acumen. He is putting himself and the lives of everyone at the auction – not to mention the kingdom – at risk by making this big scene."

"Not going to try and talk your way out of it?"

Matthias shook his head. "Of course not. I am a capable mage, and the High Forgemaster and my king have need of me. I will be there. Though... I have an odd request for you."

"Oh?"

He pressed his lips together in a thin line. "From what I overheard at court this morning, you and Ur Kirov have been assigned to guard the Voivode together. His Majesty wants Suri by his side – I shall give you one guess as to why – and I shall be assisting the Forgemaster. I would like for you to watch out for Kirov."

I frowned, confused. "Watch out for him? He's like... nine levels higher than me."

"Perhaps. But he has a naïve streak," Matthias said. "And while I count him as a dear friend, I fear he is overconfident about the wisdom of His Majesty's plan. Unlike you, he cannot come back to life if he perishes..."

"I get it," I said. "And sure – I'll keep an eye out for him. You guys saved me and Karalti back in Bryos. I owe you one."

Matthias smiled and patted me on the arm. "You owe me nothing, rytier. You are the caretaker of a very special young Solonkratsu and have already been indispensable. But come – let us break our fast together. I suspect we will be more likely to live out the day on full stomachs, don't you?"

CHAPTER 25

The first thing I did after leaving Vulkan Keep was buy a stock of herbs for health potions and a new weapon. The need for improved steel was kind of irrational, given that Baldr was now the literal fucking ruler of Ilia, but upgrading my gear made me feel better. It was kind of like buying comfort food, but the comforting part went into *other* people's bodies.

The best spear I could afford was the unfortunately named Alpha Rod. Yes, really. I wasn't sure exactly who had named this thing, but whoever they were, they definitely had something on the brain when they entered the item description:

Alpha Rod
Common Weapon
Slot: Two-handed
Item Class: Weapon
Item Quality: Excellent
Damage: 121-130
Durability: 100%
Weight: 3 lb
Special: +2 Str, Critical Hit Damage Bonus +8%, chance to Stun +1%
A thick spear with a large blade. The silver ash haft is firm and silky to the touch.

The Alpha Rod easily had the best stats out of anything in the local weapon store, but the woman staffing the counter leered at me knowingly as I took the girthy polearm in hand. "Here you are, sir. And if you use our weapon to bring in the Slayer of Taltos, will you recommend us to the Volod? It would be a great honor for my father, the smith."

"Oh, absolutely," I swung the polearm a couple of times, testing the balance. "I'll be sure to give His Majesty a blow-by-blow description of how I reamed the Slayer of Taltos with my new Alpha Rod."

Karalti waited for me outside, surrounded by a crowd of awed NPCs. She was hamming it up for them, strutting back and forth and accepting worshipful offerings of food and coins. Some of the dragon groupies were praying.

"*Thank you, thank you,*" she was making a rare broadcast to the gathered faithful. "*The emissary of the gods accepts all offerings of fish and tasty meat-kebabs! Extra blessings for lamb!*"

"Okay, 'Emissary of the Gods', time to saddle up," I muttered, reaching up to clap her on the shoulder. A few people gasped.

"You dare touch the sacred draak!?" A plump nobleman in purple silk and a spiffy hat took a step forward, a hand on the hilt of his rapier.

"She's *my* dragon. Don't make me smite you, for in my hands, I wield the mighty Alpha Rod." I wrapped a hand around the rope harness I'd made as a temporary saddle and pulled myself up as Karalti crouched down. As I hauled myself onto her back, I felt a familiar itch just before a yellow 'water' drop icon began to flash out the corner of my eye. The fucking Pee icon. "Ugh. *Why* does this game tell me when to pee?"

"*Wat?*"

"*For some fucking reason, there's this HUD icon that alerts me to the need to relieve my bladder.*"

"*Well, if there wasn't an alert, how would you know?*" Karalti bobbed her head goodbye at the flash mob congregation and nosed through them. NPCs gasped and reached out to touch her as she passed. I had the passing urge to kick their hands away, but they weren't doing her any harm.

"*It's just so arbitrary,*" I said. "*For one thing, why do I have to pee in a video game anyway? For another, the pee meter could have filled at the palace in the morning, but no. It has to be here, in the middle of the street. And I don't think Taltos has any public toilets.*"

"So you just get your thingy out and pee on a wall. That's what the other man was doing."

I rolled my eyes skyward. *"I'm not a fucking animal, and I'm not pissing against walls in the middle of the goddamn street."*

"You are too an animal! Humans are made of meat, like everyone else."

"Oh, that's right. You're an apex predator." I groaned aloud. *"Literally everything you say sounds like something a serial killer writes on his holiday cards. Now give me a second. I have to message Suri."*

"Okay."

First, I checked for a reply from Rin, again. She was still a dead signal. I searched my map for her icon, but came up blank. At a loss, I sent my trusty Beserker companion a voicechat invitation. To my surprise, she actually picked up.

I decided to kick things off in a mature note. "Hey gurrl. How's it goin' over dere?"

Instead of speaking, Suri sent me back a couple of emoticons in our HUD window: a giant middle finger and a dog. I actually laughed out loud.

"No, in all seriousness though," I replied. "We should probably make a game plan for tonight. You know as well as I do that it's going to be a screaming howler monkey shitshow. The Volod's answer to 'suspected terrorism' is to try to bait Kanzo out into a situation where all the prospective targets can be massacred at once. Because video game mission logic, I guess."

"Okaaay. Well, I'm dress shopping right now. Can we vid-chat after I'm done?"

I didn't know what was funnier: that Suri was out dress shopping, or that she didn't know what a video game was but still used words like 'vid-chat' without any sense of recognition or irony. "You didn't ever strike me as the dress-wearing type. I can join you, if you'd like?"

"I'm the 'wear whatever the fuck I want' type. And no. At best, you'll be bored shitless."

"Aww, come on. I love going shopping with the girls."

"I shop alone. You can see the dress at the auction."

"Don't worry, I'm just teasing you. Do you happen to know if Taltos has a civilized man's toilet available to the public?"

"No. But I'm sure you can drop into the Armory and they'll make you a diaper."

I sent *her* the middle finger emote this time.

After weapons, our second stop was the saddlemaker's – except that when we got to the entry to the Tanners' District, it was closed. No fewer than ten guards were lounging outside the portcullis. Two of them were riding hookwings. There were also three large mastiff-type dogs lounging in the shade. For the time being, they didn't look particularly ferocious.

"Let's see how that Negotiation skill is levelling up." Annoyed, I rode up to the guards, tapping Karalti so she turned side-on to the small crowd of men. "Excuse me, sir. I need to get in there to do some trade with one of the locals. King's business."

The guards eyed me warily. Only one of them spoke up. "No one's allowed in or out of the silverskins' ghetto. That's our orders."

"Are your orders flexible?" I asked, with a wince.

"I'mma set the gate on fire if they don't let us in." Karalti pawed the ground, wings and crests rising. *"I want a proper saddle."*

The guards looked the posturing dragon, then at each other. The first man nodded. "Ten rubles says they're flexible for the likes of you."

"Ten? You'd skim ten rubles from the agent of the Volod and the Emissary of the Gods herself?" I pointed angrily at Karalti.

"Heresy!" she squawked aloud.

For a moment, they all glanced at Karalti uncertainly, and then, without another word, one of the guards turned around and unlocked the winch that turned the portcullis.

"Good hustle, Tidbit." We watched them work, and when the gate was open enough for her to slink underneath, I flattened myself down against her back and we went inside. The portcullis came down a lot faster than it went up. It hit the ground behind us with a rattling boom.

The Tanners' District was now a ghost of itself. The neatly paved streets were nearly empty, and all of the industry we'd seen during our stay with Rin had vanished, locked away behind shuttered windows and closed doors. I felt like we were being watched from the narrow row houses. Human soldiers hung around the main intersection in tight cliques, staring suspiciously at the few Mercurions who were outdoors. Those Mercurions were taking no chances: they wore concealing cloaks, broad-brimmed hats and their signature masks. They had hunched shoulders, and their heads swiveled to track us as we passed by.

Guilt crushed me down like a cigarette stub into an ashtray. I knew, technically, this mess wasn't my fault. I couldn't even entirely condemn Andrik for wanting to protect his people and consolidate his power as a feudal king... but like a cigarette, the whole thing left a bad taste in my mouth.

"I really think Rin is right about Kanzo," I remarked to my dragon. *"That Kanzo is being blackmailed and he's being forced into this. But... damn, Karalti. I don't know if I did the right thing by helping her run. She could be out there, making bombs or some shit, and it's my fault if she is."*

"Yeah, it is." Karalti replied cheerfully.

I scowled. *"Gee, thanks."*

"Nuh-uh. You decided Rubber Lady didn't do anything bad, and if she did, then you were wrong. And that's okay."

"Is it, though? The NPCs – I mean, the people here – basically have real feelings and real suffering. I feel like I'm in over my head. I'm too dumb to work this shit out without a quicksave function."

Karalti hissed through her side teeth, making a pitiful sound like a deflating balloon as she shook her head. *"Stop saying that. It's not true. You're not dumb."*

"I sure as hell feel like it."

"My blood sings the song of Pride, the Words of creation and destruction," she replied testily. *"The clanmates I choose to link my blood with are not stupid."*

The sudden sharpness - and maturity - that I heard in my dragon's voice jolted me out of the confusion and self-pity that was creeping up on me. Karalti sounded so... adult.

"You're right. I'll try and think myself out of this hole later."

I took us by Rin's shop, and my heart fell when I saw the state of it. The door had been smashed, and what little we could see of the inside was trashed. Two burly *Joh* Mercurions loomed beside the entry. They wore sleeveless leather brigandine armor and carried wickedly sharp javelins. Their silver teardrop masks were identical, the mana swirling with sigils that gathered into the image of a single eye with a spiral pupil.

"Stay back, *sang'hi*," one of them called as we came to a stop. "And keep moving. You are not welcome here."

"I'm Rin's friend." 'Friend' seemed like a bit of a stretch, but I cared about her. "I just wanted to know if she managed to get out-"

"That is none of your business. We are protecting the Master Crafter's goods. *Bat'haxalta et'.*" The other one jerked his head toward the street.

"Righty-o. Well, you gents have a lovely day," I said. Karalti bristled, but I shook my head and twitched my heels against her ribs, signaling for her to keep walking.

"*These guys must be keeping their spare javelins up their asses,*" I said to her. "*Not that I blame them.*"

"*Mm.*" Karalti swung her head, scenting the air. "*I hope the saddle guy will talk to us.*"

The saddlery was attached to a stable that was set up for creatures Karalti's size. There were a pair of toothy, feathered, griffon-like creatures lashed to hitching posts at the front – quazi, I guessed. They chirped and clattered their beaks at us as we rang the bell at the gate. After several minutes, a slender, heavily robed Mercurion peeked out from around the corner of the building at us, her face obscured by a smooth dish of metal.

"I'm here to see Mikhail. I have a commission for him," I called to her – or at least, I thought it was a 'her'.

'She' did not reply, except to vanish back around the corner. Nearly fifteen minutes passed before I could hear anything but the murmur of speech from inside the main house attached to the stable. The sylvan Mercurion reappeared, accompanied by a hulking man in a heavy leather apron. Mikhail was also a *Joh* Mercurion, the largest and most obviously masculine of their race's six different body types. He had a high ponytail of silver hair, and as he strode toward us, he pushed his mask up onto his head. He looked alarmingly like Sephiroth of Final Fantasy fame... something that momentarily gave me a twinge of nostalgia. I'd grown up playing my grandparents' games, and that game - and character - was one of my favorites.

"Sorry to spook your clanmate," I said through the fence. "I'm looking for a saddle for this girl here. I heard you're the best."

"I am," he said simply. "And my name is not Mikhail. It is Mix'hxian. Mikhail is the name the *sang'hi* give me. I prefer Mix."

The middle part of his name sounded like a wooden clicking sound, so I was grateful I didn't have to try and pronounce the whole thing. "I meant no offense. I'm Dragozin Hector of Tungaant, and this is Karalti."

"Karalti." Mix echoed the name as he unlocked the gate and threw it open. "The silhouette cast by the moonlight when it touches an object."

"Sorry?"

"That is what her name means in *Tlax'it*," Mix rumbled. "We are both People of the Blood. We still share some language with the dragons."

Karalti gaped her jaws in the imitation of a human smile. "*Kochi gul-gabi!*"

"*Kochi suna, sulunkraati.*" The Mercurion bowed his head, and motioned for us to follow him into the workshop behind the conjoined house-stable complex.

"*What does that mean?*" I asked Karalti. "*I still know shit-all about Mercurions.*"

"*It means like... uhh... your face is awesome? Like when you tell me I'm pretty. And he told me I'm pretty, too.*"

I blinked. "*You told him he's pretty?*"

"*Yeah! Because it means his clan did a good job making him. That's what you say when they take their mask off like that. They only take it off when they wanna get to know you.*"

"*How do you know this?*"

Karalti chirped out loud, flipping her wings against her ribs. "*Rin told me about it! She said that masks are really important for Mercurions, but she doesn't wear one as much because she's Starborn.*"

"*Huh. She explain why?*"

"*Kind of. She said that the masks show what House you're from, and if you don't wear one, it's like showing off. You could offend someone and start a fight. She said that Mercurions like to fight a lot, so...*"

"So you don't want to be flaunting your family's goods on the street." I chuckled. *"Weird. You know, I'm worried about Rin. I wonder if these guys know where she is, or if she's okay."*

"I dunno. But even if they do know where to find her, I don't think they're going to tell us."

"No? Why?"

"Sang'hi is a really rude word.

CHAPTER 26

Mix's open-plan workshop had an array of works-in-progress laid out on saddle forms. They were obviously of high quality, and beautifully made. Three other Mercurions were here. I couldn't remember the names of their body types, but one was tall, thin, and androgynous, while the other two were stocky, short but feminine, and similar in build to Rin. They paused in their work, watching us in inscrutable silence.

"I have never made a saddle for a Solonkratsu," the craftsman said. He collected a long measuring tape from a workbench stacked high with cured leather hides of various animal species. "However, I believe I can adapt a quazi saddle blueprint to fit her."

"How long will it take? And what's the cost?"

"The base price is 80 olbia. If you do not want it tooled, it can be done quickly." Mix hung the ribbon over his shoulder and looked more closely at Karalti. "Hmm. There is already one unique challenge for this project – her wing membranes. We will not be able to use a tightening strap around her abdomen unless her membranes are pierced."

Ouch – 80 olbia was pricey. Karalti's crests flared, and she reared her head back, looking at me nervously as I slid to the ground. "I know the dragons I saw in Ilia had small holes for tack cut into their wings. Any other options?"

He shrugged. "Extend your wings, *sulunkraati*, and I will make an assessment."

Karalti shook herself out, and then lifted and stretched her wings. She kept the tips folded in so that they didn't snap out and strike the ceiling. Mix walked around her, asking her to kneel down so that he could see the shape of her back and wings from in front and behind. I could see the problem too. The edge of the thick membranes went nearly one-third of the way down her tail. I watched on with my arms crossed, and when Karalti met my eyes, I nodded and smiled.

"The wing piercing would be the most efficient route," he said slowly. "However, I have concerns. Her membranes are too soft. The dragons you saw most likely had the holes made when they were freshly hatched, then stretched and tempered as they grew. That is how skin works. Even if I cut the holes and cauterized the edges, they would become prone to tearing. She would experience cycles of tearing and healing until they scarred."

I frowned, thinking back to the dragons of the Eyrie. Their wingholes for their saddles had been thickly scarred and tough-looking, and there was probably some technique to creating them that I didn't know. "Right. What are our other options?"

"A tail cinch is sub-standard. Too many moving parts." The Mercurion reached up to run a smooth, alabaster hand over the dorsal ridges at the base of her tail. "As for other options... Hmm."

"Wait." I joined him by Karalti's hindquarters. "Are these dorsal fins of yours sensate, Karalti?"

"*What do you mean?*"

I took out my dagger, and rapped the edge of a fin with the hilt. "Feel that?"

"*Nuh-uh.*"

"What if we pierced holes through these?" I asked the crafter. "Could they be used as anchor points?"

"Those could be used as anchor points, though we would have to drill through them and weld the saddle attachment rings in place," Mix mused. "Though a screw-on clasp would also work to allow for replaceable rings... and that would also mean a lighter saddle. Yes, with ingenuity and proper tension, that would be possible."

The thought of drilling into Karalti's dorsal ridges made me nervous and a little queasy, but it was better than weakening her wings. At her current small size, even small holes could be a liability. Not to mention, I didn't want to do anything the way the Skyrdon did if I could avoid it. That wasn't just out of conceit – in the event of us having to ever fight one or more dragon knights, our tactics, gear, and abilities needed to be wildly different than anything they were used to having to deal with. I rubbed the base of her tail. "What do you think, girl?"

"*Drilling sounds scary. But I'll do it.*" She leaned against my hand. "*I wanna fly with you more than anything. Because then you'll love me, right?*"

"*What do you mean 'I'll love you'? I already love you.*"

She flattened her wings back against her body, shifting from one foot to the other like a new hatchling. "*Yeah, but you'll love me the best then.*"

"*I'll always love you the best. Don't you worry about that.*" I clapped her on the leg. "Alright, Mix. Let's mark her up and get started."

We blocked in between 11 a.m. to 5 p.m. for crafting. While Mix and his spouses – plural – and kid worked on the structural parts of the saddle, I had to drill the holes we'd need through the bony dorsal ridges of Karalti's back.

"Ready?" I knelt beside her out in the yard. She lay on her side, one wing tucked underneath her, her spine arched toward me. That meant I could drill down from the top instead of having to hold the tool upright.

"*Yeah. I'll tell you if it hurts.*"

The drill Mix had given me was basically a steampunk power drill with a long diamond bit. It was powered by a small capsule of green crystal mana. Resolutely, I set it against the dark scales of my dragon's back, sweat running down my forehead, and gently depressed the trigger.

Karalti flinched as the drill bored through the thick keratin ridge on her back, and I pulled away. "Hurt?"

"*No. It's okay,*" she said. The tip of her tail flicked on the ground, sending up puffs of dirt and dust. "*Just feels weird.*"

"Right." Nervously, I resumed my work.

Karalti lay there placidly as we started to bore through what I had always assumed was solid bone. But the fins weren't actually bone – they were more like very thick fingernails, keratin mixed with the black nacre-like substance that gave her dark scales their camouflage. They were extremely tough, but we weren't going to paralyze her by drilling through them, provided we weren't too close to her spine.

"*It doesn't hurt at all,*" she said once I was about halfway through. "*Makes my bones feel funny, though.*"

"Better this than your wings, then." I wet my mouth – it was dry with anxiety – and kept drilling. "You want to try flying after we get this on you?"

"*Yeah! Flying is the best thing ever!*" Her tail began to twitch harder. "*We should go to the auction that way.*"

"If you think you're strong enough to carry me and our gear." I sucked a tooth as I felt the drill bit sink into the ridge, then punch through. "There. That's one. Five more to go, and then it's on to potion making."

"I decided on what Path I want, by the way," Karalti said. *"Is it a good time to talk about that?"*

"Sure." I started on the next hole. Mix had marked the exact places I needed to drill. This activity wasn't technically a Crafting skill, so nothing was levelling up while I worked on this. Only the leatherworking part would raise my skill EXP.

"Well, like I said, flying is the best thing ever... so I want to take the Path of Alacrity," she said shyly.

"Yeah, I like that Path, too." I smiled, leaning onto the drill as it ground out a round hole about an eighth of an inch in diameter. We had to bore them out, then widen them with a chisel bit. "Why do you like it?"

"Because I want to be faster. And it has more magic... you get some bonus Lexica with it."

"You like magic, huh?"

"Yeah." She heaved a deep sigh. *"And there's a spell I want later, too."*

"Which one?"

She hummed in her throat, and her toes curled. *"I don't wanna tell you."*

"You don't? Why not?"

"Nuh-uh. Not telling. But can I choose a spell at Level 9? And take the Path of Alacrity?"

"Sure." While I worked, I bought up the Path descriptions and looked over the Skills, curious to see what spell she might want. There was a relatively long list, but none of them leaped out at me as being particularly special. An enhancement for her breath weapon, polymorph, a teleporting spell, and a tracking spell. I recognized the tracking and teleportation spells – they were the same magic that Knight Commander Arnaud and his team had used to track and rescue Rutha and I when we were stranded on the coast of Zaunt. This was probably a veiled game-speak way of ensuring she ended up with the teleport spell. "So, you sure you want Alacrity? Want me to lock it in?"

"Yeah!"

Before I confirmed it, I went into her submenu and had a look over the Path ability summaries, ensuring they were what I also wanted.

Path of Alacrity Abilities

Level 5 - Split Turn: Burn 5 mana points per second to immediately change momentum while rolling. This allows for 90 degree and 180 degree turns in any direction. 2 bonus Lexica.

Level 10 - Wings of Deception: Create a brief illusory decoy in midair and teleport a short distance in any direction, then attack your distracted enemy for double damage. 1 bonus Lexica.

Level 15 - Death From Above: Dive at an enemy and strike their weakest point while continuing to move at full speed. x2 damage, sharply increased critical hit rate. A successful hit causes the Bleeding (normal hit) or Hemorrhaging (critical hit) debuff. 2 bonus Lexica.

Level 20 - Parabolic Mastery: Your dragon has mastered her control of gravity, allowing her to stall herself in midair and recover from tumbles that would send other dragons falling out of the sky, even while injured. In addition, her wings become stronger: Wing injuries become 50% less likely to occur and 50% less disabling in the event they are injured. 1 bonus Lexica.

Level 25 - Skydancer: Your dragon has unparalleled abilities of evasion and maneuverability while flying. She gains steep bonuses to Stamina, Evasion, and Dexterity, and gains the Burst Flight ability that allows her to briefly launch through the air at near-supersonic speed. 2 bonus Lexica.

The other Path was essentially a combat-focused path that allowed you to turn your dragon into a tank, but it was better suited to someone who needed their dragon to do all of the heavy lifting while they were in the air, literally and metaphorically. For an armored knight who was their dragon's personal assistant, spotting attackers and protecting their vulnerable wings, the Path of Power was probably better. The Path of Alacrity was better suited to a mobile DPS unit like me.

The Path of Alacrity would lead into the Shadow Wing advanced path at Level 30. That AP was focused on precision attacks, stealth, and crippling abilities that were a good compliment to my own – and, I hoped, a good compliment to an acrobatic aerial partnership. I selected the Path, and paused to confirm.

Karalti shivered, and closed her eyes. Her head flopped onto the ground. The Path selection added 10 more points to her Dex, and 5 each to her Str and Sta, just like that.

While she digested the information, I had the HUD read out her new ability description:

Split Turn

The Path of Alacrity turns dragons into masters of the sky and their own bodies, allowing them to perform aerial feats that should be impossible for a creature of their size. Split Turn is one of those feats.

Normal dragons possess awesome momentum in the air, but relatively little dexterity due to their size and weight. However, your dragon partner can now literally turn on a wingtip, cutting the air like a swallow. While using Split Turn, your dragon burns Mana at 5 points per second to speed her flight and allow her to change the course of her forward momentum with supernatural dexterity. She can fly around sharply angled corners, u-turn while in the air, and perform a vertical 'figure eight' turn to completely change direction.

Both of your dragon's wings must be undamaged to use Split Turn. To safely ride your dragon during Split Turn maneuvers, you must have a Dragon Riding skill of 5 or higher. If your skill level is lower than this, you risk having an accident, falling off your mount (if unsecured), or sustaining injury (if secured). If your dragon exerts more g-force on you than your body can handle, you will suffer damage, penalties, and debuffs appropriate to the level of force.

"Looking good," I said. "So, my plan for training is to take some small, short flights, and work up to longer ones. We have to increase your strength and stamina before we get too ambitious. Sound okay with you?"

"Yep." Karalti had ceased moving, and lay in the weak sun like a gleaming sculpture of black opal, her eyes closed. "I need to meditate for a while on this though... It's a lot of changes."

"Think you'll be ready for tonight?" I began to bore hole number five.

"*Uh-huh.*"

"Good." I sighed, setting the drill against the mark for the last hole. "Because I'm a hundred and twenty percent certain that tonight is going to suck."

CHAPTER 27

Despite its everyday realism – the sights, smells, and sensations of an early industrial-era city, with magic and monsters – there were things in Archemi that reminded me that it was a game. The crafting, especially. Watching Mix fit and craft the saddle was like watching God create something à la Genesis, with parts precisely cut and hammered together at a pace that was impossible IRL. All the leather shapes fit together like a puzzle. I knew there was no earthly way an item of this complexity was able to be created in five hours or less... but somehow, it worked. And the NPCs thought nothing of it.

"This turned out well," Mix said to me, as he buckled the finished breastplate across Karalti's keel and patted it fondly. "You really want no other restraining straps than these ones on the stirrups?"

"Nope," I said. "That's why I made twenty health potions while you were busy. The whole point is to learn without training wheels."

Karalti bobbed her head and made little gurking noises of excitement as she flexed one wing, then the other. Eighty gold had bought us a sleek, long saddle that was sculpted so that I could lie down, stand, crouch, or ride astride. There were grips to the front and back, points for lashing gear, and iron footrests to either side of Karalti's ribs that allowed me to buckle my feet in and take a jockey position on her back. The short swallowtail end was held flat by the heavy brass dorsal rings that kept the saddle under tension. Our ten-slot saddlebags sat forward of the rings, but behind the shallow cantle – the scooped back of the saddle.

"You're crazy, *san'harik*," Mix remarked, locking the last strap in place. "But I am satisfied with this saddle's design. When she grows and you need another, let me know."

About twenty minutes later, with barely half an hour to spare before we needed to be at Kobayaz, I knelt on Karalti's back on the edge of the tallest building in the Tanners' District. It was a massive granary and warehouse complex that backed against the city walls, at least fifteen stories tall

"I always joked around that if my parents made me go to prom, I'd have jumped off something tall to avoid putting on a tuxedo." My voice echoed behind the concealing half-mask of my helmet. I could barely hear myself. "Maybe we can just fly back to Vulkan Keep and rejoin the questline tomorrow or something?"

"I don't think that's how that works," Karalti replied.

"Probably not." The wind howled over us up here, chilling my skin even through layers of armor and clothing. My hands sweated on the saddle grips, and I was trembling with about six parts excitement, one part cold, and three parts sheer, gut-wrenching terror.

I'd flown dragonback before, but that had been a very different experience than what we were about to do. For one thing, Talenth - the ex-Knight Commander's dragon - had been about a hundred feet long, with a back big enough to carry six people. Karalti's back was about as long as I was tall. For another, Talenth's saddle had tie-down straps, plus an experienced rider guiding him. Karalti's did not, because neither of us really knew what we were doing. Getting on my dragon in the middle of a fight and gliding twenty feet to the ground in broad daylight had been one thing. Straddling her back the way I would a racing bike, on the edge of a granary a hundred and fifty feet off the ground was quite another.

"Now... Let me think..." I said aloud. "Head down, ass up when you're diving. I think that's right."

"*Uhh... I guess?*" Karalti shifted restlessly from side to side. "Who told you that?"

"*This airforce pilot I knew. But he might have just been hitting on me.*"

Karalti giggled. "*Okay... you still wanna go?*"

"*Yeah. Let me do one last thing.*" I drew a deep breath, focusing on the Mark of Matir, and invoked Blessing of the Raven. The energy of the Dark God hit me like a shot of caffeine to the brainstem. When I opened my eyes, the bonus skill EXP buff icon floated at the corner of my eye.

"*Okay.*" I stared out over the city and narrowed my eyes. "*My body is ready.*"

The dragon bunched like a sprinter beneath my thighs. Even at her Level 5 size, I could feel awesome, fiery power surge through her body. She relaxed her wings out to the sides, letting them catch in the breeze. As she did, I felt her second heart speed up and fall into sync with the first. Dragons had two hearts, and while I didn't yet know much about the biomechanics of why, I suspected that one of them was basically just for flying.

My chest and ears thumped in time with the rhythm. I buckled my feet in, backed my ass up, put my face against the base of Karalti's neck, and drew a deep breath. Anticipation built into an eye-of-the-storm sensation, the feeling of being so excited, so wound up, that your mind was empty and calm.

"Hold on! And don't fall off!" Karalti wiggled to test her traction, and before I had time to reply, kicked out from the battlement and threw herself into the open sky.

Anyone who has ever felt really good torque knows that roller-coaster thrill: your teeth step back in your head, your skull pounds, your guts feel like they got left a mile behind you on the road. You can't do anything but cry out with shock. It's arousing. It's addictive and unsettling and terrifying. It's a high so intense that you will always be chasing it, no matter what happens.

"HOLY SHIIIIIT!"

We fell about twenty feet before Karalti gained lift. I howled with wild laughter as my stomach lifted up behind my eyes, then fell out through my asshole. Her wings pumped to either side of my knees, and all the blood in my body rushed down into my legs as she began to climb. When she levelled out, I slid back into the shallow scalloped seat of the saddle, and for a moment, I regretted telling Mix that I didn't want restraining straps. Then she dropped a wingtip and rolled gently to one side, and my lizard brain screamed at me that this was It. I was dead, I was going to fly off and burst like a ripe tomato when I hit the ground.

Karalti sensed my sudden terror. She straightened up so quickly that she nearly pitched me off. *"Hector! Are you okay!?* What's the matter?"

Time had slowed, and for several seconds, I couldn't reply. My eyes were watering from the ferocious wind as I stared out over the city. It was beautiful. Taltos glowed orange and charcoal from up here, bathed by the light of the setting sun. *"I'm fine. Fly properly, just like how you would without a rider. Just try not to do anything too crazy."*

"Okay. Lean with me... I felt you pushing back against the turn before." She rolled to the left again, circling in and beating her wings to climb back up. My heart skipped a beat as the torque shifted back,

then forward again. The muscles of Karalti's back surged under my hands and against my knees, and every time she lifted and dropped, I felt like I was going to fly off into the wind.

My entire body thrummed with tension, hands white-knuckled and shaking against the grips. "*This is fucking incredible! Oh my god! Why did I let myself get this far away from the ground?!*"

"*We're not that high, silly Hector.*" Karalti's voice was thick with mirth, but warm as well. "*You having fun?*"

"*This is the second-most awkward hard-on I've ever had!*" I was yelling telepathically for some reason.

Karalti bellowed joyously, and before I had time to adjust my position, she rolled sharply to the left and veered into a strong, cold stream of wind. Her wings filled with air, and suddenly, we jolted upwards, higher and higher. My stomach pulled down, and I barked a cry of excitement that turned to manic, wild, howling laughter. When she topped out and beat her wings to join the swiftly moving coldstream, she picked up speed. Tears were pulled back along my cheeks, my heart raced, my fingers pounded in time with my pulse. I was terrified, moved, and exhilarated all at the same time.

It was the best I had ever felt in my entire life.

"*This is amazing!*" I shouted, as we thundered over the city wall, heading for the country estate marked on our minimap.

Karalti's ribs flexed like a bellows as she settled into a glide. She was panting, neck straight, her horns held tightly to her skull. I tried to minimize my drag the way that I would on the back of a motorcycle, flattening down. We passed carriages and hookwings the size of Matchbox cars on the ground, winged over a crossroads inn and a small cluster of summer homes, and continued toward the Kobayaz Estate. Notifications began to trickle in.

[[You have reached Dragon Riding 2!]]

[[Karalti has learned Laden Flight 1!]]

[[You and Karalti are a good match! You earn +10% skill EXP for Riding: Dragon and Laden Flight thanks to skill synergy!]]

[[Would you like to learn about Skill Synergy?]]

"Not right now!" There was already a lot to get used to beyond the act of holding onto my dragon's back. The game's interface had adapted to being in flight. An Augmented Reality display had appeared, overlaying the terrain of the air and sky and helping to keep me oriented on the horizon. This gyroscopic jet fighter-style vision was not something I'd had before the Trial of Marantha. When I scanned the patchwork of fields below, the AR highlighted landmarks of interest – places where we could do sidequests, landing zones, even a couple of random monsters prowling a ruined hut. I could zoom in with my vision, too – to about 200% magnification, which I figured was also something I'd gained from my dragonrider mutations.

My stomach plummeted as Karalti suddenly jolted and lost altitude. When she dropped again, I looked to make sure nothing had happened to her wings. They were fine, but her wingbeats were off-rhythm. I banished the HUD and refocused on her. "You alright?"

"*This is hard!*" Her breathing was becoming more labored, the muscles of her back and shoulders shuddering with effort. "We gotta practice more!"

"*Time to land, Tidbit,*" I said. "*We can walk the rest of the way.*"

"*No, I can make it!*" She rallied out of sheer stubborn pride, pumping her wings to stay in the air stream, and then angled her head toward the manor yard. Kobayaz was at the back of an orchard, with a cluster of buildings surrounding a central court. There was a crescent-shaped carriage yard out front, currently filled with an array of vehicles.

"*You've hit your limit, girl. If you run out of stamina, we'll fall out of the air.*"

"*I know how much stamina I have!*" she replied hotly. "*I'm starting the descent. Get your head down!*"

I bit my lip and held on as she angled into a shallow dive and swooped down toward the carriage yard.

As she deepened, I really began to feel those Gs – the blood rushed to my head and left me dizzy. I tucked down and stuck my butt up, trying to look past Karalti's shoulder. What I saw made my heart skip. People were running out of the house and cluttering up our landing zone. They pointed and waved at us, jumping up and down.

Dragon riding lesson number one: people are fucking stupid.

"Get out of the way!" I growled, hanging onto the saddle grips for dear life.

Karalti snarled with frustration as she came in low, and I knew she was still going too fast. My eardrums popped, and I flinched just before she swung her back legs and tail forward, back-winging, flapping madly to halt her momentum. Her mana gauge burned down as she hit her new Split Turn ability, and that was all that stopped us from careening to the dirt in a cartwheel of broken wings and necks. Squawking like a hatchling, she tripped and skidded forward onto her keel as screaming guests threw themselves out of the way.

The landing was harder than I expected, and I'd been expecting a hard landing. It sent me sprawling forward, but because my feet were locked into the stirrups, I didn't go flying. Instead, I pitched over Karalti's shoulder, jarred my legs, and banged my face down against her armored scales. My nose burst like a grape on impact as we slid to a stop in a spray of dirt.

"Holy shit. Holy fucking shit." I groaned, struggling back into a seated position. Every one of my limbs was like jelly. "Shit. Shit, Karalti. Are you okay?!"

"I'm alive!" she squeaked. She pushed herself up with her forearms and wing claws and hopped forward a few steps, shuddering with *exertion "Only lost a little HP. Are you okay? I smell blood!"*

'A little HP' was about twenty points for her, and fifteen for me. I got a couple of Mint Potions out, and patted her neck to get her to turn her head around so I could feed them to her. As she chugged them, people began to gather around us, open-mouthed and babbling with excitement.

I pumped a fist, stashing the empty potion bottles in my Inventory, and then set about unstrapping myself from the unfamiliar saddle. "Good job, Tidbit!"

Karalti whipped her head from side to side, her throat clicking, tongue hanging out. Shaking, I slid off her back, hanging onto the saddle to drop onto the ground. I was so wobbly that I stumbled a couple of steps to the side.

A young woman in a canary-yellow and white dress closed in at the front of the admiring crowd. Her eyes were as big as saucers. "You're the hero working for the Volod! Can I touch the dragon?"

I glared down at her, blood pouring out of my face, and uncorked another potion. "Do you just touch random people on the street, lady? No, you can't." I drank this potion down myself and tossed the bottle into my Inventory as well.

"Get out the bloody way!" I heard a familiar voice call out. Suri. She was shoo-ing people left and right, clearing the twittering crowd ahead of herself.

"Did I do okay?" Karalti nuzzled at me urgently as I dropped down, licking my chest and shoulders.

"You did great on all counts. We just flew ten miles in ten minutes. That training's paying off." I reached up to rub her jaws and throat with one hand, and set my nose back in place with the other. I was so high I barely felt it.

"Yeah!" Karalti ducked her head down and dropped her wings, cheeping like an overgrown chick. I smiled, looking up as Suri reached the front of the pack. At the sight of her, my petting hand slowed, and my eyes widened.

When Suri had told me she was going dress shopping, I figured she was joking. You know – 'dress shopping', as in, shopping for armor. But no. Suri sashayed toward us in a sheer ankle-length gown that hugged her every curve. It was sleeveless, with thin straps and a very deep neckline, so deep I wasn't entirely sure how it was staying on. The fabric looked like a swirl of monarch butterfly wings had been sewn together around her body. She was wearing gold rings in her ears, nose, and lip. Her axes were on her belt, and her huge sword and scabbard were slung over one shoulder, an odd counterpoint to the dress and jewelry.

"Nice landing. I like the blood." She came to a stop in front of us and struck a pose: hands on hips, chest out. The dress slid over one of her legs, baring it up to mid-thigh. "What'dya think, soldier? Look alright?"

My first thought – beyond *"Holy shit, she's gorgeous what the fuck do I say"* – was the sudden terror that Archemi might have a 'Hide Your Awkward Boner' minigame. Karalti's body stiffened behind me.

"I, um, uh, wellll..." I tried to subtly adjust myself without using my hands. "Is it just me, or is this new armor of mine really hot all of a sudden? Hoooo. Ahhhh. Excuse me for a moment."

I turned, marched on the spot until the pain stopped, then turned back. "There we go. Better."

"*What are you doing?*" Karalti demanded. "*We were talking!*"

Suri arched a scarlet eyebrow, and glanced down at my crotch. "I guess that answers my question."

"Hang on a second." I patted Karalti on the neck, and pointed up at my face. "Excuse me, ma'am. My eyes are up here?"

Suri smirked. "Could have fooled me, given how much time they've spent resting at tit-level over the last couple days."

Okay, that one actually got me to blush. I glared back at her and gestured at her chest. "It's just that I can't help but wonder how you don't float away into the sky like a hot air balloon."

Suri let her lips part and wet them, leaning forward in a way that made it very difficult to continue looking at her face. "Probably for the same reason you don't bust the cup off your armor every time you think you're gonna see a nipple."

"*Stop it!*" Karalti lunged past me at her, snapping and slavering.

I was not expecting to be suddenly shoved from behind. Her elbow hit me in the shoulder and sent me face-first into the gravel. "The fuck, Karalti!"

"Mine!" Karalti snarled at Suri as she backed away. Drops of white napalm splattered on the stones and in the garden bed, where they sizzled. "*Get away from him!*"

Suri held her hands up. "Whoa there, Sunshine."

"Karalti! Cool it!" I scrambled up to my feet, confused and shaken. "What's gotten into you?"

"*Stupid party! Stupid Suri!*" Karalti's eyes blazed with hot, humiliated anger. She snapped at me, narrowly missing my face. "*Stupid YOU!*"

"What?" I tried to go to her, but she irritably flicked me back with a wing. "Come on, Tidbit, we just-"

"Don't you 'Tidbit' me! I didn't put this saddle on so you could... so you..." Karalti couldn't finish whatever she was trying to say, and spun around with her nose in the air. Scattering people with her tail, she stalked off down the driveway, roaring at a pair of hookwings who tried to bob their heads at her. The dinosaurs screeched and backed into a carriage, nearly knocking it over.

"I... what?" I stared after her in bewilderment.

"Your little dragon's in love with you, Hector," Suri said, suddenly close beside me. "You hadn't figured that out?"

"In love with me?" I reached up to untie my hood from my helmet and pushed it back. "I know she's attached to me at the hip, but... She's a completely different species. Not to mention, she's basically my kid, and that is all kinds of weird."

"Yeah, but she's not your kid, is she? She's a moody teenager the size of an elephant." Suri clapped me on the arm as I blinked. "C'mon. This is just one of those things she's going to have to work through."

"But... What if she doesn't come back?" I felt – and sounded – as young as Karalti actually was.

"She will. She's gonna go write in her diary about how much she hates you, sing some pop songs, and then she'll be back and trying to crawl up your arse again." Suri gently took me by the elbow. "Come on, Casanova. We've got your nose to mop up and our primaries to protect. They're waiting for us."

CHAPTER 28

I let Suri guide me up the stairs to the gate leading to the manor courtyard. Nobles, courtiers, the king's advisors and spies and religious allies mingled among disguised soldiers. The butler and servants dashed around the garden looked stressed - everyone looked kind of stressed, actually – but the real guests had turned up in gowns and porcelain heels, fur-trimmed coats and wigs and foppish hats. They were drinking wine and nibbling on nuts and fruit while uniformed guardsmen lounged boredly at the fringes. The other half of the crowd were also richly dressed, but in ways that could readily conceal weapons. These guests were also polite, but wary, alert, and not drinking anything.

The elegant entryway into the manor itself was manned by guards and a pair of Knights of the Red Star who were frisking everyone who went inside.

"Kingsman." One of the tattooed knights – a woman – stepped forward to greet us. "You're allowed to bring your arms and armor in, but I must inspect you for magical contagion. Curses, hexes, suchlike."

"Sure." I held my arms out.

"Do I need to go through processing again?" Suri asked.

"No, my lady." The knight took a thick golden wand off her belt, and ran it up and down my body like a metal detector. It crackled with energy, and glowed blue when it passed over my backpack.

"Please let me look at your magical items," she asked.

I gave her a thin smile, and began pulling things out. Some of them, like the alchemy potions, easily fit in a real bag. Others, like the seven-foot-long Spear of Nine Spheres, appeared in my hands like a magic trick. When she passed the device over it, the golden rod turned white. The knight raised her eyebrows, but seemed unconcerned. Maybe the Spear wasn't cursed after all.

"Alright. Thank you." She nodded to us, and then looked past me to the next approaching guest.

"Damn," I said once we were inside. "Never seen one of those devices before."

"We call those Samarthi'diva in Dakhdir," she said. "They measure magical force in sigils or items. A mage can enspell it to look for particular types of magic. That cruddy old spear of yours must be something special to glow like that."

"It will be, assuming I can get it fixed."

We passed another doorman inside the Grand Hall, and turned down a gold and white marble corridor, following a babbling hum of noise. Suri walked ahead of me, and I couldn't help but stare at the way the dress slid and shimmered over her ass and legs. It was hypnotic, but checking her out was a guilty pleasure. When I tried to reach out telepathically to Karalti, all I heard was a furious whine.

We broke out into an enclosed garden. It was painfully noisy. Musicians played fiddles and drums, jugglers twirled stacks of plates on sticks, dancers spun ribbons of silk, and people crowded together in laughter and chatter. Other than the guards stationed around the walls, I was the only person in armor.

Dammit. I should have worn something nicer. My parents had drummed it into me that good Korean boys were always well-dressed. Because of this, I'd stuck to grunge fashion on principle, but I currently felt like That Guy who'd turned up to prom with his shirt untucked and no tie.

"So, what are your thoughts on tonight's shenanigans?" I asked Suri. We didn't pause at any of the food or drink stations, heading instead for the back of the garden. "Ready for a fight?"

"Always. And I think this place is a bloody powder keg waiting for a match," she replied. "But they've taken precautions, I'll give 'em that. About one in every ten guests here is a soldier from the Vulkan Garrison. There's a couple of mages, too. Toth has a Sage with him."

"Father Matthias. He's a good man."

"Hopefully he's a good bodyguard," she replied tersely. "Anyway, you and me have been assigned to the noble targets because His Majesty thinks that we're more likely to take a bullet for our primaries. You've got the Duke. Unsurprisingly, I have Andrik."

"Matthias told me about that. How do you feel?"

"How do you think?" Suri replied quietly. "I dressed to look nice, sure, but the little weasel's been eyeing me like a fresh rack of lamb. There's different types of ogling, and some of them I'm okay with, and some of them I'm not."

I swallowed the impulse to ask if whether or not my kind of ogling was okay. This wasn't about me. "Want me to tell him to get fucked?"

Suri made a sound of disgust. "He's a blue-blooded royal cunt. He'll have you staked if either of us say 'boo' to him. If that wasn't the case, I'd do it myself... though backup is always appreciated."

I looked around, but couldn't spot Andrik. "Aye aye, comrade."

Suri's stride faltered, and her back stiffened. She turned on me, and I nearly ran into her chest. "What did you just call me?"

I blinked. "I... uhh... was being a smartass?"

The corner of Suri's eye twitched as she tried to hold my gaze, but after a couple of seconds, it faltered. She looked... shaken?

"Don't ever call me that again," she said, her voice barely loud enough to be heard. "Not even as a joke. I know you didn't mean anything by it... but... please."

I leaned away from her. "Uhh... okay? No worries. I thought that was standard address in the Pacific Alliance?"

It was her turn to look puzzled, and then I remembered: she didn't know. She had some kind of VR amnesia.

"It's... You're only the third person to ever talk about this shit to me," Suri reached out and grabbed my shoulder. Hard. "Australia. The Pacific Alliance. This 'Total War'. Sometimes, I admit it... I get flashes, hunches about something just out of my reach. But mostly what I remember is what was done to me by the other Starborn I knew. They used to sling that word around while they were torturing me."

My skin prickled with a rush of fear – and anger. I dropped my voice to a hiss. "What? Players were torturing you? Inside Archemi? Did they have blue halos like mine, or gold, like Rin's?"

Suri looked down. I saw her throat work, and then she let go of me. She turned her head away, then reached up to push a lock of hair back behind her ear. Her fingers were trembling.

"Oh hell, I'm sorry," I said. "I was just asking because... Well, this has some major implications for like, the entire world and the Devs... uh... the Architects. It's hard to explain–"

"Don't. Please." Suri shook her head with small, rapid shakes. She was no longer able to meet my eyes. "Look – I know that there's something beyond this world, alright? I know you and Rin and those 'Architects' know something I don't about Archemi. And I don't want to know what it is, okay? Some things should just be left alone."

"I'm sorry," I repeated. I wasn't sure what else to say. The only explanation I could think of for how Suri was even here was genuinely awful. I was about to try to comfort her when the crowd parted, and Kirov came striding toward us.

"Hector!" He boomed, throwing his arms up. He was dressed in his armor and helm, the bronze disks and red lacquer mirror-polished. "A pleasure to see you again! Ahh, and I see you have worn your best clothes for the night's festivities! But rytier, you appear to have some blood on your face."

"Figured I'd warm up before the Slayer got here." I shook his hand and clapped his arm, glancing back at Suri.

"My goodness, Lady! You look incredible!" Kirov turned to her next. "May I plant a kiss upon your hand and pay my respects?"

"No, thanks. Not right now. I better get back to Andrik," she said, backing away from us. "Excuse me."

I rubbed the aching bridge of my nose. Nice one, Hector. You've managed to screw both the women in your life in the space of thirty minutes, and not in the sloppy, happy way.

"Oh, well. Still, that reminds me! Have you met the Voivode yet?" Kirov was apparently oblivious to Suri's misery as he pivoted back to me.

"No sir, I have not," I sighed.

"Then come! I, Ur Kirov, shall introduce you to the luminaries of Taltos!" Kirov was flushed in the cheeks and nose, and clearly had a bit to drink. Before I could ask him 'can we not?', he had looped his arm through mine and dragged me off into the snake pit.

Kirov pulled me along the floor like an overeager dog straining at his leash, coming to a stop in front of a trio of people dressed in long, thick robes trimmed with gold, silver, and fur. The woman had a pinched, button face and wrinkles around her lips; the older man was balding and beaky, and the other had the scowling, blocky features and paunchy belly of an old soldier gone to seed.

"Your Grace, may I present you with the man who faced the Slayer in single combat and nearly brought him to bay!" Kirov burst into their conversation like a wrecking ball, throwing a heavy arm around my shoulders. "Dragozin Hector, this is the Voivode of Czongrad and his lovely wife, and this is Lord Rasiv Braska, master of the Royal Treasury."

"Uh... pleased to meet you." I was already searching the room frantically for some way to get out of this.

"A pleasure," the Voivode replied. He had a droll voice and piercing gray-green eyes. The hand he offered me was soft and limp, but dry as crisp new dollar bills. "Nearly brought him to bay, you say? What prevented you from doing so?"

"It started out as single combat, but it didn't stay that way." I spotted my salvation across the room: an interesting-looking NPC who had a vendor marker and a HUD highlight. He was an unusually tall, patrician Lysidian man with short, neat, silver hair, and he was standing beside a display table laid out with items of jewelry and weapons.

"You're the Starborn who is shepherding us tonight? Aren't you the barbarian man with the dragon?" The Voivoda of Czongrad asked me. She had a shrill voice to much her lemon-pucker mouth.

"Yes ma'am, that's me." I pointed over at the table. "Speaking of security detail, I should really go and see what that guy's selling. He might have items that could, uh, even the odds a bit in case the Slayer shows up and brings some friends again." I faked a smile and backed up. "Excuse me."

The Voivode looked like he wanted to argue with me, but before he had a chance, I extracted myself out from under Kirov's arm and fled.

This was literally the worst kind of party I could think of. I didn't hate all parties – I liked the kind where I knew everyone in the house, and we sat around with booze and video games and anime and had a good time. But this fancy-pants formal crap? This shit was a special level of Hell.

I held up a hand to a waiter who tried to offer me wine - I didn't drink on the job - and fled to the vendor. As I got closer, I was able to see the sign at his table, and felt my spirits lift. He sold stat and ability-boosting accessories, not something I'd seen around the city.

"Good evening, sir," he said to me when I was close enough. "And what a sight for sore eyes. I've been looking for you and those like you since I arrived to trade in Taltos."

"I bet you have," I replied. "Adventurers, or Starborn?"

He winked at me. "Both. Now, what can I help you with?"

"Can I see a list of items and their bonuses and prices?"

"Of course." The vendor held up a long hand, and my HUD came to life, displaying a virtual shop window. It was similar to all the other stores I'd used: a grid display of items. If you hovered over one by thinking about its item name, you got its stats.

This guy had two categories of items: equippables and consumables. I looked over the equipment first, and several of them caught my eye.

Brawler's Wristband

19 Armor

5% Evade

-3% Magic Defense

+5 Attack Power

+2 Str and Con

250 gold olbia

Can be upgraded.

Simple wristbands studded with enchanted green crystal.

Black Belt

+20% HP

+5 Str

200 gold olbia

Cannot be upgraded.

A black cloth belt from Tuungant worn by the monks of Burna. It fortifies health.

Witch's Bracelet

+10% magic defense

+2% magic power

350 gold olbia

Can be upgraded.

A finely made silver bracelet with crushed bluestone crystal worked into the metal.

Besides these three, he had elemental resistance rings, a necklace that increased attack speed, and earrings that boosted defense. I really wanted the Brawler's Wristband and Black Belt for me and the Bracelet for Karalti - but damn, they were expensive. Trying not to openly wince, I navigated to the vendor's consumables, and found an array of mana crystals that could be worked into weapons to give them different elemental effects. These were not as expensive as the accessories, but still pricey. The cheapest, the Cinderstone, still cost 50 gold pieces.

"How do you attach these mana crystals to weapons?" I asked.

"Ah. Well, you can't attach these stones to most common weapons. Once you are Level 20 or so, the world of magical weapons begins to open up to you," the vendor replied. He looked a little crestfallen that I hadn't immediately jumped on anything.

I considered that for a moment, then unequipped the Alpha Rod and swapped it back for the Spear of Nine Spheres. "Like this weapon?"

The man was visibly startled at the sight of the Spear. His eyes widened as he looked over the battered weapon. The Spear of Nine Spheres wasn't terribly impressive - but it obviously meant something to him.

"Aesari design..." he murmured. "Do you know how much this is worth?"

"No?" I'd floated the Spear at the Weapon Shop just to see how much they'd have paid for it, and it had been no more than 10 silver rubles.

"An artifact like this is worth a fortune," he whispered back. "To the right buyer. Say... two thousand olbia?"

Two thousand gold was enough to buy us better equipment. A lot of it. I thought back to the message I'd received this morning about Baldr somehow taking over Ilia, and swallowed. Karalti's saddle had maxed us out. We had 3 copper litz left to our names. But even as I thought about it, the Mark of Matir twitched.

"It's not for sale," I replied weakly. "But I'll remember your offer. Sorry to say, I can't afford anything right now-"

"Then it is just as well that someone is interested in sponsoring your quest to bring down the Slayer of Taltos, isn't it?"

A woman I hadn't heard - or seen - padded up beside me, light on her feet. She was rail-thin, dressed head to toe in scarlet. Red slippers and gloves, red breeches, a form-fitting doeskin tunic cut to her razor curves, and a red capelet and hood that was drawn up around her face. The reds varied between a dark burgundy and a brilliant scarlet. She was very small-breasted, practically flat. Her arms were slender enough that I could have put my hand all the way around her bicep, but her legs were corded with hard muscle. She showed no skin at all, including her face. She wore a full-face white ceramic mask with angelically beautiful, realistically sculpted features. The mask crawled with small red sparks, like embers.

Uh-oh. One of the unspoken rules of RPGs was that anyone who dressed in only one color was bad news. "And you are...?"

"A potential patron." Her voice was soft and raspy. "Call me Red."

CHAPTER 29

The vendor looked between me and Red, blinking in obvious confusion.

I flashed her a toothy smile. "I already have a patron, thanks. The Volod."

Red's mask had human features: serene, feminine, and mysterious, the eye holes shrouded with black silk. There was no way to tell who – or what – she was. "I'm well aware. Would you walk with me?"

"No," I replied. "No offense, but I avoid keeping single company with obvious assassiny-types."

Red dipped her head in acknowledgement and reached behind her back. I tensed, but she came up with a pouch, not a blade. She flourished with her fingers like a magician, rolling the small clinking bag on her palm, and opened it to pull out... a rose. With a long stem, AND thorns.

"Some say there's no difference between mummers and assassins, but what is entertainment without the scent of danger?" she rasped, extending the flower to me. "For your lady."

"Uhh... thanks?" I took it gingerly, but didn't sniff it. There were more drugs than cocaine that could get into your body through your nose.

"You're welcome," Red replied. "Now, perhaps a minute of your time?"

My monkey brain screamed two words in regards to this woman: 'hell' and 'no'. But rational, non-monkey Hector could see the advantage of gathering intel. "Sure. But we stay here, inside the manor."

"Of course." Red bowed gracefully to the accessories guy, and paced off ahead of me, lithe as a gymnast.

"What do you want?" I asked her, once we were out of earshot of anyone in particular. "Because you're clearly an uninvited guest, and half the Knights of the Red Star are here tonight. All I have to do is say the word, and your ass is grass."

"An interesting expression," Red replied. "As for what I want? Hmm. Averting the genocide of the Meewfolk of Vlachia would be nice. I should also like to get revenge on my father for all he did to me, remove the usurper of Vlachia's throne, and have my nails done - in no particular order. I come to you about only two of those things."

Damn. This lady had big brass ones. "I'm guessing it's not to talk about your daddy issues and get a manicure."

"No."

"Good, because I suck at nail polish. I always get it all over my cuticles."

"I overheard the Volod discussing the eradication of the Meewfolk tonight, while your lovely Dakhari friend was freshening up in the ladies' room," Red remarked, pushing open the door that led into the garden. "He was working out the specifics with Lazrov Urgas, the Captain of the Vulkan Garrison. Our sovereign will be going ahead with that order if tonight's charade does not provide him with a scapegoat. I don't suppose you knew that."

"Well, *I* overheard him talking about how he wants to watch Suri peg me on the back of my dragon while he jacks off with a pair of salad tongs," I replied. "See? I can make up straight-faced bullshit as well."

"Unlike your sexual fantasies, what I just told you will soon come to pass." Red almost sounded amused. "I would urge you to carefully eavesdrop tonight and make up your own mind."

I frowned. "You sound pretty sure about this."

"I am. Non-humans are already being turned back at the border," Red continued in her whisky-and-smoke voice. "Mercurions have started to vanish from the Tanners' District. Rumor is they're being interrogated and killed. The International District - Cat Alley - is in bad straits. Children are being removed from their parents there. I want you to consider if what will soon happen there is worth having on your conscience."

"And what's the alternative?"

"Accept a down payment, enough to buy one of the baubles you were lusting for. Leave tonight, retire to a fine inn with your friend and your dragon, sleep easily until morning, and live happily in the knowledge that you chose the lesser evil."

"And wake up to a bloody social purge and riots in the streets?" I snorted, looking up at the eaves of the manor roof. Karalti might have been up there, her scales bending the starlight and rendering her invisible in the shadows. "How about 'no'?"

"Are you sure? Because-"

"Apparently 'no' wasn't strong enough. So let's try 'go fuck yourself'." I jerked to a stop, ready to call my spear to hand. The garden was less crowded than it had been earlier. Strangers were glancing at us, probably mistaking our hushed, tense conversation for a lover's spat. "There's no such thing as the 'lesser evil' when you're talking about treason and social unrest, and Suri is going to tell you the exact same thing. I don't know who you are, but the only thing that's going to stop this insanity is Kanzo's head."

Red flinched slightly at the name. It had surprised her?

"As you say," she replied stiffly, hopping onto a marble bench. "Then you had best attend the auction, hadn't you?"

"After I hand your ass over to the Volod." I hadn't finished speaking before I lunged forward, my spear appearing in my hands.

Red jumped backwards into the air - springing up ten feet or more - and landed silently in the branches of the oak in the center of the courtyard. She jumped easily, almost lazily, and tilted her head before vanishing completely. There was a rustle of leaves... then nothing.

"Shit!" I swore loudly, turning heads. Two guards had advanced a couple of steps from their posts, looking around in surprise. The few drunken guests who had noticed the argument were doing that dumb cow stare that groups of people did when they were confused. I looked around, but whatever Red had used to vanish masked her completely. No sound, no smell, no trace of her presence. She had quite possibly teleported.

"You motherfucking, goat-sucking...!" I slung my spear back over my shoulder and stormed off back into the main building, picking up into a jog. I nearly slammed into a waiter carrying a tray of empties. The sound of breaking crystal followed me as I stormed forward into the glittering cocktail throng, searching desperately for Kirov, Andrik, or Suri.

"Suri - where the hell are you?" I messaged her.

I got my answer as I squeezed between an irate dowager and her pimply teenage boy-toy. The doors to the main auction hall were open, though they were still roped off. Beyond the ropes were round tables with place settings. Standing right in front of the ropes, about to be admitted in, were Andrik and Suri. As I pushed toward them, they and a few other select guests went inside. Behind me, a bell tinkled, silencing the room.

"Ladies and gentlemen!" the doorman called. "Please form a line at the door and prepare to take your seats! Your invitation contains your seat number, which we will collect at the door..."

I spotted Kirov hanging back, talking with his buddy Ur Pavel, the thin, buggy-eyed knight from the morgue. Their heads jerked up as I balled up on them.

"Guys, there's a problem," I said, trying to keep my voice down. "I think something's about to go down at the auction."

"What? Why?" The smile wiped from Kirov's face. Same with Pavel.

"Some woman just tried to buy me off and get me to leave," I said. "She called herself 'Red'."

"Who does she claim to represent?" Pavel asked.

"She didn't tell me. But she had a serious assassin or spy vibe." I gestured urgently to the guests pouring into the auction hall. "This is nuts. We have to call this off."

Kirov shook his head stubbornly. "No, we cannot. The Volod hoped to lure out the Slayer's comrades, and that is what is happening."

I leaned toward him. "Kirov, listen to me. They're going to try to kill Andrik."

The Knight's dark eyes glinted with concern. "Of course they are. We have mages and snipers on the rooftops, guards on the grounds, and every tenth guest here is either a knight of my order, or one of our soldiers. His Majesty has armor on under his clothing, and his cloak offers good protection against magic, poison, and other effects. Believe me, *rytier*... We were expecting this."

"There're tables everywhere," I fretted. "And glass. Even if one in every ten is a soldier, that still means ninety percent of people in that room are civilians."

"Fear not. We are the King's swords and shields," Pavel said. He clapped me on the back. "Now go. You and the Voivode are at a table near the door. We have not seated all the important guests together."

Nearly everyone was inside now, and Suri had still not replied to my P.M. I sighed, resisted the urge to spit in annoyed disgust, and tromped in after them. I'd played enough games to know a set-up when I saw one.

The auction hall was the old ballroom of the manor, set out with rows of round wooden tables. Tiered plates tottered with little open-faced sandwiches, baklava, Turkish delight, macarons and cream puffs. I was at the Voivode's table. I sat to his left, and the Captain of the Vulkan Keep garrison sat to his right.

"Why did they put us all the way back here?" The Voivode muttered, arms folded against his chest. "This is a disgrace."

"For your safety, my lord," the captain replied for the hundredth time. He also had his arms crossed, but unlike the noble couple, he was watching the room like a hawk.

"It means you're closer to the door in the event of an emergency. The King and His High Forginess are near exits, too," I added. I'd made a sweep of the crowd myself, but was now watching Suri at the back of the room. She was seated next to Andrik at a table near another entry to the ballroom. Thanks to the Trial of Marantha, I could see everything going on there. Their expressions, where Andrik was putting his hands - or almost putting his hands - and I could even read their lips.

"It remains a serious breach of protocol. You do not seat your vassals at the back of the room," the Voivode said, with a sniff.

I chewed morosely on a pistachio macaron. It was good, a cookie with the perfect combination of chewy, crunchy, and creamy. I sighed with relief when the Auctioneer emerged from behind a curtain, and the room – and the Voivode – fell silent.

"*Holgyem et Arain.* Ladies and Gentlemen, thank you for attending Kobayaz Estate tonight," he said, in a high, reedy voice. He was sharply dressed but round as a plum. "I am your host, Ephraim Terer, and I shall explain how tonight's event will proceed..."

He began reading out the rules for the auction - signs only, no shouting, all proceeds go to the widows and orphans left behind by the murders. While no one was looking, I shoveled the entire plate of macarons into my Inventory, gaining ⟦Assorted Macarons x 10⟧. They'd be perfect for mopey binge-eating later in the night.

"And now, High Forgemaster Agoston Toth would like to say a few words." The Auctioneer stepped aside as Toth took his place in front of the podium.

"*Holgyem et Arain.* I would like to thank you all for your interest and generosity toward us, the Church of Khors the Maker, and the faithful and good people of Vlachia," he rumbled, raising his voice to be heard over the room. The burly lion of a priest was in the same ceremonial robes he'd been wearing when we'd met him at the church. "We have lost a number of our finest brethren to the Slayer of Taltos - doctors, smiths, teachers, the founder of our largest orphanage, and so tonight the Volod himself, His Majesty Andrik Corvinus the Third, has put forth some of his family treasures to raise funds for those left behind..."

I tuned him out, looking around the hall for anything suspicious. If Suri and I were right and the priests had been murdered according to the virtues of their church, then what was left? We'd had Wisdom, Honor, Hospitality and Courage so far... that left Self-Reliance, Discipline, and Honesty. Of the two, Self-Reliance seemed like the more difficult one to stage. And Toth - or the Volod himself - were the only feasible targets. I watched Toth intently, and jumped when my HUD beeped.

"*Sorry I didn't reply before,*" Suri messaged. "*Andrik has been taking up all of my time.*"

"*I noticed.*" I sent it off, and immediately regretted how curt I sounded. "*Listen, something's up. Get ready to drag him out of here by his goatee. If he dies, we fail our quest and this country will go downhill, fast.*"

Toth finished his speech with a prayer, holding up a hammer and using it to bless the auction table and the assembled people. I definitely tuned that part out, and tried one of the sandwiches. Chicken and asparagus, cream cheese, soft rye bread... not bad. I arched an eyebrow when Toth kissed the hammer and laid it down on the auction table.

"The very first item of the night is, in fact, this holy relic that the High Forgemaster created especially for this auction," the Auctionmaster said, once Toth had started back for his seat. "It is made of Mithril and Titanium, and was forged using the ground scales of a dragon which were given freely to the Church some two hundred years ago. We will start the bidding at 250 olbia..."

Tense, I watched Toth move back to his table, which was ringed by guards from the Church. Most of the other 'guests' who sat at the tables to either side of him had the tense, wary look of warriors. Kirov was seated at that table, and so was Matthias, who watched the proceedings with the glazed expression of a man who was bored to tears.

"*How does it look from your angle?*" I asked Suri.

"*Looks fine so far.*"

Suri's P.M. was pushed aside by Karalti's telepathic voice. "*Hey, so, I still hate you and everything, but some bad people just snuck into the grounds.*"

I drew a sharp breath. "*Sitrep?*"

"*Six, tall, they got weapons. I think they're Meewfolk. They're coming from the north and heading for the house... Uh-oh...*"

"*Get them if you can. Be careful.*" I leaned in towards the Captain, who glanced at me in consternation. I kept my voice to a hissing whisper. "Sir, we've got a situation. My dragon just spotted six intruders coming over the north wall. She's going to engage."

The Captain paled. He nodded, rose quickly, and exited the room. Once he was outside, I heard him bark orders at the guards outside.

The waiters were still circulating. I noticed that they were avoiding the Volod's table, and that neither he nor the High Priest were letting the waiters serve them drinks. One caught my eye as he passed by Toth's table, carrying a single bottle with an unusual color on a tray. The opaque glass, usually green, had a weird red tint. A non-mutant probably wouldn't have noticed, but I sat up straight, trying to get a proper look.

"Five hundred! We have five hundred rubles over here!" The Auctioneer was warming up now, brandishing his gavel. "Five hundred and twenty! Five hundred and forty!"

The waiter passed too close to one of the church guards, who caught him by the arm and quietly rebuked him. The man - human, pale, bald, sweating like a pig - nodded and bowed, withdrawing from the table and bumbling straight into the chair of the next guest.

I saw his expression – calm, resigned, even serene - and lunged up to my feet as the bottle toppled and fell to the floor. "Get back!"

Three things happened all at once. The bottle smashed, releasing a cloud of gas into the air; Father Matthias threw himself from his chair and tackled the waiter to the ground; and the assassin exploded.

CHAPTER 30

The suicide bomber took out the floor, the ceiling above Toth's table, and the tables around it. I saw Suri throw herself over Andrik just before the shockwave engulfed me and flung me to the ground.

[[You are Deafened!]]

[[You take 25 bludgeoning damage!]]

[[Party Member Suri is gravely injured!]]

People - and parts of people - and tables showered everyone and everything. Groaning, I rolled over on the ground, armor crunching over bits of broken wood and stone. I could feel the gravel shifting underneath me, but I couldn't hear it. In my HUD, an icon of a musical note with an X through it had appeared, along with a 30 minute-long debuff bar.

"Suri!" I scrambled up and forward, barely noticing the red flashing warning in my HUD as people shoved past me, stampeding for the doors. There were at least twenty bodies on the ground, and all around me, people were going to their knees, clawing at their skin as seams of light crawled on and *through* their flesh. The stench of blood and mana was all around us.

I couldn't see her, but Suri's name and player halo were highlighted in among the smoking mess, and they were flashing red with warning. Her HP was draining away second by second, down to a sliver by the time I waded through the wreckage and pulled the splintered remains of a table off her body.

She had put herself between the blast and the Volod. He was okay - unconscious, but alive, and his NPC halo was stable. Suri was not. She was sprawled in the wreckage of several chairs. Her beautiful dress was torn to shreds... and her left arm was gone. She was bleeding out from the stump of her elbow. The game had not been merciful enough to knock her out. She stared at the ragged end of her limb with bewilderment. Her lips and the skin around her eyes were pale with shock.

"Fucking fuckity fuck-" I continued to curse. I pulled a Moss Tincture from thin air and poured it onto the wound. Suri flinched, lips moving, but I couldn't hear her. I shook my head and put the Moss Tincture flask to her lips. "Drink! You're going to be okay!"

She swallowed, eyes rolling to look up at my face, until her gaze slipped past me. I dumped a second potion on her, healing her another 70 HP. The status updates continued to narrate to me telepathically as I worked to save her.

[[Suri has a critical injury: severed arm. Her Max HP has been reduced to 180!]]
[[Suri is stable! Current HP: 148/180]]

Suri stiffened and flinched as I took out a healing poultice to make up the 32 point gap. She yelled something, shoving me back a step.

"I can't hear you!" I bellowed, probably far too loudly. "I'm deaf!"

"TURN THE FUCK AROUND!" she shot back by P.M.

I jumped and spun back to face the main room. "Oh, shit."

The bodies of the dead and dying had Stranged - but instead of an army of ghouls, they were sliding across the floor, drawn toward a nexus of magical gravity that smashed them into one another and merged the corpses into a tottering tower of flesh and sharp bone. A [[Gibbering Flesh Amalgamation]]. One that contained the remains of the High Forgemaster... and Matthias.

"Get Andrik and any other survivors out of here!" I spun my spear around and fell into stance.

"I can fight-"

"Don't give me this Black Knight 'tis but a scratch' bullshit! The Volod will *die* if you don't get him the fuck out of this room!" I felt cold energy swirl through my body and condense in my limbs, winding them taut. "Go!"

And with that, I Jumped right into the fray.

The Flesh Amalgamation undulated from side to side, and as I sailed through the air toward it, half a dozen eyes erupted on the surface of its body. It lashed out with a pseudopod, but the clumsy strike missed as I twisted in midair and drove the spear down with my full weight behind it. The blade sunk into the slithering mess like butter, and blood sprayed from the wound. I carried the maneuver through and bounced away, wrenching the weapon free from the thing. I felt a dim wail that rattled the floor and shook dust from the ceiling.

[[x3 damage! You hit Amalgamation for 401 HP!]]
[[HP remaining: 4599/5000]]
[[Amalgamation uses Hideous Screech! You are immune!]]
[[Suri is Stunned!]]
[[Suri shrugs off Stun with Battle Fury!]]

I landed and skidded over the blood-covered floorboards, keeping an eye on my adrenaline level as I ran back in. Long, ropy tentacles sprung out of the Amalgamation's body, lashing out in all directions. Some were at head height, some were intended to sweep my feet out from under me. I skipped over them and then executed my new Blood Sprint chain. The first two moves were familiar: Blood Sprint's dash carried me in close enough to stab the monster deep in its side. I tore the blade free, landing several bleeding cuts in quick succession, and then triggered the Death by a Thousand Cuts finale.

"You gonna *die*!" A shadowy nimbus pulsed along the weapon, ruffling my skin with an unpleasant sensation that churned my guts like an icy claw. The curse seemed to suck the light out of the space around the Abomination, marking it with a stain of darkness. It cringed back as its attack power diminished, and I drew a deep breath as the sliver of power flowed back into me.

[[Flesh Amalgamation is Cursed! -2% Attack power!]]
[[You gain +2% Attack power and +5% damage reduction from your opponent's attacks!]]
[[You deal 617 damage to the enemy!]]

The thing punched me with a meaty 'fist' the size of a small cow before I'd even had a chance to recover my balance. The blow sent me tumbling, then crashing into the surviving tables. Little crustless sandwiches and fancy cookies went everywhere as I skidded through shattered crockery on my back and sprawled onto the floor.

[[You take 221 bludgeoning damage! HP 338/559.]]
[[Gibbering Flesh Amalgamation uses Horrid Screech! You are immune!]]

"Fucking bullshit-!" Ranting under my breath was surreal when I couldn't hear anything except the ringing of my own punctured eardrums. I scrambled up and away, trying to keep moving. Not being able to hear the monster meant it couldn't paralyze me with its screeching, but I lost the advantage of being able to hear it telegraphing its moves. In the dust and smoke and haze, that could be fatal, and almost was when another gelatinous tentacle - as thick as a tree trunk and studded with sharp, broken bones and chair legs -

slammed down across a table I was using for cover. It smashed the solid oak into kindling.

I slammed a couple of Bonebreak Poultices, healing a hundred HP as I circled and ran back in. I sprung up like a cricket, flipping midair, and Jumped onto the monster as I had the first time. The thing twisted and flailed, but it missed the agile strike and tore the ceiling open instead. It clipped my leg as I followed the Jump through and leaped away, sending me careening off course midair.

As I fell, Leap of Faith kicked in - time slowed enough that I could right myself in the air. I spun around to land with knees bent and weapon ready.

⟦x3 damage! Critical hit!⟧
⟦Flesh Amalgamation is immune to critical hits! 401 Damage!⟧
⟦You take a glancing blow! HP: 412/559⟧

The Amalgamation tensed up in a way that my gamer brain was instinctively familiar with: 'Area of Effect attack imminent'.

"*Hector!*" Karalti's voice pierced the battle fugue as I began to run a circle around it, putting broken furniture between us. "*What's happening!?*"

"*I thought you hated me.*"

"*I do! But not THAT much.*"

"*Big monster. Lots of HP.*" I saw the monster stiffen, and triggered Shadow Dance.

The Gibbering Flesh Amalgamation's body erupted with splinters of wood, bone, and absorbed weapons, blasting everything in a thirty-foot radius like the grossest nail-bomb in history. Most of it went through my temporarily-gaseous form, but I took a few shards to the chest when I rematerialized. Twenty-three HP down the drain.

Karalti called to me again. "*I'm coming! Hang on! Suri is coming, too!*"

"*What!? Stop her! She only has one arm!*" Panting, I ran back toward the Amalgamation and Jumped, this time with the intent to use Obscuring Veil - the new Jump combo chain I'd forgotten about in the excitement - but the creature did something I'd never seen in a video game before. It anticipated my move. As I plummeted toward it, a huge mouth unzippered along its side, gaping into what could have almost passed for a fang-lined grin.

"GOAT BALLS!" I couldn't change my trajectory fast enough.

[[x3 damage! You deal 401 damage! Amalgamation is immune to critical hits!]]'

[[You are entangled! -50% maneuverability!]]

[[Amalgamation has swallowed you whole!]]

The flesh horror slammed shut around me like a Venus flytrap, plunging me into darkness. And suddenly, I *really* missed Umbra Burst.

[[Amalgamation uses Engulf! You take 100 damage!]]

Pain blossomed in about half a dozen place on my body at once. It was fucking *chewing* me! Revulsion crawled up the back of my throat. I slammed down three Moss Tinctures as my health dropped down into the red, bringing it back up to half after the last attack. I had eleven potions left.

[[Amalgamation uses Engulf! You take 100 damage!]]

Fuck. Shadow Dance allowed me to become immaterial enough to allow blows to pass through me, but it unfortunately didn't allow me to phase through barriers. I struggled with everything I had, plunging the spear into the monster's body like a butter churn.

[[You deal 120 damage to Amalgamation! HP: 3060/5000]]

[[Amalgamation uses Engulf! You take 100 damage! HP: 414/559]]

And then it occurred to me - I now had Whirlwind Butcher III. And it wasn't affected by the entanglement penalty.

I couldn't see or hear, but I felt dark, savage strength gather in my body, then ejected explosively as I tore my spear up and around through the belly of the monster. I was inside it - so all six blows hit, and they tore it to shreds.

[[You deal 758 damage to Gibbering Flesh Amalgamation!]]
[[Karalti uses her breath weapon! 450 damage!]]
[[Amalgamation is on fire!]]
[[Suri uses Primal Rage! Suri loses control!]]

I felt the boss monster rumble through. The side of it split, and it spat me out into the open air. I twisted like an acrobat and landed, only to look up and see one of the weirdest sights I'd ever witnessed in my entire life.

The Flesh Amalgamation was crowned with white fire, and lurched as it sizzled and popped with a smell that was alarmingly similar to barbecued pork. Karalti had torn a hole in the ceiling and was raining Ghost Fire down on it from above. Suri had stripped her flimsy dress down to her waist and torn off a long strip of it, which she had tied around the bloody stump of her left arm at the elbow as a makeshift tourniquet. She was boiling with a red aura, and her face was a mask of uncontrollable frenzy as she ran in, topless, with an ax, and leaped bodily onto the Amalgamation with no apparent regard for her life.

"No! Whyyy!? You have a hundred and eighty HP and NO FUCKING ARMOR!" I yelled in frustration as I shook red goo off myself and sprinted back into the battle.

[[Amalgamation hits Suri for 75 reduced damage!]]
[[Suri's rage builds as she is injured! Damage reduction and attack power drastically increases!]]

[[Suri hits Amalgamation for 440 damage!]]
[[Amalgamation hits Suri for 55 reduced damage!]]
[[Suri's rage builds as she is injured! Damage reduction and attack power drastically increases!]]
[[Suri hits Amalgamation for 660 damage!]]
[[Amalgamation takes 100 Fire damage!]]

Oh wow. Okay. *That* was why. But even with crazy berserker DR, she only had 50 HP left and could only take a few more hits with that amputation in play - and I bet that this ability of hers would cost her afterward.

As I ran, I planned my next moves. And then I sprung up to Jump.

The Amalgamation didn't have to turn to see me - it had eyes everywhere. As it had last time, a gaping maw split along its side, but I didn't carry Jump through into its meteoric strike this time. I used it evasively, springing off the edge of its meat-mouth, and then triggered my other new ability: Shattering Darkness. Dark energy rippled along my spear, then blasted forward as I stuck the huge monster with the very tip of the Alpha Rod. An icy blast of shadow sped down the haft and blew into the Amalgamation, sending thin spikes of black ice through the entire mass of its body.

[[You used an Ice attack! It's super effective!]]
[[You deal 500 Freezing damage to Amalgamation!]]
[[Amalgamation takes 100 Fire damage!]]
[[Suri hits Amalgamation for 660 damage!]]

The overkill stacked up in a single round. Simultaneously burning and freezing, the Amalgamation emitted a shrill roar that rattled my teeth. Suri's final ax blow sent cracks through its frozen body. It rumbled, slowly expanding with bursts of magical light, and then exploded into chunks.

[[You have defeated Gibbering Flesh Amalgamation!]]
[[You gain 1000 EXP!]]
[[Congratulations! You are Level 12!]]

"*Dun dahh da dah da*-ow!" I pressed a hand to one of my ringing ears as a small spike of pain flashed through it, then pulled it away with a grimace as I realized it was covered in blood and slime. "Eww. Fucking gross, man."

Suri staggered up bare-breasted, gore-streaked, her remaining hand clenched around the haft of her ax. She panted through her teeth, her gold eyes blazing. It was like staring into the face of War personified.

"Well. Th-th at was a bit nasty, wasn't it?" The woman tried to lean on her weapon to rest, and stumbled to her knees. She swayed for a second, and then fell flat on her face.

I ran to her side just as Karalti dropped through the gaping hole in the ceiling, sending dirt and broken tiles, plaster, and wood everywhere. She landed on the remains of the Flesh Amalgamation as I stopped beside Suri and felt for her pulse on IRL instinct.

"*Are you okay?*" My dragon squeaked.

"I feel like a refugee from a German porn set, but I'm okay." To my great relief, Suri's heart was strong. I checked her in the Party menu: she had healed some HP, but she was still under 180 because of the severed arm. Her stamina was zero, and her status was 'Unconscious'. I guessed that was a symptom of the Berserk Rage ability she'd used. "Come on, we have to go outside and see who survived. Search the monster. But... be respectful. My friend was sucked into that."

"*Okay. Well, it's good that I don't hate you anymore.*" Karalti hopped off it, and began to delicately nose through the remains.

I felt heat from above, and looked up to see that the ceiling was on fire. Great. With a heavy heart, I slung my cloak off and crouched down. I used it to cover Suri up, then went to loot the Amalgamation.

[[Gold Ruby Ring x 3]]
[[Gold Necklace x 4]]
[[Broken Plates x 10]]
[[Iron Sword x 4]]
[[Green crystal Mana x 6]]
[[100 olbia]]
[[Petko Matthias' pipe]]

The last one was genuinely painful. I pulled the pipe out of the sticky mess and wiped it off. *Matthias. You poor son of a bitch.*

"*Hey! I found something!*" Karalti said from behind me.

"What?" Swallowing my grief, I stashed the pipe and turned to face her.

Karalti trotted over, and spat something into the palm of my hand. It was a ring with a grinning cat's face, just like the one we'd found on the rogue outside of Kanzo's laboratory.

"Well, what do you know," I muttered, turning it around. "It's our old friend, the King of Cats."

CHAPTER 31

"I am truly sorry I did not take you seriously. I have failed my nation, my king, and Father Matthias." Kirov was slumped in a chair, with his sword resting over his knees and his helmet by his feet. He looked like he'd been gutshot.

Kirov, Suri, and I were all bunkered in Suri's quarters - a suite that had clearly been lived in longer than the one Karalti and I currently occupied. My dragon was out hunting.

"The guy had the explosives stitched up into him. There's no way anyone could have known." I wrung out a cloth, and wiped it over Suri's face. She was in bed, covered up and mostly well, though she was still passed out. A check of the wiki had revealed that the Berserk Rage ability inflicted a fatigue penalty equal to the amount of Adrenaline used to power the ability. In Suri's case, that was nearly all of it - which meant she'd be out until we did something about her arm and her health and stamina could start to regen normally.

"That bottle of mana and reagent was probably smuggled in days ago. I should have believed you in your entirety," Kirov replied miserably. "You are the guardian of a sacred *draak*, and you have proven yourself to be a mighty warrior, as is Suri. I admit, I had my doubts about her..."

"About Suri?"

He nodded. "The Volod, well... He is something of, how should I put it? He can be something of a cad, and she is fair of face and form. I'd wondered if he hired her because of that."

"What you just said is more insulting to Suri than it is to the Volod." I dropped the cloth back in the bucket of warm mineral water beside the bed, then reached out and felt Suri's temperature. Her forehead was hot. I was worried about that arm - blood poisoning was a feature of this VR.

"What I mean to say is that His Majesty is inordinately fond of the company of beautiful women, and that, well... He's done it before."

I snorted. "Call it like it is, then. He's a fuckboy."

Kirov's tattooed face twitched. "That is... vulgar."

"So is assuming shit about people based on optics." I pulled my pack around, and began to withdraw items from my Inventory: my alchemy set and some of the herbs I'd bought. I settled a mortar and pestle in my lap, threw in some Holy Basil and Green Moss, and then added some powdered Birch Bark as a binder before starting to grind. The three ingredients formed the basis for a simple Blood Cleansing potion that helped ward off the Infection debuff. Like real blood poisoning, the debuff could kill a player if you didn't head it off.

"You are once more correct." The lines around Kirov's mouth deepened, and he sagged even more deeply into his chair. "I am a disgrace."

"No offense, but if you want some bread to go with your whine, I'm not the man to talk to." I scowled as I beat the potion ingredients together, then added {[Pure Alcohol]} to the mixture. "Look, shit happens. We both lost a friend, but we've got terrorists to catch and a murderer to put down. Matthias threw himself on that bomber to save people's lives. We owe him our best until the job is done."

Kirov hunched. "I know what you speak is the truth. Perhaps I just needed to hear it from someone outside my own head."

"That's usually how it goes." I mashed the plant matter into the alcohol. The mixture turned a bright lime-green color as the plant matter broke up into the potion. Not particularly realistic, but satisfying.

[You have made 2 x Sweet Basil Tinctures]

I took two of my empty flasks out, and bottled the liquid. One went in my Inventory for later, and one went to Suri. I wet a new rag with it, and applied it to the stump of her arm.

Just as I was doing that, the door opened. A small, wizened old woman with her hair wrapped up in a scarf came bustling in. She had piercing dark eyes and a bounce in her step. She carried a brown leather doctor's bag in one hand. "A-ha! If it isn't Ur Kirov!"

"Elder Mashka." Kirov stood up and bowed respectfully. "Elder, this is-"

"I know who the dragonrider is, boy. Don't you think everyone in Vlachia does by now? *Bozye mada.*" The old woman rolled her eyes, but her expression softened when she lit on Suri in her bed. She bustled over.

"Rytier Hector, this is Mashka Kali," Kirov said weakly. "She is the Palace Alchemist."

"AND the Field Medic for the Knights of the Red Star," Mashka added crisply. "AND the Senior Medical Instructor of the Vulkan Garrison."

I smiled ruefully as the old woman pushed in, bumping me aside with her hip. "I never would have guessed."

"Let me see... hmmm..." Mashka pursed her wrinkled lips as she checked Suri's vitals, then her arm. "I have a Limb Restoration decoction, but it will make her ill."

"Alchemical?" I asked.

The woman gave me a waspish - but curious - look. Then her gaze fell on the mortar, with its bright green potion. "A student of the art, are you?"

"I'm muddling along," I replied. "Only had some really basic training from some village herbalists. The rest is self-taught."

She grunted. "Yes, the Limb Regrowth potion is alchemical. She's Fireblooded, which means she isn't likely to transform into some nasty beastie, but she will be unwell. The limb regeneration takes four hours, and the illness will last twelve."

I rubbed my chin in thought. "I don't suppose you'd be willing to share the recipe?"

"At a glance, I can tell your Alchemy skill is not high enough for you to craft it, though we could fix that." Masha turned back to Suri. "For now, study its effects."

Masha rummaged through her bag, and took out a small, oddly shaped vial that contained a small amount of bright yellow liquid. Visually, the main difference between alchemical and herbal potions was that alchemical potions always glowed, as this one did.

"She will not Strange?" Kirov's eyebrows furrowed.

"There is always a small chance the cure acts as a poison. In her case, it is unlikely. A fever and the sweats is the worst she can expect, and that's a small price to pay for the cost of a limb." The old woman tipped Suri's head up, set the uncorked potion to her lips, and slowly let it trickle in. She followed it up with a plain herbal ⟦Stamina Potion⟧.

Suri's face scrunched in pain, and then she groaned under her breath.

"Don't let her push herself. Probably a difficult job with this particular woman, but she can't afford to exert herself for the next four hours. It is best that she sleep all through the night and into tomorrow." Masha nodded, and snapped her bag closed.

"We'll do our best to keep her down," I said. "Did I hear you make an offer to teach me Alchemy, ma'am?"

"I'll consider it, though you must pay for tuition." The brisk little woman turned to face me. "People never seem to value the wisdom they are given for free."

"Deal," I said. "But not until she's okay."

Masha smiled, then gave us a tiny nod and hastened off the way she'd come.

"I ought to leave too. I must face my Brothers and the Volod, and determine what the future holds for me and my family." Kirov rose, the round plates of his armor clinking like coins.

I cocked my head. "You have a family? I didn't know that."

He smiled faintly. "A wife and a little daughter, yes. Good luck, and thank you. Believe me, *rytier*, the story of you and Suri's battle against the foul creature that killed so many will be spread around the city come morn."

"Mama always told me I'd be famous." I flashed him a big sloppy grin, which lasted until he closed the door behind him. Then it abruptly fell away. I slumped back with a sigh of relief, and looked down at Suri. When I saw her looking back, I jumped about a foot inside of my own skin.

I straightened up in my seat. "Oh, shit, Suri! Hi! You're looking very..."

"Stumpy?" she croaked.

"I was going say you looked 'pruned'," I replied. "You know, like a rose bush. You cut it back for the winter so that it grows out in the spring. That means when your arm grows back, there'll be like... four of them."

"Three more fists to punch you in the face with." She groaned, shifting around on the bed. "You got me a limb regrowth brew?"

"Sure did. Masha - the Healer - said you'd feel like a gaping crusty ass for about twelve hours." I folded my arms, resigned to remaining on duty.

Suri sighed. "That'd be right. So, you saved my ass, huh?"

"You saved mine," I replied. "You and Karalti. I have to say, for someone who doesn't like to respawn, you came running back in like a suicidal maniac."

"It's my job."

"You didn't even think to equip your armor, though?"

"Primal Rage only works without armor. One of those Berserker things." Suri was beginning to look quite flushed and hot. Her cheeks were reddening, and her hair was damp and sticking to her brow.

I wrung out the rag from the bucket, and dabbed her forehead with it. Her lips parted, as if she were about to say something, but then she seemed to think better of it and relaxed back against the pillows.

"You need some water?" I asked.

Suri nodded, eyes closed. I got up, and went to the dresser to pour her a cup from pitcher.

"Thanks," she said. "For not letting me die."

"Well, I remember you telling me that you never wanted to." I shrugged. "I get it. I have phobias too. For me, it's bugs. Not like...big bugs. Little bugs that get under your clothes and bite you and shit. Ticks, scorpions, shit like that. I fucking *hate* ticks."

"I'm not afraid to die," Suri said. "I'm scared of where I end up when I come back."

I turned back around, and found Suri looking away from me toward the window. "What do you mean?"

For close to a minute, she said nothing.

"I was born in a prison, a place called Al-Asad. Or... I *think* I was born there," she said, haltingly. "Al-Asad is a labyrinth that was turned into a dungeon out in the Bashar Desert. It's about a week's ride out of Dalim, the capital of Dakhdir. The Sultir – our Emperor – imprisons the worst of his enemies out there."

"You... were born in a prison?" I came back with the cup and sat down beside the bed again. "What do you mean by 'I think'?"

"Because my first memory is from when I was about twelve or thirteen years old." Suri's eyes were closed, tracks of perspiration running down her face and neck. "I don't remember my parents, or of even having parents. I don't know even what their crimes were.

Point being, though, I died all the time in there. I've probably died about twenty, thirty times."

I held the cup out, and helped her drink some water. "That's not good."

"There's worse things than death." Suri sprawled back. "The Starborn I told you about... they had golden halos, like Rin's. It started with just the two of them, but they brought friends now and then. Those fuckers treated me like garbage."

My ears started to ring. I had to fight down the urge to stand up and pace. "You remember their names?"

"No, never saw them. It was like their names were masked. The main two... one was a Mage and the other was some kind of Warrior-path guy." Suri sighed. "These guys told me I was in Al-Asad because I was a war criminal. They called me names, like 'Comrade' and 'Australian' and suchlike... And they're the only other people besides you who ever talked about this 'Total War' and 'Pacific Alliance' stuff. I figured it was like... some kind of schizo delusion, you know? I'd never been in a war. I'd never left the prison."

The implications of what Suri was telling me settled like a lead blanket over my shoulders. There were a couple of possibilities. One was that Suri was a real human, like me, but a Pacific Alliance citizen who had been uploaded during the military GNOSIS/OUROS project and somehow ended up here, in the fun civilian game program. Option B was that she'd been constructed out of multiple datasets by a couple of sick-minded Devs. The end result was the same either way.

"Fuck," I said. "That is so fucked up. How did you escape?"

Suri frowned, the muscles of her face twitching. "If you're imprisoned in Al-Asad, you can't gain any levels or take a Path. The only things I could increase were my stats. So I trained whenever and however I could. Punching straw, fighting for scraps, fighting for the fun of it... I got my ass kicked, and died and respawned all the time. About a month ago, something weird happened. I remember that I'd managed to get myself this old piece of *injera* and some locusts and had cooked it all up. I was sitting down to eat when the world blacked and I passed out. When I woke up, I didn't realize anything had changed. But later that night, some guy tried to pick on me for some you-know-what. I killed him before he had his cock out, and I got a pop-up message telling me I'd gotten EXP. I gained a level from killing that bastard. Then I got all these messages telling me I could choose a Path. I opened up my menu, and there were all these new options and shit. So I took Warrior, and began to train up as hard as I could. I never saw the golden-ring guys after that, either."

The server reset. I sat back, cradling the cup in my lap. My fingers felt numb, ringing like my ears. "Yeah. That *was* about a month ago."

"Some of the other guys in the hole were able to start taking levels too, of course," she said, shifting restlessly under the blankets. "But they didn't come back to life if they died. I did. I got revenge on all the ones who'd fucked with me, and teamed up with some of the better men. We decided we'd try and break out. The prison was next to these moldy ruins, and we ended up digging our way through to them. I almost made it that first time, but this fucking monster came out of nowhere and nailed me."

"Fuck."

"Yeah." Suri grimaced, swallowing. "But the worst part? When I died, I woke up in my cell. If I die, that's where I go. Straight back to prison."

I frowned. "You should be able to set new spawn points. All Starborn can do that."

"I can't." She shifted again, pushing the covers down her chest. "Menu... says I should be able to. But it's grayed out and shit, and-"

"Hey, shh. Calm down a bit. You need to stay warm." I pulled the covers back up over her chest. "Drink more. Can you hold this yourself?"

By way of reply, Suri took the cup in her hand. It shook as she brought it to her mouth and began to drink with needy, shuddering gulps.

I watched her in numb silence, emotions swirling through my mind like a storm. So many things had clicked into place with that abbreviated, almost sterile version of all of the horrors that had happened to her, and nearly all of those revelations made me want to go back into the real world so that I could go to Ryuko HQ and blow it up a second time. Me and Rin were going to have a talk.

"Thank you," I said.

"For what?"

"For trusting me. That's some heavy shit."

"Too heavy for most people. Like I said, some things are better off left buried." Breathing hard, Suri dropped the empty cup. She cracked her eyes open and looked up at me. "I figured you'd be like those Gold Rings and their mates when I first met you, you know. You started going on about the war and everything, but I'm okay with being proven wrong. You're alright, Hector."

On impulse, I reached out and clasped her hand between mine and squeezed. Suri smiled faintly, and squeezed back.

"You're literally the toughest person I've ever met," I told her. "You're brave, and smart, and smoking hot, even when you don't have a fever."

She chuckled, grimacing with discomfort. The fever was in full swing, but her severed arm had started to grow back, if the shape under the loose bandages was anything to go by. "Lay it on... uhhn... too much thicker and I'll throw up all over you."

"I'm serious." I let go and stood up. "After this, when you're feeling better and this whole Slayer thing is sorted out, let me take you out to dinner."

"Dinner, huh?" The woman smiled faintly. "I'll think about it once I no longer feel like puking. How's that sound?"

"It's not a 'no'." I smiled back.

"It's not a 'no'," she replied. "I just feel really crook, and if I think about food for more than a second, it'll definitely become a 'no'."

I squinted. "Crook? I'm sorry, but I don't speak Austrababble."

"Sick, you idiot." She flopped back against her pillows in exasperation. But not just exasperation - she looked disheveled and exhausted.

"You need to sleep, Suri. But speaking of crooks, though - I found another one of those cat-face rings at the scene," I pulled it out from a pocket. "Well, Karalti did."

"Nightstalkers," Suri muttered. "Hold onto it... and when I'm awake, we'll... we'll talk about the Stalkers. Go pay them a visit."

"No worries. Get some sleep." I looked down at Suri, and swallowed the urge to lean down and kiss her on the forehead. Instead, I flipped the ring in my hand, and headed for the door.

It was time to check in with His Majesty. And then I had some training to do.

CHAPTER 32

Even though it was late, I had a feeling the Volod would be awake. I found Andrik in the hidden parlor to the side of his throne room, the same place where we'd had our first audience.

Andrik was rumpled, sprawled in his fine red velvet armchair with a glass of wine and a sullen scowl. He stared at the fire, while the Captain of the Kingsguard, Garen, sat patiently in the corner. He had his sword over his knees, a shield by his other hand, and appraised me warily as I walked up and stood at ease beside the Volod.

"How is Suri?" Andrik asked. Up close, he looked ‐ and sounded ‐ exhausted.

"She'll recover," I replied. My voice was quiet in the closeness of the room, which was dark except for the fire blazing in the hearth. "I came to give a report on what happened at Kobayaz."

"We know what happened. The man had a device that killed Toth, obliterated one of the greatest sages of my kingdom, twenty soldiers and ten other guests, including Lady Andreas Lustival, a beloved opera singer who has set the trends for the ladies of the court for going on fifteen years now. Then their corpses amalgamated into some revolting beast which you, Suri and your dragon slew while my men ran away like little girls." Andrik scowled, and took a deep swallow of wine. "Did I miss anything?"

"I tried to warn your men that something was going to happen," I said. "There was a hostile agent at the Auction House. She called herself 'Red'."

"'Red'? What did she look like?"

"Tall, extremely thin, dressed all in red, as the name implies. I think she came in as one of the mummers."

"I don't recall seeing her. Was she human?"

I shrugged. "Couldn't tell you. Definitely an odd one, though."

"And who did you warn?"

"Ur Kirov and the Commander of the garrison," I replied. "They told me that every precaution was in place."

"It was. But none of us thought that someone would be so desperate to sabotage this event that they would do something this extreme." Andrik shook his head, and had another drink.

"There was another thing," I said, holding out the ring. "My dragon found this in the remains of the monster."

Andrik frowned as he took the ring and held it up to the fire, turning it around so that he could see the details.

"It's a syndicate ring worn by members of the Nightstalkers." I parroted back what Suri had told me about it. "The head of the Syndicate calls themselves-"

"The King of Cats," Andrik said quietly. "Yes... I know."

He handed the ring back to me, and sighed, gazing off into the flames. "Garen?"

"Yes, sire?"

"You may leave us." Andrik waved his hand back toward the door.

The Kingsguard stood, armor rattling. "Your Majesty?"

"I will not say it again. Leave."

The older man glanced between us, then picked up his shield and clanked his way over to the door. He let himself outside, and when it closed, Andrik waved toward it again.

"Go and stuff some wax in the keyhole, Tuun," he said. "I do not want anyone eavesdropping."

I shrugged, and did just that, warming up a candle and using the soft wax to plug up the small hole. When I came back, Andrik sat up in his chair and reached for the bottle on the table beside him. "You know that I am the younger of two brothers, do you not?"

"I have heard that His Majesty lost a brother some years ago," I replied carefully.

"Don't be coy." Andrik sloshed more wine into his glass. "This is my castle, Hector. I know full well what kind of gossip gets shared around here. One of the oldest and juiciest pieces of gossip involves Ignas and what happened to him. Everyone knows the reason why the Corvinus Throne warms my behind instead of my brother's bony arse. Sit down. Do you want a drink?"

"Sure." Refusing Andrik while he was tipsy and brooding seemed like a bad idea, so I got a second glass and a chair and pulled it up next to him.

"*Discipline*." Andrik shook his head he poured my wine. "That was Ignas' favorite word. 'A man is nothing if he has not built himself on a foundation of self-discipline and temperance'. He used to say that to me whenever he thought I was hunting or whoring too much. Ignas was very much our father's son."

"Okay." I bought the drink to my lips, but didn't touch any of it.

"Well, what is it they say about moral men?" Andrik snorted, swirling the wine in his glass. "I told you about the properties of Corvinus Rubies, and that my dynasty is the only one who can use them to imprint memories. Well, Ignas had always been known for his love of the arts, and he kept the company of several notable artists in court, including this one Meewfolk dancer. I can't remember his name... Rhan'ah or something. The short version of a long tale is that my pious, terribly disciplined brother was not only been screwing this Meewfolk male, but recording his experiences onto a ruby so that he might replay and relive his bestiality over and over."

I winced.

"Father found the stone," Andrik continued. "And that was that. He marched into the lunchtime banquet, tore Ignas' coronet off, and screamed at him to pack his bags. I'd never seen a man become so furious in all my life. Ignas broke down and begged forgiveness, but how could he be forgiven for such a thing? He was the Crown Prince, and he was already engaged to Princess Ahrem, the flower of the Jeun Empire. That same night, my brother committed suicide."

I nodded, taking a moment to digest what he'd said. "How'd he kill himself?"

Andrik snorted, sinking down into his chair. "He walked into the sacred furnace at the heart of the Keep, the one which warms the ground and walls. Baked himself into charcoal. That was three years ago to the day."

"You think he's alive?"

"They pulled the remains out of the furnace," Andrik said. "But the handy thing about self-immolation is that it makes the dead harder to identify. When I went to view him, the first thing I thought to myself was 'that can't be my brother'. Ignas was tall and lanky. This man was too short and broad. The attending priest said that was because the body shrinks and contracts while burning, but... I remain skeptical."

"Did you tell your father?"

"Of course, but he didn't want to hear it. The old man died of grief not long after. He'd already lost Mother when I was a babe, and now this." Andrik shook his head, looking down at the ground between his feet. "And here I am, stuck with a crown I never wanted, faced by the need to marry and produce heirs well before I was ready... We have some manner of monstrosity threatening us in the East, and now we have Ilia baying at our doors – no fault of yours, I assure you. The alliance with Jeun collapsed with Ignas' death."

"Why are you telling me this?" I motioned to him, the untouched glass of wine in the other.

"Because I don't think Ignas is dead," Andrik replied. He jabbed a finger toward the ring. "A year ago, I started hearing this name, the 'King of Cats'. He is the leader of one of the largest underground gladiatorial circuits north of Dakhdir. That vice is illegal, but there is a great demand for bloodsports. Vlachia, Dakhdir, Shalash, and even Meewhome partake of underground fighting events. The syndicates can be useful to a monarch, and so most savvy nations play host to these brigands under the terms of a gentleman's agreement."

In other words, you tolerate organized crime because the Dons give you a cut of their profits. I kept that observation to myself.

"I was assured by my contacts that the Nightstalkers were nothing but a small gang of pit fighters. Then there was a change in leadership, and suddenly, the Nightstalkers are competing with the biggest syndicate in Vlachia, the Rose Knives." Andrik's brow creased. "I tried to learn about this King of Cats, but we found nothing. I sent out word that I was interested in a meeting. When that failed, I tried an assassin. My man's head and spine were returned to the Keep and laid out on my Chancellor's bed. Meewfolk assassins are fond of that display."

I struggled not to grin. "Maybe they thought the Chancellor was hungry."

Andrik shot me a dark look. "Do you think this is funny?"

"No, sir." I shook my head. "You think the King of Cats is Ignas?"

"Well, there are two things that occurred to me about the Nightstalkers," Andrik replied, looking back to the fire. "They're supposedly very wealthy now. And above all, they're terribly *disciplined.* Almost like a small army, you could say."

"Yes, sir." But even as the old 'yes sir-no sir' speech fell from my lips, I was thinking of what Andrik might be leaving out of his story. Like I'd told Suri, I had a problem with authority.

"Regardless of whether or not the King of Cats is my not-so-immolated brother, the fact remains that he has now been implicated in the murder of my citizens. He must be brought to justice." Andrik drained his glass and set it aside. "It's good that you came alone, actually. I have a proposition for you."

"Oh?" I set my untouched glass down as well.

"Yes. You are a servant of Matir, are you not? Or, what do you call him in your land? Burna?"

"I wouldn't use the word 'servant'. More like 'franchisee'."

The Volod shrugged. "Regardless, you serve his tenets and believe in his message. Therefore, I invoke the *Kara Bukat-talom.*"

I frowned. The words were Tuun - they meant 'Moon Pact', and with them came a wash of racial knowledge. The *Kara Bukat-talom* was a pact of secrecy made under oath before Burna, used to discuss clandestine matters. Breaking your word after swearing one made you a pariah and gave the aggrieved party the freedom to avenge themselves in any way, and if they informed the faithful of Matir that you'd broken your word, they'd join in the hunt. I knew, somehow, that this wasn't just a 'he said, she said' thing, but a status mark, like the King's Mark that told the guards of Taltos that I worked for Andrik.

"Okay." I bowed my head, rubbing the Mark of Matir with my other hand, and summoned the words for the oath out of my Tuun racial memory. "*Bukat Talom den Kanbuchen.*"

"Good." Andrik nodded. "Under the restrictions of the oath, I will pay you another five thousand olbia if you bring me the head and one hand of the King of Cats. If it is Ignas... I will add another five thousand."

That hardly surprised me. As soon as he'd invoked a sacred oath under the God of Darkness, I knew he'd been about to discuss something like this. I made a show of considering it, then shook my head.

"Your Majesty, please hear me out," I said. "You and I share some things in common, even though you're a noble and I'm not. I'm a younger son from a strict family with an older brother. His name was Steve."

"Odd name for a Tuun."

"Yeah." I brushed it off. "Me and Steve were polar opposites. He was tall and handsome. I had short legs and bad skin. He was smart, and good at everything he did, and I was dumb and had trouble concentrating at school. My parents were always really proud of him, and always ashamed of me. And I lived up to their shame, too. I did stupid shit... drugs and bullying and dangerous riding. But that wasn't my natural state, you know? When we were kids, we loved each other to death. We shared a lot of the same interests and sense of humor. As we got older, he began to believe what our parents said about me. He started to look down on me, like I was some lost puppy that just needed a firm, guiding hand to set me on the path of sensible financial decisions and good grades. We hated each other."

Andrik's expression of sly skepticism faded as I spoke. He looked down. "Yes. It was the same with Ignas and I. We were very close as children... not so much as adults."

"Yeah. Well, both of us got sick," I continued. "Sick enough we were going to die. And you know what his first thought was? Me. We hadn't spoken in five years after I disowned my family in a huge, nasty fight. But when we were dying, his first thought was to find a way to help me. And he did. So if the King of Cats really is your brother... I'm just saying to give him a chance. Thanks to Steve, I've been able to do more with my life in the last month than I did in the previous twenty-six years. If he was alive, I think he'd be proud of me. And your brother? If he sees that you've been a good, wise, stable king, maybe you can talk him around. You don't have to give to him except your time and some empathy, you know what I'm saying?"

The Volod nodded. Then, to my surprise, he pulled a silk handkerchief and dabbed at the corners of his eyes.

"My goodness," he said. "That certainly touched something. I will take your heartfelt words to bed with me and think on them, you can be sure of that.

I nodded, and almost reached out to clap him on the shoulder before I realized that was probably not a good idea. "In any case, I will be looking into the King of Cats angle. If he turns out to be some random asshole, I'll see what I can do about removing him from play - assuming he's guilty."

"Of course. However, speaking of that, you ought to turn in yourself. Who knows what the dawn shall bring." Andrik held a finger to his nose as he sniffed, then stood without looking back at me.

"I need to do some training first," I said. "Karalti and I just started flying together."

"Is that so? Well, the parade ground is yours to use," he replied. "I can mark it on your map, if you require."

"Sure." I nodded.

Andrik concentrated for a moment, and sure enough, the location icon appeared.

"Enjoy your evening," he said. "Was there anything else?"

I was already edging away when he asked, and suddenly remembered something: the 'quest' I'd gotten to learn about the Ravensblood Ruby.

"Yeah, actually. One thing." I turned back. "What can you tell me about the Ravensblood Ruby? Like... what makes it so special?"

The Volod regarded me shrewdly. Then he snorted.

"It is nothing more or less than the heart of Taltos, and perhaps all of Vlachia," he replied. "Despite its grandiose name, it is not a very large stone... perhaps the size of my thumb. It is an exceptional Corvinus Ruby. Since we found it some five hundred years ago, Vlachia has never fallen to any of its enemies. We have fended off barbarian hordes, the Jeun Empire, Dakhdir. Perhaps more mysteriously, it is said to contain the memories of the dragons themselves, including dragons who travelled here, to Vlachia. Most of the Church's lore of dragonkind was extrapolated from a written interview with my grandfather about the contents of the stone. He did not pass down the Words to activate what he saw, unfortunately."

"Huh." I scratched my stubbly jaw. "I wonder why it is that only your family can use these stones?"

"They say we are descended from the demigod Taltos, for whom this city is named. He was the son of Khors and a human woman." He smiled, nodding again. "It gives us some native resistance to magic, as well as... a few other quirks and features. Now, I really must be off to bed. Enjoy your training."

I bowed from the waist. "Enjoy your sleep, Your Majesty. I'll definitely be thinking about what you said."

"As will I." And with that, he swept out of the room.

CHAPTER 33

I walked from the Great Hall to the parade ground in the bitter wind, spear in hand. I'd stripped my gear down to the bare minimum, leaving the rest in our suite. I had my two primary weapons - the Spear of Nine Spheres and the Alpha Rod - some healing potions, our cash, and essential quest items that I either couldn't unequip or didn't want to.

"Karalti," I called out to her, mind to mind. *"It's time to come back and talk, Tidbit. I know you know where I am."*

For a couple minutes, all I heard was telepathic grumbling. I kept my ears pricked and my eyes keen, waiting, and was about to message her again when I saw a familiar, winged shadow cut in front of the moon and then vanish again.

Karalti slowly wheeled around in a crescent, sweeping great clouds of dust from the smooth stone of the drilling yard as she came to land. She dropped into a series of neat hopping steps, tucking her wings in against her sides. Her eyes gleamed brightly in the golden light that Erruku cast over Archemi.

"You alright?" I asked aloud.

Karalti turned her head, grunting and huffing.

"You need to use your mouth-words, girl." I set the end of my spear on the ground, leaning on it.

"Is... Suri okay?" she asked, after a short pause.

"Yeah. She's going to make it. She's tough."

The dragon's nostrils flared and then sealed as she snorted, and then she turned her muzzle back toward me.

"Look, I'm sorry I split my attention between you and her at the party," I said. "But at the same time, you have to meet me halfway. You need to really believe me when I say that you're one of the best things that's ever happened to me, Karalti, and that's never going to change. Neither is the fact that I'm human, and you're a dragon. It doesn't matter how we feel about it - that's the truth. We're going to have a different kind of relationship than I would with another human."

Karalti paced on the spot, chomping her jaws together as she wrestled with my words and herself. Just then, I remembered what Suri did to placate Cutthroat. I smiled at Karalti and put the Spear down. Then I stood up and held my arms out, and bobbed my head.

Karalti turned her snout from side to side, looking at me with one eye, then the other. She took one step toward me, and then she spread her own arms, mantled her wings, and bobbed her head quickly. She drew one leg up, and then dropped into a sweeping bow - a ton of weight perfectly balanced on three toes.

"*You dance back,*" she grumped.

Grinning, I bowed as well, and as she plunged and reared her head, I did my best to mirror her, dancing slowly to the left as she set the pace to the right. As we moved, she came closer, winding in until I could wrap my arm around her neck and grip her arm with the other hand, my face buried against her wing shoulder.

"*I'm jealous. I know it's bad.*" Karalti ducked her head, and crooned low in her throat as we embraced. "*My Words are Words of pride, because pride is part of Darkness... pride and jealousy. I don't like that you like Suri, but I like her, and I... like you.*"

"Yeah." I petted her scaly forearm. "I know. And you'll be okay, okay? So will we."

"*Yeah.*" Karalti hung her head.

I stood back, and on impulse, I caught Karalti by the muzzle and gently pulled her head around so that I was looking straight into her eyes. By moonlight, they seemed especially luminous. They were very much like her mother's, but innocent and hopeful instead of wise and pain-stricken. It was hard to meet her gaze for long, because I could feel the churn of emotions she was experiencing: the puppy love and confusion, the instinct she had to form pack bonds clashing with the instincts of a predator driven to challenge and drive away rivals and threats.

"Seriously," I said. "I promise."

Karalti made a little gurgling sound, then stretched her nose forward and licked me right up along the face.

"Urgh, what-!" I let go of her and wiped dragon drool off my nose. "Why?"

Giggling, my dragon paced forward, eagerly licking at my head and and hands as I tried to shield myself. Her head darted back and forth, while I laughed and cursed her and backed away. I let her smack her nose into my palm, and then hooked my fingers into her nostrils and pushed. Karalti squealed, shaking her head. "*Nooo, don't!*"

"Then don't lick my faaaace!" I pretend-whined back at her.

She beamed at me, jaws agape. "*Then stop being made of meeeeat.*"

"You have teeth the size of my thumb now. That joke is... in poor taste." I played a little rimshot on her wing, and she groaned.

"*You're the worst,*" Karalti grumbled. "*You wanna try flying again?*"

"Yeah, but first, we need to do some groundwork." I nodded. "Then I think we need to go and grind you up to Level Six. You said you found some monsters outside the city?"

"Yeah! They're down by the valley river, in the forest. Slimy dead people called mavka and frog things called vodniks."

"How much EXP do they give?"

"Uhh... about 80 and 170 each, I think."

I looked at our sheets, and did a rough calculation. I had a bit over a thousand EXP to go before I hit Level 13, and Karalti needed 934 before she reached Level 6. We'd need to kill nine mobs. "Are they tough?"

"Kinda. They don't like fire."

"Perfect. I cut down on weight, so you should be able to fly longer." I nodded, and bent down to pick up the Alpha Rod. I spun it in my hand and tucked it back under my arm. "You want to do it?"

"Yeah!" Karalti bounced up and down.

"Awesome." I clapped her on the shoulder, and went around to swing up into the saddle. "Because I'm about to try the stupidest thing I've ever done."

We soared over the valley river in near silence. The only sounds were those of the night: frogs croaking, the wind rippling over Karalti's wings, the slosh and gurgle of the shallow, salty water below. I hung forward over my dragon's shoulder, searching the stagnant marsh for our next target - preferably a vodnik.

We'd already killed eight monsters: five [[Mavras]], three [[Vodniks]]. Karalti was 25 EXP from leveling up, and I was 121. We were up to Dragon Riding 4 and Laden Flight 3 respectively, and with every point invested into the skills, flying became easier for both of us. Despite all of this, I still hadn't been able to work myself up to jumping off Karalti's back from a height.

Down below, I saw a motion in the stands of tall cattails. I tracked the rustling and swaying, and the glowing crosshairs in my HUD darted in to auto-target it. Yep - it was a vodnik, a hulking, orc-like, amphibious demihuman carrying a large rock as a weapon.

"*There,*" Karalti said. "*See it?*"

"*Sure do.*" I drew a deep breath, and squeezed the haft of my spear. This time, this strike, was going to be the one where I did it. "*Buzz it as close as you can. I'm going to try to jump.*"

Karalti dipped her wing, and I drew a sharp, excited breath as the horizon tipped thirty degrees. I'd learned to relax while leaning into her momentum, just like I would have on a motorcycle. The more relaxed I was, the easier it was for her, and the less likely I was to fall off.

"*You really gonna do it this time?*" she teased.

"*Hell yeah I am.*"

Like a hawk, Karalti swung around and lined up at the unsuspecting Vodnik. I swallowed, and got ready to stand.

"*Keep it steady.*" Drawing deep breaths, I drew one foot up underneath me, got some weight on it, and braced to leap. "*Here we.... GO!*"

This was a test of the game's limitations: namely because I had no idea if Jump worked while plummeting from a short height onto the back of a monster. If it did work, I'd stab and bounce, as I generally did when I called the maneuver on the ground. If not... *splat.*

Biting down the urge to scream 'DEATH FROM ABOVE!', I got my feet down, and half-Jumped, half-fell off Karalti's back.

It was a long way down - thirty feet or more - and I was moving at speed. I stayed calm by focusing down the length of the spear as the crosshairs disappeared, and....

WHAM.

The spear plunged through the unsuspecting creature's body, taking it right in the back of its neck. The bloody weapon thrust out through the monster's sternum. The impact rattled my teeth, but I got the notification I'd been dying to see.

[[You have landed a devastating blow on Vodnik! X5 damage!]]

[[You have taken 80 impact damage!]]

The monster slumped and clawed at the spear blade sticking out through its body, eyes bugging with shock as Karalti flew back in. Her jaws opened as I pulled my weapon free and got the hell out of the way.

"CHAAAAAAR!" White fire blasted over the Vodnik like a furnace, crisping it. All that was left after the flames died was its loot bag.

[[You have defeated Vodnik!]]

[[Congratulations! You are Level 13!]]

[[Congratulations! Karalti is Level 6!]]

[[New Feat: Banzaiiii!]]

Karalti came in to land, splashing water everywhere. Her form rippled and twisted, and then she grew - but not as much as the last five times. From levels one to five, she had almost doubled in size. This time, she only grew an extra three or four feet in length.

"Hell yeah!" I sloshed over to her, limping a little. "Did you see that! Times *five* damage, baby! Woo!"

"I saw!" Karalti beat her wings exuberantly, nearly knocking me down. *"Oops. Wings are bigger now."*

"This will make flying *so* much easier." To my great relief, the saddle had grown too. Like human armor, the accessory stretched or shrunk to fit whoever it was equipped on.

"I have more Lexica!" Karalti crouched down to let me up. *"Enough for a new spell! And more strength, too!"*

"Excellent." I mounted up, still riding the adrenaline high, and chugged a potion. "Alright - you should be able to take off from the ground, now."

"I'll try! Hang on!"

Of all the things I was sure to do, it was hang on. I stashed my spear in my Inventory to make use of both hands.

Karalti waded to shore, and when she was on drier land, she broke into a run into the wind. On instinct, I flattened my body down. It was a good call.

The dragon picked up speed, both hearts pounding against the walls of her chest, and then kicked herself up as she scooped with her wings. It was like trying to ride an earthquake. Her back bucked up and down, and it was all I could do to not bang my nose and knock myself out as she labored up into the sky.

"Yeah! We did it!" She was panting, her tongue flapping out the corner of her mouth... but we were in the air and gaining height.

"*We need to put you on a treadmill, Tidbit. Make you run laps around the parade ground.*" But even though it was still hard work, I could feel how much stronger she had become - and how much faster. She'd gained 15 points of Dex in that one level.

I dumped my ability point into Umbra Blast. I hadn't thought I'd need that ability, but during the fight with the Flesh Amalgamation, I had missed it. Then I opened up Karalti's sheet.

Karalti - Queen Dragon

Level 6 Juvenile

Strength: 54

Dexterity: 68

Stamina: 30

Will: 24

Wisdom: 8

Intelligence: 16

HP: 949

MP: 64

Affinity: Darkness/Life

EXP: 1934 (1645 to next level)

Lexica: 14 (4 points to spend)

Spells: 4

Skills:

Acrobatics: 8

- Aerial Acrobatics: 9

Dive: 5

Laden Flight: 4

[[Karalti has two unspent skill points!]]

Abilities:

Gift of the Blood: Allows a dragon to utilize magic and other supernatural abilities.

Eviscerate: A power attack with the front claws.

Ghost Fire: 195-285 fire damage; sticky fire that burns underwater.

Bite: 237-255 damage.

Gore: A dragon's unarmed attacks do double damage and cause Bleeding.

Split Turn: Burn 5 mana points per second to immediately change momentum while rolling. This allows for 90 degree and 180 degree turns in any direction. 2 bonus Lexica.

Spells:

Bioscope: Analyze an enemy and learn their strengths and weaknesses.

Sense Aether: Detect and assess magical effects, artifacts, and locations.

Dark Focus I: Double power of next magical attack.

Dirge: A curse that slowly damages enemies every turn and has a chance to cause the Deaf and Mute debuffs.

Sixty-eight dex? I whistled out loud into the wind as we cut the air.

I'd already planned what spell I wanted her to take with this level - Haste. I probably couldn't yet withstand the forces that sped Karalti up to supernatural speeds, but if something ever happened to us, I wanted her to be able to get away. I didn't know if dragons could respawn, and I never wanted to find out.

CHAPTER 34

We ended up sleeping on the floor of Suri's suite, with my back curled up against Karalti's belly, warmed by the shelter of her wings. I woke up to bright light, the sounds of clattering and shuffling, and pushed Karalti's wing to see Suri's copper-skinned back as she pulled her shirt over her head. She had a lot of scars.

"G'morning, sunshine," she drawled. She didn't turn around while she tugged the shirt down and slung a short leather vest on over it.

I glanced at her bare right arm. It was back, fully formed. The only sign that she'd lost it was the difference in color. The skin below the elbow was noticeably lighter and smoother than the rest of her.

"Morning. You're looking better." I sat up straight, yawned, and cracked my back. It was more a reflex than anything - since arriving in Archemi, I'd had no actual back pain at all outside of combat.

"I feel like a dog's breakfast, but I have my stats and HP pool back up to scratch, so I'm not complaining." Suri flexed the new limb, then began to don her armor and gauntlets.

Karalti stirred beside me, stretching and yawning. She opened one eye to peer sleepily at Suri, then grumbled and yanked me back in against her chest like a kid with a teddy bear. "Mmmm."

"Ack!" I fell back over, struggling against the iron grip. "Leggo!"

"*No. Mine.*"

Suri laughed, watching me flail around. "Aww, look at it. True love."

"True something." Resigned, I sighed and let myself be hugged as the dragon curled around me possessively, her tail twitching back and forth.

"So." Suri sat down on the edge of the bed to slide her plate gauntlet up along her freshly regrown arm. "You found another Nightstalkers ring, if I heard you right?"

"Right."

"That's what I thought. The good news is that I can get us a meeting with the King of Cats," she replied.

I raised an eyebrow. "I'm sorry, but did you just admit that you can get us a meeting with a local crime boss?"

Suri nodded. "Yeah."

"How?"

"*It's because she's a thieving-*" Before Karalti could finish, I whapped her on the edge of her wing with my knuckle. She snorted and pulled her wing away.

"None of that," I scolded. Then I realized I'd spoken aloud. "Sorry, Karalti said something to me in private."

Suri glanced down at her in confusion. "The Nightstalkers are a pit fighting syndicate. They do some smuggling on the side, but it's mostly about the sport. Well, I fought for a syndicate down in Dakhdir - Dhul Fiquar, the Rose Knives. Ever heard of them?"

"I hear they're the biggest syndicate in that country," I replied, gently prying Karalti's claws from around my midriff. "Man, you think you're getting to know someone, and then you find out they're a foot soldier for the fucking Mafia."

"I wasn't a foot soldier for *anyone*, asshole. I was a gladiator." Suri wrinkled her nose at me. "Fighting's how I survived in the city after I broke out of Al-Asad. I told you I tried to become a dancer. Well, it was at a place called the Tiger's Den. They ran fights out of the basement there. The guy I beat up on my first night dancing tried to murder the bookie."

"Bookie as in bookmaker?"

"Yeah. Well, I ripped the knife out of the guy's hand and stabbed him to death. Saved the bookmaker's life, and Dhul Fiquar picked me up as talent. They loved me – I was strong enough to take on middleweight and heavyweight men in the ring. It was a real hit."

"Huh. The more you know."

Suri nodded. "Well, point being, I made syndicate connections as soon as I wandered into Taltos. If you're not in a rival gang, it's polite for visiting syndicate members to pay a house call to the big players in any city they travel to. You go introduce yourself, have a drink, pay your respects. The Nightstalkers are currently the biggest syndicate in the city. I know where they hang out, and if we play it right, I'm pretty sure we can meet the boss. It's good that we're both foreigners."

"Why?"

"Because their base is in Cat Alley. The 'International District', where the Meewfolk live." Suri stood and hooked her axes onto her belt. "They don't like locals, and the locals don't like them, but that's where we have to go. The earlier, the better."

"Not at night?" I asked.

"Nope. Meewfolk are nocturnal, and nights are when the fights happen. The pit bosses do their admin in the morning, sleep all day, then run events from after sunset until the next morning. If we get there before nine, they'll be wrapping up whatever went down yesterday."

I poked Karalti in her armpit. "Come on, girl. You heard the lady."

"*Bleh.*" Karalti yawned again, but she finally let me go.

I picked myself up and yawned as well, then swiped my HUD and equipped my armor. I was alarmed to see that nearly all of my stuff was gone, until I remembered that it was in a pack in my room. "Mind if we stop by my place?"

"Nope. But should get going already."

The three of us walked down to the Royal Stables, where rows and rows of riding beasts were kept in communal pens. Cutthroat's was easy to find: it was the one where most of the other hookwings were cowering back against the far wall.

It was just after feeding time, and Cutthroat was licking out the bottom of an empty trough. Two other, far more dainty hookwings watched her nervously as they gulped down their meals from the next trough over. The bigger hookwing looked up once she had cleared every scrap of meat, smacking her jaws, and her baleful golden eyes fixed on the rapidly vanishing food in the other trough. She didn't even really bother making a serious challenge to the twins – she just reached out with a claw and began to pull Meal Number Two toward her.

The smaller dinosaurs screeched with rage, and one of them snapped at her arm. As its jaws closed in, Cutthroat lowered her head and headbutted it right in the snout. It yelped and backed away. The other one was now alone. Victorious, the coal-black hookwing dragged the trough close enough to pull a mouthful of entrails from it, snapping them up and swallowing them down. Her eyes narrowed with pleasure.

"Same old psycho," I chuckled. "How are you two getting along?"

Suri held a hand up to ward me back, and strode over to the bolted gate. She threw it open and strode in, scattering hissing hookwings to all corners of the corral. When Cutthroat saw who it was, her throat swelled, and she left off the food, bobbing her head and making a weird sound. *Gurk gurk gurk.*

"Wait... is she about to...?" That was all I got out before she regurgitated the guts she'd just stolen onto the ground in front of Suri's feet. I jumped back against Karalti. "Eww! Dude!"

"She's trying to feed me. She thinks I don't eat enough." Suri remarked. She took Cutthroat's tack off the hooks and saddle tree.

"That's fucking *nasty*!" I hung back, watching on in a mixture of admiration and horror as Suri threw the saddle blanket and saddle onto Cutthroat's back.

"They do it for their mates to show they will be able to provide for chicks. It's a courtship thing." Suri said. "She's basically my wife now."

"That's so romantic." Karalti sighed with longing.

"Umm, sure." My stomach churned as Cutthroat lowered her head and began to lick up the steaming pile of meat she'd just vomited onto the ground. "If you ever do that to me, I'm disowning you."

I watched as Suri mounted. She was looking more confident in the saddle these days, and watching the pair gave me a warm glow. For all her antics, Cutthroat would always have a place in my heart. When push came to shove, she'd always been there to back me up.

Karalti was bigger than Cutthroat now, so she took the lead. People actively got out of our way, watching on in awe as she strutted by. Once we were outside, she broke into a graceful lope, lighter and faster than the hookwing's bulldozer gallop.

"You going to be able to stay cool during this?" Suri asked me, once we'd cleared the gatehouse at the end of the road. "You're not going to turn into Mr. Law and Order all of a sudden, are you?"

"Of course not. Anything I should know?"

"Keep your purse down the front of your armor. Pay for things in copper coins, and don't flash any silver or gold. Don't stare any Meewfolk you meet in the eye without blinking. If they look at you, sort of squint your eyes slowly, nod, and leave it at that. They tend to talk without making eye contact, so don't be weirded out if they're looking somewhere else other than you."

"Huh. Alright." I watched the street as we cantered by. "You've never met this guy before, right?"

"No. Just one of the pit bosses and some of his lieutenants."

"Were they all Meewfolk?"

"No. Pretty diverse lot, actually. That's normal for syndicates... Champion fighters and coaches come from all over the world."

I chuckled. "Did you have a name in the ring? All fighters have ring names, don't they?"

"Yeah, they do." Suri replied. "They called me *Libiwat Asada*, the Red Lioness. You don't speak Dakhari, do you?"

"Nope."

"'Al-Asad' means 'Of the Lion'. The lion is the Sultir's Clan symbol, and they named their dungeon after it. It was a bit of an in-joke."

"Nice. How'd you avoid the authorities in a city of that size?"

"Dalim's underworld is literally underground. Nearly all the crims are Fireblooded," she replied. "They took me in, and for most of that first month of freedom, I was too scared of the sky to go outside much."

"Really?"

"Yeah. There's two things that scare the piss out of me: wide open spaces, and giants."

"Giants?"

"Yeah. I hate big things, you know. Shit that towers over you. Gives me the creeps."

Cat Alley – officially known as the International District - was easily the shittiest and most heavily policed part of Taltos. The neat cobblestone roads and clean apartments gave way to a ramshackle sprawl of huts, crooked stone buildings, stalls, and lean-tos. On the way through the gate, we saw soldiers harassing a group of sour-faced Meewfolk. The humans were making them turn out their backpacks and pouches onto a table, searching for stolen goods and weapons.

Even so, the area was lively. Street vendors sold baked fish, fried insects, live chickens, rats, and ducks. Human preachers held small crowds on street corners. Surprisingly clean Meewfolk children chased each other or played games by the edge of the sluggish canal. The river ran underneath a series of bridges in the middle of the district.

"We're in the Women's Quarters right now," Suri said. "Men live on the other side of the water."

Suri reined Cutthroat to a slow walk as we crossed a bridge and turned down one broad curving street, which ended in a dingy walled courtyard. The spike-topped wall was covered in faded notices and wanted posters, graffiti, and moss. Five guards - three Meewfolk, one Mercurion in a battered mask, and a human - lounged beside a heavy oak and iron door, or played cards at a rusted metal lattice table nearby.

"Easy, girl." Suri murmured to the dinosaur as she snorted and grunted, eyes darting from one face to another.

"Telling Cutthroat to calm down is basically an exercise in futility. You know that, right?" I whispered to her.

"Sure, but it's worth a try. Let me handle this one."

"Oh, look. It's the dragon man and the Dakhari bounty hunter," the human called out. He was a big rough scar of a man, with a twisted lip, a big crossbow, and a bandoleer stacked with ammo for it. "Heroes of Taltos, renowned across the land. Not that you've done much about the Slayer. What's your business here, kingsmen?"

"My business is with your boss," Suri replied. "I'm Suri Ba'Hadir, the Lioness of *Dhul Fiquar*. Me and Hector need some face time with the King of Cats."

"Dhul Fiquar? The man squinted at us both. "That supposed to fuckin' mean something to me?"

"Yeah, it should. And if it doesn't, this will." Suri brandished her hand with the gold Nightstalkers ring. I lifted my hand to show the same.

"Come back at night. There's no rousing in the morningsss." One of the Meewfolk rasped. He was relaxing on one of the chairs at the table, his hand of cards folded against the top. Unlike the human, he carried no weapons other than his own claws, but he looked tired and strung out.

"We're not here to rouse. We're here to shift bluff," Suri said.

"Shift bluff?" I asked her by P.M.

"Trade information," was the terse reply. *"A rouse is a fight."*

The human grunted. "Give me one good reason the king would want to see you."

I urged Karalti forward a step. "Because Red made me an offer, and we decided to take her up on it."

Suri looked over sharply. The guard's thick brows arched with intrigue. Red's involvement with the Nightstalkers had been an educated guess on my part, but it seemed I'd hit the nail on the head.

He jerked his head to one of the Mercurions. "Glick, go in and give the boss their names. See what she says."

Glick bowed their masked head, then opened the gate and paced inside.

We dismounted, and I lay a hand on Karalti's shoulder. *"I need you to stay out here and watch Cutthroat for us. Alright?"*

"Alright. You don't need to tie her or anything. She'll follow me." Karalti looked down at the guards, flaring her horns.

"You sure?"

"Yeah. I'm bigger now, so she listens to me."

Suri started to lead Cutthroat to a hitching spot, but I caught her arm and shook my head. "Karalti says she'll take care of her."

Suri shrugged, then nodded.

Another ten minutes or so passed before the Mercurion returned. He beckoned us forward with two bony fingers, and we followed him through the gate into a compound that was similar to a Chinese *hutong*. The path turned left, and we passed under an Asian-style hip-roofed gateway that opened into a courtyard. There were a number of houses here, all of them in bad shape. Some of them were clearly relics of an older Taltos, built out of worn black limestone. Others were distinctly foreign, with steep gabled roofs supported by carved wooden pillars. There was little in the way of walls and rooms. Meewfolk lounged on the bed-sized windowsills of these houses, sleeping in the open air, or watching us suspiciously as Glick led us to the biggest house in the compound.

This house was in better condition than the others, but you could smell the old booze and sweat from the doorway. The Mercurion opened the door ahead of us, walking with a light, dancing step, and came to a stop at the bar where he flourished and bowed to the only person there.

Red was dressed almost exactly the same as she had been at the party. She reclined elegantly against the edge of the long wooden counter, her body a study in sharp points and long, lanky curves. She was wearing a different mask today: instead of a serene Mona Lisa smile, this one had the grimacing face of a Japanese demon. Her head swiveled toward as we approached.

"Hi, Red," I said through clenched teeth. "You really know how to throw a party, you know that?"

Suri frowned and stared at us. "Wait. Do you know each other?"

"Hector and I met at a party once." Red pushed back from the bar and beckoned us to follow her. "Come. The king is expecting you."

CHAPTER 35

Red led us through the building and down a flight of hollow wooden stairs, as graceful and quiet as a ribbon of smoke. The hall had the dreary, grimy look of a shuttered nightclub, with dirty floors and clusters of empty, dirty tankards, paper, and straw. The refuse was being swept up by the morning cleanup team.

"What's this place called?" I asked Red, following behind Suri. We naturally fell into letting her take point - she was the tank, and I was the guy who could almost see behind his own head. It was natural that I followed up the rear.

"It isn't called anything," Red rasped. She still had that gravelly, pack-a-day voice. "If someone wants to drink and find a fight, they know where to come."

At the bottom of the stairs was a basement lined with kegs and barrels. Red strode to the far wall and vanished right through it.

"Whoa," I said. "Illusion."

"Yeah." Suri nodded her agreement. "Probably keyed to these rings."

She passed through, and I followed. The illusory wall had to have been fairly solid, because there was a noticeable temperature drop on the other side. Behind the curtain was another part of the Lethos Cellar complex - what looked like an ancient mineshaft. Clusters of brightly colored glass lamps hung from the ceiling, lighting a path that led down to an ancient cistern. A solid beam of light shone down from overhead, illuminating the center of what had once been a round, shallow reservoir for water. Now it was a fighting pit with a fence built around the edge.

"Does fighting pay well?" I asked Suri.

She eyed the ring with an odd expression on her face. Nostalgia. "If you're good at it."

"To the death, or...?"

"Depends. Death matches pay better than anything else, though."

I smiled faintly as we cut around the arena and headed down a narrow stone passage. "I'm guessing they didn't call you 'Lioness' just because you came out of Al'Asad."

Suri chuckled. "Nooope."

Red strode to a door at the end of the tunnel and knocked twice before opening it. I nodded to her, and paused as my HUD chirruped. I had a message - when I glanced across, my heart jumped when I saw who it was from.

⟦You have one unread private message from Rin Lu⟧

Dammit. Talk about shitty timing. I pushed the notification back with a thought, and followed Suri into the room while Red held the door.

The office beyond was cool and sweet smelling, offset by the soft sound of trickling water. It was beautifully furnished, with antiques from every part of Archemi blended into one seamless artful composition. A purple divan was partly hidden by jade and pearl-inlaid ebonwood screens; fringed colored lanterns lit the dingy place with blue, red, and yellow light. At the back was a firepit, which burned high and clean behind a large mahogany desk and the lean, tall figure who sat behind it. As we crossed the floor, he stood and came around to greet us. He was almost six and a half feet tall, broad-shouldered and narrow-hipped, and dressed like an assassin in layers of dark, soft leather. His face was thin and handsome, and even with a short salt-and-pepper beard altering his features, the resemblance to Andrik Corvinus was unmistakable.

"You're looking pretty good for a dead man, Your Majesty," I said, with a bow.

"Your... Majesty?" Suri's head turned sharply toward me, then she looked back to Ignas, the King of Cats, and her eyes widened. "Ignas? Ignas Corvinus?"

Ignas gave us a sad, small, thin-lipped smile. "I can count the number of people who know my name on one hand. That's because everyone else is dead. I say this to you only because you enter my residence carrying my brother's mark, so you must pardon this old man for his concern."

Red had stayed by the door, and crossed her arms as three Meewfolk rogues materialized from the shadows, lingering close by. I hadn't seen them, hadn't sensed them, and my HUD hadn't picked them up until they revealed themselves.

"No problem, Your Majesty. And don't worry about your safety: your brother's a dick," I said to him. "I signed up with him to catch a murderer, not become one."

Suri made a choking sound in the back of her throat.

Ignas' mouth quirked to one side. It wasn't exactly a smile. His white-gray eyes were very level. Wise, cold... and as Andrik had said, disciplined. "What do you mean?"

"I can't tell you because he swore me to a pact," I replied. "Take a guess."

"He hired you to kill me?"

"I can't say."

"Fair enough." Ignas blew away a strand of imaginary hair, then chuckled and shook his head. For a moment, he almost seemed like the wise, good-natured man Matthias had described, but the fleeting humor was very short-lived. "So - I have been up all night, and as I'm sure you understand, I'm quite tired. I will make this short and simple. You have come to me about ceasing my activities now that Andrik's evangelical council is all but dead. The answer is no."

"What? Just like that?" I said.

"Yes." Ignas replied. "Just like that."

Suri stepped up, but I held a hand up. Eyes narrowed, she jerked her chin, then stood back.

"Well, good thing I'm not here to try and stop you. Red over there made me an offer the other night," I said, motioning back over my shoulder. "I'm interested."

"Then you should have listened to her during the event." Ignas shrugged his shoulders minutely. "It's not a light-hearted offer I make in accordance with your whims."

"No. Defeating the monster you made out of those people at the party wasn't a light-hearted decision, either," I said. "But when Andrik tried to bind me to an ancestral vow to get me to kill you, I started having second thoughts. I had an older brother I owe my life to. Fratricide is way beyond my comfort zone."

"But the persecution of my people is tolerable?" Red snapped from behind us.

"Ebisa." Ignas' eyes flicked up past my shoulder. "You know as well as I do that personal grievances surpass societal concerns in all men, Mercurion or otherwise. Come here and join us."

Red - Ebisa - stalked over to us and slouched against the edge of the desk, her arms and ankles crossed.

"We worked out the pattern to the assassinations," Suri said. "You were having those men killed to mock the virtues of the church."

"Virtues none of those men adhered to in their pursuit of power and self-interest. Abel and Darko were despotic theocrats. Toth, Orban and Erik were hypocrites and perverts." Ignas lifted his chin, then turned his face to look back at the fireplace. "Khors, the Forge Father. God of artists and crafters, the builders and smiths and potters who make any nation great. He is a good god, worthy of worship. And yet, Khors is only one of the Nine. Without the others to balance out the material power of his church, he quickly becomes an overbearing patriarch mired in tradition. The crafting done in his name becomes soulless, or worse - bent toward nothing but war and control."

"The last two virtues left are discipline and honesty," I said. "My guess is that the Duke is discipline, and your brother-"

"Is honesty," Ignas finished. "Well, at least he hired astute investigators. But were you astute enough to be able to deduce that he has no intention of rewarding you? The men he hired you to protect are now almost all gone. Even if they had survived and you bought Andrik the Slayer in chains, he would have turned on you in the end."

I grinned and shrugged. "Now that you mention it, I had wondered."

Suri folded her arms. "So the affair, the suicide, everything was faked?"

"Of course," Ignas replied. "Andrik's assassins were hounding me within hours of my framing and disinheritance. Friends of mine helped me source a body from the morgue, which we spirited into the castle and used to fake my death while I escaped."

"How did he frame you?" Suri asked.

"It is commonly believed that only the Royal Family can use Corvinus Rubies - that is not true," Ignas replied. "Anyone with magical ability can use them, but the Words of Power are jealously guarded family secrets. They are conveyed only to the heir of the throne on the day he achieves adulthood. My brother spied on us during the ceremony between me and my father and learned the words - using a Mercurion-made automata, ironically."

"Kanzo's listening devices?" I frowned.

"Indeed. It was that device that convinced my brother to become Kanzo's patron," Ignas said. "Once he knew the command words for our family jewels, my dearest brother hired a Dakhari *magus* to ensorcell a ruby with lurid illusions. Andrik had tried to dig dirt on me for years, you see. He had failed to unearth anything that could have me disinherited, so he settled for making something up. When the recording was shown to my father, he believed that only I had the Words required for the rubies, and I'm sure you know the rest."

"I'd wondered why you were using Kanzo," Suri mused.

Ignas reached out, and lay a hand on Ebisa's shoulder. "That is not the only reason."

As one, we both looked at the masked Mercurion woman.

"Andrik used Kanzo's listening device to take the throne," Ignas said. "And in the process, Kanzo not only gained a great deal of wealth, he gained the Words for his own use. Andrik is a boor and knows nothing of *sang'ti'tak*, Mercurion artificing, and naively assumed that Kanzo would not be able to do anything with his knowledge of the rubies. Instead, Kanzo used this and his new-found fortune to commit a grave sin against his own kind."

"Why didn't he just marry and do things the normal way?" I spread my hands. "I mean, he's a Mastercrafter, maybe the best Artificer on the mainland... that has to make him an eligible bachelor, doesn't it?"

"Two reasons," Ebisa said stiffly. "For one thing, he is nearly thirty-six years old. He is elderly by the standards of our race."

I scratched my head. "Thirty-six is elderly?"

Ebisa nodded. Her sculpted porcelain mask gave no hint to her expression. "We are born adult, self-aware, and invested by the knowledge of our clan - ideally. But the mana which animates us decays; our lives are fleeting, and thus we are driven to make all that we can, to leave a legacy of our *sang'ti'tak* to our descendants. He has perhaps eight months of life left."

"And the second reason is that he is clanless, right?" Suri asked.

"Yes. He is from Tlaxi'ca Tisaksa, the House of the Wasp, but was stripped of his House name and title for stealing blueprints for *sang'ti'tak* from the Clan vault," Ebisa said. "There are Tisaksa in

Taltos. His clan status is a matter of public record, and a clanless *juchi* cannot marry."

I rubbed my eyes. "So the 'kicked out of my clan because of my love and peace' thing is bullshit?"

Ebisa looked down, clutching her arm with a thin hand. "Somewhat. He refused to fight in the Zaunt Civil War, but not because of his ideals. The only things Kanzo cares about are himself and his creations. Not even them. His entire life, everything he has done, is to protect and gratify himself and his pride. Everything."

"Gods. Poor Rin," Suri murmured.

Ebisa barked a bitter laugh. "Poor *Rin*? Oh yes, he loves Rin, the miracle child of her Clan. She's Starborn... a one-in-a-million among our people, destined to be able to live again and again. He was so *proud* to have her as his apprentice, because she makes him feel even more important than being an Artificer for the Royal family. Kanzo treats her like a trophy, but she... he never..."

"Take off your mask, Ebisa." Ignas dropped his voice.

Ebisa's shoulders hunched, and she drew her arm in closer to her chest.

Ignas squeezed her shoulder, and gestured to us. "By their expressions, you know there shall be no judgment here."

She nodded slightly, then reached up to push back her hood, revealing a smooth, hairless scalp of silver silicone. She had the usual backswept crystalline wings in place of ears, but they looked different to any I'd seen on other Mercurions. They were curly and fancy, made of red stained glass and soldered metal. She unhooked her mask, and let it fall into her hand before lowering it.

Ebisa's face matched the rest of her scarecrow body. Her skin was drawn tight over her skull. Her nose was thin-bridged, with cheekbones sharp enough to cut glass. The overall structure of her face was one of was eerie beauty... but she had no lips, and more alarmingly, no eyes. In place of eyes, she had four polished Corvinus Rubies, two to each side. It made her face look utterly alien.

"He had to *make do*," she hissed. Without lips, the grim slash of Ebisa's mouth peeled back from her metal teeth with every word. "That's what he always told me. He had to *improvise.* So that is what I am. His *improvisation.*"

"Establishing a body and brain complex enough to sustain an intelligent consciousness is extraordinarily difficult," Ignas said sadly. "But the formulations and magic required for it are not unknown, and can be obtained by rogue artificers desperate enough to make the effort. But there is no such thing as true Life magic in the world... only the Words that simulate the complexity of life."

"And he does not know all of them, and nor did he have the resources to properly equip my body." Ebisa finished. "So not only am I *juchi*, I am an abomination. I require Corvinus Rubies to continue living, and no Mercurion will look at me, even other *juchi.* I am forever without any one of my own kind, even in friendship... which was surely Kanzo's intention. This way, I could be certain that the only one who would love me was him."

"I think you look kind of badass, to be honest," I said.

Suri elbowed me sharply. "So you're what is being used to blackmail him?"

Ebisa put her mask back in place, hooking it over her ears. "I *am* the one blackmailing him – not that he believes me."

"Meaning?"

"He thinks I'm doing this against my will," Ebisa spat. "He thought that I was happy in his little laboratory, entirely reliant on him to continue living. I learned where he kept the rubies I rely on to live, and I escaped."

Suri frowned. "Kanzo is murdering because he thinks Ignas will free you?"

Ebisa drew herself up straight. "Yes. He operates under the threat that I will be revealed to our people and he will suffer their judgment. The Mercurions will cast his name from our archives here and in Zaunt. His blueprints will be burned, and no children will be modeled on him. His works will be destroyed. Even his darling Rin will purge all memory of him and find a new Master. No one will remember Kanzo, and nothing terrifies a narcissist so completely as erasure. He will do anything - *anything* - to leave his legacy. And so he shall: as a kingkiller and assassin, which is a lesser fate than what he has been offered if he does not comply. At least this way, he knows he shall be remembered for *something.*

CHAPTER 36

"Well damn." I put my hands on my hips. "Guess you aren't fucking around."

"There is too much at stake." Ignas shook his head, regarding Suri and I with a critical eye. "I don't suppose you know what caused this rift between brothers to start with, do you?"

"Nope," Suri replied. I shook my head.

"Not merely a case of simple jealousy, I assure you." Ignas squeezed Ebisa on the shoulder and left her where she leaned against the desk, walking around it to sit down. "Andrik has never been a self-disciplined man. From an early age, he was always prone to fancies and laziness. He was smart, but would fail repeatedly at simple things - arithmetic, writing, magic - simply because he wouldn't follow through on the work required. He was always looking for the pill to cure his woes and struggles."

I privately winced to myself a little. *That* sounded awfully familiar. I'd been like that before the Army.

"You must realize that this is the reason why religion appeals so strongly to Andrik," Ignas said. He began to fill a pipe with tobacco, and my chest panged with the memory of Matthias - and the sharp reminder that this man had been responsible for his death. "It has nothing to do with piety. When we were boys, he got it in his head that if he prayed to the gods, they would fix his problems for him. Anything from a toothache to his homework, he hoped that he could pray it away. Of course, that's not how it works. Or it wasn't... until he joined this, this *cult*."

"Wait. This just took a sharp left turn," I said. "What do you mean, he joined a cult?"

"Exactly that," Ignas said. "He joined a cult. I was never able to dig into it very far, because he went to pains to hide his involvement, but I found small signs that I raised with our father. The problem was that the main symptoms of his involvement with this organization were, in my father's eyes, 'good' things. Andrik lost weight. He became more aggressive, more confident, interested in matters of state. He began to devour information on magic, philosophy, statecraft... all of it with a peculiarly radical slant. He changed very quickly from a foppish young milksop into a shrewd courtier, which pleased our father but raised my hackles."

Suri had her resting cop face back on. "So how do you know he was in a cult?"

Ignas shrugged. "I found his shrine of worship. A week after that, father came into lunch, screaming about 'filth' and waving a Corvinus Ruby with a very clear recording of me sodomizing a talented male Meewfolk sword dancer. I was disowned and disinherited on the spot... and thus we share this moment."

"Can you describe the shrine?" she asked.

Ignas's brow furrowed. "It was a nook inside of a walk-in closet in Andrik's room. I went to view it after my spy – his valet – reported that Andrik was up to something in a part of his suite that he had forbidden the servants to enter. But it's strange – I remember elements of what I saw, but I could not describe the shrine to you. I know that he had taken the Ravensblood Ruby – our crown jewel and a relic of the Church of the Maker – and had it set up in some ritualistic fashion. There was a deer's heart there... but the rest, it is like my memory rejected the sight of it. I recall that there was a symbol on prominent display, and that it terrified me beyond all reason."

Me and Suri looked at one another, then back to the king. "Do you remember what the symbol was? Like, do you think you could draw it?"

"I am afraid I cannot," he replied heavily. "I can tell you now that it was no symbol associated with The Nine. Not even a shrine to Rusolka is as dark as what I saw that day."

"Your Majesty, this adds a whole new dimension to everything," I said. "May I make you a counteroffer?"

He twitched his shoulders. "You may try."

"Call a truce. Leash your attack dog, and tell Kanzo to hold off on the next target," I said. "I'll investigate this cult issue for you and we'll get evidence of his blasphemy. That's going to discredit him badly enough that if you step in, you'll be able to take the throne again. No one else has to die, and if we're caught, it's no skin off your back."

"Not a bad idea," Suri drawled. "My pit bosses told me to come to Taltos because the King of Cats was known to be a fair and trustworthy business partner. I'm willing to put my money on you and throw in with Hector."

Ignas clenched his pipe down between his teeth. "No. By the time you have enough evidence to convince the Council of Lords, all of the Meewfolk of this city will be staked on the walls, the Mercurions murdered and drained for their blood, and this nation will be on an unstoppable course toward becoming a corrupt theocracy."

"You're living proof that humiliation is a devastating tool in the hand of a monarch," I said. "If you prove you were framed and that Andrik is a fratricidal scumbag, you have a more legitimate claim than you would if you killed him."

"None of what we have undertaken is being done lightly or without consideration of the consequences. If we even pause in our efforts, more innocent citizens will die by his hand. He has already closed the Mercurion's quarter, and this district is next. Andrik must pay for his crimes against me and Vlachia, and I will not miss the chance to take my country back for the sake of your convenience."

"Then we have no choice." I shrugged. "We have to kill Kanzo."

Ignas put his palms against the top of his desk and pushed himself up to stand.

"I want to let you both free," he said quietly. "I do. But there is too much at stake. I'm still willing to purchase your non-involvement for the duration of the upcoming events, but if you continue to threaten me, I *will* retaliate."

Ebisa slowly straightened up from her slouch.

"Go ahead. I'll respawn at Vulkan Keep, and we'll spill this entire thing to Andrik. This place will be crawling with soldiers within an hour." I pulled the collar of my armor down, baring my neck, and pointed at it. "Here you go - clear shot."

"I never said anything about killing you, Starborn," Ignas replied coldly. "If Kanzo dies before he achieves his final aim, you will never know peace again in Vlachia or the kingdoms of our allies."

"I have a dragon outside who will torch this place if you so much as lay a hand on either of us." I crossed my arms.

The man's eyes narrowed. I could see the gears turning in his head. When Ebisa made to draw a dagger, he shook his head sharply.

"You're a strong negotiator. I can respect that," he said. "What is he offering you both that I cannot?"

"Sanctuary without threat of extradition," Suri replied to him. "We're fugitives: me from Dakhdir, him from Ilia."

Ignas nodded slowly.

"He is lying to you," he said firmly. "Because I know for a fact that Vlachia has extradition treaties with both of those countries. By the terms of those treaties, he MUST send you back to face justice for whatever crimes you may or may not have committed in those nations. I myself oversaw several extraditionary processes as Crown

Prince. Suri – if you are a veteran of the syndicates, perhaps you know of Malak the Harpy?"

Suri's expression shut down into an implacable poker face.

"He was one of the outlaws extradited to Dakhdir by my decree," Ignas continued. "I believe the Sultir made an example of him."

Suri jerked her head in a small, stiff nod. "He threw him into Al-Asad, and he used to complain about being sent back to Dakhdir from somewhere. But he never said which country, or which king."

Well, shit. I looked between them, thoroughly disconcerted... and found myself thinking back to the mass attack by the Ilian Mercenaries in the University District. The guards had arrived late. The street had been empty, like an ambush. I'd put it down to the Mata Argis... but...

"If your safety is paramount to you, no wonder you refuse my money." Ignas bowed his head and spread his hands. "In that case, I shall reframe my offer. In the course of my work with the Nightstalkers and other similar organizations, I have developed a strong network of smugglers, forgers, and other specialists. Let our schemes take their course, and I swear on my father's blood that I will offer you and yours sanctuary."

"How?" I asked.

He regarded me patiently. "I am not yet a King, but I am a ruler within a commercial empire that spans three countries. We are fully capable of assuring your safety. The Nightstalkers and their affiliates are mobile, discreet, and are not beholden to treaties with any nation, least of all the likes of Ilia. We could even arrange for you to travel to Meewhome."

"Is it anything like the International District? Because if so, that's not a perk. No offense intended."

"It is a tropical archipelago, actually. Here: let me make this offer official."

Ignas bowed his head, concentrating, and a new Quest notification jumped in the corner of my eye. When I pulled it over, my eyebrows lifted. This was not a type of notification I'd ever seen before.

Quest Alternative (The Slayer of Taltos): Stalkers in the Night
You have discovered that former Crown Prince, Ignas Corvinus the Third, is alive and well. After faking his own suicide and spending a year in exile, he has returned as an underworld figure in Artana's profitable underworld fighting circuit. Not only that, but he claims his deceitful younger brother, Andrik, lied to you about his offer of reward and sanctuary.

Ignas is offering to match his brother's rewards, on one condition – that you abandon the hunt for Kanzo, the Slayer of Taltos, and allow Ignas to execute the master stroke of his plan. His goal? To pull Vlachia back from the clutches of his brother, a heretic guilty of betraying his own blood for the sake of power.

Reward: *15,000 gold olbia (half up-front), EXP (progressive), +500 infamy in Vlachia. The Nightstalkers and allied Syndicate factions go from Poor to Good (Protected status).*

Special: *If Ignas becomes Volod of Vlachia, your reward may change.*

Special: *This is a co-current quest with the Slayer of Taltos. If you accept, you will have to fulfil the terms of* **one** *quest – Andrik's or Ignas'. The other quest will automatically fail.*

If Ignas succeeds in his plan to retake the throne, you will suffer no faction-based penalties for switching quests and will gain Very Good (1500) fame with both the Vlachia and Nightstalkers factions.

If Ignas fails in his scheme, you will suffer faction-based penalties from both Vlachia and the Nightstalkers and allied Syndicate factions.

If you reject this quest, you will suffer faction-based penalties from the Nightstalkers and attain a Nemesis (Ignas Corvinus).

Wow. Okay. I scanned the quest, lips parted in disbelief. Suri had a similar expression on her face. I'd figured out that Archemi's AI adapted your questlines to your decisions as time went on – but I'd never seen anything like this. It wasn't the quest forks that bamboozled me so much as the *uncertainty*, the 'Ignas might win, or he might not' aspect. I'd been playing the Slayer questline like a story, expecting it to be basically predetermined... but this ripped that notion out from under me. I'd forgotten something in all of this. The NPCs were smart enough – self-aware enough – to fucking outsmart and outplay *each other*.

"Well?" Ignas said.

"Wait." I licked my lips and held up a hand. "I need to think about this."

Suri gulped. "Me too."

He shrugged. "Take your time."

To my surprise, Suri actually drew in close to me, huddling up before PMing. "*Shit, Hector... I don't know what to do. He's right about those extradition treaties, I'm sure, but I don't have any reason to doubt Andrik. I haven't seen a hint of him reneging on his deal. He's a spoiled brat... but... do you believe this guy or not?*"

"Hang on." I reviewed the Special information again, frowning. "*Karalti?*"

"*Huh? What is it?*"

"*Tell me that I'm smart.*"

There was a pause. "*Wat?*"

"*Encourage me,*" I said. "*Tell me I'm smart and I'm not a dumbass, and that the hunch that I have is something important.*"

"*Uhh... you're super smart! You can hold onto me while flying, and... and you jumped off and hit the frog thing! And you're a good dancer.* And *you fought off all those Mata Argis for ages.*"

It was weird – but it helped, hearing this voice in my mind choke down the self-doubt that was clouding my intuition.

I messaged Suri again. "*If Andrik gets his way, and we kill Kanzo, we are going to earn the wrath of the Nightstalkers and their allies, plus, there's a chance that Andrik isn't going to live up to his half of the bargain. If we support Ignas and he fails because Andrik stops his own assassination, we're doubly shafted.*"

Suri sucked on one of her teeth, staring at her own display. "*Right. That's what I mean. It's a gambit.*"

"*No. It feels like a gambit, but it's not.*" I pressed my lips together. "*Putting aside the fact that he killed someone I liked... The best objective outcome for all of us is that Ignas becomes king. If we choose to support Ignas, Ignas is more likely to become Volod. Players - Starborn - are agents of fate. Therefore, we get the maximum benefit if we intervene. So, probability-wise... I think we should throw in with him.*"

The woman drew a deep breath. Then she nodded. "*For once, you're not a total dumbass.*"

I suddenly realized that Suri was close enough that I could smell her perfume: sandalwood and honeycomb. Her shoulder was just barely touching mine. She looked up, and I met her golden-eyed gaze. Her lips parted a little before she stood back from me.

"You know, I never liked Andrik anyway." Clearing her throat, Suri turned her attention back to Ignas. "You're a ruthless son-of-a-bitch, Ignas, but you're a sportsman. You wouldn't have become the King of Cats if your word wasn't pure fuckin' gold. I'm in."

"You killed one of my friends at Kobayaz," I said to him. "Father Matthias. The way he and those other people died was terrible."

Ignas's confidence flickered. "I know. And I knew Petko. He was a good man... my friend, and one of our agents in Andrik's inner circle."

"We were as shocked as you were." Ebisa shrugged her bony shoulders. "We don't instruct Kanzo on how to take out any of his targets, except that they must be done in such a way as to mock the virtues of Andrik's church and avoid harming civilians whenever possible. We certainly didn't tell him to mutilate priests or destroy Kobayaz. When I talked to you, I only expected the Forgemaster to die. My scouts were in position to distract the guards in case Kanzo was spotted. When they returned with tales of monsters and fire..."

Ignas bowed his head. "Indeed. We have lost control of him."

"Yes." Ebisa uttered a testy sigh. "Kanzo has automata the size of a kitten that can deliver a fatal sting on a man's ankle. He did what he did because he feels nothing for the lives of others. His narcissism demands he make a scene."

"Maybe you guys should have thought of that before." I pulled the quest back into focus and hit Yes. "But for better or worse, I'm in."

The elder Corvinus looked over us both, then let out a tense breath. "Good. You have my word, and I assure you it means a great deal more than Andrik's."

CHAPTER 37

"How do you feel?" Suri said to me, as the door to the tavern slammed behind us. "About betting on Ignas, that is?"

"There's two things I hate more than anything else," I replied. "Liars and bullies. Ignas doesn't have clean hands, but if what he told us is the truth, then Andrik needs a good drop-kicking. Plus, you know how Ignas was talking about him being a part of some cult?"

"Yeah?"

"Well, this is complicated, but bear with me. So, you know that global notification we had yesterday morning? A guy named Baldr Hyland becoming the Grand High Poobah in Ilia?"

"Yeah? What about it?"

"Baldr is Starborn, and he tried to murder me in cold blood over that broken spear of mine," I replied. "He's also probably possessed by the ghost of a fucked-up Architect. The how and why isn't stuff I want to discuss out here... but the short version is that Architect, Ororgael, is a bad seed. He's also the Architect at the center of a cult, and he's been known to meddle in world affairs."

"Like empowering a weak-willed prince to usurp the throne from someone who would stand up him?" Suri nodded slowly. "Possible. Kind of a stretch, though. It's all circumstantial. He could be in a cult to Rusolka on the side, or a demon. We don't know."

We exited the gate, and I smiled when I spotted Karalti at the iron lattice table. She was sitting upright on her haunches, her tail lashing stiffly behind her as she watched one of the Meewfolk rogues dexterously switch a series of three cups around and around. When he stopped, he spread his fingers.

"Which cup do you think the die is under, oh ssscaly one?" He asked her. "One, two, three?"

Karalti's eyes narrowed. "*Inside your cheek.*"

The Meewfolk's chipped and pierced ears flattened back. He put a palm against his chest, clearly affronted, but leaned away in alarm as Karalti ducked her head down and put her snout in close.

"*Cheeeeeek.*" She let her jaws part, showing him two rows of fire-polished, backswept fangs.

The other guards laughed as the Meewfolk spat the die he'd palmed from the shell game onto the table. Karalti giggled.

"What happened to watching Cutthroat?" I pointed over at the hookwing. She was lurking near a crooked tenement building on the other side of the cul-de-sac, growling as she paced back and forth along the edge of the weeds that grew beside the wall. Her head was snaking constantly, nose darting in and out of the grass. The feathers of her chest and winglets were slaked to her body with filthy city mud.

"*Oh, she's fine. She's been hunting rats,*" Karalti said. She bobbed her head to the bouncers and got to her feet, shaking herself out in a leathery rustle of wings. "*She's too big to catch them, but that doesn't stop her from trying.*"

"Cutthroat! Come on!" Suri called out to her.

Cutthroat stood tall and turned her head, quorking in her throat when she saw who was calling her. She was about to trot over when there was a rustle in the grass. She spun back around, chomping her jaws from side to side as she charged into the weeds... and ran herself right into the side of the building with a dull *thump.* Dirt and chips of brick and stone came raining down.

"Oi! Get over here!" Suri stalked over as the cross-eyed hookwing shook her head and smacked her teeth together. When Suri gathered her reins, Cutthroat turned her head and nipped at her arm – then squawked when Suri slapped her muzzle away. "Oh no you don't. You bite me, and you're gonna regret it for the rest of your life, you bloody great chook."

"See? They're a good match!" Karalti lashed her tail happily as I got on board, watching Suri rant on as she climbed up into the saddle. *"All Suri has to do is dance and puke for her–"*

"Don't," I said. *"Just let that train of thought stay at the station, thanks."*

We rode out of the cul-de-sac, and only once we were clear of Ignas' hideout did I remember something – Rin. I whistled to Suri. "Hey – Rin sent me mail. Can you keep an eye out for surprise assassins?"

"Sure." Suri jerked her chin up in acknowledgement.

Stress built in my chest as I went to my mail and opened up the message from Rin.

"Hi Hector." The window narrated the letter to me in Rin's voice. *"I'm okay thanks to your warning. I got out through the Cellars (>__<).Can I trust you with something? Best regards, Rin."*

I couldn't help but smile at Rin's old-fashioned formality. *"Hi Rin - Sorry for the delay: we were in a meeting. And sure."*

There was a few minutes pause while we slogged our way back toward the canal bridge. Just when I thought she'd backed out, I got a new alert.

"Don't tell anyone yet, but I'm in contact with Kanzo," Rin messaged. *"But after what happened at Kobayaz, I'm having second thoughts. What he did was really messed up and our people, the Mercurions, are suffering in the Tanners' District. He keeps trying to justify it, so... I'm willing to cooperate and have him arrested, okay? Can we meet somewhere public? I'm desperate to talk to someone who isn't crazy (;__;)."*

I winced. Perfect fucking timing. *"We shouldn't meet. P.M is safer. I don't know if we're being followed, but there's a good chance that Andrik is following us somehow. Look, Rin... our quest has changed a lot. I'm willing to talk to you about it, but I don't think we should meet face to face. Let me and Suri find somewhere safe to settle in, and we can set up a party chat."*

"I know it's a risk, but I'm lonely and scared, and I really just want to be around some people I know. I think Kanzo might do something even more terrible. He's crazy, Hector. I need to be somewhere else. I can be discreet, I swear. Maybe we can go to lunch? I don't eat any more, but... you know. I still think about food. It would be nice to see some people eat |(;A;)/"

I sighed. Fuck. There was no mistaking the terror and fatigue in Rin's voice. *"Okay. Give us fifteen minutes or so. We'll meet you in the Main Square, location TBD. I'll make coordinates once we settle in."*

She sent me back a heart emote. Aww.

We were just passing out of the gate leading into the Meewfolk ghetto. I tapped Karalti's shoulder, steering her in closer to Cutthroat and Suri. "Hey, Suri - would you like to go out to lunch with me?"

"What? She asked, voice lifting with surprise. "Now?"

Karalti tensed under my hands.

"Yeah. As in, let's go eat a meal and meet up with Rin. She's okay, and she found Kanzo. I told her we'd RV in the Main Square, where she can blend in with the few Mercurions who are outside of the Tanners' District."

"Oh. Right." Suri flushed, turning her face away from me. "Sure. Where do you want to go?"

Even *I* wasn't dense enough to miss Suri's disappointment.

"It uh... I mean, I'm not asking you out *just* so we can talk to Rin," I said quickly, tripping over every other word. "I mean, I also just want to take you out to lunch for *you*, if you'd like to go out with me? For lunch. You know. Food. For two humans... you know, hanging out and talking about royal conspiracies together?"

Slowly, Suri nodded. "You know, actually, I *would* like that."

Wait. She said yes? I couldn't believe my ears. But was this a yes-yes or an 'okay'-yes? Regardless, it was like one of those corny movie moments where the sky opens up with sunbeams and a chorus of angels. My back broke out into a nervous sweat. It was weird – I hadn't felt like this around Rutha.

"Great! What uh, what food do you like to eat?" I stammered.

"I know a good kebab place off Osteria Utca. Like, really good." Suri chuckled under her breath. "Cum-your-brains-out good."

"I thought you said sharing food was gross," Karalti grumbled.

"We're not throwing up on each other, Karalti. We're having lunch." I thought back. *"Fuck. She's flirting with me. What do I do now?"*

"You tell her that Karalti is the most beautiful queen in the world and you don't need anyone else. Just Karalti."

I sighed and rolled my eyes. *"We've been over this. I thought you were okay with the human-human relationship need?"*

Suri arched her eyebrows, then frowned in hurt confusion. "What? You don't like kebab?"

Oh fuck. "No! No way, I love kebab!" I squeaked. "Karalti just asked me a question, sorry. Do they have beer at this place?"

"'Course they do. Every restaurant here has beer."

"Thank god." I patted Karalti on the neck. *"Come on, Tidbit. Try and remember what we talked about last night,"* I said to her.

Karalti began to mutter under her breath like a pissed-off parrot, which sounded remarkably similar to a demon talking through an old radio.

We broke out of the squalor of Cat Alley and into the traffic leading into the Market District. It was going on one p.m, the busiest time of day, and the Main Square was packed with people enjoying the clear hot weather. Hawkers hawking, farmers selling produce off cats. Jugglers were performing for knots of people while pickpockets prowled. People streamed in and out of the great market, the church, the many small stores clustered around the fountain sculpture of Taltos in the middle of the plaza.

"Suri, do you know the address of the kebab joint?"

"Grazi Utca 32."

I quickly relayed our destination to Rin, and she sent me a thumbs up. Once that was taken care of, I returned my attention to Suri.

"By the way," I asked. "What do *you* think of this whole thing with Ignas?" I asked. "You never really said."

"He's alright. I like him more than Andrik," she replied. "Bastard tried to cop a feel at the auction house."

"He what?"

She made a scooping motion with her hand. "Whoopsie, right up under my ass. If he wasn't the King, I'd have decked him."

If I hadn't disliked Andrik before, I definitely did now. It was kind of weird to feel protective of an ex-pit-fighter Berserker with seventeen more Strength points and four levels on me, but I did. "If he tries it again, I guess I'm going to end up getting staked, but I promise you the Volod won't have any teeth left."

She smirked, riding out into the town square. "Cute."

I scoffed. "Cute? In case you hadn't noticed, Suri, I am an A-grade cut of man-beef, hewn from the plump loins of an enormous bull with really big... uh... horns."

Karalti chuffed, rustling her wings in agitation. "*More like an A-grade load of bullshit.*"

Suri's eyes danced. "Horns, huh? Plural?"

"Yeah, and like, I totally don't mean to boast but, in addition to having at least *two* dicks, I have a green belt in Taekwondo." I put on my best dumb Chad voice for that one, and Suri laughed. But it was the last straw for Karalti.

"*Mine!*" The dragon snorted a thin stream of fire from her nostrils as she broke into a run. "*Mine, mine, MINE!*"

I nearly fell head over ass, because I'd been too busy acting like a peacock and wasn't hanging onto the saddle. I caught it just in time, bouncing and flapping around until I caught both grips and got my knees down.

"Karalti! Why!?" I called to her as she barreled into the Main Square. People jumped out of her way with yelps and screams. "We had such a great time last night - I thought we'd sorted this out!"

"I'll show you why! She can never do what I can do! Never!" Karalti roared, a sound that boomed out across the entire market, and beat her wings stiffly by her sides as she built up speed. She was headed straight toward the great big fountain in the center of the plaza.

"Karalti! Stop! Bad dragon!" I got my feet into the stirrups just in time as she flung her wings open, sending people and crowds of pigeons running to either side, and kicked herself into the air.

She had barely gotten her wings under her when the entire fucking fountain exploded.

CHAPTER 38

The blast swallowed us like an open mouth, turning the world to noise and fire. The explosion blew Karalti out of the air and flung her away like a ragdoll. I lost my grip on the saddle, vaguely aware of spinning, falling, and then impacting the unforgiving ground.

When I regains consciousness, I couldn't see. My eyes were gummy with blood and dirt, and my legs were numb. That wasn't good. I swiped my wrist over my face, rubbing the dust away. When my vision cleared, I thought – for one terrified moment – that I'd somehow been ejected from Archemi and back into the real world, the Total War, and that I had woken up in the ruins of a building devastated by a nuclear explosion. But then I saw the broken body of a dragon sprawled in the wreckage of human bodies and market stands.

"No! Karalti!" I tried to get up, and my arm and leg just kind of folded underneath me, bending in places they weren't supposed to bend. It hurt, but the pain was distant, pushed away by raw panic as I dragged myself over to Karalti's side. Notifications were streaming in about both of us.

⟦Karalti is in a critical condition! You must restore HP equal to one quarter of her total HP! HP: 10/949⟧

⟦You have sustained Internal Bleeding! 3 HP per second damage until healing is applied!⟧

⟦You have a broken arm! You cannot use two-handed weapons or physical skills until healing is applied!⟧

[[You have a broken leg! 50% movement speed until healing is applied!]]
[[Karalti's wings are broken! Karalti is suffering internal bleeding!]]
[[You are in a critical condition! You must restore-]]

"I fucking know already!" Frantic, I raided my Inventory for potions and dragged myself up to Karalti's head. She was down to 7 HP by the time I reached her. The explosion had erupted almost directly underneath her, and her chest and abdomen were pierced by shards of wood and stone. She was unconscious, and trickle of blue blood ran from the corner of her mouth as I forced her jaws apart, uncorked a potion, and poured it down her throat. Then another, and another. She had 949 HP, which meant I had to restore at least 238 points to stop her from dying. I only had three Moss Tinctures and no Bonebreak Poultices – healing a total of 210 HP.

As I drained the potions into her, a voice began speaking from all directions at once, like a loudspeaker.

"Here me, citizens of Taltos!" Kanzo's voice rang out sharply and clearly across the plaza. "I am the one you call the Slayer, a weapon in the hands of corrupt and unjust terrorists! Well - no longer! I will not be used by you *sang'hi* bastards anymore! Whoever among you took my daughter from me, know this! For every day onward that my people are held captive in the Tanners' District and my child is held captive by the so-called 'King of Cats', I will detonate a bomb - just like this one - in locations around Taltos!"

Karalti moaned, drawing a ragged breath. I used my good arm to pull pieces of shrapnel out of her, and was confused when two pairs of arms reached past me to start helping: slim silver hands, and gauntleted ones.

"Here. Drink." Suri crouched beside me, holding a potion bottle to my lips. I shook my head.

"G-give it to Karalti," I said. "She's dying–"

"YOU'RE dying," Suri snapped. "Drink the fucking potion."

While we argued, Kanzo's voice continued to rant on over the sounds of fighting and screaming. "Heed my words, King of Vlachia, King of Cats, whoever you are - none of you shall know peace until my child is free! You will be tormented as I am tormented! You will suffer as my people are suffering! You think to oppress me?! I am Tlaxi'ca, and while I would choose peace, I was bred for war!"

"I respawn. I d-don't know if she d-does. Give to her. Please," I rasped.

"Christ." Suri went to the dragon, who was starting to struggle and moan on the ground, and tipped the potion down her neck. Karalti swallowed weakly, then shuddered and opened one eye.

"Some of the bodies are Stranging! Help!" I heard Rin shout.

Kanzo's message was on repeat, drowned out by my pulse. My vision blurred, darkening as the edge of my HUD throbbed red. Then Suri's arm snaked around my back, and I breathed in her deep honey and sandalwood scent as she propped me up.

"Here. Last one." Suri touched my lips with another glass vial, and the herbal smell of a Moss Tincture wafted to my nose.

I swallowed, and then shivered as my HP jumped and the ache of broken bones receded. I felt the disjointed edges of the breaks in my arms and legs realign and then seal. As Suri lay me down against Karalti's flank, the world came back into focus – the sounds of battle, the moaning of mana-animated undead, shouting, and the sound of steel striking stone.

I groaned. "The fuck is going on?"

"Zombies. The Volod's soldiers are coming to back us up. Sit tight." Suri stood, pulling her greatsword from her back, and then ran off into the fray.

Zombies? I wasn't staying in place if there were zombies running around. Gritting my teeth, I reached out to my dragon as she stirred on the ground. "You alive, girl?"

"Yeah. Kind of." Karalti's telepathic voice was strained. *"I'm sorry. This is my fault."*

"There's only one person whose fault this is, and that's Kanzo." Anger gave me strength, and I rolled to hands and knees. *"I don't care if Andrik and Ignas hate my guts for the rest of eternity – I'm going to pull that self-absorbed motherfucker's heart out through his asshole."*

There was a girlish scream from behind us. Drawing a deep breath, I pushed myself up, searching for my spear. You could drop weapons in Archemi, and I saw the Alpha Rod highlighted by my HUD about twenty feet away, close to where Rin and Suri fought a crowd of shambling undead – thirty or more of them. Cutthroat was hanging back because of the mana in the air, barking fearful cries of warning. The shuffling corpses – some still bleeding, some missing limbs - pulsed with magical light. Shards of mana crystal had erupted from their skin and hands, like claws made of glass and frozen blood.

Karalti tottered up to her feet, panting. She and I were both in the deep red: 280/949 HP for her, 81/680 for me.

"Use Bioscan on those zombies," I panted, and broke off at a jog to retrieve my weapon.

Karalti concentrated, and the seams of opalescent material between her scales went from multicolored to a brilliant blue. *"250 HP... no MP. They're weak against Fire and immune to Darkness."*

"Got any fire in you?"

"I think so."

I scooped my spear off the ground and spun it around before angling it down along my arm. The freshly healed bones ached, but they were functional. *"Blast 'em."*

The dragon shook her head and roared in challenge as she broke into a limping run, her damaged wings held in against her sides. She thrust her jaws forward, and her throat swelled just before blinding white liquid fire burst from her mouth. Karalti's Ghost Fire ability had a narrower stream than the typical yellow flamethrower-blast of other dragons I'd seen, but she could wield it like a whip, lashing the stream up, down, or to the sides.

The gout of flame lanced past Rin and struck the zombie that had broken past the defensive wall of her turrets. It made a weird whistling sound as the flames caught it, and its skin caught like it had been dipped in gasoline. Rin stumbled back away from it – she clutched a crossbow in her hands, holding it up like a shield.

[[Karalti used a fire attack! It's super effective!]]
[[You deal 523 damage to Mana Zombie!]]
[[Mana Zombies use Entrap! Suri is Entangled!]]

Suri had hacked her way through a hoard of zombies and was stuck inside of a twenty-strong mob. They had gathered around her in a knot of moaning, clawing bodies, forcing her to strike them away with her feet and the hilt of her sword. Her HP ring was draining, one Bleeding attack at a time.

"Karalti! Protect Rin! I'm going to break open the pack for Suri!" I grit my teeth and charged.

I burned ten precious hit points to Dash in, because it gave me the boost of speed I needed to chain Blood Sprint and Blood Storm – a sacrifice that paid off as I slammed into the mobs and blasted them back. Five targets on a good hit meant 50 HP in the tank. They were immune to Darkness, so I swung the polearm around, triggering Whirlwind Butcher during the Sprint cooldown. That maneuver threw enemies like skittles and blasted the mob to pieces, killing the zombies Suri had already injured.

With room to move, Suri was once more in her element. With a roar, she slashed once, twice, and then channeled a burst of boiling red energy into a downward blow that cut a zombie in half and cracked the pavement under the blade of her sword. She pulled it free and whirled on me, teeth bared.

"What the fuck are you doing here?! You have barely any HP and no fucking pots!" She snarled, belting another zombie that lurched toward her.

"Same thing you were doing when you waded into a boss fight with one arm and no bra," I snapped back. A trio of zombies ran at me, slashing with their crystalline claws. I dodged on reflex, Jumping back into the air, then reversing course to rain down Obscuring Veil on them. The Dark energy fell like freezing needles – they were immune to the Blindness debuff and the bonus damage, but they still took the normal damage from the physical strike as I came down.

"Mass them up!" Suri called to me. "I can hit 8 at a time with Bull Rush!"

"Why didn't you use that before!?" I bounced back and dodged the clumsy zombie swipes. Suri tanked the blows, but they had a hard time hitting me. Compared to them and Suri, I was prancing around like Tinkerbell.

"I did! They have a special entrapment ability when there's more than six!"

I led the zombies into a waltz, dashing to the side – ten more HP gone – then Sprinting into them again as soon as the timer vanished. I only hit three with the combo, restoring a tiny sliver of HP, but had to Dash again to avoid getting stuck in the crowd. Once they were rounded up and shambling in a group, Suri dropped the sword, pulled her axes, and ran at them from behind. Crimson light coiled and snapped into an energy shield that she used like a battering ram to plow through the rank. This ability had Knockdown, and it floored eight zombies to the pavement and split the mob. Whirlwind Butcher took out my side; her ax tornado took out the others.

[[You have defeated 28 Mana Zombies!]]
[[You gain 337 EXP!]]

Soldiers were pouring out of the streets that fed into the main plaza, with several hookwings. Backup – thank fuck. I sagged down to one knee, exhausted. Suri ran back toward Rin, and I turned to see Karalti spending the last of her fire on the few remaining zombies attacking her and Rin. Mutated victims of the bombing were scattered around them in a ring, their chests and heads plugged with arrows. And Rin was backing away, terrified.

"Run!" She screamed, just before she broke into a sprint away from the center of the plaza.

"What?" Confused, I looked back at the approaching soldiers and waved, then forward again, freezing as five guards broke rank and bodily tackled Rin to the ground. "Hey! Wait–"

Suri and Karalti were as startled as I was as at least fifty guards swarmed us. I was knocked down from behind, struggling as soldiers piled onto me. My head was forced down; my spear was torn from my hands, and they were pushed back behind me. "Wait! We're working for the Volod!"

"We know who you are," one of the guards retorted.

"You want a piece of me, you cunts!? Here it is!" Suri roared.

[[Suri uses Primal Rage! Suri loses control!]]

"Hector!" Karalti cried. The hookwings were encircling her, and she was out of Ghost Fire and low on HP.

"Get out of here! Karalti! Get away!" I shouted, struggling against the crush overhead. It was getting hard to breathe, and I writhed and bucked to no avail as a pair of manacles were clamped around my wrists.

Flexing her injured wings in a panic, Karalti tried to take to the air, but was taken down by nets and bolos flung out by the cavalry. The weights dragged her back down, honking with pain and terror. Someone ran up with chains that crawled with magical sigils and snapped them around her ankles. She blasted someone with the last of her Ghost Fire.

"Karalti!" I screamed in real fear now, thrashing on the ground.

Suri was next: she fought like a demon, felling soldiers left and right, but there were just too many of them. I lost sight of her as the platoon crowded forward.

"You're under arrest for aiding and abetting a terrorist and conspiring against the Crown of Vlachia!" A woman's hard voice pierced the fugue of cursing and screaming. "Stop resisting, or you will be made to comply."

"Fuck you! You want it? You fucking take it!" I bellowed back. "Suri! Rin! Karal-"

The boot to the back of my head drove my nose into the pavement, and I didn't even get to say her name one last time.

CHAPTER 39

Thunk. Thud. Thunk. Thud.

The world rumbled and swayed and grunted as I faded into consciousness. My head was pounding, my pulse hammering in my temples and fingers. My throat was dry and tight.

"Uhhgggh... fuck." I shifted around on what felt like blankets, itchy and coarse against my bare skin. I tried to push myself up on my hands, but as I did, the damp wooden floor beneath me lurched. I dropped back down with a groan.

Thunk. Thud. Thunk.

The rumbling I heard was the sound of wagon wheels bucking over rough stone. We were moving steeply uphill. I cracked my eyes open and stared up at the iron-reinforced ceiling. I was naked, alone, and being taken somewhere in a prison wagon - great. There was nothing good about this. I needed to move. I needed to find Karalti.

I gritted my teeth, and rolled onto the side that hurt less. "*Karalti? Where are you, Tidbit?*"

⟦You are Incarcerated by the City Guard! Private messages are currently disabled!⟧

Trying to speak to her caused an odd sensation: a sense that my words hit an invisible barrier between her and I, as if I - or Karalti - was trapped inside a glass bubble.

"Ugh." I spat, trying to clear my mouth of the dirt and grit I'd picked up from rolling around on the ground. "This fucking *game*."

Slowly, I sat up and took stock of my predicament. The compartment I was in was maybe half again as long as I was tall, and it reeked of old sweat, piss, and terror. There was a rusty grate in the floor in the far left corner, and a small barred window about five feet off the ground on the wall to my right. I had 20 HP left - no more broken bones, thankfully - but I was laboring under no fewer than 6 debuffs: Hunger, Thirst, Chained, Incarcerated, Exhausted, and the fucking Pee Meter. I was also half-naked. They'd left my pants on and stripped everything else. Armor, weapons, items, all gone. And so were Karalti, Suri, and Rin.

I got to my feet with some effort, weighed down by heavy chains. Keeping balance with the wall, I shuffled over and tested the crusty grate, looking for a weakness. The bars were unfortunately sturdy. Resigned, I whipped out Hector Jnr and got busy fixing Archemi's most awkward debuff, and was about halfway done when someone knocked on the wall where I was resting my other hand.

You know what happens when someone lets go of a firehose while the water's on full blast? Yeah. "Fucking shit-tits!"

"You're a real poet, aren't ya?" Suri's voice croaked from the other side of the wall. "You should've become a bard."

"Jesus Christ! I just pissed all over my... my everything." Scowling, I shook my hand.

"Stop telling me about your golden showers and go look out the window, eagle eyes. Tell me if I'm seeing what I think I'm seeing up on the wall of Vulkan Keep."

I kind of awkwardly wiped everything, then straightened up and went back to the window, bending down to look out. We were on the hairpin road leading up to the castle, just about to turn the bend that led into the gatehouse. When I looked up at the portcullis, my blood turned to ice.

Kirov hung limp along a long metal stake mounted on the wall like a flagpole. The sharp end jutted out from his mouth. But even worse were the bodies mounted alongside him: Stefin the Jeweller, his eyes still bugged from terror and agony, two women, and three children. All staked, and left out for the crows.

I squeezed the bars until my knuckles groaned, clenching and unclenching my jaw. "I see Andrik's fucking death sentence, is what I see."

"That's what I figured." Suri sounded as exhausted as I felt. "Volods, Sultirs, Emperors... royals are all the fuckin' same. He's probably going to stake us, too. If I end up back in Al-Asad-"

"Don't say that." I drew a furious shuddering breath, and pushed back from the window to pace back and forth inside the narrow space. "I won't let them send you back."

"You can't. I've already tried breaking the window and the piss grate on my side. No luck, and I'm up to 42 Strength after my last level. So what I was gonna say was... if I end up in Al-Asad, don't give up on me. I'll find a way out again, somehow. I dunno. Maybe it'll be easier to break out now that these Architects are mostly out of the way."

"I won't give up on you, and I won't give up on Karalti." I rolled my shoulders, balled and unballed my fists, and wracked my brains for a solution as we turned and climbed the final hill toward the keep. "If I have to bust through the walls like the fucking Kool Aid Man, I will. These motherfuckers don't know who they're dealing with."

"The Kool Aid what?"

"The Kool Aid Man. You know. He's this giant jug full of juice that breaks through walls and screams 'OHHH YEAAAH!'."

"Right. Think you could start by breaking through the walls of this prison wagon, then?"

I took a moment to compose my best nerd voice. "Weell, *ackthully*, there's more to life than just muthcles? And I hypothesize we're going to have to use our *brains* for thith dilemma?"

"Christ." I was pretty sure I could hear Suri's eyes rolling around and around in her head, like the wagon wheels. "How are you managing to take the piss when we're about to die?"

"I *was* taking a piss when I was so rudely interrupted."

She groaned. "If you keep talking about your fetish, I'm gonna start telling you all about *my* trip to the grate."

I pressed up against the wall. "I'm just trying to warm up before King Ramrod gets busy with those stakes."

Suri barked a short, bitter laugh.

"*Biznasck*! Shut up in there!" A guard pulled up beside my window on his hookwing, banging his spear against the bars before riding off ahead.

"*You* shut up." I gave him the finger, but he didn't see it. "Asshole."

In all honesty, I had no idea what to do - other than joke around to stop myself from going insane with anxiety and rage. Death by stake was not exactly my idea of a fun time, but I couldn't believe an NPC was capable of inflicting that kind of torture on players. There had to be some real-world law against that, something that would prevent it from happening. We were just going to have to wing it once we were inside the castle, and hope that one of us could think of something.

The wagon stopped thunking as we rumbled over the drawbridge, and then smoothed out even more once we were headed through the grand gates leading into Vulkan Keep proper. Guards were pacing by the wagon on both sides now, so I hung by the wall and ground my teeth, waiting for the right opportunity. I'd escaped imprisonment twice in Archemi already. I was sure I could do it again.

We didn't go inside a building: we went underground, moving past the hookwing stables to somewhere deeper under the Keep. When the wagons stopped, I heard Suri shuffle around in her nest of chains, moving away from the back wall toward her cell entry point.

"Stop it! Let me go!" A high, girlish voice cried out from up the line. Rin.

"You there - help the mages with that dragon. It won't carry itself!" A thickly accented voice demanded of the other guards. "You

- put the disruptor to that silverskin's head. If she does not comply, you stun her like a cow."

Fuck. I had no idea what a 'disruptor' was, but it sounded like magictech.

Suri was next out. She launched herself at the guards with a shout, cursing in three different languages as she fought. A mostly-naked Berserker was still a Berserker, and I tensed with excitement as one guard gargled and fell while others shouted in alarm. But once again, there were too many of them, and not enough of us. Suri was bought to ground, and I clenched my jaws together at the sound of her being beaten into silence.

Twenty nearly-silent minutes passed before a heavy fist thumped against my door. "You! Stand facing the back wall with your hands up. If you do not comply, then the lives of your women and your dragon are forfeit."

I frowned. There was a good chance they were forfeit anyway, but I remembered the words that Karalti's mother had said to me not long ago. *"Herald... you are a creature of shadow. Be subtle and be clever."*

I drew a deep breath, turned around, and put my hands up.

A key turned inside a heavy lock, and then the door opened out, admitting two guards. They took me by the elbows, and I let them walk me out - not resisting, but not doing anything to help them, either. We were in a loading-dock like area that had a low stone platform and multiple doors leading further underground. There was no sign of Rin or Suri - save for Suri's blood on the ground. The Captain gave a terse nod when he saw me, then spun on his heel and clanked his way toward one of the doors, unlocking it ahead of us.

The guards frogmarched me through a series of dimly lit tunnels - winding tunnels with deep S-curves and defensible murder holes. Several steel doors and a flight of stairs later, I found myself entering through a secret door into the Great Hall, where Volod

Andrik Corvinus the Third sat in his throne, contemplating a huge magical circle that had been drawn straight onto the flagstones. Karalti was in the middle of it, wrapped up like a tamale in layers of blankets and chains. When she saw me, she whimpered - but it was clear she couldn't move.

I kept the insults and angry words locked down deep inside as I was taken around Karalti to join Rin and Suri, who had been made to kneel in front of the staged area that contained the Corvinus Throne. There were other people here besides the Volod, flanking Andrik to either side: to his left was Garen, the Commander of the Kingsguard, who was dressed in full black dragon plate armor. He had his hands wrapped around the hilt of his greatsword, the point resting on the floor, and was now flagged as a combatant. He had a violet HP ring with a skull beside it, as did the other five Kingsguard who ranged around the throne.

To Andrik's right was the Voivode, Janos Lanz, and a well-muscled, olive-skinned man with piercing green eyes I didn't recognize. He was old enough to have gray streaks in his curling hair, and was wearing robes and an apron similar to the ornate clothing of Forgemaster Toth. I could guess this was his replacement.

"You know, I really would like to be wrong about foreigners for once in my life." Andrik said. He sat with one ankle crossed over his other knee. He was dressed in his scorched armor, his ruby crown, and had a jeweled longsword resting over his lap. "I hired you in good faith. I offered you hospitality in *my* castle-"

"Yeah. You did. And you just broke hospitality," I snapped back.

The guard on my right slapped me over the back of the head. "Silence."

Andrik's pale eyes glittered with rage. "I host you rabble *in my home*, and what does my spy report? Not only were you were seen entering a known hideout for the Nightstalkers - the organization associated with these terrorist acts - but you were seen laughing and fraternizing with them, shortly before you detonating explosives in the Main Square. Then you and *THAT*-" he pointed down at Rin, "-began slaughtering *my* people, in broad daylight.

"I have a name!" Rin replied hotly.

"You are the Slayer's accomplice." Andrik rose to his feet, the sword in hand. It was slightly too long for him, and the tip of the blade scraped the marble floor as he took a step forward. "And you, all of you, were working with her. Hiding her. Conspiring against me."

"Mate, you've lost your fuckin' mind." Suri's voice was thick and stuffy. They'd broken her nose.

"You mean to tell me that the series of convenient escapes that have occurred since *he* arrived are coincidences?" He pointed the sword at me, and I leaned back. "That you and this fugitive dragon thief *didn't* warn this Mercurion to escape her home? I know you Starborn are capable of communicating with each other over distances. How did Kanzo set up explosives at the auction house? How is he moving around the city? I'll tell you - he is aided and abetted by terrorists and foreigners, and YOU!"

The 'you' was clearly directed at Suri and I. And in that moment, I made my choice.

"Well, you caught me." I jerked my head and sniffed. "She had nothing to do with it though. It was me."

Suri turned her head sharply. So did Rin.

"Yup. Guilty as charged. I've been sucking the mana out of Kanzo's cock all this time." I pumped a fist as enthusiastically as the chains allowed for. "Fuck the police! Screw monarchy! This is Vlachia, son! Guns, gloryholes and freedom - yeehaw!"

"Oh - so you admit you are complicit? That was unexpected." Andrik's eyes narrowed as he turned toward me. "You see, I had a discussion with someone from Ilia, someone whose opinion I greatly respect. They warned me not to trust anything you said, but to expect you to deny and defer blame. Do you think being honest will bring you mercy?"

"I think it should help you lay blame where blame's due." I shrugged. "Suri didn't know. She was just doing her job."

She scowled. "Hector-"

"I did message Rin behind Suri's back. I let her off the hook, twice." I held up my hands. "I did fight Kanzo, and let him escape. I didn't kill Red on the spot at the party, and I did go to Cat Alley and speak to Mister King."

Andrik was looking increasingly smug.

"But you know what I *didn't* do?" I continued. "I didn't frame my older brother as a furry-loving pervert so that I could usurp his throne for myself, and *then* try and hire someone to kill him when he came back from exile as the ironically named 'King of Cats' to kick your ass."

Before I'd finished speaking, the Mark of Matir flared with a sharp pain, and in the corner of my eye, a violet and black 'X' icon appeared. The vow of secrecy I had taken had been broken. Now, I was a marked man.

Andrik had affected amusement right up until the assassination conspiracy part, and then his expression froze into a hard, cold, calculating mask.

"Yeah, that oath you put me under? Fuck it." I said, shrugging off one of the guards as he tried to cuff me across the ear. "You made me, the Herald of Matir, swear under the Kara Bukat Talom-"

"Silence him!" Andrik snapped at the guards behind me.

"-and you offered money for me to kill Ignas Corvinus!" I spat, nearly shouting his brother's name in his face as I struggled against the soldiers, trying to avoid being knocked out.

"Your Majesty? Does he speak the truth?" Voivode of Czongrad, Janos Lanz, stepped forward. the new Forgemaster had turned ashen.

"What? Of course not. It's desperate nonsense." Andrik, barely holding his calm, waved it off.

Suri bared her teeth. "Oh no, it's true alright. Ignas is alive. The King of Cats is Ignas."

I was hit in the head enough times that I lost track of up and down. They must have knocked me out - because I blinked, and in that second, I went from being up on one knee to lying on my face on the floor.

"He's not lying!" Rin exclaimed. "I met him as well. He's blackmailing Kanzo so that he will take revenge on Andrik for-"

"SHUT UP!" Andrik turned away from me and lunged toward Rin, the sword raised. "SHUT UP, YOU SIMULACRA BITCH!"

"No! Sire! Her blood-!" Ur Garen charged forward to intercept his king.

Before he got there in time, Andrik struck Rin across the face with the flat of the blade, pitching her to the ground. She fell with a short scream, and kept screaming as he began to kick her, over and over again. Chained as she was, she was defenseless.

"Lay off her, you rat-bastard!" I pushed myself up, only to be taken down again. Oof: I only had 15 HP left.

"Stay back, Garen! And give me that!" Andrik wrenched a spear from the hands of one of the attending soldiers. Suri and I shouted and struggled as more soldiers came in to back up the ones holding us, while the Voivode, the priest, and everyone else watched on in mute horror as Andrik began to beat Rin with the haft of the spear. She hadn't been high on health to start with: each blow took off a sliver of her HP.

[[Rin is in critical condition!]]

"RIN!" I felt Matir's power surge in my body, prickling up from the Mark as I prepared to use Life for Life. It would give me enough energy to get these fuckers off me, and then... then...

"No! Just find me!" Pinned under three soldiers, I couldn't see Rin - just hear her, as her voice weakened and cracked. "Don't... here... just... fi-!"

There was a horrible dull crack as Andrik broke the spear haft over Rin's body.

[[Rin Lu has died.]]

"You fucker!" I didn't want to listen to what she'd said. I snarled aloud as a surge of feral, furious strength rolled through me... strength that froze me as the guards hauled me upright, and I saw Andrik throw the broken spear away. He had the point of his sword pressed to the back of Suri's neck. "You-!"

"She's next if you BOTH DON'T SHUT UP!" Panting, red-faced, he punctuated each word by pushing with the blade. "I want that Mercurion bitch staked out over the gate leading into the Tanners' District. NOW."

Even with a greathelm obscuring Garen's face, I could see him hesitate. "Sire, she's-"

"STAKE HER OVER THE FUCKING GATE!" Andrik screamed back at him.

"... Yes, sire." Garen stiffly bowed his head, cutting around us to approach Rin's body, but no sooner had he bent down to pick her up than her corpse pixelated and vanished, leaving only her gear behind. "Uhh..."

Suri grunted against the floor, flinching as the point of the sword dug in at the base of her skull. "She's Starborn, you idiot."

Andrik's cheeks flushed a red so dark it was nearly purple.

"We must speak to this King of Cats." The new Forgemaster had a deep voice, thick with concern - and disgust. "If there is no truth to what this man - who is branded with the Mark of one of the Nine - has said..."

"There *is* no truth to it! My cat-fucking sodomite of a brother is dead!" Andrik turned on him, teeth bared. "*I* am your king! *I* am a descendant of Khors himself!"

The Voivode's face was wooden, his mouth a grim slash in his face. "I must concur with the High Forgemaster. There must be an appearance, and when the truth is satisfied, an execution."

"Yes. Execution." Andrik's cheeks were still burning. Breathing heavily, sweat running down from under the silver band of his crown, he took the sword away from Suri's neck. I let out a breath I hadn't known I'd been holding. "Though there are worse things than death for a Starborn, aren't there? Hector, I am giving you one final ultimatum."

The Volod withdrew back to his throne, and plopped down. He took his crown from his head, and with his fingers, popped out one of the rubies from its setting. Several people around us gasped.

"This ruby." He wrapped a fist around it, nostrils trembling. "Will contain a message from me to this self-styled king of filth. If he is Ignas, he will be able to receive the message, and he will know where to come to face me. We will wait in the appointed place. You will have two hours to deliver this ruby and return. And if you can't, I am sending your dragon back to Ilia, to her rightful owners. If you fail in your mission, or if you run, you will never see her again."

Karalti bugled behind me, a shrill cry of distress that Andrik ignored as he whispered against his fist and concentrated. There was a soft flare of red light between his fingers... and then he threw the gem at me. It hit me in the chest and clattered to the floor.

Quest Update: The Slayer of Taltos/Stalkers in the Night

You have 120 minutes to find Ignas and deliver his brother's message. Run.

CHAPTER 40

"*Rin! Are you alive? Where the hell did you respawn?!*" I P.M'd Rin as I raced Cutthroat down the road from Vulkan Keep at full speed, holding onto her saddle with my knees like a jockey as we churned up dirt on the way down to the city gate.

"*I'm okay! I'm sure that hurt, but yay for terminal amnesia! V(^__^)v*" She texted back.

"*Listen: I have two hours to deliver a Corvinus Ruby with a message to Ignas and get back to the castle. Andrik is summoning him to the Keep. I just spent fifteen getting the fuck out of Vulkan Keep, and I'm a good fifteen to twenty minutes from Cat Alley. I'm on the fastest hookwing I know-*"

"*You can't go straight to the International District! (O_O)! It has to be a trap!*" Rin replied. "*Not to mention, wherever you met Ignas, he's not going to be there anymore.*"

I'd had a horrible gnawing feeling about that as well. Ignas wasn't the sort of guy to take risks - like waiting in the same place where agents of his crazypants brother had visited earlier in the day. "*Shitballs. Any idea where he might have gone?*"

"*No, I don't... but I know someone who can help.*" *There was a pause, then a second message.* "*You're not going to like it... (>_>);*"

"*It's fucking Kanzo, isn't it?*" I steered Cutthroat out of the way of incoming traffic, belting past them toward the open gate.

"*Yeah... I respawned in his location. After the bomb went off, the King of Cats contacted him and told him to get to a meeting to get his 'daughter' back. They said they were going to release her.*

He's still here... I bet the two of us could convince him to take us to the handover."

"*When's this handover?*"

"*In about thirty minutes, down in an old underground ossuary. But you can't go straight to me - Andrik has spies everywhere. Head for the University District and go to the morgue.*"

"*The morgue?*"

"*Trust me. I'll guide you once you're there (^c^).*"

The University District, in the north, was much closer to Vulkan Keep than the International District - less than a ten-minute ride between the city gate and the target. I still had 55 minutes on the timer. Cutthroat heaved for breath as I vaulted to the ground, squawking in confusion when I abandoned her without tying her to anything and ran for the morgue.

I clattered down the stairs, pushing past a startled doctor and his assistants. "*Okay, I'm here. What do I do?*"

"*Go down the main stairwell and turn right. At the end of the hall, you'll see a pair of copper double doors with a bas relief of Saint Minos on them. That's the entry to the chapel. Run through the chapel and take the last door you see on your left. Don't panic - remember, Archemi is a game. OUROS doesn't give quests that players can't possibly accomplish.*"

"*You're assuming OUROS gave this quest. Ororgael gave me the Spear of Nine Spheres quest, remember?*"

"*Yeah, but Michael isn't here.*"

Panting, I cut down the right-hand corridor. It wasn't long, and I saw the doors Rin had described. "*I think Andrik is part of the Cult of the Architect. I think that's why and how he's king. It's how he's getting away with shit like staking key NPCs and beating players to death.*"

"*What?! Why?*"

I pushed the doors open into a simple, rectangular stone chapel, where a startled priest in blue robes was holding a service for a very dead old lady and her grieving family. They stared at me in open-mouthed shock as I ran by them, checking over my shoulder to see if I had a tail. Sure enough, there was a long shadow quickly approaching down the hall – a shadow cast by someone or something I couldn't see. *"In a minute. Door on the left: what next?"*

"Ummmm, go in the door furthest from the chapel on the left. That's the embalming room. There are two doors there - you need the one to the right. Then you go down some stairs. There should be a metal door - you want to go in there. It's the crematorium."

"Why the fuck am I going to the crematorium?"

"Because my map says there's a trapdoor there that leads into the Lethos Cellars," she replied. *"Tell me about Andrik?"*

"When we met Ignas, he told us Andrik betrayed him after he learned that his little brother was in some cult." I cut through the door, pushing past a trolley with a sheet covered body, and took the door to the right. This one was able to be locked from my side - I slammed the bar down, and kept running. *"He didn't know what cult, because he couldn't remember anything about it: the symbols he saw, the shrine Andrik had to his 'god'... they were wiped from his memory. All Ignas remembers is that he was disturbed by it. And have you seen the Taltos city entry bug?"*

"The screwy NPC code? Yeah. NUMFETCH errors aren't too uncommon. Those happen when an NPC... umm... oh."

"When an NPC umm-whats?"

"Well... NPCs are generated via the radiant AI system, right? Sometimes, ATHENA creates a non-viable NPC, so it's, umm, digested and replaced. The NUMFETCH error happens when the system tries to replace an NPC with a copy, but the original NPC hasn't been deleted properly. I guess... that could also happen if an NPC was hacked and partially replaced, and the system wasn't sure how to handle it?"

"Oh. Fantastic." I felt a thrill of fear, because *I* was a fucking 'NUMFETCH error'. And that begged the question – who might

have hacked me? "*So, not only is there something screwy about Andrik, but Karalti and I were attacked by a big ambush of Ilian mercenaries - well, sort of mercenaries. They were fanatics. We pinned a guy to interrogate him, and he killed himself rather than talk.*"

"*Oh my god (@__@)!*"

"*He was carrying a brooch,*" I said, pulling up in front of the metal door. "*The Ryuko company logo, kind of. My guess is that this is Ororgael's little 'Cult of the Architect' joke at Ryuko's expense.*"

"*Oh no. That's not good.*"

"*No, it's not. Andrik is probably sucking Baldr-and-or-Ororgael's cock as we speak.*" I wrenched the door open, and a blast of heat engulfed me from inside. "*I'm not sure OUROS has as much to do with this as it should.*"

"*Right. Okay - are you in the crematorium?*"

"*Yes ma'am.*" There was a woman in a leather capelet and plague mask there, and she stared at me dumbly as I slammed the door behind me and dropped the crossbrace to lock it.

"*The trapdoor is... umm... drat... where did I see it...?*"

Frantically searching the room, I spotted it - a thin seam, visible by the reddish light of the roaring furnace where the city of Taltos burned its dead. "Found it."

There was a booming rapport on the front of the door. "Open up! We have an emergency! A fugitive is on the loose in the morgue!"

I Shadow Danced past the bewildered morgue worker and felt around the crack for the entry into the trapdoor. I found it, and just as I was hauling it up, I saw the NPC run to the door and start to lift the crossbrace.

Common sense told me to rush over and kill her before she let my pursuers inside. My conscience told me that if I did, I was no better than Andrik, Kanzo or Baldr. As usual, my conscience won out.

I raised my voice. "Hey! Stop that! Back off from the door, now!"

The Morgue Worker looked back uncertainly. The people - or whatever those shadows had been - banged a second time.

"I work for the King. Trust me - don't let anyone inside. They're monsters." I saluted to her, opened the hatch, and dropped inside.

It was perfectly black in the musty basement below. I fumbled a torch from my Inventory and lit it, revealing a basement cluttered with pipes, old mortuary equipment, parts for the crematoria roaring overhead, and stacks and stacks of compressed charcoal. "*Okay - I'm in. Where to now?*"

"*Great! Head north: you should find a grate that leads down into the undercity ruins. Cut back, then follow the left-hand tunnel down and then head toward my marker. We're going to keep moving toward the ossuary.*"

I checked my map. "*I don't see a marker.*"

Oh - wait a second. Let me turn tracking back on /(.__.)|"

"*Wait? You can turn player tracking on and off?*"

"*Sure you can. Just think 'player tracking off' when you're in your HUD. Sorry - I thought you knew (=^__^=).*"

Dammit - that would have been useful any number of times in the last month. Annoyed, I called my mini-map and waited until Rin's golden arrow pin appeared. The passages were mapped out for me. "*What's an ossuary, anyway? Some kind of bird?*"

"*It's a mausoleum where the bones of the dead are interred. Don't worry, though: just follow my marker. Be careful to announce yourself when you get close. I haven't told Kanzo you're coming.*"

Upstairs, I heard the squeal of metal and raised, angry voices - male and female.

"*Fuck.*" I hissed through my teeth, and followed her directions, the torch in one hand, my spear in the other. There was now only 45 minutes left on the clock. "*Hold on, Karalti.*"

Rin's marker was moving. I found the grate she was talking about, kicked it out, and extinguished my torch before sliding inside. It was a tight fit, armor scraping against the sides of the mossy drain. As I neared the end, a familiar damp, cold, stale smell wafted to my nostrils - the smell of the Lethos Cellars.

I dropped out of the end of the drain into knee-deep, slowly moving water. It wasn't a sewer channel, because it was clean. The tunnel looked quite a lot like an old mine shaft, with stone supports holding up a gently curved ceiling. Water ran and dripped everywhere, slowing me as I waded forward. I was wary of monsters... this seemed like the perfect place to hide everything from fish-men to slimes and giant maggots.

When I reached a dry tunnel, I clambered out, shook myself like a dog, then started to run. I was a hot panting mess by the time I broke out into a circular chamber stacked from floor to ceiling with old bones. This had to be the ossuary.

"*Okay. I'm here. Kind of.*" I checked the map - Rin wasn't far away now. "*I'm heading up on your position.*"

"*Alright - we're almost at the meeting site. I'm glad this meeting is going ahead for your sake... but I'm sad it's going ahead. Kanzo is desperate to get his* juchi *bastard back.*"

"*Don't call her that to her face, or this whole thing is a bust.*" I ground my teeth, hurrying through the halls of bones, and peered around a corner to see torches gleaming barely a hundred feet away. The flickering light they cast bounced off a vaulted ceiling overhead, like an underground church. I moved my head from side to side, focusing my eyes, and zoomed them in to see Rin idling by Kanzo's taller, tenser form. When she spotted my light, she waved to me.

I only advanced when I was reasonably sure this wasn't some kind of ambush. As my circle of light joined theirs, I got a good look at the Slayer of Taltos for the first time since almost killing him. Compared to how he'd been during our tussle near the orphanage, he was a mess. His clothing was torn and patched, and his silver mask had a giant crack running through it. Whatever magic allowed Mercurions to see through them without eye holes apparently still worked, because his face tracked me as I approached.

"Long time no see, Mister Slayer." I swallowed down the dark impulse to leap on the man and throttle him. "Nice bombs. I really enjoyed getting blown up, arrested, and forced into being here today. How's the murder business going?"

"Spare me your snide lecture, *sang'hi.* I'm not proud of what I've done." Kanzo drew himself up arrogantly. "I did what I had to do for my daughter's sake."

"Like bombing Main Square back into the stone age?" I asked. "You know that the Volod and Voivode weren't there, right? Or are you just killing any human in your path right now?"

Kanzo's hands clenched into tight fists. He took a step forward, light rippling in an uneven wave across the surface of his mask. "You self-righteous-!"

"Hector, Kanzo, please." Rin put herself between us, facing Kanzo. "Call a truce for now at least, okay?"

I put my hands up. "Sure. I'm a big boy. I just want Kanzo here to know that the only reason I'm not tearing his dick off and choking him with it is because the Volod is holding the most important people in the world to me hostage, and it's all thanks to his uncontrollable urge to breed."

Kanzo rattled something off in the clicking-and-snapping language of the Mercurions, only to be sharply rebuked by Rin. Whatever she said got him to back down, but he continued to radiate fury, like a grumpy little sun.

That was enough poking the bear for today. I sized them both up, leaning on my spear. "How did you two manage to find each other so quickly? Seems like you weren't telling me and Suri something important, Rin?"

Rin flushed a vivid, deep blue. "I... I was going to, before we got blown up and arrested. When I escaped the workshop, I went into the Cellars. I... umm... I ran into some monsters, and I died. I'm not very good at fighting, especially just by myself. When I respawned, I woke up in Kanzo's camp. I think it shocked him almost as much as it shocked me. Well, it happened this time, too."

"Andrik is almost as much of an animal as this King of Cats," Kanzo muttered. "Beating my poor little Rin to death."

"You feel alright now?" I asked her, brows furrowing.

"Yeah. I don't really remember the whole 'being beaten to death with a spear' thing very well. But because of this, I decided to multiclass into a Mage Path..." She trailed off, spotting something behind me.

I turned my head slightly to adjust my blind spot. Directly behind me, two torches were bobbing up and down in the darkness. One torchbearer was tall and broad-shouldered, the other painfully thin. My keen vision picked up the shadows of at least five Meewfolk who split into the shadows in the doorway, moving on silent, padded feet.

The arrogance left Kanzo's body: his shoulders loosened, his fingers uncurled. He came up beside me, enmity forgotten. "Ebisa! Ebisa, is that you!?"

I grimaced at the raw pain in his voice, keeping an eye on the quest timer. I had just under fifteen minutes left before I had to be out of here and back on the way to the castle. I took the ruby and clenched it in my fist.

"I need to speak to the King first," I said quietly. "I'm on a time limit."

"I haven't seen my child in over three months!" Kanzo hissed back.

Rin turned on her Craftmaster. "Be quiet!"

Kanzo flinched like he'd been slapped. "Rin-?"

"I don't want to hear it." Rin turned her nose up at him and, to my surprise, reached out and clutched my arm as the King of Cats and his lieutenant drew near. They were both cloaked and hooded. Ignas was wearing a bandit bandana across his lower face. Ebisa had broken with the red theme today. She was dressed head to toe in black leather, with a matte-gray fox mask that was nearly invisible in the darkness of the underground.

"Well, look who it is." Ebisa was entirely inscrutable except for the acid tone of her voice. "Dragozin. 'Father'. And you... you must be Rin. I've heard all about you, though I never had the chance to meet you."

"I'm pleased to finally meet you, too." Rin put her hands together, palm to palm, and bowed gracefully from the waist. "And I'm sorry we were never introduced... or I would have spoken earlier."

Ebisa crossed her arms. "Of course you weren't. That would have meant Kanzo would have had to admit his abject failure as a craftsman, and no self-respecting narcissist could ever bring himself to do *that*."

Kanzo advanced a step, reaching out to her. "Ebisa... how can you say such a thing about me? I've been worried to death since you were-"

"Kidnapped?" Ebisa turned her attention back to Kanzo. "Only in your wildest fantasies. *This* man has been more of a father to me than you ever will be. This is Ignas Corvinus, the true king of Vlachia, and I am *working* for him."

Kanzo pushed his own mask up with a trembling hand. His beautiful face was wide with shock and pain. "Working? You work for this... this *sang'hi*?"

"Yes. And by extension, so do you." Ebisa drew herself up, looking down at him.

"*You* used me?" Kanzo's voice shook as he took a step forward. "*You* made me kill those humans?"

"Yes." Ebisa moved back away from him. "Because when *I* escaped that accursed containment tank and your laboratory, I ended up in Cat Alley. And there, I tried to find my way by contacting other *juchi*, other bastards. And you know what happened? They were so disgusted that they tried to kill me. The other *bastards* thought I was an abomination!"

"You're not an abomination! You're my miracle!"

"Yours?" Her whipcord body tensed. "Is that why you locked me away in a vat?"

"You weren't going to be contained for long! It was a temporary measure until-"

"Months." Ebisa reached back and pulled a dagger from her belt. "I was in that vat for *months*."

"Because you weren't breathing properly on your own!" He retorted. "How can you blame me for creating you, nurturing you, teaching you? I gave you everything I could!"

"You created me as a plaything to gratify your own vanity, and you expect me to be grateful?"

Kanzo regarded his 'daughter' bleakly. "Every Mercurion alive was created for one single purpose, Ebisa - cannon fodder. That's all our taboos are for: they ensure that the same body-plans are made over and over again. Short-lived, uncreative, inflexible cannon fodder for a war that has been raging two centuries. But you? You are something new, something better. You can live longer, be cleverer and have a memory better than any Mercurion in known history. You don't have to be... an..."

"Outcast?"

"No! You have the potential to be the greatest artificer this world has ever known. You can show them we can be better!"

"And maybe that's not what I want to do," Ebisa replied. Every word landed like a whip crack. "Maybe I *like* working for

Ignas. Maybe *I care* more about politics and community and the welfare of Vlachia's people than I do about showing your enemies that I'm 'better' than they are. Maybe I *enjoy* my chosen Advanced Path. Did that ever occur to you?"

He sighed. "And here I thought I'd created an improved design... a person capable of learning all I have to pass on. But you're bitter, twisted, like every *juchi* I've ever observed. I have failed."

Before I could interrupt, Rin swelled up like an angry kitten, stalked over to Kanzo, and slapped him so hard that his head snapped to the side and he stumbled.

"You jerk!" she shrilled.

"Look, I'm sorry to interrupt the family reunion, but I have something really important and time-sensitive to give His Majesty." I said. "Sire, your brother has demanded to see you. He gave me this, and told me it has the coordinates for a meeting so that he can expose you as being someone other than his brother. Which seems kind of dumb to me - unless he plans to lure you into a fatal trap. Point being, if you don't go there at the appointed time, he's going to execute me and Suri, send my dragon back to Ilia to become a broodmare, and declare a pogrom on the Mercurions and Meewfolk. We have to act - there's no more time to sneak around in the shadows. And if you can prove your identity, I'm sure you're going to have the support of Janos Lanz and the new Forgemaster."

I held out the ruby. Ignas and Ebisa looked at each other.

"How unfortunate. He is not here in person." the man said. He removed his half-mask, and my heart sunk. This guy looked like Ignas, walked like Ignas... but he wasn't quite Ignas.

"Christoph is His Majesty's doppelganger," Ebisa said, with a shrug. "While I hate to pull aside the curtain of deception so soon, you surely didn't expect that the real Ignas Corvinus would attend a meeting that was as potentially dangerous as this one?"

"I..." I looked back at Rin, who had her hands to her mouth.

"Fortunately, you have recourse, Dragozin. Give it here." Ebisa held out a hand. "I can read it."

"No." Kanzo ran forward, trying to intercept us. "No, if there is some fell magic in that stone, it could infect you—"

"Then let it infect me. It is *my* decision to make, not yours." Ebisa snatched the stone off my palm, removing her mask with her other hand. When she bared her alien face, Rin gasped. Ebisa sneered knowingly.

"Nonono! I'm sorry!" Rin squeaked. "I just... the composition of your features... they took me by surprise—"

"Believe me, kitten, I am less surprised by your reaction than you are by my face." Ebisa reached up and plucked out one of her gemstone eyes — the inner right. She palmed the bigger ruby and inserted the new one. It was too small to fill the socket, but it flared to life as she spoke. "*Bahn, Odam, Vorhis.*"

The stone's light flared, and Ebisa's hands dropped to her sides. She went very still, like a doll... and like a doll, she had no eyelids and didn't blink.

"Tell us where Andrik is going to meet Ignas," I urged her, moving in closer. "Because I'll go with you to wring that asshole's neck."

"Well, I would, but there's a problem." Ebisa grimaced, and reached up to remove Andrik's ruby. "He hasn't recorded anything. This stone is blank."

CHAPTER 41

I stared at Ebisa in disbelief. "What do you mean, it's blank?"

"Empty. As in, there's no recording." She frowned. "Clever little weasel."

I wasn't sure if I was going to scream or explode. Some childish part of me railed that this wasn't fair, that the bad guys weren't allowed to be this smart, this manipulative. That they had to play by the rules. I'd heard from someone here before only a couple of days before - Rin, sobbing that Kanzo had gone and acted on his own, beyond the norms she expected would contain him. I'd been working on that basis, too.

"Ebisa, can you and Fake Ignas here make recordings onto those stones?" My voice came out hard and cold.

"Certainly," Ebisa said.

"Then record a message. A challenge, from Ignas to Andrik. And I'll take it back." I flexed my shoulders and cracked my knuckles. "Ignas doesn't even have to attend personally. We set Andrik up. And then we kill him."

A sly smile spread over Ebisa's lips. "I like the way you think, Dragozin. I know the perfect spot, too - the Imperial Crypt under the Church of the Maker, in the center of town. Ignas always said that if he were to choose one place to face his brother-"

"No!" Kanzo stomped his foot, fists balled by his sides.

There was a pregnant pause.

"No? What do you mean, 'no'?" I turned to face Kanzo. "We're doing this. If he'd left Karalti out of it, I'd be perfectly fine with staying out of politics and letting him go his happy little way. But that fucker is holding my dragon hostage. *My* dragon. I've got thirty minutes to do something about it."

"Ebisa, I made you to be a scientist!" Kanzo was aghast. "A crafter! Not some... some human prince's assassin!"

"As you so graciously noted before, I am very bitter and very twisted." Ebisa's rough voice oozed sarcasm. "But by the look on Rin's pretty face, she's about ready to join me as an honorary *juchi*."

"I didn't mean it that way, Ebisa! You are my daughter! My miracle!" Kanzo replied hotly.

Ebisa's features froze. "And you are nothing. Leave us."

"No! I will not let you go through with this nonsense after everything I did for you!" Kanzo stormed toward us. "Give me that stone!"

Ebisa teleported as Kanzo lunged at her, zipping to one side in a flicker of shadow. He blundered into one of the pillars supporting the vaulted ceiling.

"You are no longer necessary, Kanzo." Ebisa drew a second dagger from behind her back. This one was a very finely-made weapon, with a thin blue glow humming around the edge of the blade. "Leave, before I remove you."

Kanzo looked between us, nostrils flaring – but wherever he turned, he saw only hostile stares. Even Rin was glaring at him, though she looked to be on the verge of tears.

"Rin, please," he begged. "You cannot let them do this. You cannot be a part of this!"

Rin clasped one of her own wrists, kneading it anxiously. "You know... you never asked me."

"What?" Kanzo did a double-take. "Ask you what?"

Her piercing blue gaze flicked down. "How *I* felt about this. How *I* suffered. What I felt when I found your lab... or how I feel now that I've met Ebisa and seen her pain. You never asked me what I wanted, or thought about whether this would hurt me... and

I don't understand why you made Ebisa if you knew what other Mercurions would do to her. You knew, or you wouldn't have hidden her away. Now she has to live with what you did, and you..."

"You are Starborn and perfectly formed, Rin, but you are not of my creation," he replied. "Rin, you must understand, I lost everything when I left Zaunt, I-"

"What about her? Did you ever ask Ebisa how she felt?" Rin motioned to Ebisa. "Did you ever ask her what she *wanted*?"

Ebisa snorted. "Not once."

Kanzo glanced at her. "It wasn't the right time. When she was older-"

"Get out." Rin pointed at the door, still staring at her feet. "I never want to see you again."

The elder Mercurion hunched back. And then, without a word, he turned and fled.

"Are you sure that's a good idea?" I said. "That guy has killed a lot of people."

"The blood he spilled stains *my* hands." Ebisa's husky voice was oddly subdued. "He was merely the tool I used for the executions. Now, come – we must record that stone, and then you must return to the Volod. And I will give you something else, too."

Ebisa sheathed the enchanted dagger she had been holding, and offered it to me.

"This?" I took it hesitantly, and had a look at its stats:

Ravenstar Dagger

Magical Weapon

Slot: One-handed

Item Quality: Excellent

Damage: 36-45

Durability: 100%

Weight: 1 lb

Special: +30% chance to cause Bleeding; +2% chance to instantly kill any human/demi-human opponent.

An engraved dagger belonging to the House of Corvinus, believed to have been forged by Taltos, the demigod son of Khors.

"This is Ignas' heirloom dagger," she said. "His gift to me when he made me his lieutenant. Present it at court with the stone, and Andrik will have no choice but to answer his brother's summons. Make sure you have witnesses.

"Will Ignas show?" I glanced at Christoph, who shrugged sheepishly.

"I think he will, yes," Ebisa said, rolling the empty stone in her palm. "Assuming Andrik accepts. If he does, Ignas is an honorable man, and what happened at Kobayaz and in the plaza today broke his heart. He knows this has been a long time coming."

I arrived at Vulkan Keep with five minutes left on the clock. It touched 4:59 as I raced Cutthroat in through the gates, sped past the guards, and rode her up the staircase that fed into the dragon-sized doors of the grand hall.

"Halt! You canno-!" The guards leapt in front of us, crossing their halberds over the threshold. Cutthroat blasted through them like a cannonball.

"OH YEAHHHH!" I shouted on the way past.

Andrik was holding court for the day: he lounged in his throne at the back of the room, listening to a Minister reading off a long parchment scroll. There was an entire crowd of people assembled inside the vaulted throne room, and every one of them turned to stare and gape as the Giant Velociraptor Express came roaring into the building. Andrik stood up from the throne in shock. The

Kingsguard encircled him warily. We pulled up just behind the minister, who yipped a girly scream as he stumbled out of the way of the steaming, snorting hookwing.

"Your Majesty. Please pardon the intrusion, but I have a message from your brother." I kept Cutthroat on a tight rein so that she didn't dart her head and snap.

A gasp went up around the throne room. Andrik's eyes narrowed. Then, quite abruptly, he laughed.

"So the Tuun can speak to spirits now?" he said, raising his voice to be heard over the murmur of his assembly. "Tell us: does the Maker's furnace keep him warm in the afterlife?"

A murmur of uncomfortable laughter went up behind me.

"Actually, he just challenged you to a duel. Catch." I threw him the stone.

Ur Garen moved in front of him and snatched the ruby out of the air. The knight examined it, frowned me, and then offered it to Andrik.

I could watch the sea of shocked faces in my peripheral vision while I stared down the Volod. "Your brother, Ignas Corvinus, accuses you of conspiring to strip him of his rightful title and family name to attain the throne of Vlachia. He demands satisfaction at the time and place of his choosing. The location and time are on the ruby."

"You don't really believe this man, do you?" Andrik snapped. "Garen! Strike him down! I will not put up with this nonsense!"

Garen slowly drew his sword, but stopped when I pulled out my trump card: the dagger. "Ignas also told me to tell you that the Maker's furnace isn't as hot as you thought it was."

"The Ravenstar." Ur Garen took the dagger from my hand and pushed the visor of his helmet up, revealing weathered, troubled features. "This was thought to have been lost. So it's true... Ignas lives."

Andrik came forward and snatched the knife away. He drew the glowing blade and regarded it impassively.

"There is only one legitimate Corvinus in Vlachia," he said quietly. "Me. Even if Ignas lives, he was disowned and exiled, and if he is here, in *my* city, in *my* country, then he is an outlaw who has committed vice and banditry and who has murdered scores of innocent people."

Garen grimaced. "Your Majesty... if he has issued a formal challenge to your honor-"

"Contain yourself, Ur Garen. I will indeed face him in the field, and prove myself against this perverted bastard. As I told you, Hector – it does not become a monarch to hide in his castle while a battle rages on."

There was a light in Andrik's pale eyes that I didn't like at all. He was planning something. "Where's Karalti?"

"Downstairs, in the dungeon, being prepared for transport," Andrik replied. "I suppose you fulfilled the terms of our agreement, and I am a man of my word. Garen, go escort our dragonrider back to his mount."

"Me, Your Majesty?" The big knight frowned. "But I am oath-bound to remain-"

"Did I stutter? Go with Hector to the dungeons and unlock the bindings on his dragon, now." Andrik said, waving us off. He held onto the dagger, clutching it as he swept past us. "Lords and Ladies of the court, my Hand will take over your concerns. I must attend to this crisis immediately. Please excuse me."

Garen was clearly torn about what to do, and his confusion only made me warier. Bodyguards weren't ordered to abandon their primaries like this.

"Tomaz, you are in charge until I return." Garen nodded sharply to his second-in-command, then motioned me with his head. "Come, Tuun. And bring that dinosaur with you before she soils the Great Hall."

Cutthroat was slowly stalking one of Andrik's dogs. She hissed when I caught her reins, giving the animal one last hungry, glowering look before padding off after us.

"So, be straight with me. Is Karalti in the dungeon, or are you about to try and jump me?" I asked to Garen as we cleared the door.

"Jump you? No. She truly is in the dungeons. My honor would not permit you to come to harm, now that you have satisfied His Majesty's orders."

We went down to the caves that housed the stables first, where I hitched Cutthroat, and then into the dungeon area where we'd been unloaded from the prison wagons. Rage simmered deep inside my chest, rising for my throat as we ventured underground. This place was too much like the bowels of the Eyrie for my comfort.

"Andrik's been weird lately," I remarked.

"I must admit, Tuun... you are correct." Garen nodded. "His Majesty has been acting strangely."

"How so?"

The Captain of the Kingsguard narrowed his eyes. "Well... his general conduct, I suppose. The unfortunate incident with the Mercurion, your draak, and Ur Kirov. He has also been sleepless, consumed by a strange fixation on the Dakhari woman, and he spends a lot of time in his laboratory as of late. He is typically an enthusiastic hunter, but-"

Suri. Where the hell is she? "His... laboratory?"

"Oh, yes. His Majesty is a keen student of the magical arts. I have never seen the inside of it."

"Seems legit," I replied. "Where's Suri? The Dakhari?"

"Last time I saw her, she was restrained in a cell down here, awaiting the Volod's judgement." Garen sounded - and looked - increasingly uncomfortable. "She is safe, though not comfortable. It seems... out of character for His Majesty to imprison a woman this way, especially one who has been so instrumental in the investigation into the Slayer..."

I fought the urge to hit him over the back of the head and run off to find her - and rescue her. But I couldn't. We had to play the long game. "The problem is, it's not out of character. Andrik's been acting strangely, probably because he believes Ignas is alive."

"Believes? No, he knows. You bought the Ravenstar back to Vulkan Keep. There is only one person you could have received it from."

"You knew Ignas, right?"

The Captain's mustache drooped with his expression. "Of course. I served their father and watched over both princes. Their mother died giving birth to Andrik. Their father - the Nine guard his soul - never bonded with his younger son, while Ignas was much loved by the court."

I heard Karalti before I saw her: the heavy breathing, the rustle of leathery wings against scales. My heart began to pound, and - hanging back behind Garen - I took my spear in hand. "So what will you do when Andrik meets Ignas?"

"I will adhere to the letters of my vows. I do not serve the Volod - I serve the office of the Volod," The older man said stiffly, unlocking a heavy door. "If you hope to seed discord between myself and the throne, you will fail."

"If you consider 'the truth' to be 'seeding disapproval', sure. Between me and you, I'm pretty sure disrupting bullshit is part of my job description as the Herald of Matir."

Garen grimaced with disapproval as he swung the door open.

Karalti was curled in a ball on a hard stone floor and a smattering of straw, contained by a magic circle that blazed with sick violet light. Her eyes were closed, and she was shivering and twitching in her sleep. The corners of her mouth were turned down. Her eyes rolled underneath their lids. She didn't rouse as we entered. That was not normal for her - she was a light sleeper, instantly alert at the slightest sound. The air that came from the doorway was bone-chillingly cold, and the Mark of Matir burned on my hand when the icy breeze touched it.

"Karalti? Karalti!" I turned on Garen. "What is this? What have you done to her?!"

"I don't know what this is. Please, stay back." The Kingsguard clanked his way into the cell, his hand on his sword. "This circle reeks of foul magic. This wasn't what was used to pacify her earlier today..."

The Mark snapped with a flash of pain, like the burn of a hot wire touching skin - and at the same time, I saw a pair of shadows peel from the walls. "No! Stop!"

Before Garen had even completely turned around, the shadows cross-cut the room, and the Level 25 knight lurched on his feet as his body crawled with thick frost. He half-turned, half-fell toward me. When his knees hit the ground, his entire body shattered.

Karalti whimpered. It was the last thing I heard before the shadows darted at me. I'd barely gotten the Alpha Rod in front of me when they locked their eyes on me.

[[Void Wraith uses Abyssal Gaze.]]

I looked at them before I could stop myself. My skin crackled, and there was an awful, painless sucking sensation through my body. This wasn't Darkness element. It wasn't anything. Before I had even really realized what I'd seen, I fell to my knees.

[[You take 1030 Freezing damage!]]

[[You take 1031 Freezing damage!]]

[[You have been killed by Void Wraith!]]

[[You are dead.]]

CHAPTER 42

I woke up to darkness, and the smell of old dust and dried flowers. It was cold, the air stale and dry. And I was buck-ass naked.

Fear spiked through my chest as I struggled up to my hands, feeling around in the pitch blackness of where the hell I was. My hands felt strange - like they weren't really attached to me. Like they weren't really my hands. Intellectually, I knew that was ridiculous. They were attached to the arms that were attached to... well... *me.* But as I fumbled around on the floor, I couldn't make the instinctual connection between those hands and the rest of my body. It was like trying to move things around with a pair of rubber chickens.

What the fuck is wrong with me? I sat back, rubbing my eyes with my wrists. My vision was frizzing at the corners, spitting with random colors. *I can't sit here. I need to get my shit together... I have to go rescue... umm...*

Fuck. I had to help... Tidbit. No, that wasn't her real name. It was K... K... K-something. I froze with it on the tip of my tongue, but where there should have been an instant draw from my memory, there was nothing. I could picture her in my mind: a gawky little hatchling with an adorable puppy grin. Tidbit... my goddamn dragon. She was... what? Level 3 now?

A small breeze kicked up, rattling dirt and small stones across the floor, and I suddenly remembered one thing - the Void Wraiths. Panic squeezed my heart in a tight fist as I groped around for anything that might help me, and was surprised to lay a hand down on something long and metallic. My HUD highlighted it in the darkness. It was the Spear of Nine Spheres.

"Oh. So you've decided to be soul-bonded after all, have you?" I focused on my hands, trying to reconnect with them. It was the strangest sensation, because they weren't numb. They just felt like... 'not me'. "Still at 17% durability, I see."

Wonderful. Sudden onset Alzheimer's Disease, no clothes, no fucking idea where I was, and a weapon with 15 base damage at Level 13. I could probably kill some rats with it, provided they were normal sized rats. Then I could employ my mastery of Leatherworking to make myself a rat-skin thong and wreak vengeance on the world. It would serve Whats-His-Face the Bad King right if that was the last thing he ever saw. I couldn't remember his name, either.

I used the Spear like a cane, sweeping it ahead of myself as I began to cautiously explore the room I was in. I froze when the spear clunked against a large, rectangular block of stone - a coffin-sized block of stone.

"Shit." I jerked away in case some unseen animated corpse came lurching out. "Dear God of Darkness - if I'm supposed to be your Herald, why the fuck didn't you give me darkvision?"

A ghostly light kindled to life behind me, throbbing like a slow heartbeat. I felt a bead of sweat run down my temple - or at least, I hoped it was sweat. Slowly, I turned around.

The glow emanated from a nine-pointed chaos star-like symbol: the symbol of Matir. It was about half a foot long, glowing brightly enough that it illuminated the mummified flowers I'd smelled before, along with an offering of coins and jewelry on the remains of a small, hexagonal altar set above the sarcophagus. Curious, I gingerly touched the rune, and was rewarded with... nothing. No darkvision, no sudden magic power. The only thing that happened was that the dim light steadied out.

"Weird. But okay." I frowned, flexing my fingers. Now that I could see them, they felt more connected. They looked normal, and as the seconds passed, I found myself syncing back up. Once I was sure my hands weren't about to fall off, I searched the altar for any clues, and glanced up when I noticed a trio of inscriptions in different languages.

One of the engravings looked like it was made of funny squiggles and shapes, almost like a magical script. One was more like Sumerian or Babylonian Cuneiform, with lots of triangles and straight lines. And the last one – a flowing vertical script similar to Mongolian – was *my* language, Tuun. And even weirder... I could *read* it.

In darkness you were conceived;
To the darkness you were sworn.
In the darkness you have found your peace,
And through darkness shall you be reborn -
Here lie the fallen of Kalla Kulesi, who joined us in our battle against the Trauvin.
Matir's Blessing be upon these Honored Dead in their nest of loving earth.

I slowly recited the passage, stumbling over the translation at points. I had no idea what a 'Trauvin' was... but I could read. And *that* was strange.

Heart hammering, I turned to look at the rest of the crypt where I'd somehow respawned. It was small, barely ten by ten feet, with only two tombs. One was missing its lid, the other was not. There was a rusted iron gate at the end of the room I hadn't yet searched, leading out into the inky blackness beyond. There was no corpse in the open sarcophagus, but there was in the closed one. I only got a glimpse of the skeletal face and empty eye sockets before my naked skin crawled and I slid the lid back into place.

"I don't get it," I said. "There's nothing here."

The room did not reply.

Frustrated, I searched around, using the dim light to try and spot anything I'd missed in my first minutes of terror. The gate wasn't locked, but the outside area beyond this tiny room was so dark as to be impenetrable. A cool wind moaned from somewhere outside. The place would be crawling with monsters. I wasn't walking out there naked, with a shitty spear and no light.

Panic began to set in. I felt disconnected and floaty as I paced back and forth, at a loss for what to do. *My dragon... she's trapped in that circle, and she's helpless. One of your friends is in a cell, and she has to be terrified. The others are going to meet the bad guy, and he's going to bring those fucking murder-ghosts as backup. They're expecting treachery, but not an undead that can kill the head of the Kingsguard in a single hit. King What's-His-Face going to wipe the floor with them.*

I looked back out into the darkness, mouth dry with fear. *What do I know about Matir? Fuck. He... he hates the undead. I remember that.*

The rune's light was starting to fade. I walked back to it, searching the altar for anything that might help. None of the jewelry was magical, but I found myself looking back to the sarcophagus - the one with the body. The thought of raiding the coffin squicked me the hell out. In some games I'd played, it had only been mildly disturbing. In a full sensory immersion scenario, it was as creepy as it would have been IRL.

"He hates the undead, so that prayer and the sigil... they're probably a protective spell for the dead to keep them from being animated or to guard against ghosts or something? I edged toward the coffin. "He's the god of the normally-dead. So the 'death is a natural part of life' thing, and the dead don't take their belongings with them, so..."

I pushed the lid open properly this time, exposing the ancient corpse.

It was wizened, dry, but recognizable as male. He was fully dressed. I couldn't really make out much detail, but his heavily-armored hands were resting on his sternum, the knuckles touching. There was something dignified about him... even serene.

My HUD - super bright against the near-blackness - immediately began to highlight things of interest.

[[Belt of Tiger's Spirit]]
[[Barrier Shirt]]
[[Blindfighter's Fold]]
[[Sanctified Cold Iron Gauntlets]]
[[Ancient Kamanocha]]
[[Boots of the Winding Path]]

Kamanocha. That was a Tuun word. A Kamanocha was a very special kind of dagger from Tungaant... but I couldn't bring the specifics to mind. *Fuck. I am even still in Taltos?*

Agitated, I bought up the summary descriptions for each item and had the system read them to me:

Belt of Tiger's Spirit
Magical Item
5 Armor
Slot: Belt
+5 bonus against fear
+5 bonus to intimidate checks
An ancient Vlachian shaman bound the spirit of a tiger to this leather belt, which was made from its skin.

Barrier Shirt
Magical Armor

125 Armor

25% chance that backstabs, critical hits and sneak attacks will be treated as normal attacks, with no bonus damage.

Light armor

Body slot

82% durability

Armor to protect against those who would fight dishonorably.

Sanctified Cold Iron Gauntlets

Magical Armor/Weapon

50 Armor

Item Class: Relic

Item Quality: Exceptional

Damage: 65 x 2 Bludgeoning

Durability: 55% (-2 damage)

Weight: 10 lb x 2

Special: Darkness element. x3 damage against the Undead. x2 damage against monsters weak to cold iron. +20 bonus Adrenaline Points.

These skillfully forged, heavy but flexible full-arm gauntlets are the traditional weapons and armor of the Baru, warrior-monks in service to Burna. They appear to be completely made of pitted cold iron, yet they have no rust.

Blindfighter's Fold

Magical Item

Glasses Slot

Special: Obscures normal vision while granting the Blind-Fighting ability.

Created in a ritual by a Khatvaana, a priest of the Left Hand Path in the cult of Burna, the Blindfighter's Fold is an important teaching tool used to train Baru for the ranks of the Dark Moon Brothers.

Ancient Kamanocha

Magical Weapon
Item Class: Relic
Item Quality: Masterwork
Damage: 50-74 piercing
Durability: 100%
Weight: 0.5 lb

Special: Mercy Strike - This weapon has a specific, special enchantment. If the dagger is drawn to commit an act of euthanasia, this knife deals x15 piercing damage to the target. If the weapon is ever used to strike a target in an act of aggression - offensive or defensive - this enchantment is lost and can only be regained by taking it to a temple of Burna.

Special: Brittle - This weapon is made of specially tempered bone that is as hard as steel when used to stab, but is still weaker than metal against certain forms of stress. Tuun bone weapons take x2 damage from bludgeoning weapons or crushing damage. Slashing with a Kamanocha degrades the weapon quality normally. If they are used to Pierce, they take no loss to durability. Tuun bone weapons cannot be reforged.

A long dagger made from the chemically and magically tempered bone of a human femur, Kamanocha (Kah-mo-notch-ah) are special ritual tools carried by Tuun as religious heirlooms. Kamanocha are created and consecrated by priests or monks for specific purposes, and may not be drawn or used for any other purpose lest the spirit of the person who donated the bone.

Baru traditionally carry a special Kamanocha which is used only for acts of euthanasia so that the monk may grant terminally ill or injured people a swift, painless death.

Boots of the Winding Path

Magical Armor

Item Class: Artifact

85 Armor

Durability: 78%

Weight: 3lb

Special: +10 movement-related checks on unstable surfaces; +5 Stamina

Boots made of hookwing leather and enchanted to be supernaturally resilient. There are small metal cleats on the soles that make them suitable for hiking in mountains and wilderness.

"Holy shit," I whispered. Now that I looked, certain things about this corpse were recognizable. His hair was long - very long, separated into two narrow braids that reached past his knees. This guy was Tuun - and he had to be a *baru,* one of Matir's warrior-healer monks. But that made no sense. Tuun weren't from this continent - we came from Daun, the Western continent on the other side of the ocean. There had been no migration between Daun and Artana before the invention of airships. Had there?

"Vlachian cloak, Tuun gear... but we don't bury our dead in Tungaant," I muttered aloud. "We do sky burials with giant insects. This baru was injured really badly when he died. Broken ribs, crushed skull. He died fighting. A hero? Yeah... but a hero in Vlachia who was given a burial in pre-Khorsian times.... which means I *have* to be in Taltos. Somewhere in the underground."

Call me old-fashioned, but I didn't like the idea of robbing graves, especially now that I was marked as an oathbreaker. But as I studied the body, there was no sense of judgement from either him or Matir. Instead, I could almost hear the monk whispering to me. *Take them.*

Reverently, I lifted out the knife, and then carefully removed the other objects. I pulled on the chain shirt and belted the Belt of Tiger's Spirit on over it. The gauntlets were powerful weapons, but they were obscenely heavy. I equipped them anyway, testing out the range of motion. As the description said, they were surprisingly flexible, allowing me to properly ball my hands into fists. I put on the blindfold last, acutely aware that I was now wearing everything but pants.

The blindfold didn't help me see - but the world around me opened up in a silent rush without the need for vision. When I tied it on, I could somehow sense the location of nearby objects. The edge of the open sarcophagus, the small altar to Matir, the body of the fallen *baru*... I knew exactly where they were. It was more like sonar than darkvision, but it was almost as good as seeing in the dark.

Feeling more confident - if no less breezy downstairs - I went back to the altar and gathered up the offerings of jewelry. The rings were ordinary treasures, but I could sell them once I had Tidbit back and this shit was over and done with. I no longer had an Inventory to store items, so now I had rings on along with everything else - except underwear.

I belted the Kamanocha on my hips, then pushed toward the iron gate and brought up my mini-map. It was mostly a big blank space beyond the door - a big round space with little nooks and narrow corridors coming off it. I stepped out, and as the sound open up, I could 'see'. What I perceived made me gasp.

Dragons.

There were six colossal biers arranged in a ring around this room, and each stone platform held the skeletal remains of a dragon. They were all curled up the way that Tidbit liked to sleep: balled on their side with their tail wrapped around their body, one foreclaw clasped over their snout, the other arm, wing, and both legs drawn up. I wandered over to the closest one, awe-struck. Taltos had used to be a dragon city... and I'd respawned in one of their tombs.

There was an inscription at the base of the bier. I crouched down to have a look, but this one was not in three languages - only one, the sticks-and-triangles script. *Is that draconic script? Draconic writing?*

I moved out into the dragons' crypt, turning and waiting to face each corridor to see which one was the windiest. That was the one I chose. When I left the security of walls, the Blindfighting ability was less useful - for a couple of minutes, I had nothing but the disturbing groan of the wind rattling through ancient tomb corridors to guide me. The tunnel was easier to navigate than the open tomb. I broke off into a jog, trying to put the pieces of my memory together as I headed back up, toward the surface.

Thirty minutes or so later, my HUD chirped. [[You have a new message from Rin Lu.]]

"*WRU??*" It began. "*We're in the Imperial Crypt and Andrik will be here any minute now! \(O.O!)/*"

Andrik. That's right. "*I died. Andrik had some crazy-powerful monsters guarding my dragon.*"

"*OMG! Is Karalti okay!?*"

Relief washed over me as I heard her name again... and with it came a few lost memories. She wasn't Level 3 any more - she was just barely Level 6. I knew there were other things I'd forgotten, but piecing the gaps together was going to have to wait. "*I don't know. I hope so.*"

"*What monsters did you fight down there?*" Rin asked after a minute or so.

"*Two 'Void Wraiths'. Ring any bells?*"

There was a short pause before she replied. "*No way.*"

"*Yah way.*"

"*Void Wraiths shouldn't be in Artana! They shouldn't even be able to spawn yet!*" She messaged back. "*You're sure!?*"

"*They hit me for over 1000 points of freezing damage by looking at me, so yeah.*"

"*Oh no! Void Wraiths are endgame monsters. Minimum Level 40 (T__T)*"

"*Do they have any weaknesses? Restrictions?*"

"Umm... they're incorporeal undead, so they'll be weak to Dark and Light magic, immune to Time, Gravity and physical hits... but even if we somehow magically had Shadowfall or Deliverance at our level, I-I know if we could beat one unless it was REALLY nerfed..."

There was a slight pause before she sent another message. *"Hey! You just appeared on my map! You must be close /(TwT)/"*

I was heading up a flight of hollowed out stairs. When I glanced at my own map, I saw Rin's icon. It was dim, meaning she was on a different floor to me. I wasn't sure how many I had left to go. *"I see you, too. I must be under the Imperial Crypt. That's good news for us re: wraiths - this place is consecrated to Matir and there's magic active on the premises. That's why I respawned here, I think. BRT."*

"OK... but hurry! I think Andrik is here, and-"

"*What?*" I picked up my pace as much as I could, breaking out into what looked to me like part of the Lethos Cellars. "*Rin?*"

There was no reply.

CHAPTER 43

I ran through the levels of cold catacombs, through halls stacked with old bones, reliquaries, and - eventually - torches. There were no monsters down here, the undead kept at bay by the many small, active wards that flared to life on the walls whenever I passed them. As I got closer to Rin's blinking marker, I heard the sound of steel clashing against steel, shouts and screams... the sounds of combat.

I wrenched open the first door I found and squeezed into a narrow corridor barely wide enough for my shoulders to pass - like a maintenance shaft, or some kind of secret channel for sneaking behind the walls of the Imperial Crypt - effectively the basement of the biggest church in the city - to eavesdrop.

Wincing, I shuffled like a crab down the confines of the passage, chafing all the way. I still didn't have any pants, which made this more of an adventure than I would have preferred. The sounds of combat grew louder, but there was little light and no sign of an exit. I was beginning to think I needed to go back when I finally realized what this stupidly tight corridor was for. Above my head, about eight feet off the ground, was a ventilation panel.

"Hmm." I narrowed my eyes while I considered how the hell I was going to get myself and the Spear out through such an awkward exit. I experimentally reached up to jab at it with the blunt end of my weapon. As I did, there was a weird *whomp* sound that cut through the air with a wave of bitter cold, and a hoarse feminine shout - Ebisa's voice.

"No time." I clamped my teeth together and started to bash the grate in earnest. The plaster around it crumbled, and the wire dented with every blow. A dozen hits, and I knocked it out to the ground. I threw the Spear through first, jumped up, Spider Climbed the wall, and pulled myself through.

I slithered out to land on awkwardly on an altar, scattering candles, flowers, a white silk runner and an urn to floor. I desperately lunged out to catch it. It smacked into my palm, and had I not been wearing the Cold Iron Gauntlets, it would have stopped. Instead, the delicate porcelain slid along the leather and thick iron plating, toppled to the floor, and shattered in a cloud of ash.

"Oh my god," I moaned, trying not to breathe as I backed up, dusting myself frantically. "I am *so* sorry."

There was nothing I could do for the remains of Volod Wizimir the Second, so I pulled the silk runner, beat the ashes out of it - wincing the entire time - and tied it around like a girdle. Or a diaper. It was better than nothing.

The Imperial Crypt wasn't a single room - it had no fewer than six interconnected chambers, about the size of a ranch-style home. I ran toward the combat, and turned the corner to see a scene out of a schizophrenic's nightmare.

More than thirty people were brawling in the tight confines of the crypt. Ebisa, Rin, a dozen Nightstalkers rogues fought against a line of soldiers without faces. They wore the silver and orange uniforms of the Taltos City Guard, but their faces were shifting, morphing walls of pixelated blackness. Reality distorted subtly around the soldiers as they moved. Even worse, they were almost soundless. These ⟦???Soldiers⟧ didn't grunt, didn't cry out in pain. There was something almost hallucinatory about them, but their steel was very real. Longswords tore through fur and flesh with ferocious strength.

I stormed in, blasting straight into the back of one soldier with the Spear. The Spear punched all the way through his chest. I followed up with an Umbra Burst, blasting a streak of energy up along the polearm that engulfed him and two other [[???Soldiers]] nearby. They thrashed without sound, clawing at their faces, and then collapsed into black dust - like pinprick holes in reality that danced, then vanished.

Void creatures. They have to be. And ironically, void creatures were weak against the Darkness element.

[[Warning! Your primary weapon is badly damaged! Durability 15/100]]

"About time you showed up!" Ebisa snarled. She was being driven back toward me, battling two [[???Soldiers]] with unnatural speed. Her limbs glowed with magic - a Haste buff. "Push through the mob! Help Ignas!"

"Where is he?" I called back, searching the pack for Rin. She was hanging back by the edges, casting spells from behind a glowing blue barrier while her turrets tanked for her.

"Head west - they're in the Founders Vault!" Ebisa teleported behind a soldier and plunged her knives into his neck. "We got separated - these freaks just appeared out of thin air and cut us off! Ignas is alone in there!"

I plowed my way through the scrum, belting a soldier across the jaw with a fist, pushing another away from me with the Spear of Nine Spheres, and sprinted toward the Founders Vault - the only room with tombs instead of urns. Huge, ornate steel coffins with life-sized statues stood behind them, dressed in layers of scrollwork. The Kingsguard had been decimated, the survivors shivering and groaning on the ground. Ignas and Andrik battled in the center of the room. Ignas with a light mace and shield, dressed like a master thief; Andrik in his ancestral armor, a mageglove, his sword and the Ravenstar dagger. He was fencing against Ignas's heavy blows, his sword wreathed in flames. His glove glowed brightly. *Andrik is a Spellsword?*

"How can you commit such deeds? In front of our ancestors, our blood!?" Ignas caught a blow on his shield, pushing the sword away before it caught the wood. "How can you act so dishonorably toward the men who protected us!? Against me? Against our home?"

"How could *you* stoop so low as to murder my citizens? Are you *that* petty about being outmaneuvered at court?" Andrik could move faster than Ignas. He was younger, faster, and he had magic. "Father always praised your wisdom, but a very wise man once told me that victory belongs to the strong."

Even as Ignas threw his brother's sword back, Andrik barked a string of Words that sent a bolt of freezing energy into Ignas' body, knocking him back toward the biggest sarcophagus at the end of the room. The tomb was flanked by a pair of thick pillars. An androgynous, veiled statue stood behind it, arms spread in a gesture of benediction.

"I did what I had to do to reclaim this kingdom before you destroy it!" Ignas snarled with effort, swinging in. His mace clipped Andrik in the shoulder, but the weapon rebounded off an invisible barrier, sending out a cloud of blue sparks. Andrik didn't slow. He pressed forward, herding his brother toward the back of the room. "You are a pretender! A vile heretic who would corrupt this place as your 'Master' corrupted you!"

Andrik scoffed, dodging "Master? I don't have a Master. *I* am the master of my destiny and the destiny of Vlachia, not you!"

I dropped into a crouch, but as I passed the threshold, I paused as both of my arms throbbed with a strange pulsing sensation. Confused, I looked down and saw sparks of deep, indigo-black energy crawl through the seams of the iron gauntlets. They were warning me. Something was wrong here.

Void Wraiths, I thought to myself. *Where the fuck are the Void Wraiths?*

Ignas feinted and tried to break past Andrik, but the younger Corvinus didn't let him. They were two thirds of the way down the vault now. Andrik was definitely pressing his brother toward the back of the room.

"You thought you could look down on me!" Andrik panted. "But now look at you!"

"I never looked down on you." Ignas eye briefly caught mine, but his expression didn't change. "And if you surrender now, I will show you mercy, brother."

"Becoming a common thief didn't teach you to lie any better," Andrik sneered. "And besides... Mercy is weakness."

I broke off from the shadows into a sprint, Shadow Dancing to cross the distance and power the blow I dealt Andrik from behind.

The Spear hit him in the back of the neck, and there was a shattering sound as his magical shield discharged and blew out. The explosion threw me back and sent both brothers stumbling forward onto the sarcophagus.

⟦Your primary weapon is broken! It can no longer be used in combat!⟧

The Spear spat and sparked in my hand. Cracks had appeared along its length, discharging small puffs of mana gas. I threw it aside in frustration and rolled up to rejoin the fight.

"No! Leave us!" Ignas barked at me. He was grappling with Andrik. The Volod had lost his sword, and was straining toward Ignas' face with the dagger – the one that could cause instant death on contact.

"You bought a friend, did you? Well, so did I!" Andrik snarled a string of foul-sounding words as he pinned Ignas against the sarcophagus, and I saw the shadows cast by the pillars stir.

The wraiths! I equipped the Blindfighter's Fold, plunging the room into darkness – but I knew where they were about to emerge. The pools of shadow were drawing life energy from Ignas and the injured Kingsguard.

"What foulness is this!?" Ignas struggled, weakening by the second.

"Don't look at them! Keep your eyes shut!" I ran forward.

I sprinted forward, determined to disrupt the summoning – and as I did, the statue above the sarcophagus moved. The long veil and shroud fell away, and Kanzo leaped down from the niche onto Andrik.

"Wh-!?" The Volod toppled under the Mercurion's weight.

Kanzo took Andrik to the floor, stabbing at his neck. Red blood sprayed across the stones, but not before the king – choking with confusion and rage – plunged the Ravenstar dagger into Kanzo's chest. The Mercurion's blue-on-blue eyes flew open, and he toppled to the side.

"Damn you!" Andrik pushed himself away. He managed to get to his feet, but stumbled back against the sarcophagus and slid down it as the Void Wraiths slowly rose from the floor. Their forms were like cutouts of reality. Vaguely humanoid, vaguely reptilian, impossible to look at. Impossible *not* to look at.

I squared up and thought of Karalti in that circle of magic, and prepared to fight, but the wraiths didn't advance. Their billowing faces turned down to regard Andrik as he gurgled on the ground, clutching at the blood that poured through his fingers.

"N-no." His voice strained with effort - and fear. "No! I did everything he asked of me!"

"***He** does not tolerate failure.*" The Void Wraiths had voices that slithered across your skin with an oily, moist sensation that made me come up in gooseflesh.

As they slowly moved in toward Andrik, Ignas backed away from them, panting with fear.

"No! I got the dragon! Ignas can't become the Volod!" Andrik croaked, trying and failing to push himself upright. "I won! I-I just need a little more help! That's why I called-"

"We have given you a great deal already," one *Wraith whispered.*

"Why is the dragon still in the circle?" the other asked.

"She is inaccessible to us."

"She cannot receive our gift."

They began to close in on him.

"Were you planning to double-cross Him?"

"The Architect?"

"No!" Andrik watched them, terror-stricken. "No!"

The sounds of fighting behind us had died off, and I turned my head as I felt someone approach - Ebisa and Rin, and one of the tougher Nightstalkers had survived. Everyone else was dead.

Rin gasped. "Kanzo!?"

"Ignas!" Ebisa took a step forward.

"Don't look at the Wraiths!" I hissed, holding up an arm as they surrounded Andrik, pinning him against the tomb. Kanzo had folded up around the dagger still buried in his chest.

"Kill him!" Andrik screamed, eyes dark and wild with hate. "Why are you menacing m-me when you could *kill Ignas*!!!"

"This place is anathema to us."

"We are hungry."

"We sense weakness."

"Victory belongs to the strong."

Andrik struggled up to his feet. He was milk-white from blood loss, but terror drove him to stand and stumble away. "I served him well! I did everything-"

The Void Wraiths flew at him. Andrik got off one blast of fire before they twisted reality around themselves and merged into his body like a virus.

CHAPTER 44

"Brother!" Ignas cried out in anguish.

"Mercy! MERCYYYY!" Andrik was engulfed by the shadows, clawing at his face as his entire body distorted and blurred.

⟦Warning: The Void draws near! HP regeneration is no longer effective! The effect of healing items is halved!⟧

⟦Void Horror is weakened by Holy Ground! Level halved!⟧

"They're Stranging him! Preemptive strike before they take him over!" I dashed forward, jaws clenched, fists raised to strike.

Rin chanted a spell as Ebisa and Ignas rushed from the sides. A Haste buff hit me like a splash of cool water, and suddenly I was faster, keener, and better able to dodge the whip-like lash of void energy that cracked out from Andrik as he stumbled to his knees.

Insectoid legs burst out of Andrik's back - his own ribs, extending and forming joints that lifted him back off the ground. His legs snapped and reformed, and his howls of pain and terror became garbled as his head caved in like rotten fruit.

I drove my knuckles into the still-forming ⟦Void Horror⟧ in a one-two punch, crushing malformed flesh.

⟦You used a Darkness attack! It's super effective! x3 damage!⟧

⟦You deal 747 Darkness damage to Void Horror! HP: 6253/7000⟧

As soon as the Void Horror finished forming, it emitted a pulse of anti-energy that sucked the strength out of my limbs. I began to feel sick. My nose and eyes ran, my joints ached, my temperature spiked. It felt like the first day of HEX's five-day life cycle. A Curse debuff appeared on the inside of my blindfold, along with a 60-second countdown.

⟦Void Horror uses Harbinger! You are marked for death!⟧

God dammit, Karalti - I need you! Relying on my blindsense and aided by the Haste buff, I dodged to the side. A pair of spiked limbs struck the floor instead of my body.

Ebisa came in from my left, swiping at the Horror's body with her daggers. She landed the blows, but the monster backhanded her and sent her flying. She hit the far wall and bounced, falling to the floor.

"Normal attacks don't do any damage!" Rin called. "You have to use Dark or Light element magic!"

"Just as well I'm a specialist!" I shouted back, circling and feinting to draw aggro instead of taking an attack turn. Fifty seconds left. "Rin, was that your Haste spell?"

"Yes!"

"Then just keep buffing. I can take it!"

Ebisa pushed herself up with the help of the wall, and Ignas ran to her. The pair of them staggered off to join Rin at the front of the vault while I danced with the Void Horror, drawing its attention away from the escaping NPCs.

The creature slashed and thrust and stabbed with two of its skeletal limbs as it slammed the other seven deep into the stone floor. Now anchored, it hoisted itself upward, pulsating like a rotten black heart. Ignas and Ebisa had almost reached the door when that heaving core tensed up and emitted a wet, gurgling bellow.

⟦Void Horror uses Antigravity!⟧

The entire place dissolved into chaos as the Void Horror made Up become Down, sending me, Rin, Ebisa, the sarcophagi, even loose dirt and grime, all hurtling towards the ceiling. Rin's shriek of shock and surprise pierced the air as the polarity of gravity reversed even as my innate gyroscopic ability kicked in. Instead of slamming hard into the ceiling, I dropped onto it on my feet and ready.

[[Rin take 65 damage!]]
[[Ebisa takes 91 damage!]]
[[Ignas takes 65 damage!]]

The coffins did more than just open. They all but exploded, ejecting their dusty, wizened contents through the air, scattering the remains of the royal dead onto the 'ground' around and on me while the Horror recovered below. With my feet firmly planted on the ceiling, I ran at it and Jumped

I couldn't actually strike it with Jump. Jump, Blood Sprint, and most of my other heavy-damage strikes required a polearm to be equipped. But there was one attack I could use with any weapon - Umbra Burst.

"KI-AHH!" I activated it and slammed into the [[Void Horror]] with fists of cold iron. Dark energy rippled around my arms as I bounced away. The Horror was immune to the Frozen debuff inflicted by the maneuver, but it took massive damage.

[[You used a Darkness attack! It's super effective! x3 damage!]]
[[Void Horror is immune to Blindness!]]
[[You deal 2988 damage! HP: 3265/7000]]

The antigravity effect ended, dumping us back onto the floor - and as I fell, the Haste buff timer ended. I landed on my feet like a cat, but the Horror's polarity change was instantaneous, and it caught me with a long, hooked claw and began to drag me in toward it. The blindfold was still on, so I couldn't see its mouth, but I could feel the frigid breath scalding my bare legs with cold. Even as it hauled me forward, other legs stabbed out into the corpses on the ground. Fresh or dry, it didn't matter to the Void Horror: power pulsed through its limbs, and the corpses got to their feet. We had 25 seconds left.

[[You take 135 damage! HP: 49/738]]

"*Spera, Cil, Kain*!" Rin shouted. Her voice shook, but Haste suffused me again, speeding my limbs.

Two more hits.

Ignas snarled with frustration. "How do we lift this curse?! We only have twenty seconds left!"

Rin's turrets began firing on the crowd of [[Breathless]] now shambling toward her, Ignas and Ebisa. I tuned out the sound of combat, barely inches away from the crackling, frigid body of the Void Horror. I kept my face forward, staring into the unseen mouth about to engulf me.

The creature lifted me up. And as soon as the toe of my boot froze, I triggered Umbra Blast a second time.

The energy of potential - of Life - flashed through my body and blasted out through my hands. 118 base damage times my Will modifier, times three.

[[You used a Darkness attack! It's super effective! x3 damage!]]
[[You deal 2988 damage!]]

The Horror screeched, and flung me away with a whip-crack of its barbed tentacle. Even Hasted, I couldn't correct my course in time. I flew through the air and landed in the crowd of zombies, scattering them like bowling pins. They softened the impact, but not enough. My ribs connected with a hard shoulder, cracking in toward my lung.

[[You have taken 41 impact damage!]]

"Fuck!" I coughed blood, and the sound - or smell - caused every one of the zombies to aggro on me.

"Hector! Hold on!" Someone came running toward me - it was Rin. She charged through the zombies, taking hits from every side as she bodily leaped onto me and shielded me.

[[Rin takes 102 damage!]]
[[Rin takes 88 damage!]]

"Rin! They're-" I struggled under her, only to feel her almost ram a potion bottle into my mouth. The herbal liquid poured down my throat, bringing blessed relief.

[[Rin takes 29 damage!]]
[[Warning! Mana concentrations are increasing!]]

"I'll be okay!" Her voice cracked as she fed me a second potion. "Get up!"

We had ten seconds left on the clock. Ignas roared as he charged into the pack, swinging his mace. His desperate rush cleared enough space for me to get to my feet. I was back to 120 out of 738 HP.

[[Void Horror uses Abyssal Gaze!]]

"Eyes! Eyes!" I shouted, lunging forward. The same entropic energy I'd felt in the dungeon rolled over my skin in a blistering wave, like passing through a veil of liquid nitrogen. "Fuck you, fuck you, FUCK YOU!"

Seven seconds remaining.

I Jumped as high as the vaulted ceiling allowed for and somersaulted down onto the Void Horror knuckles-first. A bone claw as long as a sword tore down my leg, opening it from hip to knee like a zipper, but not before I smashed into the monster with my fists and began beating the shit out of it. I didn't even see how much HP I'd lost.

Three seconds.

The velvety energy of Darkness pushed into the Void Horror's body and inflated it, overwhelming its entropic nothingness, and the thing that had been Andrik Corvinus shuddered.

Two... One.

The crypt rumbled around us, and my ears popped as the Void Horror wailed and inverted, shrinking in to a super-dense core that fell and shattered on the ground like charcoal.

[[You have defeated Void Horror!]]
[[You gain 1021 EXP!]]
[[Your friend Rin Lu is Level 11!]]

The undead tumbled to the ground, the source of their animation vanished, and we were left in the eerie silence of a deserted tomb. I pushed up my Blindfighter's Fold, squinting down at the floor.

"Hector! Are you okay!?" Rin ran to me, limping. Her silicone skin had long gouges taken out of it from the zombies, though she did not bleed.

"I just punched a Void Horror to death. Bitch, I'm motherfucking Sabin." I blurted the ancient meme out before I thought that through, but to my surprise, Rin laughed a girlish, tinkling laugh.

"But you didn't suplex a train!" she said.

I grinned back at her. "I'm not the only antique games collector here, huh?"

She smiled shyly. "No. And my dad loved that meme, and the game. All those games, actually."

"Help me get Kanzo!" Ebisa called to us as she ran past. "He's still alive!"

I was startled by the panic in her voice, but reacted without thinking. Rin and I both ran to her and helped her pull a fallen sarcophagus lid off Kanzo's body. At first glance, I thought she had to be mistaken about the 'alive' thing. Kanzo lay still, his silvery skin bleached chalk-white. But when Ebisa crouched down and slapped his cheeks, the Mercurion stirred. He looked up at her with eyes that were now almost a flat, dull gray. The mana - and life - that animated him was nearly gone.

"Ebisa," he rasped. "Rin. I... got to see you both... one last time."

"What are you doing here?" Ebisa's shoulders hunched as she saw what was buried in his chest - the Ravenstar, the dagger that had been gifted to her by Ignas. Her fingers hovered over the hilt, barely touching it.

Kanzo blinked slowly, laboring for each raspy breath. "I... thought about it all. And I realized... how much this means to you. You said you would come here. I decided I would hide myself and... and observe. Make a judgment. I saw Andrik for what he truly was. I... decided to kill him. For you."

Rin's face contorted with grief. "You..."

"Rin. Ebisa. Listen." He licked his lip with an iron-gray tongue. "Even if you do not... recycle my body... please take my heart. There is a memory stone in there. I put it there m-myself, when I first learned the properties of Ruby Mana. It has... it has all my knowledge. All my art lives there. Take it... use it... however you will. Ebisa... if you use it, you will g-gain my power. All you will need is... is practice."

The *juchi* reached up and removed her mask, looking down implacably at her creator.

"Please..." Kanzo gasped. "For... for the realm."

The last of the light drained from his eyes, and he sagged against the floor.

Ebisa shook her head as she stood. Rin stayed crouched down, sobbing into her hands. Ignas hung back, his stern face grave and pale.

"A liar to the end," she said heavily.

"What?" I looked over at her. "I saw him jump down and stab-"

"Not that." She bent down and pulled the Ravenstar from his chest. "I mean the melodrama. He always told me that if there was one thing worth dying for in this world, it was art. His art, specifically. He spent years of his life trying to transfer his work to his students, but he was never happy with them. They changed his work in subtle ways... they had minds of their own. So he created me. That stone he was talking about? He always intended for me to have it. This was his last, desperate attempt to convince me."

"Oh." I looked down at the ashen Mercurion. Even in death, Kanzo was beautiful... a work of art.

Ebisa looked down at Rin. "You'll be alright, girl."

"No I won't! I don't want to be alone!" Rin shook her head, her face buried in her hands. "I hate this! I hate fighting... I hate HEX! I already lost everything! My life, my d-dad!"

The other Mercurion cocked her head in confusion.

"B-Before I came to Archemi. My dad died, then I died!" Rin hunched in on herself. "Everyone's dead!"

"Oh, kitten." Ebisa crouched down, and awkwardly patted Rin on the shoulder. "Cherish the memories of your dead, but the time for fathers is past. Now, it is time to make choices about our future. You have a House, surely?"

"They're in Zaunt. And I don't want to go there. It's horrible... nothing but war and more war."

"So I've heard." Ebisa sighed.

Ignas grimaced, and walked over to the scattered charcoal on the floor, toeing it with his boot. Then he grunted, and bent down to pick something up. I went to go retrieve the Spear of Nine Spears. The metal felt fragile and crumbling, and sparked when my fingers touched it. I re-joined them, aching and bone-tired, and so did Ignas. He held out a stone to us - a ruby about half the size of a golf ball.

"Andrik was carrying this," he said. "This is the... wait. Look."

The stone had started to glow, the light building strength as I came closer. The Spear crackled in my hand, and then suddenly sparked with light. Red light. "This is the Ravensblood Ruby?"

"Yes. I've never seen it do this before." He motioned the ruby toward the Spear. "How fascinating. It's reacting with your weapon."

I held the spear up for him to look at. "This is the Spear of Nine Spheres - the weapon that bound the Nine themselves. It is the key to the seals that trap the Drachan in the north. Your Majesty, the Void Terror we just fought and the cult your brother was in are connected, and I'm making an educated guess that if we're seeing Void monsters in Archemi, it's because the Drachan are starting to shake off their chains. Ebisa, I know you don't want to follow in Kanzo's footsteps as an Artificer, but I need ask you for a favor. Please."

Ebisa regarded us levelly, then looked back down at Kanzo's body. Her brows furrowed.

"I'll think about it. Leave me." She put the gray fox mask back on, and turned away from us to point at the corner of the room. "And take your survivor. He is your key to the throne, Your Majesty."

"Survivor?" Ignas frowned, puzzled.

One of the Kingsguard struggled weakly on the ground, his leg pinned by a fallen sarcophagus. It was Tomaz - the second in command.

The new Volod of Vlachia nodded, and looked to me and Rin in turn. "Then I have one last request: that you help me take this man home. We can heal him, and put the court to order. I only hope that I can make things right after all of this suffering."

CHAPTER 45

This kind of victory was usually the kind where I took my headset off, sat back into my shitty old armchair, had a beer and congratulated myself on a story well-told. Maybe after that, I'd go back into the game and try out the different endings to see which one I liked the best.

But here, there was no headset, no armchair, and definitely no multiple endings. I wasn't even sure we were the good guys.

In the dust and haze of the ruined crypt, I watched Ebisa and Rin collect Kanzo's broken body and wrap it in a shroud, and helped them load the bodies of the dead onto wagons. I watched Ignas dejectedly sift through the corrupted remains of his brother's ashes. I felt like we'd done the right thing... but it was hard to pick a winner here. The murders had been stopped, the girls were about to be saved, peace would soon return to the kingdom. Theoretically.

I left the business of cleanup to the new Volod and his crew, jogging through the streets to the morgue. Fifteen minutes or so later, Cutthroat and I thundered through the gates of Vulkan Keep, headed for the stables. I left the exhausted dinosaur in her corral with an extra helping of food, and ran for the dungeons with a ring of keys liberated from the corpse of one of the Kingsguard.

My heart was in my mouth as I unlocked each door, following the same route that Garen had taken me. When I reached Karalti's cell, I equipped the Blindfighter's Fold, listening for any sound. There was nothing.

"Karalti!" I called to her as I unlocked the barred metal doors. "Karalti, can you...?"

As they swung in, I saw my pack and the dragon saddle on the floor, and the magic circle, deactivated and empty. Panic gripped my stomach.

"Karalti!?" I took a step inside, letting the door slam.

There was a deep hiss from behind me.

I lifted the blindfold as I turned, and saw a pair of huge, brilliant violet eyes peering back at me from the darkness. She was still chained, collared and muzzled, hunched against the wall and melded into the shadows.

"Oh thank god." I ran to her, fumbling with the keys. Karalti stayed very still as I unlocked each manacle and disconnected the heavy chains from the collar, then the headcage that kept her from breathing fire. As soon as they came off, there was a swooping rush as our mental connection re-established itself... and then the dragon threw herself at me as I reached up to embrace her around her long, powerful neck.

"*Hector!*" Shivering and hot, Karalti pressed as much of her body against mine as she could. "*Hector! That was so awful! I was trapped in this bad, bad place with nothing all around me!*"

"Shhh, Tidbit, it's okay." I squeezed her tightly, burying my face against her scales, breathing in her deep floral scent.

"*They were saying terrible things about you! And me! A-And my mother!*" The anxious dragon crooned, swinging her tail from side to side in agitation. "*Th-they kept trying to get in my head, and I-I couldn't attack them, or move, or anything!*"

I kissed her arms and rubbed her shoulders and the joints of her wings, not knowing what to do or say other than be with her. When I felt her start to relax, I looked up. "It's okay, girl. But Suri's still down here somewhere. We have to find her - she's trapped, too."

Karalti wagged her head and pushed past me, stalking toward the door. "*I can find her by smell! Come on!*"

The dragon was just small enough to squeeze through the dungeon passages, though her tightly furled wings still banged against walls and cell doors, and the spines that started from her rump and ran along her tail scraped the low ceilings. She tracked through the darkness like a scenthound, turned the corner, and came up short at a wooden door. "*There! She's past there!*"

"*Roger that.*" I crawled underneath Karalti's body and came up at her head, unlocking the door and pushing it into the room.

It was a torture room. Racks and strappado pulleys were cast into sharp relief by torchlight, along with trays of tools and rusted metal cages with built in stocks. Suri was in one of them - exhausted and pissed off, but otherwise unharmed.

"You wanna end up like the last guy who tried to fuck with me!? Come over here, mate! I'll rip your fucking balls off!" she yelled from across the room.

"I'll have you know that I never show anyone my balls until we've been out to dinner at least twice." The joke sounded better in my head than it did coming out, but it was something to break the ice as I entered, Karalti padding in on my heels.

Suri couldn't turn her head much. She was forced to bend at the waist, her wrists and neck locked into the metal stocks, her lower body trapped in the cage. She tried anyway, struggling to look up. "Hector?! Where the fuck were you?"

"I'm sorry I couldn't get here any faster. The last three hours of my life have been like some kind of Nihilist wet dream-slash-nightmare. Void Wraiths, Void Horrors, Void-this, Void-that." I pulled up in front of the cage and unlocked the two halves of the door. The lower half swung out, revealing the lock for the stocks mounted under the upper half of the door. "I'm really glad they let you keep your pants on."

"Fuckin' oath. Some cunt tried to take them off, believe me. I donkey kicked him so hard that he choked on his own dick." Suri glowered at the room while I worked. "What the hell happened? And why are you wearing a nappy?"

"A what?"

"You're wearing a bloody diaper."

"No public toilets in Taltos, remember?" I let the bottom of the stocks drop away. "And it's not a diaper. It's a *girdle*."

"It's a diaper, you shitcunt." Suri groaned with pain as she sunk to her knees and crawled out. I offered her a hand up, which she accepted. To my surprise, she leaned forward and wrapped me in a tight, fierce embrace.

"Is 'shitcunt' something you call someone you like?" I squeaked, as she crushed me into her chest.

"Depends on how you say it and who you say it to." Suri buried her face against my neck, and only then did I feel the quaking in her hands and the muscles of her back.

I returned the hug, stroking her hair, and glanced at Karalti to gauge her response. The dragon's crests were flat against her skull, but when I met her eyes, they lifted a little. She tentatively bobbed her head.

"We're okay, Suri." I rubbed between her shoulders and clapped her on the back. "Ignas won. Andrik's dead. Like... really dead. The new Volod is wrangling his court as we speak."

"Tell me on the way upstairs." Suri's voice was thick, as if she was fighting back tears. "I need a long bath and some clean clothes. And you need some fucking pants."

"Sorry, ma'am, I left my fucking pants back in my *other* castle," I replied.

Suri slapped me, but not with any force. I giggled as she stalked off, trailing behind her. I wasn't sure everything was going to be okay just yet - but it was okay for now, and as Ebisa had said, it was time to think about the future.

CHAPTER 46

Two Days Later.

As I had done just over a week ago, I woke to the blueish light of Archemi's sun dancing through the curtains across from my bed. Well, our bed.

Karalti curled around me, her wing draped across my body, her foreclaws clasped over her long, elegant muzzle. Her double heartbeat pounded a steady, slow rhythm against my back. Her lean body took up most of the bed, leaving just enough room for me to sleep.

I yawned as I pushed myself up to sit, letting the leathery blanket slide down my back. My HUD was pinging me, small blue icons pulsing at the corner of my eye. I leaned back against Karalti and pulled them across to check the time - 8:32 a.m - a quest update, and several notifications and messages.

[[New PM from Suri Ba'hadir: Want to go for breakfast before the Big Event? RV at my bunk between 0830-0900.]]

[[New Event! 12pm - The Coronation of Volod Ignas II]]

[[You have unspent skill points!]]

Quest Update: The Slayer of Taltos/Stalkers in the Night

The Slayer is dead, Andrik Corvinus III's plan for the nation of Vlachia exposed, and the true Volod of the largest nation in the East has cleared his name. The Void-touched scheme of the old king did

not come to pass, though the cost was dear. Was it worth it? Only you can answer that.
There remain some unanswered questions. During or after today's Coronation, speak with Volod Ignas Corvinus II to solve the final mysteries of the Slayer of Taltos and claim your reward.

I grunted and accepted the update, then stretched and carefully extracted myself from the circle made by Karalti's limbs and tail. When I got to my feet, she huffed out a small wheezy sigh and balled up tighter, shielding her face with a wing.

"Still too damn cute for your own good," I muttered fondly.

I went to our pack and equipped my freshly repaired and polished gear: the Naziri Chest and Leg armor, Boots of the Winding Path, and the Sanctified Cold Iron Gauntlets - or as I liked to call them, the Zombie Crushers. They were much heavier than the fine leather Naziri Gauntlets, but the discomfort of wearing thirty pounds of iron and dinosaur leather on my arms would improve my Strength over time. I could even end up as strong as Suri - I just had to embrace The Suck.

I checked myself in the bathroom mirror one last time, and let out a terse sigh before stalking back into the bedroom. "Okay, Karalti. Wakey wakey, rise and shine!"

"Uuggoo..." The dragon groaned and wrapped her wing more tightly over her face.

"Come on. Up and at 'em." I snatched my spear from where it leaned against the wall and poked her with the blunt end. "Mr Alpha Rod says it's time for you to become erect! Upright! *Turgid.* We have a coronation today."

"*You're gross.*" Karalti kicked out weakly with one of her back feet, snapping her killing claw down to try and catch the polearm. "*Bring me some breakfast?*"

I scoffed. "You can get your scaly ass out of bed and get your own breakfast, Princess. Come on, I have to go see Suri."

Karalti mumbled, flexing her long ankles and hind claws before drawing her knees up against her belly. *"So go see her. I sleep."*

"Not jealous?" I teased.

"No. I sleeeeep." She sounded increasingly petulant.

I rolled my eyes, but I could tell I wasn't going to win with her this morning. Dragons didn't sleep quite as much as cats, but they definitely needed more sleep than humans. I'd spent most of the last two days sleeping as well. "Well, you've got an hour. Then we have to join the Coronation parade."

"Uggh."

Suri's quarters were in the floor below our suite. I nervously brushed down my clothes and made sure my hair was sitting right before I knocked on her door.

"Hector?" She called.

"Yeah, it's me." Surreptitiously, I checked my breath. As always, it smelled faintly minty. One of the benefits of being a digital ghost.

I heard the heels of Suri's boots against the floor, then the clunk of a bolt being drawn back. She opened the door and smiled as my jaw practically hit the ground.

"What do you think?" She struck a pose in the doorframe. Suri was already dressed for the coronation: gold rings in her lip, nose and ears, her fiery hair styled into loose corkscrew ringlets. She wore a scoop-necked dress made almost entirely of small glass beads. They poured over her dark curves like a heavy liquid, baring her arms, most of her chest down to the sternum, and both legs to the hip.

"I... umm..." I blinked a couple of times. "Requesting permission to shamelessly objectify you, ma'am?"

"Permission granted." She linked her hands behind her back and thrust her chest out, her lips quirked in a sly smile.

I looked down, eyebrows raised, and nodded. "I'm pretty sure this is what heaven looks like."

"Kind of like the Grand Canyon, huh?"

"Yeah." The urge to brush my knuckles over the bare curves around the edge of the dress was powerful, but I managed to keep my hands to myself. "That sideboob game is intense."

"Isn't it?" Suri grinned, flashing sharp teeth. "Ignas put me on to his favorite dressmaker. Old bastard's got good taste in clothes, I can tell you that."

I shook my head with a chuckle. "I still trip out at the thought of you being this into fashion."

Suri planted her hands on her hips. "If you spent all your early life in filthy rags, you'd want to wear nice things, too. Besides, I didn't get to enjoy that last dress I bought for the auction, what with losing my arm and all."

"Can't argue that." I looked up at her, and glanced past her at her room. I couldn't see much of it, but what I did see was very tidy. She'd even made her bed. "So, you going to let me in? Or are you coming out?"

"You're coming in." She reached out and caught me by the wrist, and yanked me inside.

We made it inside the doorway, and that was as far as we got before she pushed me up against the wall and kissed me. A hot thrill flashed through my body at the contact of her lips. They were hot, sweet, as eager as her hands as she pressed her thighs against mine. I hooked a foot behind her ankle and spun her around, turning the tables, and she laughed against my mouth.

Even through my armor, I could feel the leonine power in Suri's body as she arched back against me. Her hands meshed through my hair, down my back, and gripped my belt. I ran mine down the side of her waist, listening to the beads click against the cold iron. When the metal gauntlet touched her bare thigh, she shuddered.

"So... is this breakfast, or 'breakfast'?" I asked her, speaking against her lips.

"Depends how hungry you are," she whispered back.

"Pretty damn hungry." I grinned at her, pushed the streamer of her dress aside, and pinned her hips to the wall while I went to my knees.

I'd made the difficult decision to abstain from certain types of, uhh, 'activity' while Karalti was still maturing. We had an intense connection, and short of walling her off with magic – which I never wanted to do again – it seemed like a bad idea to expose her to all the things I wanted to do with Suri. But Suri's pleasure? That was fair game. And I was learning now that there were more ways to get off than the obvious ones – like pinning a girl against a wall while she moaned and bucked and cursed me for not fucking her. There was a dark power to be found in going down on her, in the discipline I had to exercise on Suri and myself... and when she came, throwing her head back, gasping, pushing her clit against my lips, her orgasm thrummed through my entire body. The control – over her pleasure, my pleasure, my body and hers – felt good. *Really* good, and *addictive.*

"After this coronation, you and me... we're going farming," Suri gasped, once I knelt back. "We're going to level that dragon up to adulthood so fast your head'll spin."

I looked up at her from the ground. She was panting, her eyes dark, her hair tousled. Her lips were flushed, her thighs trembling and slick. I felt like I'd go crazy: all I wanted to do was turn her around, push her against the wall, and fuck her... but in the back of my mind, I could sense Karalti's innocent dreams, her contentment and comfort. It was best for all three of us that I waited.

"Think you'll be ready by then?" I teased Suri, taking her hand and leading her to the table where our breakfast waited: coffee, Vlachian citrus tea, open-faced sandwiches, lean cuts of cured meat, cheese, and pickled vegetables.

"I think so." It wasn't just Karalti who needed time. Suri had some hangups of her own... the legacy of her rough start in Archemi. She hadn't even known about them until the day before, where she'd seen me mostly naked and had some flashbacks. I was okay with that, and after some reassurance, so was she. It was all part of healing.

We spent a good hour over breakfast, eating together in the cool morning light. Sometimes we held hands, sometimes we didn't... but we talked, weaving a dance through the things we liked to do, what we believed, what we thought of the Slayer questline and what happened to Andrik. I was wrapping up the exciting finale of the fight with the Void Horror when there was a knock on the door.

"I'll get it." Suri rose and walked past me in a cloud of soft perfume. I couldn't help but turn to watch the way her hips rolled. The pleasure wasn't so guilty now.

She opened the door to reveal Rin. The young Mercurion's face was soot-smeared, as was her smithing apron and gloves. She gasped when she saw Suri.

"Oh my god you look amazing!" She jumped up and down on the spot, shaking her fists with excitement, and then hugged Suri around the middle as the taller woman bent down to embrace her.

"Are they calling us for the parade?" I ambled over, and got the same wraparound hug from Rin.

She nodded, her blue on blue eyes shining. "Yes! They... umm... they had some trouble getting Cutthroat ready, but I think it's done now. You're good to go."

"You aren't coming?" Suri asked her.

Rin bit her lip and shook her head. "No... neither me or Ebisa are really good at parades and, well, anything noisy. We're fixing your Spear today, though! And I've been busy upgrading Lovelace and Hopper with some of the magic I picked up with my last level. Ebisa helped me reorganize my ability point distribution for the Mystic Engineer class, so... yeah!"

"When do you think the Spear will be done?" I asked.

"After the Coronation, definitely." The Mercurion bobbed her head, smiling. "You guys look so amazing. I'm so proud!"

Suri ruffled Rin's hair and flashed me a wry smile over her shoulder. "Well, go get your dragon. I guess you'll be flying, so we'll meet you at the church?"

"Sure will. We'll go down for you." I wiggled my eyebrows at her. Suri's eyes narrowed, but she blushed.

Karalti was busy grooming herself when I returned to our quarters, sitting in the middle of the bedroom with one leg tucked underneath her and the other sticking straight up in the air. She looked up at me as I got her saddle ready, her forked tongue sticking out between her front fangs. *"Is it time already? I haven't gotten everything clean yet!"*

"Too bad, Tidbit." I patted the saddle. "Time to fly."

Level 6 was likely to be the last level where Karalti and I could enter a private suite together. She had to squeeze through the door to the balcony. When she hit Level 7... we were going to have to work out some different sleeping arrangements.

When we were saddled up, she glided out to the battlements of the Keep, looking out over the valley and the city just beyond it. My heart lifted as I took in the sight of the high-walls, the dark steeples, the amber and gold domes cresting the church in the center of Taltos. The vanguard of the coronation parade was working its way down the switchback road – voivodes and satraps, knights on hookwings, banners rippling in the warm summer wind. Behind them rode the Black Legion of the Vulkan Garrison, then the Knights of the Red Star on their black destrier hookwings and quazi, resplendent in their red lamellar. They surrounded the Royal Coach, the grand golden carriage that bore Ignas toward the city gate.

Behind them, Suri rode sidesaddle on Cutthroat. The huge hookwing had her head down and her shoulders hunched, skulking after the coach and radiating dejection. Somehow, the stable hands had draped her with decorative red-and-white silk barding woven through with roses. The barding already looked tattered and dirty, and quite a few of the flowers were rumpled.

"*Ready?*" Karalti asked me.

I pushed myself back along her back, settling into position, and squeezed the saddle grips tightly. "Always."

Karalti trumpeted, beating her wings stiffly by her sides to warm them up, and then launched herself from the parapets into the open sky. The torque hit me in the belly, and I whooped and laughed as she glided down in a looping spiral toward the city below.

Coronations were an involved affair, taking weeks – if not months – to set up IRL. But this was a videogame, and so Taltos had blossomed with decorated canopies and streamers after only a few days, cheering crowds, festival food, and perhaps an undercurrent of bewilderment that the populace suddenly had a new Volod.

For the duration of the ceremony, Karalti stood behind the sacred forge in the Church of the Maker, her wings held out behind the new High Forgemaster, Kaled Ferenz, as he crafted the crown Ignas would wear for his term as Volod of Vlachia. The tradition of the land was that every new king wore a crown forged from the materials of the old one. Andrik's had not been recovered, so the materials were new.

There was no choir to sing in this church. The only sound was that of the olive-skinned priest expertly banging out and shaping silver and rubies, steel and gold into a coronet. Ignas waited on a wooden throne in front of the dais where Forgemaster Ferenz worked, his long face still and meditative as he waited in his regalia with his eyes closed.

When the hammer struck metal for the last time, the grand vaulted room fell silent. Ferenz lifted the glowing crown in his tongs, then quenched it for all to see. It frothed and bubbled, and when he pulled it free, a hushed murmur went up around the crowd.

"Do you accept Ignas Corvinus the Second as your rightful King, to assume the Domain of Vlachia and all of its lands and principalities?" He called out in a loud, clear voice.

"Agreed, so be it, long live the king!" The crowd screamed back.

The High Forgemaster went to Ignas. He waited in the throne in front of the forge, heavily robed and holding a scepter and sword. When the Forgemaster placed the crown, I saw his weathered features relax with relief.

I smiled as the church erupted with cheers, and each one of the attending priests moved forward to give the new Volod their blessing. The High Forgemaster was not the only celebrant here: representatives of Matir, Veela, Solnetsi, Veles and Perun were all here today, priests who had been in hiding during Andrik's reign. He also received a musical blessing from two Meewfolk – a female pair whose outfits resembled those of Japanese shrine maidens - and a gift from a trio of Mercurions. To my pleased surprise, it was Mix and his two spouses. They presented the new Volod with a finely made saddle for his quazi.

"Nice political move on his part," I whispered to Suri. "Sure to ruffle a few feathers in court."

"Fuck 'em," Suri replied. "They'll deal."

Once all of the pomp and ceremony was over with, Ignas rose in his mantle of heavy robes, and held up the sword and scepter.

"Citizens and guests of Vlachia! These hard years of exile have taught me much," he said, his voice booming off the high ceilings. "After having my name slandered and smeared, I escaped the country, pursued by assassins hired by my brother. When I returned, I lived among the least of you. I survived only because of the grace and generosity of the poorest people in Vlachia, the fishmongers and tanners and charnel workers. These people - human, Tlaxi'ca,

Prrupt'meew - supported me in ways large and small as I pursued justice for myself and my House. I did things I am not proud of, but which needed to be done... and I am humbled by your re-acceptance of me. I pledge to return all that was given to me in my capacity as your new *Volodniy!*"

Cheers went up from the crowd, and I winced as the roar pierced my eardrums.

"I guess the motives of the Slayer have to remain secret," I remarked to Suri, listening as Ignas continued his speech.

"Politics. It is what it is."

"Think they'd be as happy with him if they knew that he was behind Kanzo murdering people and blowing shit up?"

Suri gave me the side-eye. "You gonna be the one to tell them?"

"No. I was a soldier in my past life. If there's one thing it taught me, it's that sometimes you have to kill, and sometimes good people end up dead. My conscience is happier with a handful of dead people than it would be with an entire nation of oppressed *and* dead people." I paused to suck thoughtfully on a tooth. "But you have to admit, our knowledge is a pretty serious point of leverage on Ignas. I think you and I should be keeping an eye out for assassins coming in through the windows."

"You think he'd do that?"

"I think he survived and eventually triumphed by becoming a crime boss."

Once the speech was over, Ignas swore in his new Kingsguard selected from the Raven Knights, and then nodded to us as he resumed his throne.

"Today would not have been possible without the efforts of three rare individuals. Starborn, from foreign lands, they made every effort to bring the Slayer and my brother to justice. Solonkratsu Karalti, Suri Ba'hadir, Dragozin Hector, please come forward."

We did. Suri took a knee, as did I. Karalti bowed, but then stood tall.

"You gave everything you had to a nation that is not your own," he said. "And as I promised, you will be rewarded. Therefore, I am bestowing each of you with citizenship and a noble title - the peerage of Count and Countess - along with your material reward."

I nearly choked on my tongue. So did Suri. A noble title? What did that mean for us?

"Do you accept?" He asked.

Suri bowed from the neck. "Yes, Your Majesty."

"*What do you think, girl?*" I asked Karalti.

"*I'm already a queen,*" she replied. "*I can be a Countess, too.*"

I cleared my throat and bowed my head. "I answer for both Karalti and myself. We accept, Your Majesty."

Ignas touched us on the shoulders with his sword, and two pages came forward with coronets and long cloaks, laying them over our shoulders.

⟦Congratulations! You have earned a noble title: Count (Honorary). +1500 fame in Vlachia! Read the Count/Countess article for more information.⟧

⟦New Archemipedia entry: Counts/Countesses in Vlachia.⟧

"Rise, Count and Countess Dragozin, Countess Ba'hadir." Ignas stepped forward and bowed from the waist to Karalti. He embraced Suri, whispering to her while the crowd behind us cheered and gossiped. My hackles were starting to rise by the time he came to me.

"The courtesy position of Count comes with an opportunity, which we will discuss later." Ignas spoke quietly by my ear as he clapped me on the back.

"What about Rin and Ebisa?" I asked.

The Volod stood back, hands gripping my arms. "I already offered her and Rin a peerage... they refused."

"Can't say I'm surprised." I smiled back.

"Indeed." The Volod inclined his head to me. "Now, do take a seat. Once all this nonsense is over with, we'll meet in the Writing Room back at the Keep. I've learned something I think you will be very interested to know."

CHAPTER 47

The Writing Room turned out to be the private parlor with the secret door, the same room where Andrik had asked me to kill his brother. Suri and I arrived to find Ignas examining the fireplace, running his fingers over the edge of the marble. He had shed his coronation finery in favor of the soft, dark leathers he'd been wearing when we met him at the Nightstalkers arena. Ebisa and Rin were waiting with him, sitting on a small sofa together with their arms touching. They had a long bundle resting across their laps.

The Spear of Nine Spheres emitted a silent energetic pulse as I entered the room, lifting the hairs on my arm. Ebisa stood as the door closed behind me. She was dressed for crafting, in a tight leather tunic and heavy leather gloves, apron, and boots.

"Do you wish to speak first, or should I give him the spear?" She asked Ignas.

"Go. Give it to him." Ignas turned to face me. "And take this. Catch."

He threw something at me. I caught it in both hands, and looked down to see the ⟦Ravensblood Ruby⟧.

"The Spear has some odd relationship with this stone, but only when you are holding it," he remarked. "I'm curious to see what happens now that the weapon is fixed. Perhaps you will be able to solve the mystery of the memories it stores."

"The memories it stores?" I watched as Ebisa untied the fabric, buzzing with anticipation.

"They seem to be from something that was not human," Andrik replied. "The contents of the stone mystified and captivated my ancestors, but they ever only saw glimpses of what it contains. You have insight into the draconic psyche that we do not. I will give you the command words and show you, once we see what happens with the Spear."

Ebisa unveiled the weapon, and both Suri and I gasped at the sight of it. The cracked, battered, tarnished polearm was now a glorious curve of polished blue steel. The long blade had been restored to a mirror finish, and the metal crawled with hairline seams of white magical energy. They moved in orderly patterns through the looping Damascus-style finish, sweeping up like motes of dust from wherever Ebisa's hands made contact. She had bound tightly woven knotwork around the haft for grip, and had attached a long braided cord just under the blade. She'd even repaired the shallow divots that studded the weapon: four at the base, four just beneath the head of the spear, and one on the blade itself.

Swallowing, I reached out to take it.

The Spear of Nine Spheres
Soul-Bound Weapon
Slot: Two-Handed
Item Class: Relic
Item Quality: Mastercrafted
Damage: 110-121 Slashing or Piercing
Durability: 100%
Weight: 1lb
Special: +4 Dexterity, Soul-bound, +150 HP, +15% evasion

Dancing black energy cracked over my hand as I clasped the elegant haft, but I struggled to disguise my disappointment when I saw its stats. It wasn't all bad, because this Spear was lighter than almost any other polearm I could buy. Its bonuses had improved, too -

double dex, triple the HP bonus, and it had swapped two Def points for 15% evasion, which was nice... but it did less damage than the Alpha Rod, a Common grade weapon I'd bought at the local smithy.

"Wow," I said. "This is... it's gorgeous."

"Isn't it?" Rin said. "Ebisa did *such* a good job."

"I did what I could. Had to try not to think about it too much," Ebisa muttered. "Rin helped."

"Bring the stone near it." Ignas watched on with bated excitement.

I drew a deep breath, and then bought the stone in close to the weapon. As I did, the color of the weapon's mana changed, shifting from white to red. The Ravensblood Ruby was a living heart in my hand, and as I stared at it, the sound of its beating swallowed up the room around me.

Reality inverted. Suddenly, I was flying.

A funeral procession trailed through the desert below me: a weeping, wailing parade plowing through a sandstorm. Triceratops hauled a massive stone sarcophagus toward high rose-colored cliffs. The face of the cliffs was carved out with columns and huge doorways. Dragons waited there for us, their heads bowed.

I turned, and through the scarlet fog, I saw the silhouette of a titanic humanoid figure striding behind the procession. It was an armored giant larger than the largest dragon, awe-inspiring to the Solonkratsu who had recorded his memories on this store. Was it... one of the Gods?

The recorder turned away, focusing back on the cave palace. It swung dizzily in all directions as the dragon landed and turned back to face the procession. As it watched the bleak scene, the titan came closer and closer... until I glimpsed it, looming out from the whipping clouds of sand. It was only there for a moment, a silhouette that vanished as the recording dragon closed his eyes, and the scene went blank.

I opened my eyes, back in the present, and found everyone staring at me - and the Spear. My hands were white-knuckled around the shaft. The Ravensblood Ruby was floating over it, and as I watched, it descended, and neatly fit itself into one of the divots beneath the blade. Slowly, the glow faded... but the light that crawled through the Spear remained red.

"This is... the... Ruby of Boundless Strength." The words pulled themselves from my throat, unbidden. "The key to the Ruby Dragon Gate. The tomb of Khors and... and... damn, what did I just see?"

Ignas had turned pale. "You saw the memories on it?"

"Yes." I looked down at the Spear again, and on impulse, I called up its description. "Oh wow."

The Spear of Boundless Strength
Soul-Bound Fire Elemental Weapon
Slot: Two-Handed
Item Class: Relic
Item Quality: Mastercrafted
Damage: 160-185 Slashing or Piercing
Durability: 100%
Weight: 1lb
Special: Soul-bound, +50 bonus fire damage, +300 HP, +10 Strength, +%15 Evasion.
Special: Maker's Blessing - Learn Crafting skills 5% faster.

"Interesting," Ebisa remarked. "It changed the properties of the weapon."

Ignas frowned. "Can it be removed?"

I used my finger to pry around the edges of the ruby, but it was firmly rooted. "Uhh... I don't think so."

Ignas sighed. "Well, I hate to part with another heirloom given that Andrik lost us the Scorched Armor of Lawislaw the Burned, but it seems the choice has been made for me. Such is the way of things. What do you make of the memory?"

"It was a funeral. Maybe of Khors himself," I said. "There was a huge being... like a mech from some anime."

Ebisa and Rin looked at one another.

"Can you describe it?" Rin asked.

I shrugged. "A hundred feet tall... humanoid. Kind of angular... reminded me a bit of a praying mantis."

Ebisa drew a startled breath. "*Ima'sancatul.*"

"A Warsinger," Rin translated. She sounded awed.

"A what?" Suri asked.

"They are a myth," Ebisa said. "Giants from the time when the Aesari and the Solonkratsu lived together, before the Aesari enslaved the dragons and they became enemies. The Warsingers were made to fight the Drachan."

"Do you know of any places in the desert with a high cliffside tomb or castle or something?" I asked them, looking to Suri. "That's where they were taking this thing."

She shook her head. So did Ignas.

"No." Ignas shook his head. "We have been trying to find that place ever since this ruby was first read by my House's founder. Wherever that place was, it has been swallowed by the Ati Krura Desert millenia ago. This was made during a time when the dragons had cities in what is now known as the Shalid. It's over 5000 years old."

I hefted the spear. "Well, maybe this spear will talk to me some more now. But speaking of land, what was it you wanted to talk about?"

"Ah. Well, first, let me show you something." Ignas motioned to us all. "Follow me."

He went to the wall, fiddled behind a painting, and depressed a button that slid open a section of wall. We trailed after him through a narrow stone hallway, plunging into the heart of Vulkan Keep.

Some ten minutes later, Ignas drew up in front of another recess and opened a similar concealed door.

"This is the Bedchamber of the Serene Highness," he explained, as we filtered in behind him. The splendid room beyond was furnished with dark wood, scarlet silk and velvet, gold and silver. "The Princes' quarters - not the King's Suite. Andrik kept his old rooms when he became Volod, in defiance of tradition. I would like to show you why."

He stalked through the bedroom, past the orgy-pit-sized bed, and into a smaller room. Turning on the light in there revealed rows of wardrobes. Ignas confidently went to one of the doors, slid it open, and pushed the collection of fine clothing aside. There was a cleverly hidden hatch door back there.

"This is a last resort," Ignas said. "A bolthole for the prince and others to hide if the castle was ever to be stormed. The lock can only be opened by the still-warm blood of a Corvinus scion. The blood must be fresh, so no man can just cut my throat and scrape the blood off his blade onto the sigil. Andrik and I used to play in these rooms. Rin, can you please conjure a light?"

"Sure. *Ori, El, Phaz!*" She concentrated, and a globe of white-blue light flared in the palm of her hand, lighting up the inside of the wardrobe.

We watched Ignas prick his finger, then trace a symbol behind the swinging robes and cloaks. There was a click, and he pushed the vault door into the panic room.

There was something wrong about it. A haunted, ghostly sensation swept out over me as I followed Ignas in. Suri came in afterward, shivering in her dress, with Rin and Ebisa piling in afterward. The room was about the size of a small study, eight by nine feet or so. A shrine had been set up with two tall tables flanking an altar that was a black rectangle of... nothing. Mounted above the featureless, angular block was the forked Y-symbol of the Ryuko Corporation.

"Do you feel that?" Ignas said quietly. "The... unhallow feeling of this place?"

"Sure do." Suri grimaced. "Reeks of bad magic."

"He sacrificed things in here." Ignas pointed at bloodstains etched on the stones. "We found this symbol in his laboratory as well. This is the one I almost remembered seeing... but I could not summon the image to mind."

"The Cult of the Architect," Rin murmured.

I walked over to one of the tables. There was a black leather-bound book there. I added it to my inventory. It was ⟦Andrik's Journal⟧. I had the HUD read it to me, starting from the most recent entries.

"Today I reported to the High Priestess that the murder situation had escalated and that the Tuun and dragon had made an appearance. I was told that the appearance of the Queen hatchling was a matter of great urgency for the Master," it read. *"She urged me to keep up the ruse of hospitality while she sent faith militant to seize the creature before it grows more. She ordered I do everything to facilitate the rescue operation. The Architect is about to consolidate his rightful place as Ilia's ruler."*

Then, a few pages on: *"The damn agents failed! Once again, I wonder at the High Priestess's loyalty and competence. Twenty men lost to a hatchling draak, a barbarian, and a Dakhari jailhouse whore! How could this be? At least I now know who the assassin is. Kanzo, that silverskin bastard... I should have had him killed."*

"What is it?" Suri peered over my shoulder.

"Here." I took the book back out of my Inventory and handed it to her, then ordered my narrator to search back through the entries to the ones written about a month ago.

"The Master told us that he would return, and he has!" Andrik enthused. *"Blessed be the Architect in all his might! I am truly overwhelmed by his munificence. He contacted me after his Awakening and has told me to continue in the work of the church*

and bring it to heel. Of course the Architect should wish that the Church of the Maker be the law of the land... I cannot wait to see the future we shall build!"

"Fuck," I said. "Ororgael *is* Baldr Hyland, and Baldr is now the Warden of Ilia."

"Who?" Ignas said.

"Ororgael is an Architect," Rin said from behind us. "He's bad news."

"You mean to tell me that one of the mythical progenitors of the gods now rules Ilia?" Ignas turned back to stare at her in surprise, and I realized - he couldn't see her gold Admin ring.

"Yeah. He... umm... he hasn't reached full power yet." Rin glanced nervously at me. "But he's very dangerous. I'm certain he was the one who inspired Andrik to smear you in the first place. Ororgael always said that Vlachia was too idyllic, that it needed more conflict, so... umm..."

"Could there be a more terrible foe?" Ebisa said, aghast.

Ignas' face drew into hard lines. "No. I don't think so. But we shall think of something."

"Foe?" I frowned.

"Yes. And this ties into my having granted you peerage." The Volod sighed, looking down at the blank altar. "This morning, we received a missive from Ilia. The Warden, this Baldr Hyland, is demanding that we extradite you and Karalti to Ilia immediately. If we do not, he will treat it as a declaration of war. We may soon have the armies of the Warden and the dragons of the Eyrie of St. Grigori on our shores."

A twinge of nausea made my gut tighten. "Then why did you make me a Count?"

"I promised you sanctuary, and I intend to keep my word. Vlachia does not bow to the whims of bullies." Ignas lifted his chin. "I have sent a return message stating that unless this 'Lord Hyland' can prove a serious crime was committed, I will consider it nothing but nonsense."

"Thank you. I'm honored. You didn't have to do that." In truth, I was actually kind of gutshot to know this was happening... that Karalti and I might be responsible for causing a war.

Ignas snorted. "Andrik spent half his adult life serving this Architect for power he didn't deserve. I will do no such thing. Vulkan Keep was built by dragons, to withstand siege by demons, and if he wants to break himself upon our walls, he is welcome to try. I shall be recultivating our good relationship with the Jeun Empire to the north, and I have already dispatched skilled ambassadors to North Zaunt and Meewhome. In addition to being Volod, I still lead the Nightstalkers - though Ebisa shall be the front from now on. As for you, Hector and Suri, I would like to make you an offer."

I glanced at Suri. This smelled like a quest.

"As I'm sure you have heard, the Province of Myszno has been invaded by a vampire leading an army of undead," Ignas said, pacing back and forth with his hands linked behind him.

"Right."

"I'm going to send a real force down there, not the ineffective peasant militia that Andrik deployed," Ignas continued, with a nod. "You two are now both ranked as military commanders. If you go to Myszno, unite the forces arrayed against the undead, and help lead them to victory, then the Duchy is yours. You may share it or divide it - that is up to you. But you shall become lords of Vlachia and will be entitled to form your own Houses, second only to the hereditary Voivodes and my own House, with all the benefits and riches that entails."

New Quest: Unto Death

Myszno, in the south-east of Vlachia, was formerly one of the most beautiful places in the entire country. Now it is a ruin, blighted by undeath and ruled by a powerful vampire lord.

You have been offered a grant to travel to this troubled land and reclaim it from the vampire's claws - a terrible proposition, given how powerful he has become. But with great risk comes great reward - you could become a true Count of Vlachia, with land, property, and income. Truly a base fit for a King - and a Queen.

Difficulty: Level 20+ (Extraordinary Difficulty)

Rewards: EXP, 60 Build Points, Charter to Resettle the Duchy of Racsa.

The new quest was also accompanied by an update to the very first quest I'd ever received:

Quest Update: The Shrine of the Elder Gods

When the Dark Star passes in front of the Moon, journey to the Thunderstones at Myszno, a village in the east of Vlachia - that is what I said to you, not long ago.

You have begun the journey of the Spear. Now, you know what you must do.

Reward: ???

Special: When you arrive at Myszno, seek the Baru, your brothers. Learn from them. Be prepared to accept the consequences of your decision to break the Moon Pact.

The last line caused me a twinge of unease, but it was what it was. Matir wasn't judging me for breaking Andrik's oath. If my fellow Tuun were going to attack me on principle, so be it. I looked to Suri and Rin. "What are you guys planning to do?"

"I'm going with you." Suri gave me a terse nod. "If you're a landed noble and Starborn, you're bound to the land you own, right? Like... you'll always spawn there by default?"

"Most assuredly," Ignas replied.

Suri's eyes were suddenly fierce and hard. "Then count me in. Countess Ba'hadir, at Your Majesty's service."

Rin looked between us and Ebisa, her lip in her teeth.

"Well... you guys... you're going to need someone to help with magic and crafting," she said. "But I'd really like to stay with Ebisa."

Ebisa made a tutting sound. "Then I guess I'm going to Myszno."

"What?" Ignas and Rin said at the same time.

"Kitten's right," she said, pointing at me and Suri. "These two meatheads need some subtler company. Do I have your permission to serve the realm, sire?"

Rin blushed so hard that her face turned blue. "Ebisa..."

I looked between them, and suddenly it dawned on me. In a few short days, these two were rapidly becoming more than friends. Ignas, however, could not disguise his shock. "Ebisa? Really?"

"Yes, really." She drew herself up straight. "Your Majesty, I nominate Prathorna Ghan to lead the Nightstalkers so that I might accompany these Starborn on their mission. You need something dead. This assassin will be indispensable to them."

Finally, Ignas seemed to notice the energy between the two Mercurions. "I see. Well, I cannot disagree... and I think it is good for you to spend time with another of your kind, but be ready to be recalled any day of the mission. If your king needs you, Ebisa, you will come. Until then, you have my leave. And my thanks."

Ebisa bowed from the waist. "Thank you, Your Majesty."

There was a lot to gain from having my - our - own castle. If the worst happened, and Baldr massed Ilia's forces, crossed the channel, and invaded... the further away we were, the more time we had to prepare, the better. I closed my eyes, feeling out for Karalti's presence, and sensed her in flight. She was chasing birds in the air above Mount Racosul, radiating delight as she swam through the air like a swallow.

I looked down at the back of my left hand, where the Mark of Matir waited. Then I swiped my HUD in, and nodded.

"Quest accepted," I said. "Let's go and kick some skinny vampire ass."

AUTHOR'S NOTE

Thank you for joining me on the Archemi Online journey so far. I am honestly overwhelmed by the support and encouragement of the Gamelit and LitRPG community. Dragon Seed has done really well, and this book launched with over a thousand pre-orders - I am bewildered, but grateful to you all.

If you enjoyed this book and the one before it, please consider leaving a review on Amazon. Your reviews help increase the sales of the books, which supports me (and my family!) so that I can keep on writing this series full-time.

You may have noticed that there is no pre-order for Book #3 yet - however, do not be alarmed.

The third book - Kingdom Come - involves significant kingdom building. Hector, Karalti, Suri, Rin and Ebisa must conquer and settle the corrupted territory of Myszno while Ororgael and Baldr up their game.

This will be a LOT of work on my end. I have to make sure all of the game system elements function properly. ArchOn is not a MMORPG - it's more like Dark Souls, with single-player and small group/PvP functionality vs a mega-free-for-all. I want that warfare system polished to a fine grain before I release Kingdom Come, and Amazon only lets me make pre-orders 90 days in advance. I'm aiming for an October/November release of this book.

After Trial by Fire and before Kingdom Come, I will be releasing a short, free novella-length book, Ghosts of the Past, which will reveal how Baldr/Ororgael managed to take over Ilia in just under a month. Ghosts of the Past will reveal what is happening at the Eyrie, and give insight into him and the other major villains of the series - Lucien, Violetta, and... Rutha?

When I was drafting Trial by Fire, the chapters of Ghosts of the Past were originally woven through the narrative as a counterpoint to Hector's activities in Vlachia. I decided that these chapters were distracting from the pace of the main narrative, and so I recombined them into their own crunchy 30,000 word-ish novella. This story will be FREE for Mailing List subscribers, Facebook Group subscribers, Patreon supporters, and people who follow me on Royal Road. It will NOT be made available for sale - there are too many spoilers for people not already invested in the series.

Between now and the publication of Kingdom Come, I will also be commissioning more art for this series: Cutthroat, Karalti, the girls... maybe even Hector. These artworks will be featured on my website, and you will be able to get them printed onto the knick-knacks of your choice. I'm sure Cutthroat body-pillows will be a popular option.

If you want to get your free story and be the first to know when the next ArchOn novel comes out, here are your best options:

Facebook: Definitely my most active platform, with frequent posts and live broadcasts. Join the James Osiris Baldwin Readers Group here: https://www.facebook.com/groups/HoundofEden/

Mailing List: I kind of hate mailing lists, so I only use mine to send new book releases and free stuff. If you just want to know when the next book is out, I'd recommend you join my newsletter.

Patreon: If you'd like to sponsor me, I throw in free books and advance copies to $5-and-above Patrons. You can also read my urban fantasy books at no extra cost this way, while directly contributing to the insane amount of caffine I consume to produce these majestic works of prose. Join me on Patreon here: https://www.patreon.com/jamesosiris

Royal Road Legends: The freebie, no commitment, no strings attached serial fiction option. I have a core base of amazing fans on RRL who help refine these stories into professional-quality books. If you want to be one of those early readers, follow and favorite the Archemi Online threads on RRL here: https://royalroadl.com/fiction/12117/trial-by-fire-archemi-online-chronicles-vol2

JOIN THE GAMELIT SOCIETY FOR MORE GAMELIT AND LITRPG!

Ye olde Gamelit Society is where most of the cool kids of the videogame fantasy world(s) hang out. Join me, Blaise Corvin, Luke Chmilenko, James Hunter and all your other favorite authors on Facebook here: https://www.facebook.com/groups/LitRPGsociety/

You can support the development of a GameLit/LitRPG database here:

https://www.patreon.com/GameLitRPG/posts

SNEAK PEEK: GHOSTS OF THE PAST

Two hundred dragons were gathered in the hatching chamber of the Eyrie, and their moans and the rustle of agitated wings stirred the hot air as the three candidates marched toward the Matriarch's nest of sand and stone. Her eggs rocked and chirped as the wyrmlings inside struggled against their shells. They were sheltered by the comatose body of their mother, who stared at the approaching knights-to-be with dull, stupefied eyes.

You big ol' dumb bitch, Baldr thought. He couldn't help but be impressed by the size of her - and amused that she'd thrown everything away to pin her hopes on Hector, of all people. That was Archemi's bleeding heart AI for you.

The last couple of days had taught Baldr a couple of things. Firstly, you never trusted the life of your enemies to Archemi's AI. He knew he should have known that, but he'd let himself slip into thinking this was reality. The Commander, the Matriarch, the monsters... they were here to support players. Dumb players, smart players, casuals and hardcore gamers were catered for in their own ways, by a network of realistic construct who *would* generate their stories... and give them opportunities for agency. That meant slipups. It meant sticking a guy in a jail cell instead of killing him, giving him opportunities, and Hector was really good at taking opportunities to run away. Baldr had briefly forgotten that the only thing capable of taking a player out of the game was another player. It wasn't a mistake he'd make again.

He'd already taken the time to brood on the error and process it. Now, all he cared about were the eggs, and the promise of the future he was destined for.

"*Ready, pussy?*" Baldr whispered the message to Lucien in PM. "*You remember which egg you're gonna take?*"

"*The small one,*" he shot back meekly. "*But I'm telling you, Baldr, the dragons pick the player, not the-*"

"I damn well know how it works." Baldr's hands fisted by his thighs as they drew up at the edge of the great big sandpit the Matriarch used for her nest. *"I KNOW."*

And he did. Things had been different since he woke up in Cham Garai. The most obvious change was the stone in his forehead. It didn't hurt, but he hadn't been able to dig it out, either. Baldr figured that if it didn't hurt or cause any problems, well, it weren't any of his concern. And it hadn't been causing any problems - to the contrary.

While they waited for the priests and the Knight-Commander to half-heartedly bless the eggs, Lucien drew up to Baldr's right like a whipped dog, while Violetta hung back to his left. He could see her with his enhanced vision. The blond girl stared ahead with dull, bruised eyes. Hatred radiated from her in waves, but like Lucien, she'd become passive after a week of conditioning. Baldr didn't question his sudden knowledge of operant conditioning any more than he questioned his knowledge of the game, or his new-found ability to access a view-only version of the Developer Console.

"Please, Lord Hyland. Lucien, Violetta... advance." Knight-Commander Arnaud called to them, and he and the priest of Benefar stepped back from the eggs.

Satisfied he'd heard the right tone of respect, Baldr grunted and strode confidently toward his chosen egg - the big silver one. He knew it contained a Tier 7 platinum male dragon, a buck one tier higher than the Knight-Commander's 'model' white, Talenth. Short of a queen dragon, it was one of the best in the game. Baldr ground his teeth until they felt like they'd crack as he approached it and lay a hand on the hot shell. The brain-dead Matriarch been hiding one of those queens... the Tier 8 mount that should have been his. But with the bitch down for the count, there weren't going to be any more queens out of the Eyrie. Queens were the only Tier 8 in Archemi, and only queens could breed more queens, and only then with a Tier 6 or 7 male. So the plan had changed. Baldr would get the best dragon on offer for now, then go and find Hector and his princess and fuck him up. They'd bring the queen back her and get her to lay. The odds of breeding this platinum dragon to her were pretty good - around 15%. Then he'd get the Tier 8 he'd been waiting years to acquire.

... *Years?*

Baldr grimaced as his head throbbed.

Whatever thought had been about to come next was interrupted by the wyrmling. He felt it tapping under his palm, then the crunch as its beak split through the shell. Baldr took a step back, zoning in on the egg as it rocked and split. The adult dragons would normally cheer a hatching, buzzing their wings and roaring encouragement, but the hatching grounds were eeriely silent as the three hatchlings struggled from their shells. Out of the corner of his eye, Baldr saw Violetta's blue egg shatter, while Lucien began pulling pieces of shell off his struggling white.

"That's it, lil' buddy." Baldr crooned, eyes fixed on his struggling hatchling. "You can do it."

Pieces of shell fell away, and then the dragon's sharp egg tooth split the leathery sack binding him inside, tearing through it like a boxcutter. Fluid spilled out, and then all in a rush, the hatchling slithered out onto the sands like a sculpture of living mercury. Smiling, Baldr crouched down in front of the panting, flapping dragon, watching as he struggled to orientate himself. The Developer Console told Baldr that this was a pure quicksilver Tier 7 male with maximum stats, just like he'd thought. No... *known.*

The dragon trilled as he beat his sticky wings and pushed himself up to sit, nostrils working, eyes still sealed with mucous. To the left, Violetta cried out with a stifled sound as her Tier 6 blue female toppled to the ground in exhaustion. Lucien was frantically assisting his much weaker Tier 4 female out of her egg. The little white panted and chirped, blundering into Lucien and knocking him to the dirt.

"Hey there, little guy." Baldr reached out as the hatchling pawed at his eyes, and helped him unseal the lids with a fingernail. The dragon staggered forward, lurching in against him in a shivering heap of wings and scales, and finally opened his eyes. They were the brilliant white of a lightning strike, churning with the magic that contained in his blood. Baldr's breath caught as their gazes locked, and in an instant, the psychic connection was forged.

The little dragon's jaw hung open with shock. Then he backpedaled, whining, and tripped over the tip of one drooping wing. Baldr halted his retreat with a thought, and hatchling's will buckled underneath his own. The geas that bound him to serve the Knights of Saint Grigori was still in effect. The magic was bound to the Queen dragon Lirenian's line, and as long as a queen lived, the geas was in effect. Baldr knew of the existence of the geas as well as everything else about this place - the details of the magic, the location of the Dragon Gate, the way the magic transferred to each Knight-Commander. He knew it, because he'd designed it.

For a moment, Baldr was confused by his own thought. Then his temples throbbed, and the moment of confusion passed. Frowning, he rubbed his brow, and squeezed the skin around the pearl embedded there. Yeah, hell yeah, he'd designed it. Of course he had. He remembered doing it.

"Your name's Bareon," Baldr told his dragon.

"*Bareon?*" The wyrmling echoed. "*But my blood says-*"

"Bareon." Baldr rose to his feet, keeping his gaze fixed with that of the newly-hatched dragon's.

"*Bareon,*" he echoed numbly. "*And you... you're... an...*"

Bareon didn't finished, too terrified to speak the word he read in Baldr's mind.

"Yep." Baldr nodded. "*You call me sir, boy. Only words I ever want to hear out of your scaly mouth are 'yes, sir' and respectfully worded questions. Understood?*"

Bareon swayed in place. His hatchling instincts were telling him to press against his bonded's body and beg for food, like a baby bird. His common sense was telling him to hang back. "*Yes sir.*"

"Right. Let's go see about getting you grown."

Bareon cocked his head. "*Food? Sir?*"

Baldr smiled thinly. "Yeah. Kind of."

Ghosts of the Past will be out soon! This title will NOT BE FOR SALE. It's free, but only way to get it is join my mailing list, Patreon, or read it for free (with no patronage or signup required) on Royal Road Legends.

LIST OF JAMES' BOOKS

Hound of Eden Series

Dark, gritty urban fantasy with a cosmic horror twist, join Russian mafia hitmage Alexi Sokolsky as he confronts the mad demons of the abyss, finds redemption, and saves the world. Hound of Eden is an LGBTI series.

Hound of Eden Omnibus (Books 1 – 3)

0 - Burn Artist (Prequel)

1 - Blood Hound

2 - Stained Glass

3 - Zero Sum

4 - Cold Cell (TBA)

5 - Scavenger Eyes (TBA)

6 - Morning Star (TBA)

Archemi Online

A LitRPG saga about a young dragonrider's ascension to greatness inside the virtual world of Archemi.

1 - Dragon Seed

2 - Trial by Fire

3 – Kingdom Come (April 2019)

4 - Warsinger (TBA)

5 - Blaze of Glory (TBA)

Shaman States of America

1. *Murder of Crows*

Other Titles

Fix Your Damn Book!: A Self-Editing Guide for Authors

The Expanding Universe #1 (Paperback)

The Expanding Universe #2 (Paperback)

www.ingramcontent.com/pod-product-compliance
Lightning Source LLC
Chambersburg PA
CBHW020603310726
48979CB00008B/1322/J

* 9 7 8 0 9 9 4 4 0 7 0 7 8 *